Calling Cards

Gordon Johnston

Ringwood Publishing
Glasgow

Copyright Gordon Johnston 2014

First published in Great Britain in 2014 by
Ringwood Publishing
7 Kirklee Quadrant, Glasgow G12 0TS
www.ringwoodpublishing.com
e-mail   mail@ringwoodpublishing.com

ISBN 978-1-901514-09-4

British Library Cataloguing-in Publication Data
A catalogue record for this book is available from the British
Library

Typeset in Times New Roman 10
Printed and bound in the UK
by Lonsdale Direct Solutions

ACKNOWLEDGEMENTS

I would like to thank everyone at Ringwood Publishing for giving me the opportunity to acquire the status of published author, particularly Sandy Jamieson for his belief and advice, and my editor Joanne Durning for the many helpful suggestions and improvements to my original text.

Writing a novel is a lengthy and mostly solitary process, and so the writer requires plenty of support and encouragement along the way. I'd like to thank everyone who has provided this for me – there are far too many names to list them all and I would hate to miss anyone out. But you know who you are.

Writers' groups are a tremendous resource for any would be author, and members of the Glasgow Writers' Meet Up Group have been a source of many helpful comments and suggestions as well as providing inspiration and good company over many evening meetings. I'm not the first from that fine group of writers to be published – and I'm sure I won't be the last either.

Chapter 1

Monday May 12 2008, 11:30am

Frank Gallen read the e-mail on his screen once again. There were only five short words:

Phil Whitby didn't commit suicide

He opened up his internet browser and googled Phil Whitby, finding that Whitby, 24, had jumped from the top of a tower block in the Gorbals and the case had been ruled a suicide.

This led him to two questions: who had sent him the e-mail? And why?

The name of the sender gave no clue. It was just a random selection of letters and numbers. Gallen hit the reply button and typed a short note asking for more details. An error message appeared immediately: the specified account did not exist.

Intrigued, he pulled up the internet header information and found the originating IP address, a series of numbers that he knew should identify the computer used to send the message.

Frank copied the address into a website that he had bookmarked some time ago. It told him that the message had originated from "*blu0-omc3-s15.blu0.hotmail.com*".

That helps a lot. He then tried a reverse IP directory, which promised to give a geographical location. Again he copied in the numbers and waited. A map slowly appeared and a box pointed to a location in the west of the U.S.A.: Redmond, Washington.

Frank burst out laughing. Of course, that made perfect sense for a Hotmail account. But it took him no further forward.

John Addison walked towards Frank's desk from his small room in the corner of the overcrowded office that served as the headquarters of Glasgow's West End Weekly newspaper.

'What's so funny?' asked Frank's boss.

'Come and have a look at this,' he replied, pointing at the screen.

John took one look at the map and smiled. 'Do you have a source in Microsoft then, Frank?'

'I wish. But what do you think of this message?' Frank pulled the e-mail up.

Phil Whitby didn't commit suicide

John leant forward to read it. 'Phil Whitby...' He thought for a second. 'Isn't he the Green activist who jumped off a tower block?'

'That's right,' replied Frank, not at all surprised that John remembered the story. 'I think I'll have a closer look into this.'

'It's not exactly relevant, is it, Frank?' asked John with a scowl. 'He came from Pollok, if I remember correctly, and died in the Gorbals. Both are on the South Side and this is the West End Weekly, you know.'

'I just have a feeling that there might be something in this. I don't know why. Call it journalistic instinct.'

'Well, as long as you cover the stories I'm paying you for first,' John responded. 'I know this isn't the Daily News, but I do need to get a paper out. And, talking of which, shouldn't you be at the opening of that Polish deli about now?' He glared pointedly at his watch.

'I know. It's at noon, so I've still got time. When have I ever let you down, John?' He looked up at his editor with an angelic expression on his face. Or at least as near to angelic as he could manage.

'Not more than a few hundred times,' replied John, still scowling.

'But never since I got sober, right?'

'Well, that's probably true,' he admitted grudgingly. 'Just make sure the story is in on time.'

'Yes, boss,' replied Frank with a mock salute. John shook his head as he walked away to return to his office.

'Janice, have you got a moment?' Frank called across the small room.

'What do you need, Frank?' the young woman asked as she rushed over, always eager to help.

'Two things. First, can you call me a cab? I need to get to Hyndland. And then can you pull off all the stories on Phil Whitby, the environmental activist who died last week?'

'Will do, Frank. What's your interest in Whitby?' she asked.

'I'm not sure yet. I'll talk to you about it later.'

'OK, thanks. I'll get you that cab.'

Frank closed down his computer and prepared to leave. He smiled, seeing that Janice was already on the phone while simultaneously working on her computer. He saw a keen instinct and a hunger for stories in her that made him think of himself when he was a young journalist. Frank tried to encourage Janice as much as possible, and she had always come through for him when he had given her pieces of work to do. Anyway, what 33 year old man would not want a beautiful young woman as his unofficial apprentice?

Frank walked out of the office to wait for his cab in the warm afternoon sun. He stood at the door, thinking about the mysterious message as he looked down towards the main road.

He did not notice the white van parked on the corner. Inside sat a red haired man with a smile on his face.

Monday May 12 2008, 12:25pm

Councillor Thomas Gallen looked out of his car window to a view across George Square in the centre of Glasgow. The large open space was filled with people as it always was in the middle of the day. There were busy locals rushing through, tourists with cameras taking pictures and office workers with sandwiches taking their midday break in the spring sunshine.

The black Daimler he was travelling in, the official car of the Leader of Glasgow City Council, turned the corner and stopped outside the magnificent Victorian frontage of Glasgow City Chambers. Councillor Gallen waited as his driver came around to open his door before he got out of the car and walked through the front door of the Council's historic headquarters.

Gallen felt an intense sense of pride every time he entered the imposing building that he loved so much. At 43, he was the political head of the largest Council in Scotland and one of New Labour's rising stars. And as a Glaswegian born and bred, Thomas Gallen was proud that a working class boy like himself could have risen to such a position of prominence. He wished, as he often did, that his father had lived long enough to see his political career flourish. His sudden death in 2002 had rocked Gallen; an unexpected heart attack taking his hero from him.

But the hurt he was left with was nothing compared to the intense pain that he still felt every day from the loss of his twin sister four years later.

Councillor Gallen took the lift to the second floor and walked along the long corridor to his office. He nodded, smiled and said hello to the Council officers he passed along the way, eager to retain his image as a man of the people. Finally he was behind his massive desk, with seconds to spare before his next meeting of the day. He opened the top file from the stack of papers to the left of his desk, which contained briefing papers for all of his afternoon appointments, and quickly read the summary sheet.

The intercom on the right hand corner of his desk buzzed and he heard the voice of Sandra McNair, his personal secretary.

'Councillor Gallen? David Longwell is here for your 12:30.'

'Show him in, thanks Sandra.' He steeled himself for what he knew would be a difficult discussion, then stood and put a smile on his face. The door opened and Longwell strode confidently into his office.

'David, how are you?' he said, shaking the property developer's hand.

'I'm well, Thomas. And you?'

'Can't complain, I suppose,' he answered.

'I trust that you have your speech prepared for the opening?' Longwell walked straight to the leather couch at the back of Gallen's office, adjusting the crease in the trousers of his perfectly tailored dark grey business suit as he sat down.

Gallen followed him, trying not to show his annoyance at Longwell's lack of respect for him and the office he held.

'My staff are working on it. The new estate looks great and I'll be sure to mention the leisure centre you've provided.'

'I should hope so, Thomas. My company does value our ongoing partnership and I'm happy to provide little extras for the Council. Like a brand new facility that just happens to be in the middle of your ward.'

'And in return you make a healthy profit, David,' he reminded the older man, uncomfortable with the implications of his remark.

'But not as much as we will make from the Parklands developments,' replied Longwell with a smile that Gallen instantly thought of as reptilian. 'I trust that the Kelvingrove Park scheme will now have your full backing? With Whitby out of the way you have no reason to block it, do you?'

'He wasn't the only one opposed to building in our most important park, you know.'

'No, but he was the only one blackmailing you, wasn't he?'

Councillor Gallen looked away and said nothing.

'Unless there is something you're not telling me?' asked Longwell, his face taking on an even more unpleasant expression.

Gallen looked out of the window and up at the clouds drifting across the blue sky for a few seconds before answering. 'Of course there's nothing else, David,' he finally said.

'Well then. Thursday's speech will be the perfect opportunity for you to announce the Kelvingrove Project. The press have already got wind that something is going on, so why not make it official, Thomas?'

'The press have *got wind* because you leaked it, David,' he retorted curtly, noting that the developer did not deny the allegation. 'We need to be careful. This is a sensitive political issue, especially with a demonstration planned for the end of the month opposing any and all developments in Glasgow's parks. Perhaps we should wait until that blows over?'

'You told me that Whitby was your biggest concern in case he went public with what he had on you, yes?'

'I did,' replied Gallen, hesitantly.

'That you wished Whitby could be dealt with?' Now Longwell appeared to be getting angry.

'Yes.'

'And you told me that if he was out of the way, your life would be so much easier. Yes?'

Gallen suddenly felt very worried at the glint he saw in David Longwell's eyes.

'That's true,' he admitted.

'Well, Phil Whitby is no longer in a position to use the information he had, is he?'

'No' he replied, wondering exactly where Longwell was taking the conversation.

'The timing of his suicide was fortuitous for you, wasn't it?' Longwell stressed the word *suicide* and looked at him with a smile that chilled Thomas Gallen to the bone.

'Well, yes, it certainly looks that way' he replied, unable to process the thoughts that were at the forefront of his mind. Was he being accused of ordering a murder? Surely not?

'So with your blackmailer out of the picture we can now continue with our business together, can't we, Thomas?'

'What are you suggesting, David? That I had something to do with this man's death?' Gallen's voice was shrill as he struggled to contain his rising anger.

'Of course I'm not, Thomas.'

Longwell spoke reassuringly, although Gallen still felt angry and confused.

'You must admit that you have benefitted from Whitby's demise. Indeed, if anyone ever finds out the full story they could only conclude that you are the one to gain the most.'

'This conversation is ridiculous, David. Phil Whitby killed himself and that's the end of the matter. The end,' he repeated, slapping the arm of his chair with a dull thud for emphasis.

'Are you so sure he killed himself?' asked Longwell with a sly smile as he looked at his watch.

'What do you mean?' A terrible idea came into Gallen's mind. 'You didn't...?

Longwell smiled once again.

'So now we can move ahead with the Kelvingrove Park project, can't we?' Longwell told him in a tone that offered no room for disagreement. 'Look, I have another meeting to go to. I will call you on Wednesday night and you can tell me what your speech will say. Is that clear?'

'We'll speak then,' Gallen agreed, relieved to have some time to think.

David Longwell stood and walked quickly out of the office without another word.

Gallen sat alone with his thoughts. As he turned over the strange conversation, he grew more troubled. He had always known that his relationship with Longwell was a potential risk, but had believed that the benefits for the city made it worthwhile. Now he wasn't convinced.

Councillor Thomas Gallen concluded that he had just exchanged one serious problem for a very much bigger one.

Frank Gallen walked back into the small newspaper office and sat down at this desk. The office was deserted and he wondered where everyone was. He glanced at a couple of notes left on his keyboard before checking his e-mail account, disappointed to learn that there was nothing more from his Hotmail source.

Frank knew that he would be able to finish writing the piece on the deli in five minutes, so he quickly called up the article he had started earlier. A few sentences about the history of the Poles in Glasgow and the growing numbers in the city, now that their country was in the EU. Add a little about the wide variety of Polish food on offer at Taste of Warsaw and a few quotes from the owner. Finish it all off with a recommendation to try the Kefir yoghurt drink and it was done. He sent the finished article on to John and turned to the folder lying on his desk, which was marked "Phil Whitby" in neatly printed letters.

Frank quickly glanced through all the news reports of Whitby's death, and then moved on to articles about the various environmental protests he had led, and even some pieces from far left and gay rights publications that he had written. And at the back of the file were a short biography and a note of his mother's address in Pollok. Janice was good!

At that moment, she walked out of the small kitchen to the side of the office, bringing him a black coffee.

'Thanks,' he said, sipping from the mug as she sat down beside his desk. 'Great job on Whitby, Janice.'

She smiled shyly, acknowledging his praise. 'So is there a story here?' she asked.

'Well, I got an anonymous e-mail this morning suggesting that his death wasn't suicide. What do you think?' he asked.

Janice ran her fingers through her long dark hair before replying. Frank had noticed that she always did this when concentrating on something.

'The press reports made it seem very straightforward and the police were quoted as saying that there were no signs of foul play or suspicious circumstances,' she said, sounding dubious.

'What else do we know about him that might be related to his death?' asked Frank, challenging Janice to come up with something.

'He worked for Green Glasgow Co-op, an organic food co-operative, and was involved with a number of Trotskyite organisations in his teens, but seems to have concentrated more on environmental activism and gay rights recently. I can't see anything there that could have got him killed,' she concluded.

'Was there anything that would make you think he was suicidal?'

'There's nothing obvious,' she replied, shaking her head. 'And he was one of the leaders of the 'Parks for the People' campaign. They have a big demo coming up at the end of the month, so surely he would have wanted to be at that?'

'What about his personal life?' Frank continued to probe, impressed at the huge amount of detail she had managed to take in.

'I don't know. There's so little to go on. Most of the information is about his political activism and not about him as a person.' She paused for a second. 'Maybe we should ask his mother?'

'*We*?' said Frank with a smile. 'You think that there might be a story here for *us* then?' he teased.

'Someone sent you that e-mail for a reason, Frank,' Janice responded, the teasing obviously right over her head. 'We should take a look and see if there is anything in it'

'I'll talk to his mother this evening and see if she will give me some more background. Do you want to come along with me?'

'Of course I do,' Janice answered. 'I have to go round to the Uni to see my tutor at four, but I can come back after we're finished, if that's OK with you?'

'OK, we'll leave about six then. Tea time is usually a good time to catch people at home in any case.'

'Cool, I'll see you later then. And thanks, Frank.' She smiled at him, delighted at the chance to be involved in a real investigation.

'No problem,' he replied as Janice walked away, still smiling.

Frank took another drink of his coffee and then turned to his notebook as he prepared to read through all of the documents in the file that Janice had prepared for him once more. This time he studied them, making notes as he went.

The news reports told him that Whitby had been 24 when he died after jumping from the roof of a deserted tower block in the Gorbals, near to the flat he had been renting. No one else had been involved, there were no witnesses and nothing suspicious was noted. The police had concluded that his death was a suicide and the story had run its course within a few days.

Frank also studied the articles that Whitby had written, grimacing at the lengthy rants and overblown language. They seemed to be standard far left commentaries on subjects such as global warming, identity cards and equal opportunities issues. And pretty much every perceived ill of society was blamed on the "crypto-fascist Nu Labour government" and the capitalist state. Just the usual badly written conspiracy theories and overly emotional rhetoric, Frank concluded.

And all of the articles were from small publications, which would only have ever been read by the faithful. So Whitby had been very much preaching to the converted, which couldn't possibly give any motive for his murder.

Frank then called up the 'Parks for the People' website. The main story was the demonstration that Janice had mentioned to him, which was due to take place in Glasgow Green on the last Saturday of the month. He discovered that the theme was opposition to all private sector development on Glasgow's parklands and an appeal to the Council to act in the common good by preserving Glasgow's parks for its citizens. Only slightly controversial, he decided, and the campaign was backed by a number of trade unions and civic organisations, as well as the usual plethora of socialist organisations. Again he concluded that there was nothing that could have led to Whitby's death.

Frank closed his notebook and hoped that Phil Whitby's mother would give them something more to go on. If not, the investigation would simply come to a sudden stop pretty much as soon as it had started.

Frank still had a feeling that there was more to this than was apparent on a first look. What was the secret to Phil Whitby's death? He could not stop wondering who had sent him the anonymous message. And why?

Chapter 2

The black taxi cab slowed as it travelled along Braidcraft Road in Pollok. The sprawling council estate to the south west of the city was a depressing place, even on a spring evening. Frank and Janice were nearing the end of a journey that had taken a rather circuitous route through the large housing estate.

Finally the elderly driver located the correct number and stopped the cab. Frank and Janice got out and walked up to the house, which was in the middle of a long terraced row. Frank led the way through the gate and up the path, noting a small but well tended garden with a patch of grass surrounded by a border containing roses and other plants that he couldn't name. As he knocked on the front door he saw that the nameplate read "Whitby", which confirmed that they were at the correct address.

The door was answered by a small overweight woman wearing a black dress. She looked suspiciously at the two strangers standing on her doorstep, but said nothing.

'Good evening. Are you Mrs Whitby?' asked Frank, politely.

'Who wants to know?' she replied in an unexpectedly soft voice, her hand smoothing badly dyed blonde hair that showed greying roots

'Mrs Whitby, my name is Frank Gallen and this is my colleague Janice Tracey. I'm a journalist and I wondered if you could spare me a few minutes to talk about Phil?'

'Journalists? What do you want with me?' she asked.

'Just a few moments of your time to talk about your son if you wouldn't mind, Mrs Whitby,' Frank replied, trying to put the suspicious woman at ease.

'Do you have identification?' she asked. Frank pulled out his wallet and showed her his press identification, which she studied for a moment.

'West End Weekly?' she queried, a frown on her face. 'Why on earth would you be interested in my Phil?'

'Could we talk inside Mrs Whitby?' asked Janice, smiling. 'Please?'

She stared at the young woman for a second, apparently assessing Janice as posing no threat and then sighed jadedly before leading them into the house.

Frank and Janice followed Mrs Whitby through a small dark hallway and then into her living room. The room was decorated in a rather overpowering shade of pink, and Frank noticed a large wall unit in one corner, which was covered with pictures of a young man.

Mrs Whitby slumped into an armchair, pointing towards the matching white leather sofa where Frank and Janice took their seats as requested.

'Mrs Whitby, my condolences on your son's death,' Frank started. He paused as she lowered her eyes, perhaps tired of hearing similar words so many times over the past week. He took out his notebook and continued.

'Now the reports that we have, say that Phil died in the Gorbals? Is that correct?' Frank wanted to get the woman talking, as he had always found that a conversation yielded more information than an interrogation.

'You're a journalist so you must know that much,' she replied. 'The police said that he jumped off the roof of one of the empty tower blocks in Norfolk Court. They're going to be demolished soon,' she added, almost as an afterthought.

'When did you last see Phil?' Frank probed gently.

'He was here for his tea last Sunday night as usual. He always came by at the weekend to see me. Every weekend without fail.' Frank noticed a single tear running down her cheek.

'And how did he seem? Was he in any sort of trouble or down about anything?'

'No, not at all. Phil was full of life like he always was. He was always a happy boy, even as a child, and he was in good spirits last weekend.' She paused and sobbed, clutching a gold crucifix hanging from a chain around her neck. 'I just can't believe that he would do what they said he did, Mr Gallen. Phil was raised a Catholic. I know that he didn't go to chapel very often anymore but I'm sure he wouldn't have sinned like that.'

Frank nodded, remembering his own time at Catholic schools, although he too no longer attended chapel, much to his mother's regret. Or rather, one of her many regrets when it came to her younger son.

'Was anything worrying Phil at all, Mrs Whitby?' asked Janice.

Frank was pleased to see that she had the confidence to join the conversation. He also thought that Mrs Whitby might respond more favourably to the young woman.

'No, love, nothing. His food co-op was doing well and he was excited about the big demo he was helping to organise at the end of the month. He was looking ahead. I just can't see why he would have done what they say he did.'

She took a photograph of her son from the unit and passed it to Janice. 'This was taken a couple of weeks ago. He was always a happy boy.'

Frank saw another tear run down her cheek as she stared at the picture of her son.

'What did the police tell you, Mrs Whitby?' asked Frank.

'Very little. They were so convinced that he had … jumped. Right from the start they were convinced.' She seemed unwilling to use the word suicide, so Frank also avoided it.

'And they didn't consider any other possible explanation for his death?'

Mrs Whitby became animated for the first time. She leaned forward towards them as she spoke. 'They had their minds made up before they had even talked to me. They were only here for five minutes, two PCs, and that was it. They didn't listen to me at all. I told them that Phil was happy and planning ahead. And if he jumped, why was there no note? There's always a note, isn't there?' Frank thought that she was on the verge of hysteria, so he tried to calm her.

'Well, most times, although not always,' he replied slowly. 'But there is always a reason. Now, did Phil have any money or relationship problems that you know of?'

'No, nothing like that. He didn't have much use for money really. Phil gave away a lot of what little he earned to those causes of his. And he was in a steady relationship, with a guy he worked with, and that was going well as far as I knew. He seemed happy enough anyway.'

From the way she had stressed the word *guy* Frank could tell that she had had trouble accepting that her son was gay. Another sin according to the Catholic Church, of course.

'Would you mind giving me his name? I don't recall it from the reports in the newspapers,' asked Janice smoothly, impressing Frank again.

'Mike something. I'm not sure of his surname, dear,' she replied. 'I only met him a couple of times, but he seemed like a nice enough young lad.'

Frank was certain that the name had not been mentioned in any of the reports that he had read, so they now had one new lead at least.

'Is there anything else you can tell us about Phil, Mrs Whitby?' asked Frank.

'Do you know something about Phil's death, Mr Gallen? I mean, no one else has even questioned whether it wasn't, whether he didn't...'

'I don't know anything definite, no,' replied Frank, trying not to raise her hopes. 'I just needed some more background, that's all.' He didn't want to cause any more distress to the woman, who was having as hard a time with the notion that her son had killed himself as she did with losing him.

'We should be going, thanks very much for your time, Mrs Whitby.' Frank took a business card from his pocket and handed it to her. 'If you think of anything else, please give me a call.' He stood and Janice followed him towards the door. 'We'll show ourselves out,' he said, noticing that Mrs Whitby was staring intently at her pictures once more. They walked out leaving her alone with her memories.

'So what do you think?' asked Janice as they walked back down the garden path and through the metal gate,

'She didn't give us much, did she?' Frank wanted to know how much Janice had picked up. 'Tell me what you got?'

'She seemed pretty certain that Phil wouldn't have taken his own life though. And she said that he hadn't left a note; that could be significant.' Janice was getting excited, Frank noticed. Perhaps she had visions of helping to break a big story.

'Relatives never believe that it was suicide, especially parents,' he explained, trying to rein her back in a little. 'You can understand why they wouldn't want to accept that, can't you, Janice?'

'I guess so, yes,' she replied, her brow furrowing. 'But we haven't found anything that could have possibly made him suicidal and there was no note.'

'That's true,' Frank conceded. 'Let's walk down to the main road and get a taxi back to the West End.' He knew that Janice shared a large student flat just a couple of streets from the much smaller flat off Byres Road that he had moved into after his divorce. They walked in silence for a few moments on what was a pleasant spring evening, both deep in thought.

'So who else should we speak to?' Frank finally asked, once again testing Janice.

'Mike, his boyfriend, might give us more on Whitby's mood or any problems he was having. Phil might have told him things that he wouldn't tell his mother,' she replied.

'That's the easy one. Who else?' he asked, smiling as they walked.

'It would be good to know what the police found at the scene, wouldn't it? Do you have any contacts, Frank?'

'Good answer,' he said, and this time Janice smiled. 'I do know a DC in the local station. I'll give him a call tomorrow. And I'll also call a friend on the Daily News to see if they had anything that wasn't included in the stories. Oh, here's a taxi.'

Frank hailed the black cab that was approaching them. It pulled to a stop by the kerb to allow them to get in before driving away once more.

Monday May 12 2008, 8:40pm

'Surely Longwell didn't really have Whitby killed?' The question came from Alan Mathers, whose official title was Personal Adviser to the Leader of the Council.

'Well, he didn't admit to it, although he certainly hinted in that direction. But it's already been ruled a suicide and the police have closed the case. The key thing is that Longwell knows how it would look for me if any of this mess ever became public,' replied Thomas Gallen, sitting behind the massive desk in his opulent office.

'Why the hell did you ever tell Longwell that you were being blackmailed?' asked Mathers curtly, his primary concern that he might get caught in the fall out. Loyalty only went so far and he had his own political career to think of, after all.

'I had to tell him something to stop him announcing the details of that damned Kelvingrove Park project. Whitby had threatened to go public after that leak, which came from Longwell himself, by the way. He as good as admitted it to me.'

'He does seem to know how to use the press,' agreed Mathers, concerned that they had been outmanoeuvred by the developer. And not for the first time.

'If it all comes out it will destroy me,' continued Gallen miserably. 'I would have to resign.'

'So what are you going to do now, Thomas? You know that we don't have enough support on the Council as yet for Longwell's project. It would be political suicide to go public now, so to speak.' Mathers acknowledged his ill chosen word with a grin.

'What can Longwell do if I delay?' asked Gallen.

'Depends on what reason you can come up with for not making the announcement,' he replied, turning the issue back onto his employer.

'If I tell him I need more time to get the votes lined up, then surely he will have to wait? What if I give him the choice between the possibility of losing everything now, or definitely getting it approved later?'

'It might work,' replied Mathers. 'He will continue to pressure you to deliver though.'

'It takes time to build the alliances needed; you know that Alan. This is a controversial development and I need to be sure that we will have a majority on the Planning Committee.'

Mathers had noticed that Gallen had taken to lecturing him, as if he were the master politician, and it was beginning to annoy him. Had the man forgotten who had been behind the campaign that had got him into his current position?

'If you tell him that you are nearly there, it might buy you a little time,' he finally counselled. 'But you have to make him believe that you will get that majority. And soon.'

'That's what I will do then,' Gallen announced decisively. 'I'll tell him that it will take a little more time. And I'll also tell him that any more publicity will risk galvanising support against his development.'

'That makes perfect sense,' agreed Mathers, although he doubted whether Longwell would buy it. He would have to think about another job immediately, he resolved.

'Let's get out of here,' said Gallen. 'It's been a very long day.'

Frank Gallen sat alone in the living room of his flat eating the chicken and mushroom pizza that had just been delivered and listening to an old Ryan Adams album. The somewhat melancholy air of the music chimed nicely with his mood. He hated silence and always had a CD playing when he was alone, which was pretty much every night at the moment, he reflected cheerlessly.

A letter lay on the arm of the chair, unopened. It was addressed to "Mr and Mrs F Gallen", which did nothing to improve Frank's mood.

It was now close to two years since Frank had moved from the larger flat less than a mile away that he and his wife Stephanie had bought together when they married. They had been happy for the first couple of years, he recalled fondly, but then things had become more and more strained between them. She had been unable to cope with his two worst traits: workaholism and alcoholism, and had eventually thrown him out. Their flat had been sold some months later when the divorce, which he didn't contest, was finalised but somehow he had not got around to buying somewhere else. Perhaps he had some fear of permanency, he wondered, falling into a moment of self analysis. But now the small dark flat felt like home to Frank Gallen.

It was here that he had retreated to after his dismissal from the Daily News. He remembered weeks when he had been drinking heavily, only emerging to stumble to the off licence for yet more vodka to dull the pain. It was here that he had finally reached the darkest point of his life.

One morning, or perhaps it had been afternoon, Frank had awoken lying fully clothed in the hall floor. The front door lay open, his key still in the lock on the outside. He realised that he had no idea where he had been the evening before and no memory of coming home. Thoughts of suicide filled his mind, not for the first time, and he curled into a ball on the floor, weeping uncontrollably. Frank realised that he desperately needed help. Staggering to the phone, he had called a taxi to take him to hospital.

And it was from here that he had tried to rebuild his life when he got out of rehab a month later. He reflected on the course that his life had taken; his rapid rise before the plummet to the bottom and now his attempts to rebuild things. At least he had had some money in the bank, which had got him through until John had offered him a job and given him the vote of confidence that he had so badly needed. Frank knew that he would never be able to explain to his friend exactly what that had meant to him.

He had been sober for over a year, but it didn't seem to be getting any easier at all. He wondered if it ever would, or if he would have to continue to fight the constant temptation. He smiled grimly, knowing the answer instantly.

As if on cue, a strong desire for alcohol gripped him from nowhere. He didn't just want a drink, he needed one, he had to have one there and then. It was the only thing that mattered, the only thing that could stop the awful feeling that had left him suddenly sweating and shaking, as his mind craved what he knew he could not let his body have.

Frank steeled himself against the rush of desire, the almost overwhelming longing for a drink that he felt burning in every fibre of his being. The taste, the smell, the familiar feelings were all in his mind now, taunting him and tempting him.

Frank told himself to be strong; that he had beaten the cravings many times before; that he could beat them once more. And that the feelings would pass. Breathing deeply he managed to calm himself, focusing on the positives in his new life, just as his counsellor had instructed him. And finally, minutes, or maybe hours, later, the feeling passed.

Frank walked to the fridge and pulled out a bottle of water, drinking deeply. Every craving defeated should make him stronger, he thought. More able to win through the next time. And of course he knew that there would be many more next times. Alcoholism was nothing more than a serious of tests and trials, every one of which had to be completed successfully.

One day at a time may be a cliché; but it was a truth nevertheless, Frank decided.

Tuesday May 13 2008 11:10am

The phone rang loudly, abruptly bringing Frank back from his thoughts to reality.

'Frank Gallen.'

'Frank, it's DS Ken Becker. How are you?'

'Ken. It's been a long time. Detective Sergeant is it now then: congratulations!' Frank was genuinely happy for Becker, whom he had become friendly with a couple of years earlier.

'Yeah, I got the promotion three months ago. So where have you been hiding yourself? I haven't seen you in ages, Frank.'

'I've been off the radar for quite a while, Ken. But I'm back working now.' Frank didn't know how much of the story surrounding his abrupt departure from the Daily News was now public knowledge, so he was deliberately vague.

'The West End Weekly is a bit of a comedown, isn't it?' pressed Becker.

'The editor is an old friend of mine; we were at university together. I'm just helping out for a while,' he explained.

Becker seemed to accept this at face value. 'So what was your call about? Why is the West End Weekly's star reporter interested in what's happening in the Gorbals?'

'A guy called Phil Whitby died on your patch last Wednesday. I was wondering if you could give me anything on the case. Off the record of course,' he assured Becker.

'Whitby … oh yes. The suicide in Norfolk Court. He went off the top of a tower block late at night. Is that the guy?'

'That's him,' confirmed Frank.

'Give me a second.'

Hearing the sound of typing, Frank picked up a pen, hoping that Becker would give him some new information on the case. There had been nothing since the original e-mail and Frank was beginning to wonder whether his instincts were letting him down for once.

'There's really very little to tell, Frank. It was a very straightforward suicide. He had a couple of drinks, took himself to the top of an abandoned building and then jumped,' the detective explained.

'No signs of foul play then?'

'None at all,' Becker replied. 'Nothing in his system apart from alcohol. No injuries apart from those consistent with the fall, and no one else involved. Case closed as far as we are concerned. What's your interest, Frank?'

'Just looking for some background in relation to another story, Ken. I heard that there wasn't a note, so I thought I would ask a few questions.'

'We didn't find one, but that doesn't necessarily mean anything. Not every suicide leaves a note.'

'Did Whitby have a record?' asked Frank.

Again typing and then Becker said, 'A few Breaches, all at left wing demos of one sort or another, but nothing more serious than that. There's no story here, Frank. I'm sure of that.'

'OK, well thanks anyway. I appreciate the call back, Ken.'

'No problem, Frank. Give me a shout next time you are over on this side of the river and we'll go for a few drinks'.

'I'll call you. Bye for now.' Obviously not everyone knew about his new life of sobriety.

'Bye, Frank. Take care.'

Becker had pretty much confirmed everything that Mrs Whitby had told him, Frank thought. But what did the author of the anonymous e-mail know that no one else apparently did? And why had he been the one singled out to pursue the matter?

Frank Gallen still had no answers.

Tuesday May 13 2008 1:15pm

When Janice arrived in the office, she immediately came over to his desk and asked Frank whether he had any new information on Whitby. He filled her in on his conversation with Becker and on another call he had put in to an old colleague at the Daily News, which had added absolutely nothing.

'Well I've got some information for you!' said Janice, clearly proud of what she had discovered.

'What's that then?' Frank smiled.

'I talked to a couple of guys from the Green Society at the University Union. One of my flatmates, Fiona, is going out with the Secretary. They knew Phil Whitby a little and told me that his partner is called Mike Convery!' She sat back as if waiting for Frank's reaction to her detective work.

He didn't have the heart to spoil her obvious enthusiasm by telling her that he had already found Mike's surname from the Green Glasgow Co-op website.

'Well done!' said Frank. 'Using your sources, that's great work, Janice.'

'Thanks, Frank.'

She was clearly elated to receive his praise, trying unsuccessfully to keep a smile off her face.

'So, shall we go and pay a visit to Mr Convery?'

'Now?' asked Janice.

'There's no time like the present, is there? And it's only a ten minute walk.'

'Let's go then!' she replied.

Frank didn't want to dampen Janice's enthusiasm, but he was coming ever closer to concluding that he was simply being led on a wild goose chase. He had never been keen on tips from anonymous sources: they tended to have their own agendas.

Perhaps Mike Convery would give them something more to go on.

Janice and Frank arrived at Green Glasgow Co-op's shop on Park Road and waited until two customers had completed their purchases of fruit and vegetables before approaching the one member of staff behind the counter. A sign in the window announced that the Co-op specialised in organic produce and they appeared to have a wide selection on show, not that Frank, who lived almost exclusively on sandwiches and takeaways these days, was any expert. The smell of fresh fruit and vegetables was almost overwhelming.

'Can I help you?' asked the young assistant. His eyes, not surprisingly, were focused on Janice. Frank wondered whether the multitude of piercings in his ears, nose, lips and eyebrows constituted some sort of a breach of food hygiene regulations.

'I'm looking for Mike Convery,' said Frank.

'Are you a friend of his?' the young man asked suspiciously, now looking at Frank.

'No, I'm a journalist,' he replied. 'I'm looking for a quote on a story about environmental campaigns running in the city and I was told that Mike is the man I should talk to.'

'Hang on a minute,' he replied, walking to a door that seemed to lead out to the back of the small shop. 'Mike, you've got a visitor' he shouted.

Mike Convery walked through a few seconds later. Frank saw that he was dressed in tattered denims and a red t-shirt with a hammer and sickle motif. An earring with a CND symbol dangled from his right lobe. Could he be any more of a stereotype, he thought cynically?

'Mr Convery, could I have a word?' asked Frank.

'And you are...?' he asked, seeming wary of the sudden interest in him.

'Frank Gallen from the West End Weekly and this is my assistant Janice Tracey. I wanted to have a word with you about Phil Whitby. Could we talk in private please?'

'Let's go outside,' said Convery. 'I could do with a cigarette break anyway.' He led them through the main door and back onto the pavement to the front of the shop. Convery pulled a packet of Marlboros and a cheap lighter from his pocket before offering the cigarettes to Janice and Frank. Both declined.

'Doesn't exactly go with the healthy organic image, does it, Mike?' Frank asked, smiling.

'I'm trying to quit. It's not easy,' replied Convery with a rueful grin. 'And now's not really a good time to try, man.' He cupped his hand around his cigarette and lit it, inhaling deeply.

'There's never a good time to beat an addiction,' replied Frank with feeling.

'Probably true.' He stared into the distance before his gaze settled once more on Frank. 'So why are you so interested in Phil?'

'His name came up in a story about environmental campaign groups I'm researching. I heard that you and Phil were close?'

Convery looked away before answering. 'We were about to move in together. We'd been partners for a year or so.'

Frank nodded sympathetically. 'My condolences on his death, Mike.'

'Thanks,' he replied, a tear evident in his eye. 'It was such a shock, for him to go that way.' Frank didn't say anything, hoping that he would continue. 'There was no hint that he would do something like that. I couldn't believe it when I found out.'

'Did Phil have any financial or other worries that you knew about?' asked Janice, again joining in confidently.

'No, nothing like that. I mean, we don't ... didn't have much money, but that was cool. And living together would have saved us a bit too.' Convery shook his head sadly.

'Did the police speak to you, Mike?' He was almost loath to ask any more questions, given the effect that they clearly had on the young man, but he pressed on anyway.

'Yes, but it seemed like they were just going through the motions. You know, ticking the boxes before they wrote him off as just another suicide. They weren't interested in learning anything about Phil at all. It was a bloody disgrace. Still what do you expect from them?' said Convery bitterly. 'Listen, why are you asking me about Phil's death? Do you know something, man?'

'Is there something to know?' Frank replied, turning the question back.

'It's just that I can't see Phil killing himself, man. I mean, I guess that's exactly what you would expect me to say, but it's so true.'

'What was going on with Phil before he died, Mike?' asked Frank gently.

'He was happy, we were planning to get a new flat and he had the shop and the parks campaign. Life was going well, man.' Convery shook his head once more. 'He just wasn't the type. Looked after himself, you know? Didn't do drugs, rarely drank and went to the gym regularly. He was there on the evening he died. I mean, why go to the gym if you're going to kill yourself?' Convery finished his cigarette, dropped it to the ground and stamped angrily on it before kicking the butt into the gutter.

'When did you last talk to him?' asked Janice.

'He left here about four to go do some shopping on Byres Road, and I called him about an hour or so later. He seemed fine then.'

'Did he talk to anyone after that, do you know?'

'The police said that he made one call in the evening. The number was saved as MM in his mobile. Phil only ever used initials on his phone not names. He was very careful being a political activist, you know?' he explained.

'Do you know who this MM is?' asked Frank, hiding a smile and wondering whether Whitby had thought that MI5 was interested in food co-ops.

'No idea. I know all of Phil's friends and comrades from our campaign, and there's no one with those initials. The police thought it might stand for Mike Mobile, but he had me stored under MC, obviously. Do you think that he might have told someone why he did it? It's so hard to accept his death without any reason. I loved him, I really did.' Convery began to weep openly and Frank couldn't help sympathising.

'Tell me what you know,' Mike said softly, tears rolling down his cheeks. 'You must be able to tell me something,' he pleaded.

'We don't really know anything, I'm afraid. We haven't found anything at all that would contradict the police. I'm sorry, Mike.' He had decided not to mention his anonymous e-mail to Whitby's partner.

'Are you going to keep looking?' asked Convery hopefully.

'We don't really have anything to go on. If we could find out who MM was that might give us something,' replied Frank.

'You need to check his laptop. His mother will have it now, I think. She told me that Phil's cousin cleared out his old flat at the weekend.'

'That's an idea, thanks,' Frank replied.

'Phil kept everything on that laptop, man. There might be something in his e-mail or on his contacts list? He never wrote anything on paper just in case it fell into the wrong hands.' More left wing paranoia, thought Frank.

'OK. Listen, here's my card,' he said, passing it to Mike. 'Please call me if you think of anything else?'

'OK, sure.' He studied the card before putting it into his hip pocket.

'Thanks for your time,' said Frank as Convery turned to go back into the shop. Janice smiled at him tenderly.

'I wonder who MM could be?' asked Janice when they were alone.

'Well, we know that it's someone Mike doesn't know about, and that makes me suspicious,' replied Frank.

'What do you mean?' she asked, frowning.

'Mike and Phil were going to live together, they worked together and Mike said that he knew all of Phil's friends,' explained Frank. 'So maybe Phil had someone that he didn't want Mike to know about?'

'Like another boyfriend you mean?'

'It's a possibility.'

'I can't see it. Mike really seemed to love him,' said Janice, frowning.

'But we don't know whether Phil felt the same way do we? His last call could well be significant in some way, Janice. And he chose to call MM and not Mike.' Frank now felt like the old and cynical journalist played off against Janice's naïve optimist.

'So what now? Do we go back to Mrs Whitby?' she asked.

'Why not?' Frank replied. 'Phil's laptop is our only possible lead at the moment, so let's chase it down. Maybe you could call Mrs Whitby when we get back and ask if she will see us again?'

'OK, I'll do that,' said Janice as they started to walk back to the office.

Kelvinbridge was bustling as always, students and shoppers rushing between the many small shops, and it took them an age to cross the busy Great Western Road. They walked back to the office in silence, each considering what they had heard from Mike Convery.

Frank wondered whether Whitby was paranoid enough to have committed suicide, just as everyone thought that he had. But something just wasn't right about this story.

If only he knew exactly what it was.

Chapter 3

Frank and Janice sat in Mrs Whitby's very pink living room in Pollok, all three in exactly the same positions as they had on their previous visit.

Frank explained their earlier conversation with Mike Convery and asked if she could think of anyone with the initials MM in Phil's life.

Mrs Whitby thought for a minute before answering.

'I can't think of anyone at all, I'm afraid, not even a distant relative.'

She was dressed all in black once more. Frank thought that she looked pale and drawn, and he wondered when she had last left the house.

'Mike suggested that you might have Phil's laptop? Could we have a look at it if that would be alright with you?' he asked.

'You can see anything that might possibly help find out what happened to Phil,' she replied. 'I've got a whole box of his stuff in the hall cupboard. Could you help me with it, Mister Gallen?'

'Sure,' replied Frank, standing and then following her into the hallway. She opened a door and pointed to a large cardboard box on the floor of a shelved cupboard that was stacked with what looked like assorted junk collected over the years. Frank saw old newspapers and magazines as well as a large number of other boxes on the shelves. He managed, with difficulty, to lift the box that Mrs Whitby had pointed out, and then carried it back into the living room.

'I haven't even opened this since my nephew brought it over on Sunday,' she said sadly, staring grimly at the box on the floor as if she didn't really want to know what it contained. 'Go ahead,' she finally said, gesturing to Frank to open it.

Frank opened the box carefully, using a pen to burst the tape on the lid. The story of Pandora suddenly came into his mind.

Inside he found a large number of political books and pamphlets, a few t-shirts with left wing slogans on them, some CDs by a variety of groups he had never heard of, and a number of smaller mementoes. Right at the bottom of the pile was Phil's laptop.

'Do you have his mobile phone, Mrs Whitby?' asked Frank.

'Yes,' she replied walking over to the wall unit and opening a drawer. She quickly located the phone and passed it to Frank. He immediately handed it to Janice.

'Can you have a look at this while I fire up the laptop?' he asked her as he took the power cable out of the box and plugged it into a wall socket. He stared at the screen, waiting for it to boot up. Finally he arrived at a blue screen which had the name Phil Whitby in the centre with a picture of him above it.

'Damn, it needs a password,' Frank exclaimed, frustrated at coming up against an obstacle so quickly, and berating himself for not having guessed that the security conscious Whitby would have protected his precious laptop.

'Which operating system is it running on?' asked Janice, who was examining the screen of Phil's mobile phone.

'Windows Vista Home Premium,' he replied after glancing back at the laptop.

'I know how to get into XP without a password, but that trick doesn't work with Vista,' replied Janice. 'We have to guess his password if we are to go any further.'

Frank was amazed: he had no idea that Janice was a whiz with computers, and he filed that little piece of information away for future use.

'Do you have any idea what his password might have been, Mrs Whitby?' asked Frank.

'None, I'm afraid. I know nothing about computers at all, sorry,' she replied, shaking her head as if he had asked her an impossible question. Frank stared at the screen, hoping for inspiration to strike.

'What if it's some weird combination of letters and numbers,' he asked, thinking back to the e-mail he had received. 'There's no way we could ever guess.'

'Most people choose a word or a name that means something to them. Why not try Mike?' Janice suggested.

That made as much sense as anything else to Frank so he typed Whitby's partner's first name in and hit the Enter button.

'No, that's not it,' he replied. It would have been too much to expect to get it first time, he thought resignedly and hit the OK button in the middle of the screen. 'Hang on: Now it is telling me: *"Password Hint: an inconvenient truth."*'

'That's easy,' said Janice quickly.

'Is it?' replied Frank, puzzled.

'Isn't that the film Al Gore made about climate change?' she suggested, smiling. 'The one that won an Oscar?'

Of course, thought Frank as he typed in 'AlGore' and this this time the laptop accepted the password. He waited a moment as the computer finished loading. 'We're in!' he said. 'So much for security.'

He saw Mrs Whitby look at him with an amazed expression that seemed to suggest they had performed some sort of magic trick.

Frank immediately opened Whitby's e-mail programme from an icon on the desktop and clicked on the Contacts item. The names were nicely filed in alphabetical order by surname so he scrolled down to the 'M's.

'There's no MM on his contacts list. Have you found anything on the mobile, Janice?'

'Phil didn't have any text messages stored, incoming or outgoing. He must have deleted them all, if there ever were any. There's an incoming call listed from MC on the day he died at 17:10.'

'That backs up what Mike Convery told us,' said Frank, nodding.

'And the last outgoing call was made to MM at 22:36,' she continued.

'Can you give me the number, Janice?' asked Frank. 'Maybe MM was a pet name or something and whoever it is has their real name on his Contacts list?' It was worth a try, anyway.

Janice read out the number as Frank sorted the list by the mobile phone field. He quickly located the number and looked to check the name associated with it.

'Mum!' Both a landline and a mobile number were listed against her name. 'Mrs Whitby, do you have a mobile phone?'

'Mum's Mobile!' exclaimed Janice.

Mrs Whitby seemed momentarily startled by the question. 'Oh yes! Phil bought me one for my birthday in February and set it up for me, but I've never used it. I don't think anyone else even has the number.'

'Could we see it please?' asked Frank.

Mrs Whitby suddenly looked stunned as the implications of the final call became clear to her. The little colour there was in her cheeks drained leaving her a ghostly white. 'Oh my God. Do you think Phil phoned me just before he died? Oh my God!' she repeated.

'Could we see the phone, please?' asked Frank gently.

She stood unsteadily and walked to the unit in the corner, rummaged in the bottom of it for a moment and then pulled out a new looking mobile phone. She sat down once again and handed it to Frank.

'He knew that I never used this thing. Why didn't he call me on the house phone? He must have known that I would be in at that time of night. If I could have talked to him then it might just have changed things.' Frank glanced to Janice, thinking that Mrs Whitby was about to become hysterical.

'Maybe he had a reason, Mrs Whitby. Maybe he just wanted to leave you a message rather than talk to you?' she suggested.

The older woman glanced over at the many pictures of her son on the corner unit and began to cry softly. She pulled a handkerchief from the sleeve of her black blouse and dabbed her eyes, quickly regaining her composure, but said nothing.

Frank switched on the mobile phone and waited impatiently for it to connect to the network. When it did it immediately started ringing, the screen indicating that the call was from the voicemail service. He answered the call and navigated through the automated menu system which informed him that there was one new message. He turned on the loudspeaker and held the phone up so that they could all hear the message.

'Mother, it's Phillip. I'm sorry but I have to do this. I have no choice.....' The call ended abruptly.

Mrs Whitby began to shake. She closed her eyes momentarily and then asked in a faltering voice if Frank would play the short message again. After he had repeated it, she leaned forward and began to talk animatedly. Somehow the message had caused an abrupt change in her mood.

'This might sound totally crazy to you but that message is very strange,' said Mrs Whitby, now speaking very quickly. 'It just sounds totally wrong. He is so calm for one thing, too calm really. Apart from that he always calls me Mum, not Mother, and he absolutely hates being called Phillip. He has been Phil to everyone from when he was a little boy. He was trying to tell me something, I'm sure. He was trying to tell me something.'

'Are you absolutely certain?' asked Frank. 'There was no one who called him Phillip?'

'I told you, he hated the name. His father was called Phillip, you see. He ran off and left us when Phil was just a baby and he absolutely hated being called after him,' she explained, still speaking rapidly.

'What is he trying to tell us?' asked Janice. 'And he didn't mention killing himself at all. Why did he have no choice? Was someone else there with him?'

'Let's not get carried away, Janice.' Frank could see that Mrs Whitby was becoming agitated once again and he wanted to keep her calm. 'The call may have sounded a little strange, but it doesn't really tell us anything new.'

She looked at him with an expression of surprise, but said nothing.

'What are you going to do next, Mr Gallen?' asked Phil's mother. 'It sounded to me like someone was making him do it. He clearly didn't want to jump. Someone had to be forcing him, otherwise why would he say that he had to do it?'

Frank thought for a moment. A strange message wasn't exactly evidence: why would you expect a suicidal man to act rationally after all? But he couldn't bring himself to shatter the glint of hope that she had taken from her son's final message.

'If I can take your phone away with me, I will play this message to the police and see if they will look into it some more. And I promise I'll get back to you if there is any news.'

'OK, if that's what you think is best,' she replied, although Frank could tell that she was somehow expecting more from him. But exactly what, he didn't have a clue.

'I know one of the officers in the Gorbals station and I will talk directly to him,' he said, hoping that this would placate her.

'As long as you tell me what he says.'

'I will do. I'll call you if there is anything,' promised Frank as he stood and prepared to leave, slipping the phone into his jacket pocket.

'Would you mind if we took his laptop too?' asked Frank. 'There might be something else of interest on it. I'd like the chance to have a more thorough look through it.'

'Of course. It's no use to me anyway,' she replied. 'Take it with my blessing.'

Frank powered off the laptop and moments later they walked out of the house, leaving Mrs Whitby to her memories once more.

'So what have you got to tell me Frank? You said on the phone that you had found some new evidence about the Whitby's suicide,' asked a sceptical sounding Detective Sergeant Ken Becker.

Becker had put on weight since Frank had last seen him and looked stressed. Perhaps there was a downside to his recent promotion? Frank quickly explained how they had found out about Whitby's final telephone call and had managed to trace the recipient. He then played the voicemail message to Becker and explained exactly why his mother had thought that Phil had been trying to tell her something.

Becker opened a folder that he had brought into the dimly lit interview room with him and quickly read through a few a sheets of paper before responding.

'First of all, well done on tracing the number, Frank. We had got as far as identifying it as a pay as you go mobile, but there wasn't a registered owner so we couldn't go any further. We also contacted Whitby's service provider and cell site analysis told us that the call was made from a location consistent with where his body was found.' He paused for a moment. 'I'm not sure that the message tells us anything new, though.'

'But Whitby called himself Phillip and referred to his mum as Mother. Why would he do that?' asked Janice, disappointed at Becker's response.

'People who are about to commit suicide aren't exactly rational,' he answered, echoing exactly what Frank had been thinking earlier. 'You would be amazed at some of the strange things people say and do just before they kill themselves.'

'So you're not going to do anything?' she asked, obviously frustrated.

'We have already closed the file as a suicide, don't forget,' replied Becker. 'His injuries were consistent with a jump. There is no evidence that anyone else was with him. And that call is consistent with a suicide too. He could simply have been apologising to his mother for what he was about to do.' Becker sat back in his chair, shaking his head and dismissing their concerns.

'But there is no evidence that he was depressed or even worried, let alone suicidal. We've talked to his boyfriend and his mother. Surely they would have noticed something about him, some change of mood?' Janice was persistent; Frank had to give her that.

'I'm sorry, but unless we come across new and compelling evidence of foul play to take to the Fiscal, then it will remain case closed as a suicide,' Becker replied gently.

'OK, thanks for seeing us, Ken,' Frank replied. He stood up and put the phone back into his jacket pocket. Janice also stood up, although somewhat reluctantly Frank noticed, but at least she had followed his lead. He shook hands with Becker and promised to call him soon and then they left the interview room.

When they were on the pavement outside the station Frank looked around at the Gorbals, wondering at the change in the area. He had grown up just a few streets away, but in a very different environment. The old council flats that they had lived in were now gone, long demolished to make way for the private flats of New Gorbals, as it was known.

Progress? Perhaps, thought Frank remembering the damp seventh floor flat of his childhood in Queen Elizabeth Square. He had watched the 1960s flats being blown up in 1993, the year after he had left school and moved out. And shortly afterwards his parents had secured a new house in Parkhead in the East End of the city after almost thirty years in the Gorbals.

'What do we do now, Frank?' asked Janice, breaking his reverie.

'Back to the office to catch up on other work, I think,' he replied.

Janice seemed upset by his answer. He knew that his young protégée was keen to find a story, but she had to learn that sometimes there was just nowhere left to go.

'What about that e-mail you received? That must mean something surely, Frank?' He could now hear the beginnings of desperation in her voice.

'Janice, anonymous tips sometimes turn out to be nothing,' he explained as tenderly as he could. 'It might just have been someone playing around or causing mischief for reasons of their own. Unless there is something we have missed here, I can't see where else we can possibly take this. I'm sorry but I think we are now at the end of the road.'

'I'll read through all of my notes for a final time when I get back,' she replied, reluctant to let go of her potential big story.

'OK. Let me know if you think of anything new.' Frank thought that he would let her consider the evidence for a short while before closing the file. She had done well, but the final conclusion would have to be that not every tip leads to a front page story.

If only life was so easy, Frank said to himself, once again becoming the cynical old journalist.

Tuesday May 13 2008 4:20pm

'Asif, can I have a quick word with you about a planning matter?' asked Councillor Thomas Gallen.

Councillor Asif Rafique looked up from the papers he was reading as he sat drinking a cup of tea in the near empty Members' Dining Room. 'Of course you can, Thomas. Take a seat,' he replied courteously.

Gallen sat down beside the slight, middle aged Asian. He quickly dismissed the waiter and leaned in towards Rafique so that their conversation could not be overheard.

'I wanted a word about some new proposals that David Longwell has been discussing with me. I know that he is in the final stages of preparing a planning application at the moment, and of course it will come in front of your Committee eventually,' Gallen began.

'Does this have anything to do with those press reports of a Longwell Homes development in Kelvingrove Park?' asked Rafique.

Gallen wasn't surprised that the Convener of the Council's Planning Committee had read the reports. He was usually up to date with pretty much everything that was going on in the city, he had found.

'It does yes, Asif,' he replied. 'But it's nothing on the scale of what was reported. All we are talking about is one block of executive apartments that will help us to attract more professionals into the city.'

'Ah, that old trick,' replied Rafique. 'Leak a story about a large development and then a small one doesn't seem quite so contentious.'

The astute Asian had clearly seen through Longwell's PR stunt. Gallen chose his next words carefully, knowing that Rafique could be a thorn in his side if he opposed the development. Or a key ally if he could be brought on side.

'There are some who will oppose any building on parkland on some sort of principle. I don't expect you to agree to a proposal you haven't seen yet, but I would like an assurance that you will consider it on its merits.' He found that he was holding his breath as he waited for Rafique to consider his request.

'I would have to be convinced of the benefits to the city. Losing even a small area of Kelvingrove Park would be controversial, as I'm sure you know,' replied Rafique.

'Of course, but I do think that the case can be proven,' he stated boldly, trying to impart a sense of confidence that he didn't feel.

'We will see,' said Rafique, although Gallen thought that he still sounded doubtful. 'Let's talk again when we have some more of the details, Thomas.'

'Of course,' replied the Council Leader. 'Thank you for your time.'

He stood and walked away, leaving Rafique to his reading. Gallen was pleased that he had at least broached the idea, although he was not exactly overjoyed at his colleague's response. Rafique had established a strong reputation within the Council and was tipped by many as a future leader. And Gallen hoped that he could eventually be persuaded to come down on the side of reason rather than that of emotion.

Tuesday May 13 2008 5:25pm

When Frank returned to his desk at the West End Weekly, he saw a yellow post it note attached to his computer screen. "See Me! JA"

He took a quick look at the large whiteboard on the far office wall that detailed all of the stories still to be completed for the week's newspaper and reassured himself that he had not missed something he was supposed to be covering.

Comforted that he was apparently on top of things, Frank approached John's office and was surprised to see that the door was closed, which was extremely unusual. He knocked and then entered the editor's office, which had room for little more than a large desk behind which John sat and a couple of old metal filing cabinets. The small office also had a number of potted plants on shelves and even a couple of larger ones in pots on the floor. As always, Frank worried that his hay fever would be set off just by walking into the office.

'Frank. I trust that you brought Janice back with you?' said John before he had even had a chance to sit.

'Of course I did. What's up?' asked Frank, confused by John's attitude. He removed a stack of papers from the seat opposite John's desk.

'While she was out playing journalist with you, the phone has been ringing off the hook and I can't find any of the advertiser files she has been working on. What's going on here?' John's voice was raised and he sounded stressed.

'Nothing's going on, John. I was following a lead on the Whitby story from that anonymous e-mail and Janice was shadowing me. She took an interest in it from the start and it has been good experience for her. If that's a problem then take it out on me, not her.'

'Who am I talking to right now?'

Frank assumed that it was a rhetorical question.

'Look, she is employed primarily to cover the admin work and I needed her here this afternoon. I don't mind her helping you out a bit now and then, but she's not your trainee or personal assistant, you know.'

'OK, point taken,' replied Frank. He knew better than to push John when he was in a bad mood. He knew that while his friend was normally a placid individual, John had a volcanic temper if sufficiently riled.

'Look, I know this isn't at all what you're used to, Frank, but I need to put out a decent paper every week to keep circulation numbers up and the advertisers on board,' John explained, looking weary. 'It's not an easy time for the newspaper industry now that so many people get their news from the web, as I'm sure you know.'

Frank recognised that John was under pressure. 'You're right, John. Look, it doesn't seem like there is a story in the Whitby death anyway. Janice is going to have one last look over her notes, which I don't think will turn up anything new. Then I'll tell her how well she has done, which is true, and explain that sometimes you have to conclude that there just isn't a story. And there endeth the lesson.'

'OK, fine.'

Frank was pleased to see that John was now much calmer than he had been at the start of their conversation.

'This did all give me an idea though, Frank. I had a look at that parks campaign's website today and there is some interesting stuff on there. Do you know about the proposals to build flats in Kelvingrove Park?' he asked.

'I've heard something about it, yes. But it won't go anywhere, will it? The Council won't give planning permission surely. Remember that plan for a night club in the Botanic Gardens? It came to nothing in the end.'

'Well, I think it will make for a good story or two,' said John. 'You know the type of thing: house builders lined up against environmentalists. Should we build on historic park land? What do local residents think of the plans? Get a bit of a public debate going.'

'OK, it sounds like it might be interesting. Leave it with me,' said Frank.

'Give me something for this week's edition, will you?' asked John.

'Sure,' replied Frank. John had turned back to his computer so Frank assumed that the conversation was over and left the office, grateful to get away from the pollen.

Tuesday May 13 2008 7:45pm

'Mum, it's Frank,' he said, standing in the middle of his small living room and looking out of the window at a group of small children playing on bikes in the evening sun. Now that's something you don't see too often in the days of video games and the internet, he reflected.

'Oh hello, how are you?' came the reply, his mother's voice sounding faint over the phone line.

'I'm fine, getting by. How are you doing?'

'Not too bad, all things considered. The doctor has given me some new pills and they seem to help with the joint pain.' Helen Gallen was in her late sixties and a combination of arthritis and angina had slowed her considerably in recent years. Not that she would ever admit it though, Frank knew.

'That's good. I'm pretty busy this week, Mum, but I'll get over to see you at the weekend. Is that OK?'

'Alright, but come on Saturday afternoon, not Sunday. Thomas, Marie and the children are coming for their tea on Sunday,' she replied sharply.

'OK, I'll see you then.'

'Bye, Frank.'

Feeling the sudden silence that took over the room becoming annoying, he put the second CD from The Eagles latest double album into his hi-fi. That's better, he thought as the music replaced the quiet of the evening.

The short phone call had been typical, Frank thought sourly. He had found that his mother usually had very little to say to him these days. Indeed their relationship had never recovered from the aftermath of the tragedy two years previously that had ripped the family apart.

Frank told himself, not for the first time, how unfair his exile was. He knew he had behaved very badly, but he had been drinking heavily at the time, and that part of his life was now behind him.

What would it take for his family to accept that he had changed, and for the better?

Tuesday May 13 2008 10:20pm

Running his fingers through his red hair, he found he had to resist the impulse to scream in frustration. The lack of any media coverage of his activities was infuriating. The world had to be told what he was doing; there was no point otherwise.

Not one thing on any of the news sites. Not a whisper. Not even a suggestion that Phil Whitby had been murdered. He shut down his computer and thumped his hand down hard. The pain did not register.

What the hell do you have to do to get the authorities to acknowledge your work? Deliver bloody bodies straight to them? Draw them a fucking map?

Even an e-mail sent directly to the great Frank Gallen didn't seem to have had any impact at all. But then maybe Gallen wasn't as clever now he was sober. Although that bastard had never been as smart as he thought he was anyway.

He realised that number four would have to be far more public. He had to do something that would register with even the most stupid of reporters. That meant greater risk of course, but it was essential for the world to know what he was doing and more importantly why.

The frustration continued to boil within him, turning to anger and then to intense longing as he thought about how and where he would strike next. It had to be soon. He couldn't wait any fucking longer.

It had to be tonight.

Chapter 4

Wednesday May 14 2008, 9:05am

> To: Gallenf@wew.com
> From: dgsh45x@hotmail.co.uk
> Date: 14/05/08 at 01:48
>> Whitby was #3. Harrington was #4.

Frank Gallen frowned as he read the second anonymous message. The name was another random series of characters, giving him no clue to the sender's identity. But two anonymous e-mails that both mentioned Phil Whitby surely had to have come from the same source, he concluded. That was the easy part of the puzzle.

But what did the message mean? Now that was the difficult part. Frank felt the hairs on the back of his neck rise, a familiar feeling that had always told him he was onto a big story.

The e-mail implied that there had been two previous deaths that he didn't know anything about, Frank realised. And if Harrington was number four, then whatever it was must have come after Whitby's death, of course.

But who was Harrington? Frank quickly checked the news feeds, drawing a complete blank. And a Google search found so many Harringtons in Glasgow that it was totally useless.

Frank then checked the websites of both the Green Glasgow Co-operative and the Parks for the People campaign. No one by the name of Harrington was listed on either. So he had no obvious connection to Whitby. This was getting even more frustrating.

Frank was alone in the office early in the morning, which was unusual as John was the first to arrive pretty much every day. But this morning Frank had woken early and, unable to get back to sleep, had decided to come into the office.

He walked to the kitchen and poured himself another coffee, wondering what to do next. Then he remembered that John was meeting with a key advertiser and wouldn't be in until later. Frank smiled, realising that he had some time to pursue the story before his boss returned.

He returned to his desk, took Phil Whitby's laptop from his drawer and logged on for a third time. His search of the machine the previous evening had revealed absolutely nothing of interest. He turned once more to Whitby's Contacts and looked under H. No one named Harrington was listed. Frustrated, he closed the computer down and put it back into the drawer.

Frank was now almost certain that there had to be something to these messages, but frustratingly he still had no idea what he was being told, or why. So the question was, where did he go next in his quest?

On a hunch Frank decided to telephone the Gorbals police station. He asked to be put through to DS Ken Becker, but was put on hold. He waited impatiently, drinking his coffee and staring at the cryptic e-mail, as if some hidden meaning would suddenly reveal itself. It didn't, of course. Finally the annoying electronic music ended and he heard Becker's voice come over the line.

'Frank. I don't hear from you in months and now you can't keep away. What's up?' Becker asked him cheerily.

'I just wanted to run a name past you and see if it means anything at all,' said Frank cagily.

'Is this something more to do with the Whitby case?'

'Just a tip I got. Does the name Harrington ring any bells, Ken?'

'Just Harrington, no first name?'

'That's correct.'

'I can't say that it means anything to me at all. I probably do know someone called Harrington of course, but can't you be a bit more specific?' asked the detective.

'Afraid not, Ken. As I said it was just a tip that said I should look into someone called Harrington,' replied Frank, sticking close to the truth.

'But this is related to Whitby, isn't it?'

Becker just wouldn't let it go. Frank sighed and decided to be honest, hoping that he could keep Becker on side just a little longer.

'There might be a connection, yes. Another crime perhaps?'

'What do you mean *another* crime?' replied the detective frostily. 'Whitby committed suicide, remember?'

'Maybe someone called Harrington has been the victim of a crime recently?' asked Frank, realising that Becker wouldn't tolerate much more.

'Not that I know of, not around here anyway. But seeing as it's you, I'll check on the computer,' replied Becker.

Frank waited expectantly for the detective to finish his search.

'The only recent entry on the system under that name is a robbery in Springburn last weekend. A Mrs Ellen Harrington. And we have made an arrest.'

Surely that wasn't what he was being directed towards, was it? 'Not to worry, it was just a hunch,' said Frank, equally disappointed and frustrated.

'I think you're being sent on a bit of a wild goose chase, Frank,' Becker said with a trace of humour. 'Is someone playing a joke perhaps?'

'You could be right,' Frank told him, although he wasn't nearly ready to drop the matter. He could dismiss one e-mail, but two in three days had to mean something, he was sure of it. His gut was screaming to him to keep going and over the years he had learned to listen.

'Frank, I was going to give you a call today anyway,' said Becker.

He sounded hesitant, Frank thought. He said nothing and waited for Becker to continue.

'A colleague filled me in last night on what you've been up to over the last while. I'm really sorry, Frank.'

'Don't worry about it. I'm doing fine now,' he replied, as cheerily as he could.

'I would never have mentioned going for a drink if I had known the situation. I hope you didn't think I was trying to say something to you.'

Frank smiled to himself. So many people he knew just did not know how to talk about his problem.

'Look, it's not a big issue, Ken. I used to drink and now I don't. And I'm feeling better than I have for years,' he explained.

'That's good,' Becker replied, sounding relieved. 'I'm glad you're well.'

'Thanks. Look I need to get on. Maybe I'll buy you a coffee sometime?'

'Sounds good.' said Becker, now laughing. 'I'll see you, Frank.'

Frank put the phone down. One more awkward conversation over, and one more person who knew his story. It was getting easier to explain his problem though, that was one thing.

But he still had no lead at all on Harrington, whoever that might be.

Wednesday May 14 2008, 11:30am

'Here's the draft of your speech for tomorrow, Thomas,' said Alan Mathers, handing Councillor Gallen a manila folder. They had been talking in Gallen's office for half an hour, but had only just got to the most crucial matter on the agenda.

'Thanks,' he replied. 'Is it as we discussed?'

'Of course. I've e-mailed you a copy too. I've made no mention of the Kelvingrove development for now. But the speech is full of praise for Longwell Homes and of the personal contribution that David Longwell is making to the regeneration of the city. I also included a reference to the strong possibility of future partnership developments in other parts of Glasgow. Hopefully that will be enough to placate him for now,' Mathers explained.

'Good work, Alan, thanks. I'll read through it and let you know if I need any amendments.' Gallen added the folder to the unsteady looking heap of paperwork that threatened to topple from his in tray.

'Has Longwell been in touch?' asked Mathers cautiously.

'Not as yet. I expect he will phone me tonight.' The Council Leader frowned. 'I just hope he takes the rationale for a delay well.'

'He should if he is sensible and it will buy us time too,' his assistant replied. *And more specifically, buy me time to get out of here.* 'But we will need to make sure that the support is there. He won't wait forever.'

'I know,' acknowledged Gallen. 'I've already talked to Rafique. He wouldn't commit, but at least he is not opposed on principle. That's a start, I suppose.'

'Good. But there's a long way to go yet, Thomas.'

Gallen nodded, acknowledging that he was not out of the woods just yet. Not by a long way.

Wednesday May 14 2008, 12:30pm

John Addison walked into the office with a big smile on his face. Frank Gallen looked up as his editor strode towards him, dressed in a very smart grey suit rather than his usual denims.

'It went well then, John?' he asked, smiling.

'Couldn't have gone better,' Addison replied. 'McInnis Cars have extended their advertising contract for another year. And I managed to negotiate an increased rate, too.'

'Wow, well done,' replied Frank, knowing that was a very important development as finances were always tight for John and the newspaper needed the advertising revenue to survive.

'Thanks. They are very pleased with the response they are getting in terms of customer numbers and with the quality of the paper too. Good news all round,' he replied.

'Keeps us all in a job,' Frank replied, smiling at his old friend.

'Talking of which, where have you got to with the Kelvingrove story? I need it tomorrow, remember?'

Frank lifted a plastic folder from his desk and opened it. 'I've pulled together a lot of background on the history of the park and that sort of thing. There's not a great deal on the Longwell Homes proposals, though: just that one leaked story but the company is not ready to make a proper announcement as yet according to their PR people. And I'm meeting Steve Findlay from 'Parks for the People' this afternoon for an interview.'

'Great stuff, Frank. Glad to see that your eye is back on the ball. Have you talked to Janice about that other matter yet?'

'No. I'll see her when she comes in this afternoon,' he replied. 'But ... I got another e-mail.' He looked to see what reaction he would get. John seemed initially to be annoyed, but then curiosity got the better of him.

'Anonymous like the last one?'

Frank nodded. 'Exactly the same format, John.'

'What does this one say?'

'It says *Whitby was #3. Harrington was #4*.'

'What the hell does that mean?' John exclaimed loudly.

'Right now I have no idea,' replied Frank. 'I don't have a clue what the numbers refer to or who Harrington might be. And I can't find anyone by that name connected to Whitby in any way at all.'

'The first one said that Whitby's death wasn't a suicide, didn't it? And now this one says that he was number three. It doesn't mean three murders, does it? And then that this Harrington is the fourth murder?' John was obviously becoming intrigued by the puzzle, thought Frank, smiling to himself.

'It's a possibility. But I talked to a contact of mine in CID and he said that the name meant nothing to him. And no one called

Harrington has been killed recently.' Frank was still wondering where to turn next. Perhaps John would give him an idea?

'Why are these e-mails coming specifically to you, Frank? Have you thought about that? Maybe that's another way of looking at it that might get us somewhere.'

'I've no idea on that either. I've never had tips like this before.'

'Well someone has chosen to contact you, Frank. There's no obvious connection to the paper with Whitby, given that he was from Pollok and died in the Gorbals. That implies that the messages must be personal in some way.'

'That's true, I suppose,' Frank conceded.

'Maybe it's someone you used to know? Perhaps it's an old contact or a source from your Daily News days?' John suggested.

'But then why make the messages anonymous? It would add to the credibility if I already knew the sender, wouldn't it? This all makes no sense at all.'

John's mobile phone rang and he disappeared into his office to take the call. Frank was left with a great deal on his mind. Who was contacting him and why?

And were there really another three dead bodies to be found?

Wednesday May 14 2008, 2:10pm

'Councillor Gallen, David Longwell is here and says he needs a minute with you.'

Gallen was surprised at the announcement from his secretary. Longwell didn't have an appointment, although the developer had said that he would telephone him.

He looked at his watch and saw that he didn't have much time before he had to leave and was on the point of refusing to see Longwell. But then he thought that perhaps it would be better to talk to him in person and to explain his decision to delay the announcement.

'Send him in, Sandra,' he finally replied after a moment's further thought. He waited as Longwell strode into his office carrying a leather brief case. This time Gallen decided to remain sitting at his desk, giving the impression of power, and so Longwell took a seat opposite him. The developer immediately got to business, ignoring the usual pleasantries.

'Thomas, I was passing and thought that we could talk about your speech,' he said.

Gallen took a deep breath before replying to the developer. 'I've talked to some senior colleagues in the Labour Group and considered what you said yesterday carefully. I don't think we are in a position to make a public announcement as yet, David.'

'Why ever not?' asked the developer.

Gallen was momentarily thrown by his calm tone, having expected a furious reaction.

'It will take me some time to ensure that there is a majority in support of the proposal within the Council. I talked to the Planning Convener yesterday and while he won't oppose the scheme in principle, he wants to see more details before coming to a final conclusion. If I can get him on side, then his committee will in all likelihood follow suit. I have to play the political game,' explained Councillor Gallen. 'And there are another couple of key players that I want to make sure are going to be supportive before we go public.'

'So you are not intending to mention my development in your speech tomorrow then, Thomas?'

Again the words were delivered in a measured tone, which worried Gallen far more than an angry one would have. What was Longwell up to?

'Not specifically, David. Although I will be mentioning that our partnership will be extended. But my political judgement is that to announce the detail now would risk galvanising support for those who will oppose the project. I think it would be much better for both of us if you give me more time to work on my colleagues.' He hoped that he sounded confident in his own persuasive abilities. 'To push forward now would be a real risk, David,' he concluded.

'I have the press on my back now, Thomas. If I can't give them more about Kelvingrove Park, then perhaps I will have to give them another story.'

Now Gallen was very concerned. He knew that Longwell could be a dangerous man to be on the wrong side of, and he suddenly had a very bad feeling that was where he was about to find himself.

'What do you mean?' he asked warily.

'I think you might want to listen to this,' Longwell said, smiling coldly. He opened his brief case and pulled out a small voice recorder. He placed it on the desk between them, pressed a button and Councillor Gallen heard David Longwell's own voice come from the tiny speaker.

'You told me that Whitby was your biggest concern in case he went public with what he had on you, yes?'

'I did.'

'That you wished Whitby could be dealt with?'

'Yes.'

'And you told me that if he was out of the way, your life would be so much easier. Yes?'

'That's true.'

'Well, Phil Whitby is now no longer in a position to use the information he had, is he?'

'No.'

'The timing of his suicide was fortuitous for you, wasn't it?'

'Well, yes, it certainly looks that way.'

Longwell stopped the recording and looked straight into Gallen's eyes without saying a single word. The Council Leader found himself unable to speak as a wave of panic surged through his body. Surely Longwell wasn't going to make the tape public? He finally found his voice.

'You recorded our conversation? Why, David?' he asked.

'I had a feeling that you might need a little more persuasion to go public with the next phase of our partnership. Now this tape could make life very difficult for you couldn't it, Councillor Gallen? You must see that.'

Gallen shook his head, understanding that he now had a second, and far more dangerous, blackmailer to contend with. And he suddenly realised that if Longwell had indeed been behind Whitby's death, he would have the material that Whitby had threatened to go to the press with.

'That is just a part of a conversation taken out of context. It doesn't prove anything.' He tried to be dismissive, but was aware how weak his words must sound.

Longwell simply ignored his protests and continued. 'Now to a journalist this recording would raise two questions, wouldn't it? Firstly, what did Whitby have on you that you were so afraid would get into the public domain?' He paused, again staring directly at Gallen. 'And secondly, how did Whitby really die?'

'You wouldn't…' began Gallen.

'Try me,' interrupted Longwell forcefully. 'I have a major interview scheduled with a reporter from the Daily News tomorrow afternoon. Your speech will decide whether I tell her about my new development, or about your relationship with Phil Whitby.' He stood and picked up his brief case. 'It's up to you to decide which it is, Thomas.'

'But how would your telling the press help you?' he asked desperately.

'Maybe the *new* Leader of the Council will be more amenable to working with me.' Longwell stood and looked down at Gallen, letting the impact of his words sink in. 'That's just a copy of our conversation, of course. And you can keep the recorder too, Thomas. Call it a gift.'

Gallen closed his eyes as Longwell left the office, and let his head sink to his chest. Confused thoughts raced around his mind as he attempted to work out what to do next.

He knew that he could not risk exposure. Everything that he had worked for, all the years of struggling for advancement within the party and the Council, it would all be for nothing. He would be disgraced. Not to mention the impact that a public revelation would have on his wife and family. Marie would surely leave him and take the children too. He could lose everything that was important in his life in one fell swoop. The sickening realisation of how dark his predicament was, left him close to tears.

Gallen tried to hold himself together; he had to analyse the situation and come up with a plan. Taking a deep breath he attempted to quell his growing panic.

He was certain that Longwell was not bluffing, so what could he possibly do to stop the developer ruining him? He quickly realised that he had no other option but go along with Longwell's demand and make the announcement the way he wanted. He had no choice but to amend his speech.

The simple truth was that Longwell had him well and truly by the balls.

Chapter 5

Janice walked into the office feeling downhearted. In her mind she rehearsed the words that she had been thinking about all morning: the words she would use to explain to Frank why she thought that they had to drop the Whitby investigation.

Hours of reading through her notes had led to nothing at all, not even a single lead that was still to be investigated. Would Frank be terribly disappointed with her failure? She could only hope that she hadn't missed anything obvious; that would just be awful.

She saw that Frank was sitting at his desk, so as soon as she had taken her coat off, she steeled herself and walked over.

'Frank, can I talk to you about Phil Whitby?'

'Sure,' he replied with a smile; that smile. 'What have you got?'

'Well, I spent last night reading through all of my notes. And I've thought about nothing else all morning. I can hardly even remember what my lectures were about because I was concentrating on this.' Janice stopped, realising that she was waffling, but found herself unable to say the words that she feared might cause Frank to think badly of her.

'And what was your conclusion?' he asked.

She took a deep breath and then said, 'There's nothing, Frank. I just can't see where we can go. Maybe there is just no story here and the e-mail was a hoax. I'm sorry, but I can't think what else we can do.' She waited, dreading his reply and praying that he would not feel let down.

But Frank nodded, apparently in agreement, and her heart lifted. 'There was nowhere left to go, so that's the correct answer, Janice. Or at least it was.' He smiled again, the slightly shy, lopsided smile that melted her heart every single time.

Janice immediately guessed that he had some new information. 'What do you mean, Frank?'

He opened the second e-mail for her to read and recounted his conversation with John.

'This e-mail changes things, doesn't it, Frank?' she asked excitedly. There was a story after all and she was helping to break it, while also getting to spend time with Frank. It couldn't get any better, could it?

'But what does it tell us, Janice? I don't know who it's from or what it means. We got nowhere investigating Whitby and I have no idea who this Harrington might be.'

She could tell that he was immensely discouraged and tried in vain to think of a solution. But all she could think of was that even frown lines did not stop Frank Gallen from being a very good looking man indeed. *Keep your mind on the job, Janice.*

'I don't know. Maybe there will be another e-mail? Someone is clearly trying to tell you something,' she suggested. *Oh well done, that didn't sound lame at all.*

Before Frank could answer, she saw someone come into the office and she had to return to the reception desk, which fortunately spared her blushes.

'Can I help you?' she asked the middle aged man who had just entered.

'Yes, my name is Steve Findlay and I have an appointment with Frank Gallen at three.' Findlay looked like a professor from an old movie, dressed in a sports jacket which had leather patches at the elbows. *Who wears them in the twenty first century*, she asked herself? He had an earnest look and she wondered what his business with Frank was.

'I'll take you through,' she said and showed Findlay into the office and to Frank's desk. They shook hands and then he took a seat opposite the reporter while Janice returned to the front desk.

Janice was determined to find the connection between Whitby and Harrington and went immediately to her PC. If she could come up with something new while Frank was in his meeting, then he could not fail to be impressed with her, she realised. With a determined look on her face, Janice switched the computer on.

'Thanks for coming in, Steve,' said Frank as they sat by his desk. 'I'm afraid we don't have a conference room, so we will have to do this here, if that's OK.'

'Sure, no problem,' replied Findlay, looking around the cramped office space with some sympathy.

'Thanks. Now as I explained on the phone, I'm doing a piece on Kelvingrove Park, the history and the future. I'm sure you've hears the rumours of a residential development in the park and I wanted to get your group's views,' Frank explained to Findlay.

'Yes, from the Daily News article,' he said, nodding. 'Something is going on, although the developers, Longwell Homes, haven't confirmed anything officially as yet. But no smoke and all that. I wouldn't be surprised if the Council or the developers leaked the story deliberately just to test the water.'

'And is that why you are planning the rally at the end of the month?' asked Frank.

'Not exactly. We were planning to have a major public event soon anyway, but this gives us the perfect focal point. We take the view that Glasgow's parks are a major asset and are simply held in trust by the Council for the people of the city. And so we oppose any private developments on parklands on principle. It's all spelled out in the press release I sent you the other day,' he explained.

'I got that, thanks,' Frank said, the release sitting in the folder on his desk. 'I just wanted a quick chat and maybe to get a couple of direct quotes to go along with it.'

'How about this?' replied Findlay quickly, leaving Frank to conclude that he had prepared his words in advance. 'Parks for the People' sends a message to the City Council. We will fight any and all plans to build in Glasgow's parks. Protect our parks for the people of Glasgow.'

'That's great, thanks. Now, just a bit of background. Could you tell me a little about your organisation, Steve?'

'Well, Parks for the People isn't really an organisation as such,' corrected Findlay. 'We are simply a broad campaign that brings together those who are in political parties and those who aren't, as well as community groups, trade unions, churches, you name it. We don't have elected officers or any real structure. I tend to do a lot of the press stuff simply because I have some experience.'

'Phil Whitby was very involved, wasn't he?' asked Frank.

'That's right, yes.'

'Was he a friend of yours?' he asked Findlay in an offhand manner.

'No, not really. I mean, we were at a lot of the same meetings together, although I didn't know him well. But he was very committed to the environmental cause. His death was a real tragedy.'

'I saw a quote from someone called Harrington on line. Is he involved with your campaign?' Frank looked for a reaction.

'No, we don't have anyone by that name. I don't recognise it at all,' replied Findlay.

'I must have got the name wrong then, I'll check later,' said Frank, pretending to make a note of his error. 'I think that's all I need for now, Steve. Maybe we can talk again just before the demonstration?'

'That would be great. Thanks for the call, Frank.' Findlay stood and offered his hand to Frank, and they walked towards the exit.

Frank had some more copy for the Kelvingrove Park story, which would please John, but was perturbed to find that another door had closed in the search for the mysterious Harrington. What next, he asked himself as they walked though the office?

Frustratingly, he didn't have an answer.

Wednesday May 14 2008, 3:05pm

'So Councillor Gallen now thinks that you had Whitby killed?'

'Very neat isn't it?' replied David Longwell to his son Daniel. He sat back in his large chair behind the mahogany desk in his plush city centre office, and watched his son working through the implications of the story he had just finished telling.

The Parklands projects would be the final crown in his property empire, Longwell thought contentedly. He would soon be able to retire with a very large nest egg. And Councillor Thomas Gallen was going to help him to accomplish his goal.

Daniel finally looked up at his father and Longwell knew that he was eager to please him.

'So Gallen has no choice but to go along with what you want. And that means he will announce his support for the Kelvingrove Project?'

'He doesn't have a choice,' replied Longwell.

'But you didn't have Whitby killed and you don't have the information that Gallen fears, do you?' asked Daniel, looking almost afraid to question his father.

'It's enough that Gallen thinks that I do, Daniel. And that recording I have could certainly sound incriminating if a journalist got hold of it.'

'That's certainly true,' his son acknowledged. 'And he knows it.'

'Anyway, there's absolutely no way he can risk calling my bluff. It would end his political career if he was wrong and we both know that he has ambitions beyond Glasgow.' Longwell smiled at his son, pleased that he had so astutely summed up the situation.

'So we keep the pressure on him and push ahead with our proposals?' Daniel asked.

'Exactly right.' Longwell had not become a millionaire by playing by the rules.

But even he had to admit that this latest manoeuvre was particularly brilliant.

Janice quickly googled Steve Findlay when she had booted up her PC and found that he was a former Green Party Parliamentary candidate as well as an active environmental campaigner. That didn't explain the patches though, she thought snidely.

She also discovered that Findlay was also a spokesperson for Parks for the People, which meant that he was part of the Kelvingrove story, she concluded. Janice wondered whether Frank would ask him about Phil Whitby and the mysterious Harrington. *Of course he will, stupid. He's an experienced reporter.*

Her curiosity about Findlay now satisfied, Janice turned to the news sites and looked for any story that was related to anyone called Harrington. A few false trails led her to unrelated or old stories, but she could find nothing that seemed remotely relevant to the second e-mail that Frank had received.

And then she hit the jackpot.

The BBC website had a new update to a story on its Scotland page concerning a murder committed during the night in Glasgow. Janice clicked on the link and quickly scanned the article.

She learned that a man had been found dead in Wellington Street in the city centre at around 2am. A single stab wound to the chest had killed him instantly, and the police were appealing for witnesses. Now that his family had been informed of his death the victim's identity was being made public.

His name was Mike Harrington.

The report described him as a 34 year old man who had lived in Newton Mearns, an affluent suburb to the south of the city. He was married, but did not have children. Harrington had been a lawyer with a leading city centre firm.

Janice could hardly contain her excitement. She wondered whether she should interrupt Frank's meeting to tell him the news immediately, but decided that she had to force herself to wait until he was finished. He was bound to be pleased with her discovery, which gave them a whole new angle to explore. And she had found it!

Frank would be delighted with her, she thought gleefully. Oh happy day!

Next, she googled Mike Harrington and came up with his entry on his law firm's website, which merely listed his qualifications, noted his speciality as property law, and named some of his clients. His hobby was listed as golf and from several other websites reporting on local amateur competitions, she soon found that he had been pretty good at the game.

Janice looked over to where Frank was still talking to Findlay and she stopped to stare at her mentor, as she always thought of him in the privacy of her mind. Mentor was not the relationship she longed for, of course, but it was a good start.

Although he was slim and not much taller than her, Frank somehow seemed much taller. Janice had always found intelligent men to be sexy, although of course Frank's dark good looks certainly added to the appeal, she thought. He was a man, so much more mature than the boys who pursued her at University. Frank was well built and she knew that he worked out regularly. Beginning to feel a little hot, she imagined his strong arms holding her, his perfect mouth tenderly kissing hers, his ...

Janice shook her head and forced herself to return her thoughts to the story. She must be professional, that would be the best way to make an impression on Frank, not wasting time fantasising like a school girl. And finding the link to Harrington would certainly help her to do that. This was the breakthrough and she had found it, thought Janice proudly.

But then it suddenly hit her: they were chasing a serial killer.

Janice realised that she now knew what the anonymous messages must mean. Harrington had been murdered, as Phil Whitby must have been too, which also indicated that there had to have been two previous murders that they had not yet discovered.

Janice suddenly felt physically sick. Her head was spinning and her stomach contorted as she contemplated her horrifying conclusion. And she also realised that it must have been the serial killer himself who had twice contacted Frank and was leading him to his victims.

This wasn't just a nice little story that she could work on with Frank and in the process try to get closer to him. Four people had been killed and there was no sign that the killer would stop there. What had seemed like a dream just a few moments ago had just turned into a nightmare. Janice sat back in her seat, feeling faint and contemplating just what she was getting herself involved in.

She looked across the office once more and saw that Frank's meeting was finishing. She waited impatiently and watched as he said goodbye to Findlay and then they shook hands. Frank showed the campaigner out of the door and turned to her. It was immediately obvious that he had seen the look on her face. She was sure that she must look terrible and she had to resist the urge to rush straight into the bathroom and redo her make up. *Professional is the key word*, she reminded herself.

Trying to keep her voice steady despite what she was feeling, she looked straight at Frank and said, 'You should come and look at this.'

Wednesday May 14 2008, 3:25pm

Sitting at the wheel of his white van, he smiled as he read the Evening Citizen. So now they had identified Harrington.

Only took them half a day. Not bad for the Glasgow police, he thought contemptuously. But then he had left the body right in the middle of the fucking city, where they couldn't miss it.

They didn't appear to have worked out the connection with the others yet, he realised. How long would that take them? The game was on now.

And what would Mister Ace Reporter Frank fucking Gallen do next? With the gift of the link between Whitby and Harrington was he good enough to track down the first two? Surely the numbers would lead him to the correct conclusion?

I guess we will find out soon, he thought and he smiled a cruel smile. Maybe it's time for another e-mail? No, forget it. He has enough information; it's up to him for now. Let's see just how good he really is.

I'll give him a couple of days before number five.

Wednesday May 14 2008, 3:30pm

What the hell was wrong? Janice looked as though she had just seen a ghost, thought Frank. Her normally rosy cheeks were chalk white and there was a crazed look in her eyes as she stared at him.

He quickly read the story about the murder of Mike Harrington and then he knew exactly why Janice was looking so shaken.

He was momentarily dumbstruck himself as the implication of the story when combined with the two anonymous e-mails led him to a horrifying conclusion: there was a serial killer operating in the city.

And he had somehow been chosen as the one to receive his messages.

But that simple deduction left so many questions unanswered and they raced around his brain. Why him? Who was the anonymous e-mailer? Why were Whitby and Harrington killed? Was there a connection or were his victims chosen randomly? And who were the other two victims?

Frank turned to Janice and forced himself to smile, trying to calm the young woman. He knew that she must have just come to the same conclusion as he had. 'I guess we've found out who Harrington is,' he said grimly.

'So do we go to the police?' asked Janice.

'We have to.' Janice's face fell. 'I know that this could possibly be a great story for us, but we have what could very well be evidence in a number of crimes.'

'But what about journalistic freedom and protecting our source?' she asked.

'This isn't just an academic discussion, Janice,' responded Frank. 'This guy, whoever the hell he is, has already killed four people and he may be planning to kill more. We have a duty to report what we know to the police.'

'I suppose so,' replied Janice, although it was obvious that she wasn't at all convinced by his rationale.

'I'll talk to John before I do anything, but I'm sure he will agree with me.' He stood and walked away leaving Janice looking crestfallen, as if she was being forced to give up something she had worked for. That might be partially true, thought Frank, but the correct course of action was clear to him.

'Of course we have to go to the police, Frank,' John said as soon as Frank had brought him up to speed. 'This is totally crazy!'

The telephone on the desk between them rang.

'Yes?' said John, answering it irritably, and then listening for a few seconds. 'It's for you, Frank. DS Becker.'

Franks heart immediately sank. He knew that Becker must have now connected the identification in the Harrington death to his earlier call and was telephoning to find out exactly what he knew.

'Ken, I was just about to call you again,' he said, taking the receiver from John, reaching carefully over a large cactus. 'I've got my editor here with me. Do you mind if I put you onto the speakerphone?' he asked.

'OK, go for it,' replied the detective. Frank reached over and managed to press the button on the handset without impaling himself. 'DS Ken Becker, John Addison, editor of the West End Weekly.'

'Hello, John. OK, Frank, I've just heard about the Harrington murder, so what's the story? How come you were asking about him before we had even identified the body?'

Frank glanced at John, who nodded, indicating that he should tell the detective the full story.

'I was going to call you, Ken, honestly. Here's exactly what happened. On Monday morning I got an anonymous e-mail saying that Phil Whitby didn't kill himself. So I looked into it and you know what I found. No clear evidence that his death was anything but a suicide.'

'Right,' replied the detective, sounding impatient.

'Then this morning I got another e-mail which said "*Whitby was #3. Harrington was #4*" .That was why I called you earlier on, asking if the name meant anything to you,' Frank explained.

'What time was that e-mail sent, Frank?'

'One forty eight am.'

They heard a sharp intake of breath. Then Becker's voice came through the small speaker once again.

'That's not long after the estimated time of Harrington's death. In fact it's before we even found the body!'

Frank said nothing and waited for the detective to continue.

'Harrington was murdered. And this implies that Whitby was too, as well as two others. Is this a serial killer?' Frank thought that the detective's voice was remarkably even, considering what he had just said.

'Certainly seems like it to us,' John confirmed.

'OK, here's what you do,' said the detective decisively. 'You tell no one about this. Repeat: no one at all. Is that clear?'

'Yes,' Frank and John replied simultaneously.

'I will contact the detectives in charge of the Harrington case. My old boss has just moved to the Murder Squad, so I'll call him too. He will want to speak to you very soon, Frank, so don't go anywhere.'

'We will be here,' Frank stated.

'We will talk soon, Frank,' and the connection was abruptly broken.

John switched the telephone off and looked across the desk at Frank. 'I want you to co-operate fully with the police, Frank.'

'Of course I will…'

'But...' interrupted Addison. 'If there is a story here, and it very much sounds like there is, I want it. Understand?'

Frank smiled before answering. 'Fully understood.'

Wednesday May 14 2008, 3:45 pm

'I've just had a call from DS Becker. You can guess why, can't you?' Frank asked Janice.

'I think so, yes,' she said in a small voice.

Frank looked closely at her and could see that she had been crying. Janice was normally a very mature young woman, but the shock of what she had discovered was a lot for her to take in.

'The police will be here soon to question me about the e-mails. Now it's important that you don't tell anyone about this. I mean anyone at all. Not even your flatmates or your boyfriend.'

'I don't have a boyfriend.'

'Don't tell anyone,' he repeated. 'Is that absolutely clear?'

'Yes Frank,' she replied, seemingly unable to meet his eye.

'But we do know that there is a major story brewing here, don't we?' Frank said, more to himself than to Janice.

Frank Gallen hadn't felt this way in a very long time. He knew that he was already in a unique position by having the inside track on the killer. No other journalist would know about the connection between the two deaths or that other murders were linked. This could be the story that restored his journalistic reputation, he suddenly realised.

'Find out everything you can about Mike Harrington for me, Janice. And look for any link at all between him and Phil Whitby. If we can get that, it might just lead us to the other two victims.'

He hoped that she would find working on the story more appealing than simply thinking about it. It was a big test and he could only trust that she was up to it. 'We have a lot more information about Whitby than anyone else will have right now, so perhaps we can find something that ties them together.'

Janice smiled and nodded her head. Frank saw some of the colour come back into her cheeks and so he left her to get on with the task.

He had to prepare for the arrival of the police.

Chapter 6

Wednesday May 14 2008, 4:45pm

John Addison's small office was cramped and hot, only just able to contain the four men sitting in it. He sat behind his desk, which was for once empty of papers and files.

Frank perched uncomfortably on a chair to one side. He had to move a large potted plant so that he wasn't obscured from the conversation. The two detectives sat opposite, taking notes as Frank finished telling them the story of the two anonymous e-mails he had received and his subsequent investigations.

'I've printed off the two e-mails for you,' said Frank, passing hard copies over to Detective Superintendent John McPherson and Detective Inspector Adam Ralston from Strathclyde Police's elite Murder Squad.

'Thanks,' replied McPherson. He was a tall man, at least six foot four, Frank thought, and he looked to be in his late forties. He was also impeccably dressed in a grey suit with a white shirt and a red silk tie. Frank remembered coming across him some years before on a story and knew him to be very intelligent, and driven to the point of obsession once he got into a case.

'Now you say these are anonymous accounts that anyone can easily create?' DI Ralston asked him.

'That's right. All you need is internet access, and it takes about two minutes to set up a Hotmail account. It looks like these were opened just to send the e-mails and then closed again immediately afterwards. There's no way at all of tracing who created them.'

'Our technical team will have a look anyway, just to be sure,' said Ralston. 'No offence.' He was much younger than his boss, in his mid thirties perhaps, but also stylishly dressed, if a little more casual in slacks and a sports jacket. Frank made a mental note to see what he could find out about him.

'Do you have any ideas as to who might have sent these e-mails, Frank?' asked McPherson.

'None whatsoever. There's no clue in them at all,' replied Frank, wishing that he had a more positive answer to give. 'But clearly they came from the killer, didn't they?' It seemed an obvious conclusion but Frank wanted to know if the officers thought the same.

'He has evidently chosen you for a reason. There's no apparent connection to the paper, as neither of the deaths occurred in the West End and neither of the victims are from the area. Could it be personal?' Ralston continued to quiz him without answering Frank's question.

'Again, I really don't know,' Frank responded. 'There's nothing in the e-mails that rings any bells. I've never received anything like this before.'

'Well, he has sent you two messages so far. Here's my card. Call me immediately if another one arrives.' Ralston passed business cards to John and Frank, who both nodded their assent.

'And of course I don't expect to see anything in print that even hints at a serial killer,' McPherson warned.

'But you will keep us up to date with your investigation?' asked John.

'I'll make sure you get copies of any press releases we issue,' he replied, and Frank noticed John frown slightly.

The two detectives stood and walked out of the office. Frank showed them out of the building and then returned to John's office.

'They didn't give anything away, did they?' he commented.

'No,' replied John. 'But then they probably don't know much more than we do at this stage. See what you can find out about the two victims, Frank. And also have a look for any unsolved murders that have been reported recently. If we can connect the two victims we know about, then we might be able to track down the others too.'

'Makes sense.' Frank nodded. 'I've already got Janice checking into Harrington. And we already know a fair bit about Whitby, so we can look for any links between them.'

'Good stuff.'

'Makes you think, doesn't it? A serial killer operating in Glasgow.'

'It's awful,' agreed John, a pained expression on his face.

'But it could make a great story,' said Frank, standing.

'Make sure that you finish the Kelvingrove story as well, won't you, Frank?'

'I'll have it finished this evening, John,' Frank assured his editor.

Wednesday May 14 2008, 5:10pm

'So what do you think, Adam?' asked McPherson as soon as they had got into the car for the short drive back to Strathclyde Police's headquarter in Pitt Street.

Ralston ordered his thoughts, recognising a test. On the surface the boss was simply asking for his take on the meeting, but he guessed that he would also expect a view on how the investigation should proceed.

'We have a number of facts that appear connected, but we don't know exactly why. And that gives us several questions to work on,' he began eagerly. This was only day three of his posting to the Murder Squad and he recognised that he would have an opportunity to make an impression on McPherson during what was shaping up to be their first major case together.

'We know that Harrington was definitely murdered, and we will work that case as normal. I've already got the team collating everything that we have so far. But the Whitby case was closed as a suicide, and on a quick look at the files, there's nothing that contradicts that conclusion. So first we need to talk to everyone who was involved in the investigation and see if they missed anything.'

There was no reaction from McPherson, so Ralston continued.

'Then there is the suggestion that there are two other linked deaths. If we can establish a connection between the two victims we know about, perhaps that will help us to identify the others. And there must be a reason for the killer, if that's who it is, contacting Gallen. Perhaps we can work out who it is from these e-mails?'

'Gallen said that there is no chance of that,' McPherson reminded him as they stopped at a red light. The traffic around Charing Cross was notoriously heavy at this time of night, the busy interchange clogged with commuters heading home at the end of the working day.

'Perhaps our technical team will have a different view,' Ralston replied. 'Gallen is a journalist, not an IT man.'

'Fair point,' McPherson acknowledged with a smile. 'What else should we be doing, Adam?'

Ralston thought for a moment before replying. 'If this is indeed a serial killer, the press will be all over it. We need to make sure that there isn't a public panic.'

'That's true. I'll talk to the PR team about how to handle it,' said McPherson gravely. 'This could be a very big case. And so early in your career with the Squad.' He paused as the car inched forward, before being stopped once again. 'But I know you are up to the task, Adam. I wouldn't have brought you in otherwise.'

'Thank you, sir,' Ralston replied with more confidence than he actually felt.

He realised that the test had now become a challenge.

Wednesday May 14 2008, 5:50pm
'Councillor Gallen, do you need anything else tonight, or can I go?'

His secretary's words, uttered from the door to his office, interrupted Thomas Gallen's thoughts as he tried in vain to find an answer to the problem that David Longwell had delivered directly onto his desk.

'No, you can head off now, Sandra,' he replied, smiling to his secretary despite his dark mood.

'OK, goodnight, Councillor,' she said, walking back out of the office.

Gallen stared at the draft of his speech on his computer screen for a long time. But nothing came to him. There simply was no way out, he concluded. He knew what he had to do; Longwell had been very clear about that.

He simply could not bring himself to believe that Longwell had been involved in Whitby's death. But did that actually matter, though? Longwell may or may not have the material from Whitby; there was no way to know for sure. But he definitely had the recording on which he had mentioned that he was being blackmailed by Whitby, and Gallen could not risk that becoming public under any circumstances.

Thomas Gallen glanced at a picture on the corner of his desk for inspiration. It showed a smiling young woman and was edged in black within a silver frame. Even his dear sister Kathleen, God rest her soul, could not provide him with any answers tonight. But he would have given anything just to be able to talk to her once more. A tear came to his eye; he missed her so much.

Of course Kathleen would be bitterly disappointed with what he had done, but somehow he knew that his twin would have found it in her heart to forgive him. And her love would have helped him through this awful predicament, he was certain.

With a sigh he turned back to his computer and located the section of the speech dealing with the possibility of future joint developments with Longwell Homes. He quickly edited the text and then printed himself off a copy of the final version.

This would mean that he would be publically committed to the Kelvingrove Park development. Gallen knew that the proposals would attract significant opposition, both within the Council and throughout the rest of the city. And he knew that he would then have to deliver, or Longwell would use the information that he had.

Think of it as a test, Thomas, he told himself. He would have to use all of his leadership skills to ensure that the plans passed through the Council so that Longwell would remain on side, and the information he had would stay private. That way everything else stays exactly as it is.

Now, could he find a way to spin the loss of a little parkland into a positive?

Wednesday May 14 2008, 6:15pm

Frank read through his Kelvingrove Park story again and made a few amendments, just the odd word here and there to strengthen the article. More a final polish than an edit, really. He wanted to get it finished and out of the way quickly so that he could get his attention back onto the story that he really wanted to chase.

"Glasgow is quite rightly known across the world as 'The Dear Green Place' because of its many superb open spaces."

"Kelvingrove Park in the heart of the city's bustling West End is a classic Victorian park. Created for the city in 1862 by Sir Joseph Paxton, it provides a peaceful, natural haven within a densely populated urban area. Its 34 hectares of public space includes the magnificent and newly refurbished Art Gallery and Museum, now the city's most popular tourist attraction. The park is also surrounded by some of the city's most beautiful buildings."

"But would a new plan to build a number of executive apartments within the park add to Kelvingrove's worldwide reputation, or should any development on parklands be vetoed by the City Council as a matter of principle?"

"The West End Weekly investigates."

That's good stuff, even if I do say so myself, Frank decided, reading his opening for a final time. He saved a copy of the story onto his own drive and then e-mailed it to John. Now he had completed all of his obligations for the week's paper and he could concentrate on the big story. But who was the killer and why had he been chosen to receive his messages?

Frank just couldn't bring himself to believe that he knew a serial killer. There had to be another reason that the killer had chosen to communicate with him. But what could it possibly be?

He looked over to Janice, who was busy at her PC sitting at the reception desk. John had already left for the day so they were now alone in the office. Time for a quick brainstorming session before they went home, he decided, checking his watch.

'Janice, can you bring the Whitby file over, and also whatever you've got on Harrington so far?' Eager to please as ever, she nodded and lifted two folders before heading for Frank's desk. He pointed to a seat opposite and she sat down with the folders in front of her.

'Let's see if we can find any connection at all between Whitby and Harrington,' said Frank. 'We've got some information we can use on both men, so let's get to it.'

'Well, we've got plenty on Whitby, Frank,' replied Janice.

'And what about Harrington?' he asked.

'I couldn't find too much about him, Frank. I've got his work details, some information from the Law Society and his old university and a basic biography. Oh, and a golf club that he was on the Committee of, but that's about all.' He noticed that she seemed brighter than earlier on and was eager to get to work. She had the right instincts to make it as a journalist, he realised, not for the first time.

'OK, we'll start at the beginning. Let's go through the basic facts that we have on each man and see if anything comes up in common. You know, it's this kind of boring background work that often throws up the one key fact that can lead to the break in a story,' he told Janice.

Janice nodded, always willing to learn. She opened the two folders and ordered the papers in them. 'I'm ready.'

He had to admit that he enjoyed passing on his experience, and that it was flattering to have such an attentive student. The idea of chasing a killer had clearly shocked her at first, not surprisingly, but she had now responded in a professional manner.

Putting those thoughts aside, Frank got down to work. He took a sheet of blank paper from the printer on the corner of his desk and drew a line down the centre. At the top of the left hand side he wrote "Whitby" and on the right he wrote "Harrington".

'OK, let's begin at the very beginning. Birth dates and places, please.'

'Whitby was born in 1984 in Pollok and Harrington was born in 1973 in East Kilbride,' said Janice after a quick glance at her files. 'Whitby was 24 and Harrington was 34 when they were killed.'

'Education?' asked Frank, beginning to fill in his chart.

'Whitby left school at 16. Harrington stayed on until 18 and then got a law degree from Glasgow University,' she replied without looking at her notes.

'Jobs we know: food co-op and lawyer specialising in property law respectively,' said Frank. 'Home circumstances?'

This time Janice consulted her files before replying. Once more her fingers were toying with her hair, Frank noticed.

'Whitby lived in a rented flat in the Gorbals and we know that he was just about to move in with Mike Convery. Harrington lived with his wife in Newton Mearns, no children. Oh, and Whitby didn't have any children either,' she added.

'Interests?' asked Frank.

'Politics, especially gay rights and environmental campaigns for Whitby. And all I have so far for Harrington is golf,' she said apologetically.

'And their deaths. Whitby jumped or was pushed off a tower block in the Gorbals. And Harrington was stabbed in the city centre. Anything else?'

'I think that's all we know,' said Janice. 'Not much is it?' she asked, looking at the two lists Frank had made on the sheet of paper. 'And there's nothing at all on there that seems to link them.'

'Doesn't seem like it,' Frank admitted, rubbing his eyes. He stared intently at the sheet of paper for a few seconds, but absolutely nothing came to him. 'Maybe something will come to us tomorrow. Let's call it a night.'

'Alright,' agreed Janice. 'I have some work I should be doing for my course, I suppose.'

'How's it all going?' asked Frank, genuinely interested.

'I'm doing alright,' she answered. 'It's very interesting and I'm learning a lot. But it definitely helps working here to get some real experience too.'

'That's good,' said Frank. 'Let's get going,' he said, checking his watch once more.

A few moments later they had locked and secured the office, and were heading home, both with thoughts of the story they were chasing filling their minds.

Wednesday May 14 2008, 7:10pm

A Michael McDermott CD was playing and the lyrics spoke of making a mess of things.

That could be my theme tune, thought Frank sardonically. He was sitting alone with a cup of coffee contemplating the day's events.

A serial killer! If he could work this one properly the story could take him back to where he belonged. It would be difficult to get any information out of the police as always, he knew, but the fact that the killer was talking to him meant that they would have to co-operate with him to some extent.

His mobile phone rang. He looked at the display to see who was calling but the number wasn't recognised.

'Frank Gallen,' he answered, standing to turn the music off.

'Mr Gallen, it's Margaret Whitby, Phil's mother.'

'Oh, hello Mrs Whitby, what can I do for you?' He was surprised to hear from her and then he wondered if perhaps she had remembered something important after they left her house.

'I just wanted to thank you. I've had the police here this evening and it looks like they are now taking Phil's death much more seriously. Whatever you said to them must have worked.' That's no great surprise, Frank thought, smiling to himself.

'That's good; I hope they come up with something.' Now he was wondering what the police might have told her, if anything.

'It would be good to have a reason for what happened.' She paused for a moment. 'This might sound strange to you, but it would really help me to know why Phil died. And to be certain that he didn't jump. I know that it won't bring him back of course …'

'No, I know exactly what you mean,' Frank said with feeling.

'I can tell that you do. Have you lost someone close, Mister Gallen?' Her words felt like a punch in the stomach. He sat down and tried to regain his composure.

'My sister,' he finally admitted. 'A drunk driver knocked her down and killed her two years ago. He was eventually caught and is now in prison.'

'I'm so sorry,' she replied, and for a moment they were both silent, each lost in their own grief.

'What did the police ask you?' Frank eventually enquired, trying to get his mind back into the present.

'Much the same as you did. Initially they seemed to be looking for a reason why he might not have … killed himself,' she explained.

She still could not bring herself to mention the word suicide, Frank realised.

'And then they asked if anyone might have wanted to hurt him, but there was no one I could think of. And they also asked whether he usually carried a wallet, which he did.'

'Why were they asking about his wallet?' Frank asked, of himself as much as of the dead man's mother.

'I'm not sure,' she replied. 'But it seemed to be very important to them. I remembered that the police gave me his phone and a couple of other things he had in his pockets not long after he died, but not his wallet.'

'I'm sure they have their reasons for the questions,' Frank said, wondering just exactly what those reasons might be. Had Whitby been robbed before or even after he died? Was that in some way significant?

'Well, I just hope they find whoever did that to Phil.'

'So do I, Mrs Whitby,' replied Frank. 'So do I.'

'Well, thanks again for raising the story with the police,' she said. 'You've really done me a big favour, Mister Gallen.'

'Don't mention it,' replied Frank. 'Goodnight.'

'Goodnight, Mr Gallen. God bless.'

Frank ended the call and laid his phone on the arm of his chair. What was the story with the police's interest in Phil Whitby's wallet? And then he wondered whether Harrington had had a wallet on him when he was found. It had taken the police some time to identify him, he remembered, so perhaps not. Was robbery a motive in the murders?

Or was the killer taking trophies?

Frank was sure he had a book on profiling serial killers somewhere. He walked over to the walk in cupboard where his books were boxed and began to look for it.

Wednesday May 14 2008, 11:25pm

'Are you coming upstairs, Thomas?' asked Marie, popping her head around the living room door, already dressed for bed.

'Not yet, darling. I need to go over my speech for tomorrow morning again.' He was sitting on the couch with a large whisky in his hand, contemplating where his speech might eventually take him. He wished that there was a reason, any reason, which meant that he could avoid speaking the words he had written earlier.

'Don't be too ...' His wife's words of admonition were interrupted by the telephone ringing. 'Who on earth is that at this time of night?' She moved towards the handset which was on the corner of an armchair.

'You go to bed, Marie. I'll get it,' replied Gallen. He was expecting a call from Alan Mathers, who had been away at a conference all day. With a sigh and a shake of her head Marie walked out of the room, closing the door just a little more loudly than she needed to.

'Hello?'

'Thomas, it's Alan. I got your message. What's so urgent?'

'David Longwell, that's what,' replied Gallen. He recounted the story of their afternoon conversation to Mathers, who was totally shocked by the story he heard.

'So what are you going to do?' he asked when Gallen was finished.

'What choice do I have?' replied Gallen taking a long drink. 'I've rewritten that section of my speech to include the announcement that he wants so much. Now I need you to make sure we can deliver.'

'That won't be easy.'

'But it has to be done. We have to get the support within the Council as well as dealing with the press and the parks fanatics. Have a think about how we can achieve that, Alan. And get in early tomorrow so that we can talk before I go to the bloody opening.'

'OK I will,' replied Mathers. Gallen could tell that he was not approaching the task with any enthusiasm.

'Look, we can make this work out for us,' he encouraged his assistant. 'We always do in the end. Now get a good night's sleep and I'll see you in the morning.'

'Alright. Night, Thomas.'

'Goodnight.' Gallen only wished that it would be as easy as that. He knew that the reaction from his colleagues within the Council would be mixed at best. Some on the left would side with the fanatics, he knew. But he might just be able to persuade the majority to come around to his side.

One more whisky before bed, he thought. God knows I deserve it after the day I've had.

Wednesday May 14 2008, 11:45pm

Janice sat at her desk with her laptop in front of her, looking out of the window from her small room. She sipped from a glass of red wine and reflected on what had undoubtedly been one of the strangest days of her life. Unable to concentrate on the assignment she was trying to finish, she finally closed the laptop and moved from the desk to lie down on her single bed.

How on earth had she managed to end up involved in the hunt for a serial killer, she asked herself?

Finding the story about Mike Harrington had been such a rush at first, and of course a cool way to impress Frank with her skills. Maybe even the means for her to get closer to him at long last. But then she had realised exactly what those damned e-mails had to mean.

Frank had managed to focus on the story throughout, but she was stuck on the horrific notion of a killer. How did he manage to remain so cool, so professional? And what had he thought of her response? She had been shaken and had reacted badly to the thoughts going through her head.

The way that Frank had looked at her at one point, it was as if he were an adult trying to comfort a child, she concluded. Did Frank really think of her as just a child, or could she persuade him to see her as a woman? God, this was awful.

Perhaps if she could find the link between Whitby and Harrington? Then he would have to be impressed and might realise that she was an adult, a female adult. She knew that he had not had a girlfriend in several months and that he must be lonely. Janice imagined him in his flat, alone like her, less than a mile away, although he may as well have been on the moon.

She had never wanted anyone the way she wanted Frank Gallen, needed him in fact. She had been in relationships before; there had been boyfriends, of course, at school and at university.

But that was the point. They were boys.

Frank was a man and that was exactly what she needed, who she longed for. He was the first man that she had truly loved and she was determined to find a way to show him that she was worthy of his attention.

Janice sat up and opened her rucksack where she had put the two files that they had worked on earlier that evening. It was late but she didn't feel in the mood for sleep yet. She moved once more to her desk and sat to read through them, start to finish, hoping that something would jump out from the words to link the two dead men. She also compiled her own version of Frank's chart, working in exactly the same manner that they had earlier. When they had been sitting together, working closely together.

But when she had finished, she still had nothing at all. The two murder victims had led totally different lives, had lived in almost separate worlds.

Maybe there was something that they were missing? Were they members of the same gym? Did they attend the same doctor or dentist? Perhaps they had a mutual friend somewhere? But how would she be able to find out any more about their lives in any case?

What if there simply was no connection between the two men, she wondered? But the thought of a serial killer choosing his victims entirely at random was somehow even more horrific.

She closed the two files and opened up her laptop. Emptying her wine glass she wondered if another internet search might bring up something she had missed earlier, now that she had more time to look closely. Anything's worth a go, she thought, pouring herself another glass of wine before she started.

First she tried googling the two names together, but that produced nothing that was relevant. That would have been too easy of course, she concluded cynically. But what to try next?

An hour later, the bottle of wine was finished and Janice was no further forward. Her searches had come up with no additional information on either man. She tried the "Parks for the People" website once more. There was a small article on Phil Whitby's death, just a standard obituary really, nothing new there. And a larger article on the demonstration at the end of the month. There was also a link to an article written by Steve Findlay on the Green Party's website about the proposed Kelvingrove Park development.

That was the guy Frank had interviewed this afternoon, she remembered. Out of interest she clicked on the link and read through the piece, running her fingers through her hair. It was well written, she thought, but seemed to be a fairly standard defence of green space. And she found that she agreed with his conclusion, which was that Glasgow has enough spare land to build houses on without giving Longwell Homes a piece of its finest park.

Something suddenly rang a bell deep in her mind and she tried to focus on what it was. The name of the developer: Longwell Homes. She had seen it somewhere else. *Think, Janice, think.*

Where had she seen the name? It was at the back of her mind, but frustratingly she could not bring it to the forefront. Sighing deeply she stared out of the window and up into the black and starless night beyond.

And then it came to her.

She quickly called up the web site of Mike Harrington's law firm, and found the page on which his main clients were listed. And there it was near the top of the list: Longwell Homes.

She had the connection!

Janice had to resist the temptation to shout out loud, to jump up and down with delight. She now knew that Phil Whitby had been campaigning against a development by a company that Mike Harrington had provided legal advice to.

She was still elated at her success. Looking for her mobile phone she was desperate to call Frank immediately and let him know what she had found. He would be as excited as she was by what she had discovered. And surely he would be very impressed with her? This could be what she had been waiting for over the last few endless months of longing.

Then she realised that it was after 1am. Damn, she couldn't call him so late. It would have to wait until the morning. But how could she sleep with her mind racing? She found Longwell Homes' website and read through the details. A family company, rapidly expanding with several developments on site in Glasgow. Nothing about developments in parks, though.

She googled Longwell Homes, came up with a number of stories about past successes and an opening of a housing development coming up in Parkhead the next day. Or rather, later today, she realised.

But again Janice found nothing that mentioned building in a park. She tried a number of other searches but discovered nothing new.

What do I have? Janice asked herself, trying to order her thoughts. The Parks campaigners seem convinced that Longwell Homes were behind the rumoured Kelvingrove development, but the company had said nothing officially.

Still it was a link between the two victims. And that was more than they had found earlier. But would it lead them to discover either the other two victims or indeed to the killer himself?

She could not wait to fill Frank in on her discovery.

Chapter 7

Frank sat at his desk, his computer open, drinking black coffee and feeling tired after a late night spent reading. He found that he had to resist the temptation to check his incoming e-mails every five minutes, desperate for another clue from his anonymous correspondent.

Frank now knew that the FBI seemed to have the best handle on serial killers, as the vast majority had seemed to operate in the United States. But even then, their profiles only gave the most common characteristics, which didn't cover all serial killers. Most were white, except the few who were black. Most were male, except the few who were female. Most were aged between 18 and 32 except the few who were in their forties or even older. Many were sexually abused as children, but a few showed no such history. And most worked alone, except the few who hunted in pairs.

But, frustratingly, he had found nothing that could help him to identify the man who was e-mailing him.

Frank turned to his computer and quickly discovered a plethora of articles on the most famous serial killers in the UK. But he soon realised that they did not match the standard profile at all. Peter Sutcliffe, the Yorkshire Ripper, came closest. He was white, male and had killed when aged between 27 and 33, although there was no known history of abuse in his background.

But Frank also read of many others who did not fit: Harold Shipman was much older. Fred and Rosemary West had worked together, as had Ian Brady and Myra Hindley.

While it was all very interesting, he had to admit that he was simply no further forward. The only common characteristics he could find were that most serial killers were intelligent and driven, and saw themselves as powerful and dominant figures, which seemed to make sense. Many had a point to make and there was often a single incident that set them off on their killing spree.

But unless you knew the killer, how did you apply the profile? It didn't seem to offer much in the way of help to him at the moment, Frank conceded.

Frank's mobile phone rang to interrupt his thoughts and he took it from his jacket pocket, checking to see who the call was from.

'Morning, Janice. Shouldn't you be in a lecture?' he asked.

'Never mind that,' she replied. 'I've got something I have to tell you!'

'What is it?'

'I had another look through the files last night, Frank. I read everything we have again and again, and I've found it! There is a connection between Whitby and Harrington: it's Longwell Homes!'

She was speaking extremely quickly in her obvious enthusiasm, and Frank struggled to keep up. But when he heard Janice's conclusion he too became excited.

'How are they connected to that company, Janice?'

'Longwell Homes is rumoured to be behind the parks development that Whitby was campaigning against, and Mike Harrington did legal work for them. I saw that on his law firm's website. This is what we were looking for, Frank!' she concluded.

'Good work,' replied Frank. 'Look, don't mention this to anyone, Janice. No one at all for now. I'll see you later on when you come in.'

'But what are we going to do?'

'I need time to think it through. We'll talk when you come in,' he repeated.

'OK, Frank. Bye,' said Janice and hung up.

Frank leaned back in his chair and thought through what Janice had learned. Steve Findlay had confirmed the rumour that Longwell Homes was behind the development in Kelvingrove Park that had been leaked to the press, which was also something that Whitby would have known, he assumed. But was that motive for murder? Surely not, as presumably all of the leaders of the campaign were aware of the identity of the company behind the rumours. What could killing Whitby possibly achieve? It certainly wouldn't stop the campaign or dampen the opposition to the plans, that was for sure.

And what about Harrington? His speciality was property law, so advising a house builder seemed like something he would do in his job. But what had he done to get himself murdered? Was he even involved in the parks project? Perhaps he had refused to work on it, which could make him an ally of Whitby? Or could he have been passing confidential information to the campaigners?

Frank forced himself to stop, knowing that it was all conjecture. He had to get some evidence of the link before he could take it seriously. Or was it just a total coincidence?

It was time to take a close look at Longwell Homes, Frank decided.

Thursday May 15 2008, 11:10am

Councillor Thomas Gallen paused and looked around the small crowd. They were applauding his positive comments about the leisure centre that Longwell Homes had provided as part of the Parkhead Central housing development. He waited for a few seconds before delivering the section of his speech that he had rewritten the day before. And he tried not to let his complete lack of enthusiasm for his own words show.

'This development we are opening today shows that the public sector and the private sector can work together for the benefit of Glaswegians. And it is not the first positive example of public – private partnership between Glasgow City Council and Longwell Homes, nor will it be the last.' He found he had to force himself to continue.

'We are currently in discussions with Longwell Homes about a number of executive housing developments in strategic locations throughout Glasgow. The first is likely to be in Kelvingrove Park, and we hope to be in a position to make a further and more detailed announcement very soon.'

Again Gallen paused, this time finding that his words had met with a mixed reception. He saw David Longwell standing to his right with a sly smile on his face. And he saw a few people shaking their heads, combined with some excitement from the journalists present. He decided to conclude his speech as quickly as he could.

'But today is about Parkhead Central and another large step forward in the regeneration of the East End. I'm very pleased to have been asked to open this tremendous new estate, not just as the Leader of the Council, but as the local Councillor.'

'So without any further ado, let me cut this ribbon.' He paused to pick up a large pair of scissors and then posed at the ribbon stretched across the road. When the photographers had their shot he cut the ribbon, the crowd applauded and the ceremony was over.

Gallen stepped to the side and spoke quietly to Alan Mathers. 'That wasn't too bad, was it?'

'This audience isn't too bothered about Kelvingrove Park, because it's right across the city,' replied Mathers, already analysing the situation. 'But the journalists have picked up on your reference and I'm sure that there will be questions. They will want details, Thomas.'

'Stall them for now, tell them discussions are ongoing or something. Just promise them a press release at a later date,' suggested Gallen. 'There are a few people here I need to talk to, you take care of the press for me.'

He left Mathers to the mercy of the journalists and went to speak to some of the local people. Many of them were members of his local party branch and all were potential voters. Ever the consummate politician, Gallen smiled as he immersed himself in the crowd.

Moments later David Longwell approached Gallen and tactfully put his hand on the Councillor's shoulder. 'Can I have a word please, Thomas?'

Gallen nodded, politely excused himself from the group he was speaking to and followed Longwell to the side of the road.

'Very good speech, Thomas. Very well done.'

Gallen found himself unable to respond, knowing that he was now tied to Longwell whether he liked it or not. And he definitely didn't like it.

'Now I will be able to give details of my plan ... sorry, *our* plan for Kelvingrove to the Daily News this afternoon. I'm so glad that you chose the correct path.'

'I didn't have a lot of choice, did I?' Gallen responded angrily.

'True, very true,' Longwell said, seemingly deep in thought. 'I will be in touch soon, Thomas.' He walked towards his BMW, leaving Gallen feeling dirty all over.

Suddenly Councillor Thomas Gallen longed to go home and have a long, hot shower.

Thursday May 15 2008, 12:20pm

Frank had spent a frustrating hour researching Longwell Homes.

He now knew that the family company was run by David Longwell with his son Daniel as one of the other two directors and his solicitor as the third. Longwell senior had started the company in Stirling and made a great deal of money building houses and flats in and around the town. From several recent press reports it was obvious to Frank that he had now turned his attention to Glasgow, as the company had been behind several very successful developments around the city.

Clearly Longwell saw Glasgow as the company's future: its HQ was now in the city centre, Frank noted.

He downloaded their annual accounts from the Companies House website and tried to follow the tables of figures. It seemed that turnover and profit were both going up: a very healthy situation given the generally poor state of the housing market.

Frank called the offices of the company seeking an interview with David Longwell himself, but was told that he would have to wait for a return call.

There was nothing else he could do, so he turned his attention back to the murders, wondering once again why the police had been so interested in Phil Whitby's missing wallet. He knew that they too would be trying to tie Whitby and Harrington together, so was this part of that process?

Was the killer taking the wallets to make identification more difficult? But why do that and then tell him the names of two of his victims? That made no sense. It had to be either a simple robbery or the more sinister explanation of the killer taking trophies, Frank decided.

Feeling irritated Frank headed for the kitchen and another cup of coffee, but found that the pot was empty. Just one of those days, he concluded ruefully. As he waited for a new pot to percolate he heard his phone ring. Hoping that it was the return call from Longwell Homes he rushed back across the office to his desk and picked up the receiver.

'Frank Gallen.'

'Frank, it's DI Ralston from Strathclyde Police.'

'Oh, hello.' Now this might be interesting.

'Have you seen the first edition of the Evening Citizen?' The question took Frank totally by surprise.

'No, I've not. Why do you ask?' As he spoke he quickly navigated his browser to the newspaper's website.

'Their front page article has the link between Harrington and Whitby. Do you know anything about it?'

'Just a moment,' said Frank as he read the story. The cat was now well and truly out of the bag, it seemed.

'You don't think I had something to do with this, do you?' Frank asked.

'Did you?' asked Ralston.

'Of course not,' replied Frank, annoyed that he even had to answer the question. 'Why the hell would I give a story like this to another newspaper? Surely you can see that's the last thing I would want to do.'

'My boss is mad, Frank. I had to ask.'

'Well, now you have your answer. And I'm sure it was no one here either. Maybe there is a leak at your end?' he responded.

'If there is, I'll find it. And McPherson will have their job if his current mood is anything to go by. Look, I'm sorry if I offended you Frank, but I had to be sure,' Ralston explained, trying to placate him.

'OK, I understand,' Frank replied. And then he saw an opening. 'What are your questions about Phil Whitby's wallet related to? Was Harrington's wallet taken by the killer as well?'

He heard a sharp intake of breath over the line before the detective answered his question. Or rather, before Ralston simply didn't answer his question at all. 'Why are you asking that, Frank?' he asked instead.

'Look, I know that Whitby didn't have a wallet on him when his body was found, and that he always carried one. His mother told me that. Now, if Harrington's wallet was missing too, then maybe the killer is collecting trophies?'

'That's not the case,' the detective answered quickly, but then hesitated for a moment. 'I can't tell you anything else, Frank. It's bad enough with what's in the press already. I simply can't give out any more information about an ongoing investigation.'

'But the two men's wallets are somehow significant to the case?' Frank persisted.

'I'm saying nothing,' DI Ralston replied after another pause.

'So you're not denying that the wallets are important?'

'I'm saying nothing,' he repeated. Frank knew that he had his answer.

'Look, I have to go, Frank. If you hear anything new, let me know immediately, will you?' asked the detective.

'Alright, I will. Bye.'

Frank put the receiver down and considered the conversation. Someone on the Evening Citizen must have a very good source in the police force, he concluded. But more importantly, just what was the significance of Phil Whitby's wallet not being on his body?

He walked back to the kitchen and poured himself a coffee from the new pot. It now seemed that Harrington's wallet had been found on his body, but Whitby's hadn't. And those two facts were somehow significant.

But why? That was the question.

Thursday May 15 2008, 1:50pm

David Longwell strolled into his office and sat down behind his desk following a very good lunch with a new contact he was cultivating. He was a contented man as he contemplated his morning's work. Things were coming together nicely he concluded. As he looked through the stack of messages that had accumulated during the morning, Daniel Longwell walked into his father's office.

'So, how did the opening go?' he asked.

'All according to plan,' he smiled. 'My plan that is.'

'Great. So, Gallen made the announcement?'

'Of course he did, just as I told you he would.' Longwell couldn't have kept the beam off his face, even if he had wanted to.

'That's great, Father. So what happens next?'

'I have an interview with the Daily News at two. I'll give them some more details and that will put the full story into the public domain. Now I need you to make sure that the planning application is on track for completion, and then we can let Gallen pilot it through the Council for us.'

'Leave it with me,' replied Daniel confidently. 'I'll go and speak to the team now.'

'Excellent,' replied Longwell. Every day his dream moved a little closer to reality. And Daniel was learning all the time, getting closer to being ready to take on the mantle of leadership when he retired.

His eye was caught by one of the stack of messages he was flicking through. Frank Gallen of the West End Weekly wanted an interview regarding Kelvingrove Park.

Now there was a name he had not heard in a long time. Longwell recalled that Gallen's promising journalistic career had come to a sudden halt last year, and that he had battled alcoholism. The West End Weekly was presumably his route back into the fourth estate.

He might be a useful man to have on side, thought Longwell. A good journalist, a contact in the local press and the brother of the Council Leader all rolled into one.

Longwell made a note on the back of the message slip instructing his secretary to set up an interview as soon as possible and turned to the next of his many messages.

Thursday May 15 2008, 2:40pm

Janice walked quickly up to the front door of the West End Weekly's office, eager to find out what Frank had made of the Longwell Homes link. She had just come out of an extremely dreary tutorial and was anxious to get back to the story that was now monopolising her thoughts. Well almost: there was always room in her mind for Frank Gallen of course.

She saw an envelope lying on her computer keyboard and immediately wondered whether it was from Frank. But as she got closer she recognised the handwriting as John's. She was disappointed to find that inside was a long list of tasks for her to complete while John was out of the office. Bother! This little lot would keep her busy for most of the afternoon. How tedious was that?

The telephone rang and she quickly picked up the handset from the small switchboard in front of her.

'West End Weekly, Janice speaking. How may I help you?'

'May I speak with Frank Gallen please?' she heard a cultured female voice ask. Janice instantly wondered whether it was a personal call. Shaking her head, she reminded herself that jealousy was not an attractive quality.

'Can I ask who's calling?'

'It's Fiona from David Longwell's office, returning Mister Gallen's call,' she replied. Not personal, business then. And Longwell Homes too. Janice could hardly contain her excitement as she put the call through to Frank. She was tempted to listen in, but decided that maybe that would be going a bit too far. Instead she stared at the light on the small switchboard, waiting for it to go off. It seemed to take forever, but finally the little red light blinked out. She stood up, took a deep breath and walked over to Frank's desk.

'So what's happening, Frank?' she asked. She noticed that he was wearing a t-shirt today, which was unusual as he almost always wore a long sleeved shirt.

He filled her in on his morning's work, while she tried not to stare too hard at his muscular body.

'Can I come with you to see Longwell?' she asked, simply willing him to say yes.

'I don't see why not,' he replied, smiling his oh so sexy smile, exciting and delighting her in equal measures.

'Did you see the Evening Citizen?' he asked.

'No. Is there something in it?'

'They have the link between Harrison's death and Whitby. The police were on to me asking if we had given it to them. Why they would think that, I don't know.'

Janice was shocked and a little worried that she would be blamed, although thankfully Frank didn't seem to be thinking that way.

'They must have a leak in their own ranks. But I did get something from Ralston.'

'What?' she asked him.

He quickly explained his conversations with Mrs Whitby and DI Ralston.

'But there is something important about the wallets?' Another puzzle, thought Janice. This story was full of them.

'I think so. But I can't work out what it could be. If I knew who the other two victims were maybe it would all make some sense.'

He shook his head in obvious disappointment and Janice longed to comfort him, to hold him in her arms. Then the telephone rang and she had to rush back to answer the call.

Thursday May 15 2008, 3:05pm

Still trying to solve the mystery of the wallets, Frank was at his desk thinking hard.

But nothing would come. He tried to distract himself by checking his e-mails, but there was little there of interest. He then checked the PA Mediapoint service, which provided breaking stories from throughout the UK. A headline caught his eye.

'Glasgow Council Leader Backs Controversial Parks Project.'

A quick scan of the contents confirmed his suspicions. So Tommy was right behind the Longwell Homes' proposal? Now that was interesting. In the past he would have expected his brother to have come out strongly against an idea like this. Glasgow's parks had historically been almost sacred to Labour politicians and the idea of a private developer building in one would have been anathema.

But of course supporting private development was now a very New Labour thing to do, and Frank knew that Tommy was anxious to impress the party leadership with his forward thinking.

If Longwell had the Leader of the Council on his side it would be very difficult for the parks campaigners to stop the proposal, he reasoned. Frank was certain that Tommy would not have come out and publicly supported the project unless he was sure of his backing within the Council. He was a very clever politician, after all.

The interview with Longwell could be very interesting, Frank thought. Longwell Homes was about to be involved in a major political controversy as well as possibly being the link between two or more murders.

Frank was now really looking forward to meeting David Longwell.

Thursday May 15 2008, 4:10pm

Councillor Thomas Gallen closed his office door behind him, looking for a little time alone following a stressful afternoon. Thursday was usually a busy day full of committee business, but being asked everywhere he went about his speech had made the afternoon seem interminable at times. It appeared that no one in the City Chambers was discussing anything other than Kelvingrove Park.

He quickly glanced through his e-mails, replying to the few that were important and ignoring the rest. On top of his in tray as always was a copy of the Evening Citizen and he unfolded the paper, wondering if he had made the front page.

His blood ran cold when he saw the name Whitby in the headline and he quickly read the story, struggling to focus on the print because of his shaking hands. But when he had finished reading the article he was totally confused. Who the hell was this Harrington and how was he connected to Whitby, and possibly to other murders as well?

And the big question: how on earth did David Longwell fit into any of this?

Gallen struggled to put the pieces of the puzzle together. If this anonymous serial killer that the newspaper story referred to had killed Whitby then it would seem logical that Longwell had nothing to do with it. And then, did that mean that he had also lied about having Whitby's videos? Suddenly the answer was crystal clear.

The bastard had bluffed him!

Longwell had played him, Gallen realised with a sinking feeling in his stomach. The developer had used Whitby's death against him, knowing that there was no way he could call his bluff with everything on the line. The blood drained from Gallen's face as he realised how he had been thoroughly outwitted.

Could he somehow turn it around and call Longwell's bluff? But he was now on record as supporting the Kelvingrove project. He knew that he couldn't reverse his position completely without losing credibility. And Longwell still had that recording of course.

Gallen walked to the drinks cabinet and poured himself a large brandy. He didn't drink often, and never during the day, but he felt like he needed something to steady himself. His first gulp of the fiery liquid burned his mouth as he swallowed it.

The only way out was to discredit David Longwell, he realised. He had to find a good reason to break the hold that the developer had on him so that he could then remove his backing from the Kelvingrove project. He could only be seen to change his position if he had a new and very compelling reason to do so. But what could it be?

It was almost as an afterthought that Thomas Gallen suddenly reacted with horror to the notion that a serial killer was operating in his city.

Thursday May 15 2008, 11:40pm

How had the Citizen got the story? Wondered the red headed man. Had Gallen given it to them?

Not that it mattered: his work was now out there. They have Whitby and Harrington, but could the police now connect the first two, he wondered?

A sudden rage consumed him, sending tendrils of fire through his veins. Surely it wasn't that fucking difficult now? How many clues did they need? Were they totally fucking incompetent?

He calmed himself a little, trying to stop the shaking.

Number five had to be taken care of soon. Not now, but soon. He fought to control the urge that made him want to kill there and then. The next act in the play was planned out in his mind in full glorious Technicolor detail. He knew just how and where he would find his fifth victim.

But then for the grand finale he would need something extra special. Everything was leading up to the moment when he finally had his full revenge.

And then the world would know what it had all been for.

Chapter 8

Sleep was still as far away as it had been when he had first gone to bed, so Frank sat up and turned his bedside lamp back on. Perhaps reading for a while would tire his mind enough to enable him to fall asleep, he reasoned. He picked up a book about famous serial killers. Perhaps it wasn't the best choice for late night reading material, he realised.

Forty minutes passed and he was no nearer to sleeping. The notion of signatures and trophies filled his mind but he could not relate any of it to what he knew about the Whitby and Harrington deaths. There were no similarities in the methods used to kill the two men, or the manner that the bodies had been found and he still had no idea what the clue regarding the victims' wallets meant.

If there were another two victims out there, then there might be enough information to connect the four of them to the one killer, he thought. But then, the link was probably needed to identify the other two victims in the first place. It was a catch bloody twenty two, he realised.

Frank's mouth felt incredibly dry so he got out of bed and walked to the kitchen. As he opened the fridge, he suddenly wished that he could have something stronger to help him sleep. Just one drink might be enough. But he didn't have a drop of alcohol in his flat, having chosen to keep temptation as far away as possible, just in case. Probably just as well, he reflected.

He lifted a bottle of water and drank from it, then replaced it on the shelf and closed the fridge door. Glancing at the clock on the kitchen wall he saw that it was after 2am, so he walked back to bed, sat on the edge and wondered what to do next to get to sleep.

Frank hated being an alcoholic.

It made him feel so pathetic, so helpless, and such a failure as a man. Millions of people managed to drink without ever letting it take over their lives, so why couldn't he? He knew in his mind that he was suffering from an illness, but that didn't help the feelings of personal weakness that sometimes overcame him.

It had been fifteen months since Frank had come out of rehab and he hadn't had a single drink since. He was proud of the accomplishment but worried that it did not seem to be getting any easier to stay sober. A while ago, maybe six years now, he had given up cigarettes, he remembered. It had been difficult at first but he had persevered. And eventually he had felt like a non-smoker.

But alcohol was different. Very different.

Frank didn't think that he would ever feel like a non-drinker. The temptations would always be there and he had to continue to fight them. He now understood that being an alcoholic was a permanent condition.

Sometimes Frank reached a complacent stage, where he was certain he had regained total control of his life. Once alcohol had controlled him, but now by quitting he had regained control. And taking it one stage further, he sometimes wondered whether he could be like normal people again. Go out for a few drinks and stop there. Use his control to have a little of what he knew that he still wanted more than anything without ever letting it lead to major problems, as it had once done.

But he had to persuade himself that was merely a fantasy. An alcoholic could not drink. That was the end of the story. And fifteen months of sobriety was too much to risk on the basis of a fantasy anyway, Frank knew.

Trying to put all notions of alcohol out of his mind, he thought about his brother. It had been strange reading about him, as if he were just another politician.

He remembered how he had idolised Tommy as a young boy. Eleven years older than Frank, Tommy had finished school just before he had started and he could still remember him leaving the house in the Gorbals every morning for work with their sister Kathleen. The twins were only sixteen at the time, but they had both seemed like adults to the young Frank. And he remembered with a smile that Tommy and Kathleen had always bought their wee brother a comic and a sweet or two when they got paid.

It was now almost two years since Kathleen's death and the pain of her sudden and tragic loss hadn't faded. But it was the fight afterwards that had led to his losing Tommy in a very different way that hurt him even more, if that was possible. How Frank wished, as he often did, that his big brother would one day be able to forgive him.

Frank finally decided to lie down once more. He switched off the light and lay in the darkness, desperate to find the release of sleep, the oblivion that would stop the thoughts that were now racing through his mind. But he could only lie watching the hands of the clock on the bedside table glowing eerily in the dark as they steadily turned.

It was well after 3am before he finally managed to fall into a light and fitful sleep.

Friday May 16 2008, 8:40am

Councillor Thomas Gallen was incandescent with rage as he finished reading the Daily News' interview with David Longwell. A series of quotes praised his farsightedness in bringing the Council to the table as a partner so early in the project. And Longwell had been clear in the interview that Kelvingrove was merely the first in a series of luxury apartment blocks to be built in Glasgow's parks, not just a one off project.

'Thomas, I asked if you wanted more tea,' Marie said, her voice raised in displeasure.

'No thanks, dear, my car is due any minute,' he replied, putting the last piece of his buttered toast into his mouth as he glanced at his watch. The children must have already left for school and he could not even remember them going, he realised.

How had he ever managed to get himself into this situation? First Whitby and now Longwell had forced him to go along with their plans. How could he have been so stupid?

'What time will you be home tonight?' his wife asked, interrupting his thoughts once more.

'I've got no idea,' he answered. 'Today is going to be hellish and I'm attending a civic reception this evening for some worthy cause or other. I can't even remember which one, but I know that it could be a late night.'

'Look, I know you have a lot on your plate at the moment, Thomas, but it would be nice to see you at home now and again, you know. And the children need you around, too.' He could tell that Marie was upset.

Just as Gallen was about to say something that he would no doubt regret later, he heard a car horn sound from the front of the house. He quickly stood up and put on his suit jacket, looking around for his brief case. Marie merely shook her head and walked out of the kitchen.

I don't need this right now, he thought. He was momentarily angry with Marie, but then remembered the secret that he was keeping from her.

Calling a curt goodbye to his wife he walked out of the front door and into the back of the black Daimler. He sat in silence contemplating the day ahead as the driver took them towards the city centre. Traffic was heavy as always and they crawled along Duke Street on the way into the City Chambers.

Gallen took out his mobile phone and speed dialled Alan Mathers, who answered on the first ring.

'Thomas, where are you?' his assistant asked.

'On my way in. We're stuck in traffic and I expect it will be another fifteen minutes or so.' He could see that traffic was taking an age to get through the crossroads at High Street.

'Did you see this morning's Daily News?' asked Mathers.

'Of course. That bastard Longwell has stitched me up totally.'

'He has certainly made it clear that you were not just supportive, but were actively involved in the idea behind these developments. There's no way out now, Thomas,' Mathers warned him.

'If only we could have held off from that damned announcement I had to make. The story about the serial killer coming out yesterday means that Longwell couldn't possibly have been involved in Whitby's death. And so he probably doesn't have those bloody videos either.'

'That might well be true, but we can't do anything about it.'

Gallen was angered once more at the dismissive tone of his assistant. It was easy for him: he was not the one whose career was on the line.

'So how do we sell Longwell's proposal, Thomas?'

'Hang on a minute.' He leaned forward to his driver. 'Just head down onto Cochrane Street this morning, John, and let me out at the side entrance. Thanks.' That would save five minutes he thought, and he hoped that he could also get up to his office without having to speak to too many people.

'Alan? Before we do anything else I want you to see if you can find any dirt on Longwell. Anything at all. If we can get something negative about him then I would have to reassess my position, wouldn't I?'

Mathers quickly cottoned on to what his boss meant. 'I get it. Something like: in light of the new information I reluctantly have to withdraw my support from the Kelvingrove Park project. It would not now be in the Council's best interests to continue its partnership with Mister Longwell given the recent revelations.'

'Exactly.' Gallen hoped that he could still rely on Mathers. 'But we need to work quickly. I'm sure that Longwell will have the planning application ready for submission very soon and I would like to be able to head him off if at all possible.'

'Leave it with me,' replied Mathers. 'I'll get on to it right away.'

'Thanks Alan. Keep me up to date.' Gallen ended the call abruptly. The car was now at the traffic lights, which had just turned to red. Gallen opened his diary and wondered just what else he would have to deal with.

Friday May 16 2008, 11:10am

John Addison walked out of his office and looked to be on his way towards the kitchen when he saw Frank coming in. As the paper was sent to the printers on a Thursday afternoon it was quite normal for Frank to come in late on a Friday.

'Morning, Frank,' said John and then he noticed the haggard look on Frank's face. 'You don't look great this morning.'

'Thanks, John. I needed that,' he replied as he sat down at his desk. 'I've just not been sleeping too well the last few nights, that's all.'

'Anything I can help with?' asked John. 'Do you need some time off?' John knew about his demons and always tried to be as supportive as he could, which Frank was extremely grateful for.

'I've just got a lot on my mind, that's all. What with the parks story taking legs and a serial killer on the loose ...'

John nodded sympathetically.

'Don't worry, I'm OK, John. And I'm seeing my counsellor at lunchtime anyway.'

'That's good, Frank. I'm here for you, don't forget.'

'Thanks, John. I mean it,' he replied. 'I'm interviewing David Longwell this afternoon,' he said, changing the subject as he turned his PC on. He decided not to tell John of the potential connection between the company and the serial killer in case it turned out to be nothing.

'The Daily News beat you to it. They got a pretty good interview out of him.'

'I know, I saw it,' Frank responded. 'But it was all pretty much big picture stuff. I'm going to concentrate on the opposition that he is likely to face. Try to get some of the arguments out before we get into the public consultation on his planning application. You know, concentrate on the local angle.'

'Sounds good,' replied John.

'Next week we will have a lot to print, what with the response to this week's article and the Longwell interview. I'll get some more from the parks campaigners too.'

''Get a view from the Council too, won't you?' suggested John. 'The local members and maybe someone from the Planning Department as well?'

'Will do,' replied Frank as John walked away towards the kitchen.

The first think Frank did was to check his incoming e-mails, but there was nothing more from the killer. He didn't know whether to feel relieved or disappointed.

He then checked the daily papers, all of which led with the serial killer story, not surprisingly. There was nothing new, apart from a Strathclyde Police statement which tried to calm the public. Ongoing investigation, no confirmation of any more deaths and a plea for any information about the two known victims seemed to be the highlights.

Frank tried once more to come up with a theory about the wallets. If the killer didn't take the wallets as trophies, what else could the link be, he wondered? Was there something he *did to* the wallets perhaps? Maybe he had a signature, Frank speculated? That had been mentioned in the books he had read. He turned back to his computer and searched for 'serial killer signatures'.

Twenty minutes later Frank rubbed his eyes, still feeling tired. He had read of staging and posing bodies, even of killers drawing on their victims as means of identifying their work. Many of these seemed to be sexual, but as far as he knew there was no sexual element to the two recent murders. He was getting nowhere fast, he concluded.

He saw Janice come into the office and closed down his browser, thinking that he would spend the time before he went to his appointment, preparing for the interview with Longwell.

She walked over to his desk. 'Hi, Frank. Anything new today?' she asked.

'No more e-mails and no new ideas, I'm afraid,' he replied. 'I just can't work out what the connection with wallets is all about.'

'Maybe Longwell will give us something this afternoon?' she suggested with a smile.

Frank thought for a moment. The more he thought about it, the more he was coming to the conclusion that the two victims' links to Longwell Homes was purely coincidental. And anyway Longwell would hardly admit to anything, would he?

'Maybe,' he said finally. 'Now let's think about the interview. What have you learned about interview technique so far?' he asked, seeing another opportunity to offer a few journalistic tips to Janice.

'We've covered the basics,' she replied as she ran her fingers through her hair. 'Preparation, having a list of questions, asking open questions and avoiding leading ones. Oh and building a good rapport with the subject, of course.'

'Pretty good,' Frank replied, impressed with her quick answer. Janice smiled, as always responding well to his praise. 'The other key thing is talking as little as possible. Let the subject do the talking; that's the way to get most information.'

'OK, so how do we approach Longwell?' she asked.

'I want to concentrate on Kelvingrove and the opposition there will be. Basically I want to get him to respond to the parks protesters' case. And get as much of the local angle in as possible.'

'And then you can slip in a question about Whitby and Harrington?' asked Janice enthusiastically

'Possibly. If I get the chance I will, but I can't just ask him outright how his company is connected to two murders, can I?'

'No, of course not,' replied Janice, frowning. 'But you can subtly drop their names in, can't you?'

I'll try.' He looked at his watch. 'I need to go out for a while over lunch. I should be back by half one. Can you book us a cab into town?'

'Sure' replied Janice, wondering exactly where Frank would be spending his lunch hour. And who with.

Friday May 16 2008, 1:30pm

'So we should be ready to submit the planning application by the end of next week,' Daniel Longwell reported to his father.

'Excellent' the elder Longwell replied, smiling at his son. 'I will let Councillor Gallen know to expect it.' He thought for a moment. 'No, I'll call him on Monday. Give him the weekend to think about things.'

'Will he still be on side, you know, now that this serial killer story is all over the press?'

Longwell nodded, recognising that the question was a good one. He was pleased when Daniel put his queries to him and happy to see that his son was getting bolder. Asking a question was not a sign of weakness, he had always told him. Information was king and the more of it you had, the better you could make a situation work for you.

'He probably knows that I wasn't behind Whitby's death now, although he might well have thought that anyway. But he doesn't know for certain whether or not we have Whitby's videos. And we still have the recording that confirms he was being blackmailed. No, he won't be able to risk that getting into the press.'

Daniel nodded, apparently confident in his father's ability to analyse the situation correctly.

'And remember that he has now come out publicly and supported the Parklands project. Add that to the interview I gave to the Daily News, and Councillor Gallen has no choice but to stay on side. He would lose all credibility if he changed his mind, as well as risking the press finding out his secrets.' Longwell smiled at his son once more. 'Don't worry. Everything is still going well.'

'I don't doubt it,' his son replied, smiling back at his father.

'And this afternoon I have an interview with Frank Gallen of the West End Weekly. Now, you know that all planning applications have to be put out to consultation by the Council?'

'Yes, it's the law.'

'Well, there will be opposition of course, but mainly from the usual loony left brigade. What I need to do is to focus their anger on the Council and away from us. It's Gallen that is giving away their precious parkland, not me. And then it is up to Gallen to make the arguments.'

'You think of everything, don't you?' said Daniel, an admiring look on his face.

'I try to,' replied Longwell. 'I certainly try to.'

Friday May 16 2008, 1:55pm

Frank sat with Janice in a waiting area just outside David Longwell's office. His lunchtime meeting with his alcohol counsellor had gone well and he was feeling better than he had in days. As always, the support helped him to get through the difficult times and concentrate on the positives in his life. Frank was almost certain that he would not be sober if he had been trying to fight his addiction alone.

The door opened and David Longwell walked out of his office to greet them.

'Mister Gallen? So good to meet you.' Longwell offered his hand which Frank shook, noting that the developer had a very firm handshake.

'Call me Frank,' he replied. 'This is Janice Tracey, who is a journalism student and is doing some work with us. I hope you don't mind me bringing her along?'

'Of course not,' said Longwell, turning to Janice. 'Charming to meet you, young lady. Please, come into my office both of you. Has Fiona offered you a drink?'

'We're fine, Mister Longwell,' replied Frank, following him into a large and expensively decorated corner office. The views across the city from floor to ceiling windows taking up two of the walls were stunning, thought Frank as he took a seat. The other two were covered with pictures of housing developments, blueprints and plans, and photographs of Longwell with an assortment of well known public figures.

'Call me David,' said the developer as he took a seat opposite Frank and Janice.

'David, as I'm sure you know, our interest is in the Kelvingrove project, which is in our area. I know the overall outline of the Parklands project, but can you tell us specifically about the Kelvingrove development?'

'After discussions with the Council we decided that Kelvingrove should be the first of our projects,' replied Longwell. 'It's a prestige development and the refurbishment of the Art Gallery arguably makes Kelvingrove Glasgow's premier park, so where better to start?'

'Can you give us some more details on the project?' Frank probed.

'We are looking at a single building with a small access road running east from Kelvin Way. The trees running down there will pretty much camouflage it from the main road. It will be a five story development with sixteen luxury apartments and two superb penthouse suites plus a small car park. We think it will fit nicely into the park and blend in well with the surrounding area.'

Longwell was smooth, thought Frank. He made it all seem like a straightforward plan that no one could possibly have any issues with. 'What about timescales?'

'Our outline planning application is almost ready for submission to the Council. There are some more discussions we need to have with them about the lease of the land. Everything has been already agreed in principle with the appropriate departments, though. And of course Councillor Gallen is helping us to ensure that everything goes to plan.'

From the way Longwell said the name, Frank was certain that he knew about his family ties.

'I'm sure you are aware of the campaigners who will oppose your planning application, David. What do you think of their arguments?' He noticed a slight frown come over the developers face, but his smile soon reappeared.

'There are always people who oppose new building, indeed who oppose progress in general.' With a wave of his hand he appeared to dismiss them at a stroke. 'The Council asked us to look at these projects because of the many good partnership developments we have already worked on together. I know that building in a park is seen as going against some principle or other to these people, but what are we talking about? One block of flats in one corner of a very large park. Now how will that affect the enjoyment that so many people get from walking in Kelvingrove?'

'There will be a public consultation of course. How will you approach that?'

'Frank, as I said we have worked very closely with the Council on this project. We are sure that with the support of the local members and indeed your brother as Leader, the majority of people will see that this is a good deal for the City. Our proposals will enhance the park, not damage it as some would have you believe. The Council is fully behind these plans,' he reiterated.

Frank wondered whether Longwell expected him to be on side simply because his brother was involved. Perhaps he knew of their relationship, but not of their history.

'But many people see a private developer building in a park as a step too far?' he asked.

'The Council clearly doesn't agree with them, Frank. As I've said it's a small piece of land and we will be very careful to ensure that our building fits in with the ambience of the park. It will be a prestige development, not some Sixties monstrosity. We think this will enhance Kelvingrove Park by adding another quality building. After all, the Art Gallery was built in the park and no one complains about that, do they?'

'Are there any major legal issues to be resolved in a deal like this?' Frank asked.

Longwell looked confused for a moment. 'I'm not aware of anything major. Once we get the planning application approved, we will work out the specifics of a long term lease of the land with the Council. I can't see what other issues there could be?'

'I know you retain a firm of lawyers to advise you on these things.' Frank mentioned the name of the firm that Mike Harrington had worked for, and Longwell nodded his agreement.

'Yes, they've worked for my company for many years now.'

'Did you know Michael Harrington well, David?' Frank asked.

Again Longwell looked confused. 'Who is he?'

'One of the men murdered recently by this supposed serial killer,' Frank explained. 'He did some work for you I believe?'

'I always deal with the partners at the firm,' Longwell replied. 'This man Harrington may have worked for them, but I didn't know him personally.'

'The other person known to have been murdered was Phil Whitby.' Frank paused and stared at Longwell. He was sure he saw the very slightest hint of recognition, but Longwell recovered quickly. 'He was one of the organisers of a march protesting against your developments, wasn't he?'

'What are you suggesting?' Longwell asked angrily.

'I'm not suggesting anything,' Frank replied speaking steadily and deliberately. 'It simply appears that the two men so far named in the press as victims of the serial killer both had connections to your company. Do you have any comment to make on that?'

'It can only be coincidence,' replied Longwell, regaining his composure once more. 'Six degrees of separation and all that.'

Frank said nothing, hoping that Longwell would continue, but he didn't. Instead the developer looked at his watch.

'I'm a busy man as I'm sure you will understand, Frank. We will have to leave it there for today, I'm afraid.' He stood up abruptly.

'Thank you for your time,' Frank said.

'Not at all. I'll make sure you get a copy of all our press releases from now on, if you leave me a card?' Frank handed him one from his pocket.

'Thank you. Have a good day,' he said.

Frank and Janice walked out of the door of the office and through the reception area to the lift. Neither said anything until they were outside the building.

'So what did you think of Mister Longwell?' Frank asked Janice.

'He's a smoothie, isn't he? And used to getting his own way too by the looks of him. Although the questions about Whitby and Harrington seemed to annoy him, didn't they?'

'I'm sure he recognised Whitby's name, although I didn't get any reaction from him when I mentioned Harrington,' Frank noted. 'I wonder what that means.'

Janice didn't seem to have anything to add.

'We're really no further forward though. Maybe the connection to his company is just a coincidence after all?'

'So what do we do next?' asked Janice.

'Let's find a taxi and get back to the office,' said Frank wearily.

Friday May 16 2008, 11:30pm

He stood outside the doorway of Blackfriars pub at the corner of Albion Street in the Merchant City. With his hood pulled up over his head he looked like just another anonymous smoker among the many forced onto the pavement because of the smoking ban.

Half way along the block he could see the Glasgow Lesbian, Gay, Bisexual and Transgender Centre. The bar looked to be busy as he had expected that it would. He stood and watched as groups of people and couples left, presumably heading for somewhere to continue drinking, or for home. Still he waited, lighting another cigarette as his cover.

Finally he saw a man, walking alone, stroll along Bell Street towards him. He needed him to turn left onto Albion Street. He felt the now familiar surge of anticipation course through his body like electricity. This was what he now lived for, the reason he put up with the sleepless nights and the awful flashbacks. But he was disappointed when the man turned right instead of left.

Whoever he was, he would never know just how close he had come to death.

He continued his vigil, fighting to control the impulses that threatened to overwhelm him. Two more groups left the building followed by two men walking hand in hand. How much longer would he have to try to keep his rage in check?

And then another single man walked towards him. Again he willed him to turn left. Come on, come on. Do it, you bastard.

Success!

Quickly he dropped his cigarette into the gutter and walked down the opposite side of the street to his quarry. Within seconds he was almost level with him. Then he crossed the quiet road, and followed the man, who did not even appear to notice his pursuer. He was staggering slightly, obviously after having had a few drinks. This was just perfect!

He pulled the plastic bag from his inside pocket and took out the chloroform soaked rag. Here's one I prepared earlier, he joked. With one last check that there was no one watching, he saw that the street was still empty.

Then he pounced just as his prey was level with a large white van. The man was a few inches smaller than him and he easily held the rag over his face as he struggled for just a few seconds before passing out into his arms. Pulling him to the back of his van he quickly unlocked the back doors, lifted him upwards and seconds later they were inside. The rag went back into the bag and the bag was securely zipped into his pocket. That was so easy, so well planned, he congratulated himself.

He picked up a length of rope from the floor of the van and pulled it tightly around the man's neck. Within a few short seconds his breathing had stopped for good. He felt the wonderful feeling of his own invincibility as he gloried in the ease with which he had just caused a human life to end with his own bare hands. Was there any better feeling than this? He sincerely doubted it.

Quickly he wrapped the body in a tarpaulin for its final journey. The concluding part of his plan was very simple: get back out of the van, hopefully without being seen, and into the driver's seat. Then take the body and leave it to be found as he had planned, making his calling card very obvious this time.

And finally, drive home to send another e-mail to Frank fucking Gallen.

The fifth out of his six tasks was now almost completed. It was almost a shame that he only had one final victim left.

He was getting so good at this.

Chapter 9

What the hell was that noise?

Frank opened his eyes, still more than half asleep, seeking the sound that had so suddenly disturbed his rest. He looked around the dark room, his eyes settling on the clock first. Not the alarm then. What the hell was it? And then his half functioning mind identified the sound as his mobile phone.

With a feeling of dread he reached for his phone knowing that no one would be calling at this time of the morning with good news. He finally managed to focus his eyes on the screen.

'John, what is it?' he answered.

'Sorry to wake you, Frank. There's been another murder and the body was left at the office door. Can you get down here immediately?'

Now he was wide awake. 'Tell me the details,' he demanded.

'Just get down here,' replied John brusquely. 'The police need you to check if there's another e-mail. I'll fill you in when you get here.'

'I'm on my way.' Frank ended the call and looked in the closet for some clean clothes. No time for a shower, so he sprayed a liberal dose of deodorant over his body and dressed quickly. Minutes later he was walking rapidly towards Byres Road in search of a taxi. Luckily he found a black cab within seconds.

The short journey only took ten minutes. Frank ignored the driver's attempt to start a conversation; his mind focused totally on what he would find when he arrives at the office.

Another victim, and only three days after Harrington. There had been a week between his death and Phil Whitby's, he recalled. The killer was escalating, he concluded, remembering a term from his reading. The time between his kills was decreasing, probably meaning that the killer was losing control. And that meant that he might make mistakes.

The taxi approached the office, stopping as a uniformed police officer barred it from getting close to the West End Weekly office.

'Just let me out here,' Frank instructed him, passing a five pound note to the driver. 'And keep the change.' He was out of the cab before the driver could reply.

The police officer now walked towards him, and from his expression he was clearly ready to tell Frank to leave the scene immediately.

'I'm Frank Gallen,' he told the policeman quickly. 'I was called for.'

The officer nodded and showed him towards the office door. He saw that police incident tape had been used to create a cordon. The scene was surreal in the early morning light, a hive of activity in an otherwise quiet scene.

Frank could see a number of men whom he took to be crime scene officers in their distinctive suits examining the body. Before he could manage to get a good look the officer had escorted him inside the office where he saw John Addison standing talking to DI Ralston.

'So what's the story?' Frank asked, looking from face to face as he waited for an answer.

'A man out walking his dog found the body just before half past five,' replied Ralston tersely. 'We have reason to believe that it was the same killer as Harrington. Can you check your e-mails for me?'

Frank sat down at his desk and turned his PC on. He noticed that even at this ludicrous time of the morning the DI was smartly dressed, and wished that he had at least had time to shave.

'Have you identified the victim? And what makes you think it is the same killer?' he asked.

Ralston paused. 'We have a name, yes, but we won't release it to the press until his next of kin has been informed. That's standard procedure.'

It had taken time to identify Harrington, and Whitby's body had no identification. So how had the police discovered the identity of this victim so quickly?

'So this time his wallet hadn't been emptied?' And there was the slightest reaction form Ralston. Just a tiny flicker of his eyes betraying an emotion behind the poker face, and a slight hesitation before he replied.

'He had identification on him, yes.'

Not a full answer, Frank recognised, but an answer nevertheless.

The PC continued its slow booting up process as it connected with the network server.

'And what about the signature? Is that how you connected this murder to the others?' This time there was a clear reaction from the detective. Frank saw John looking at him as if to ask where the questions were coming from.

'We are sure it is the same killer,' was all Ralston gave in reply.

Yes but how? That was the question that Frank needed an answer to.

Frustrated, Frank looked at his screen and saw that his computer was now ready, so he opened his e-mail account. Amongst several incoming emails was another from an anonymous Hotmail account. As the DI and his editor leaned towards the screen for a better look he opened the e-mail.

To: Gallenf@wew.com
From: hd8sh45kk@hotmail.co.uk
Date: 17/05/08 at 00:57
Please accept delivery of #5. My calling card is more obvious this time!!!

Instantly Frank knew that he had been right about the signature. But what was it that linked the victims?

Frank also thought that the killer sounded as if he was getting frustrated. Perhaps he wanted his victims to be identified and linked together? But how much had the police worked out and, more importantly, how much would they be willing to tell him?

'What does that mean, Detective?' John asked before Frank could say anything.

'Well, it confirms that the victim was another in the series, doesn't it?' he replied cagily. Ralston took a seat opposite Frank's desk, leaving John standing behind him.

The reply wasn't good enough for Frank. 'You knew that anyway from the body, didn't you? But what is his calling card?'

This time the answer was immediate. 'I can't give out details. This is a multiple murder inquiry, you know.' He leaned back in his seat and folded his arms across his chest as he spoke, the defensive set of his body language clear.

'Look, I think the killer is communicating with me for a reason,' said Frank, hoping that his gambit would sound convincing. 'This is now the third e-mail, don't forget. First he directed me to Whitby, then he gave me the link between Whitby and Harrington and now he dumps the fifth body at my office door.'

'That may well be true,' conceded Ralston.

'So if I knew a bit more about your investigation I might just be able to help you. I think he wants me to figure out the story behind his choice of victims for some reason. Why else would he send the e-mails to me?' Frank was becoming frustrated, feeling that the answer was very close but that he was not being allowed to access all of the clues that would allow him to find it.

'You know how these things work, Frank,' said Ralston, still very defensively, Frank noted. 'I can't give everything to the press or we will have widespread panic on our hands. And anyway we always keep details back from the media so we can weed out the nutcases who will inevitably call us claiming responsibility.'

'We're a weekly paper, Detective,' interrupted John. 'It's not as if we could print everything you told us immediately. And you will have to give the press a statement sooner or later.'

Frank immediately built on his boss's statement. 'Totally off the record. I promise none of the details above what is in your press statement will find their way into print. Think of me as aiding your investigation rather than as a journalist.'

'Give me some time,' he said. Frank wondered if he was weakening or simply stalling. He knew that the pressure would be on the Murder Squad and that this was probably the biggest case of Ralston's career.

The detective stood and started to walk away.

'You know where to find me when you want to talk,' said Frank with assurance. He could only hope that the detective would give in eventually.

Ralston nodded, a frown on his face as he left the office.

'So what do we do now Frank?' asked John.

'Wait on his call,' replied Frank. 'And in the meantime I'm going to make some coffee.'

Saturday May 17 2008, 9:50am

Councillor Thomas Gallen had just left for the short walk to the local primary school where he held his surgery for constituents.

It was a grey and dreary morning and he carried an umbrella, just in case. Gallen was feeling awful after several glasses of champagne at the previous evening's civic reception, followed by a couple of large whiskies when he eventually got home. His late arrival had not pleased Marie in the slightest and he was definitely in her bad books.

He pulled his mobile phone from his pocket and called Alan Mathers.

'Alan? What have you got on Longwell so far?' he asked as soon as his assistant answered. He did not have time for formalities.

'Give me some time, Thomas. It's only been one day.'

'I told you that we needed to move quickly on this one. Do you have anything for me or not, Alan?'

'I've put out the feelers within the construction workers' union and with my contacts in Stirling where Longwell comes from. I'm just waiting on them to get back to me now,' Mathers replied. 'I also had a look at his accounts for the past few years. His company keeps growing as do the profits, which is nothing short of a miracle in the current economic climate. He has no outstanding legal actions and no criminal record. Clean as a whistle,' he concluded.

'That's not what I need to hear, Alan. We need to get something on him.'

'He looks dirt-free so far, Thomas. I'll keep looking, but it might take a few days for folk to get back to me.'

'Chase them up first thing on Monday morning, Alan. I need to stop Longwell from submitting that planning application, remember.' He turned into the school playground nodding a good morning to the janitor. 'I'm relying on you, Alan.' Gallen abruptly hung up.

What if Mathers couldn't come up with something on Longwell, he thought? What was Plan B? He had always prided himself on being in control, of having thought out all possible scenarios in advance. But Longwell clearly held the upper hand at the moment.

He had to find a way to turn the tables on the developer and soon. Very soon.

Saturday May 17 2008, 10:10am

A bundle of West End Weeklies was delivered to the office on a Saturday morning at the same time as the new edition was distributed to local shops and community centres. Frank was sitting leafing through a copy, well into his third cup of coffee when Detective Inspector Adam Ralston walked back into the office.

'Hello again, Frank,' he said. Frank pointed to the seat opposite his desk and Ralston sat down. The detective looked tired, having been one of the first on the scene earlier in the morning.

'Early start wasn't it?' he asked sympathetically. 'Can I get you a coffee?'

Ralston shook his head. 'I didn't get in until midnight last night and I was called out just after five thirty this morning. My wife wasn't at all pleased, I can tell you.'

'So what's happening now?' Frank asked.

'My boss wants you to come into headquarters right away.'

Bingo, thought Frank. They had realised that they needed his help.

'I'll explain on the way,' said Ralston, already moving towards the door.

'OK,' replied Frank. 'Just let me tell John that I'm going.' Ralston nodded as he walked towards the editor's office.

Ralston was standing by the door when Frank returned five minutes later. He had promised to call John when he was finished at the police headquarters.

Frank knew that he would soon be in a unique position to write about the case. He was already the recipient of the murderer's e-mails and he was certain that he would be the only journalist to have access inside the investigation.

Hell, maybe there would even be a book in this, he thought optimistically.

'OK, let's go,' he said to Ralston and they walked out of the office together.

'We'll take my car,' said Ralston, pointing to a blue Vectra parked to the side of a number of vans and police vehicles. Frank noticed that the body had already gone, and also that there was a crowd of reporters and cameramen being held back by uniformed police officers. News of the fifth killing had obviously become common knowledge very quickly.

Frank got into the passenger's side and Ralston started the car and drove off at speed. He radioed in to let his boss know that they were on their way and then addressed Frank.

'The Superintendent needs your help on this one, Frank. We don't know for certain whether the killer is contacting you for a reason, but it is a possibility that we have to consider. It might be someone who knows you, so he wants to brief you to see if there is something you can tell us.'

'That's exactly what I said earlier,' responded Frank. Ralston merely nodded wearily.

'But he will want you to treat everything as off the record. There are certain details about the investigation that we don't want getting out.'

'I understand,' replied Frank. The Superintendent was simply trying to look as if he was still in control, which was OK with Frank. He would give McPherson his place. 'I'm not new to this, you know.'

Again Ralston just nodded and lapsed into silence for the rest of the short journey along quiet city streets. Less than ten minutes later they pulled into the yard to the rear of the Strathclyde Police headquarters on Pitt Street. Ralston parked the car and then showed Frank in through the back door. Moments later they were on the fourth floor and at the door to Superintendent McPherson's office. Ralston knocked and then they entered.

McPherson was seated behind a large desk covered with stacks of folders. Behind him on the wall were many photos and what looked like citations or awards. The senior detective stood as they entered and indicated that they should sit at the meeting table in the corner of the office. He lifted a bundle of files and then joined them at the table.

'Thanks for coming in, Frank,' he said. 'Now this is all off the record, are we absolutely clear on that?'

'Sure. As I said to you earlier I won't print anything that you don't make public in your press releases until the investigation is over.' Frank deliberately chose his words very carefully.

'Right, I'm glad we understand each other. Now, the killer may well be contacting you for a reason. Of course, it could be purely a random thing, but at the moment it's a legitimate line of inquiry.'

'So, if you let me know everything you have, you hope that I might be able to give you a lead on his identity?'

'That's the theory.' The older detective gave Frank a humourless smile. 'Let's see how it works out in practice.'

Frank said nothing as McPherson consulted one of his files and prepared to bring him up to date.

'OK, here's what has happened since we last talked. As you know, Harrington was found stabbed to death in the city centre early on Wednesday morning. He had no ID on him when we got there. His wife later reported him missing. She described him and the clothes he was wearing, so we made the connection and she formally identified the body.'

He paused and looked directly at Frank. 'But one thing was strange: the only item in Harrington's wallet was a playing card. The three of spades.'

That piqued Frank's interest immediately. 'Is that the signature then? The calling card mentioned in the e-mail is an actual card?'

'Just let me tell it as it happened, please,' said McPherson with just a hint of irritation in his voice. He was clearly not used to being questioned.

Frank nodded, then sat back and listened.

'Now it initially looked like a robbery gone wrong, so the local CID proceeded as normal. They tried to retrace his steps: who he had been with and where, that sort of thing. But that went nowhere. Harrington had told his wife he was going out for a drink with a colleague, but we discovered that the colleague was at home all night with his wife. He also reported that he hardly knew Harrington and had never socialised with him.'

Frank restrained his natural inclination to ask questions and allowed McPherson to continue uninterrupted.

'Then you gave us the link to Phil Whitby from the second e-mail. So we looked again into Whitby's death but still couldn't find evidence for anything other than a suicide. We also tried to find a link between Whitby and Harrington, but we couldn't find one.'

Frank wondered if he should give McPherson the possible link that the two men had with Longwell Homes, but he decided to hear him out. He didn't want to annoy the detective again.

'Now Whitby didn't have a wallet on him when his body was found, so we had pretty much discounted the playing card found in Harrington's wallet as being unimportant at that stage.'

Frank saw a look pass between the two detectives. Had this decision turned out to be a mistake, he wondered?

'Much of Thursday was taken up with routine inquiries which frankly led us nowhere fast. And also chasing the leak to the Evening Citizen, of course. I know where it came from now, Frank, and he has been dealt with. Apologies for having Adam ask you about it.' Frank nodded and he continued with his narrative.

'On Thursday night we managed to track down a number of witnesses who had seen Harrington in the hours before he was killed. Turns out he had spent the evening in the Waterloo pub, which explains why he had lied to his wife about where he was going.'

Frank immediately understood: the Waterloo was a well known gay bar.

And there was the link: Harrington and Whitby had both been gay. They hadn't found it earlier simply because Harrington had been married. Talk about making assumptions, he chided himself.

'That's right, Frank. Both of the victims were gay.' And so the Longwell Homes connection must have been just a coincidence after all, Frank concluded.

'Now, knowing the connection between the two men we finally had something to help us find numbers one and two, as the killer would no doubt describe them,' said McPherson. 'On Friday I had officers trawl through all unsolved murders in the city looking for any where a gay man was the victim. But we could only find one.'

He opened a folder took out a photograph. Frank saw a young, dark haired man.

'Meet Ian Ramage. 28 years old and killed by what was thought to have been a hit and run near his home in Partick two weeks before Phil Whitby's death. His body was identified the next day by his male partner.'

Again McPherson paused as Frank tried to take it all in.

'The local station's inquiry into Ramage's death was stalling when we took it over. No witnesses and no CCTV on that particular side street meant no concrete leads,' continued McPherson. 'But when we looked at the details of Ramage's personal effects it turned out that the only thing in his wallet was a playing card. The five of spades.' McPherson stopped again, this time looking as if he wanted a break.

'Can you organise some coffees, Adam? I'm parched. Frank?'

'Sounds good. Black for me, please,' he replied.

'I need to make a quick call, Frank' said McPherson, walking over to his desk. 'Let's take five.'

Frank sat back in his seat and considered what he had now been told. The serial killer was targeting gay men, but as far as he knew there was no sexual angle to the murders themselves. Thinking back to what he had read, he wondered whether the murderer had perhaps been sexually abused himself. That would possibly give him a reason for targeting gay men.

But what about the playing cards that had apparently become his signature? He now knew that the killer had used the three and five of spades so far, but the numbers of the cards did not coincide with the order of the victims, so what did they mean? The ace of spades was known as the death card, Frank knew, but he could not think of any significance for the other cards.

His train of though was interrupted as a female officer entered the room with a tray of coffees. Frank took a cup for himself while Ralston added milk to his. Seconds later Superintendent McPherson came back to the meeting table, taking the final cup and adding both milk and sugar.

'Right, where were we?' McPherson said. 'Ramage and the five of spades. OK, so we realised that the playing cards were significant after all. We still have one victim to find, it seems, so I currently have officers going through all of the recent murders in the city looking for one with a playing card in the wallet of the victim. We have to go through every file by hand as that sort of detail isn't on computer,' he explained.

'That brings us to this morning and victim number five. Meet James Stevenson,' said the detective taking a photograph from another folder.

'Stevenson was 28 and lived in Pollokshields. He was a graphic designer with a company in town and yes, he was gay too. He had told his flatmates that he was going to the LGBT Centre in the Merchant City last night to meet up with some friends, although they couldn't give us any of their names. We are going through the contacts from his mobile phone at the moment. We are also in the process of tracking down everyone who was working there last night to interview them. And officers will be there tonight to talk to the customers.'

He opened yet another folder from the pile. 'Forensics have given us an initial report from the scene. Stevenson was strangled to death, probably with a rope based on the ligature marks on his neck. There were also traces of chloroform around his mouth. And it also looks like he was not killed at your offices, but that the body was placed there some time later. We will know more after the post mortem. I have officers looking at CCTV from both the Merchant

City and the streets around your offices to see if we can find anything suspicious.' McPherson paused and Frank could tell that he was about to say something significant.

'And when we found Stevenson this morning there was a playing card taped to the forehead of the body. The two of spades.'

'So that's what he meant about it being obvious,' Frank realised. 'He was having a go because we didn't seem to have picked up on the cards.'

'It looks like it,' agreed McPherson. 'We think that he is counting down his victims using the cards. Look at the sequence: Ramage with the five in his wallet, then Whitby, then Harrington with the three and finally Stevenson marked with the two. We are thinking that perhaps Whitby's wallet was stolen before we got there and that it must have contained the four of spades to stay with the sequence. And the victim we have still to find must be the first of them all, with the six of spades in his wallet.'

'That's pretty callous isn't it? Robbing the dead?' Frank remarked.

'The body was called in by an anonymous male on a pay as you go mobile phone. Could be he took the wallet for the cash or credit cards, not realising that there was something more significant in it,' suggested Ralston.

'So what does the sequence of the cards tell us?' asked Frank. Then he answered his own question. 'The next victim will be the ace of spades. That's the death card.'

Both police officers nodded, confirming his thinking.

'The Chief has brought in a profiler to work on the case with us, a criminal psychologist who thinks he can get inside the mind of the killer.'

McPherson's manner left Frank in no doubt how little he thought of that idea.

'I prefer good old fashioned police work myself,' he commented, confirming that Frank had been correct.

'Let me guess,' Frank quickly interjected. 'He told you to look for a white male, aged between 18 and 32 and working alone. He is above average intelligence and was probably sexually abused. And as a child he wet the bed, started fires and tortured animals.'

Frank watched as both detectives' mouth fall open and he tried not to laugh. Humour somehow didn't seem appropriate while they were discussing a serial killer with five victims to his name.

'Where did you get that from, Frank?' asked DI Ralston. 'Are you an expert on serial killers now?'

'I'm correct: that's what he said, wasn't it?' he asked. Ralston nodded, still with the quizzical look on his face.

'I've been reading up on serial killers,' explained Frank. 'That's all standard FBI profiling from the States, but it describes almost none of the main UK serial killers. Sutcliffe and Christie are the closest but Shipman was much older. And then there were the couples who killed together: Ian Hindley and Myra Brady, Fred and Rosemary West.'

'Very good, Frank,' said McPherson, looking impressed. 'So profiling doesn't mean too much then, in your opinion?'

'I'm sure your expert will have a different view, but from what I've read it doesn't help too much at all in an investigation. Not like it always does in the movies, anyway,' he added.

'Well, I will continue to run the case the way I always have,' stated the detective resolutely. 'When the evidence and the witnesses lead me to a suspect I'll see whether he meets the suggested profile or not. But only out of curiosity.'

'The profiler did agree with our thinking on the cards though, Frank,' said Ralston. 'He says that there is most likely only one more victim, and he is the main target for the killer. The others are likely to be in some way symbolic, especially as there was no sexual element to his killing. But he is working towards the ace, whoever that might represent in his mind.'

'Sounds reasonable,' agreed Frank.

'OK then,' said McPherson, closing his folder and looking directly at Frank. 'That's exactly where we are with the investigation at this moment. Does anything that I've told you give you any indication at all of who the killer might be, Frank?'

Frank was anxious to come up with something, but his mind was disappointingly blank.

'I'm afraid not. I can't think of any connection. I don't know anyone who was abused as far as I know, and the cards don't ring any bells,' he replied, despondently. And he could see that the detectives were disappointed too.

'So why has he sent his messages to you, Frank?' asked Ralston.

'I've no idea at the moment, but maybe the reason only makes sense to him? We can't assume that this guy is altogether rational.'

'That could be true,' conceded McPherson.

'I can't think of anything that might link the killer to me,' Frank said. 'I've never had e-mails in this format before and I've never had a contact with a history that would suggest anything like this. Perhaps it's not personal though?'

'What do you mean?' asked Ralston.

'It would make sense for him to pick a journalist wouldn't it? But perhaps I was just a name picked at random?'

'I don't think so,' responded McPherson. 'Especially now that he has delivered the fifth victim directly to you, Frank. That would seem to suggest something more personal, in his mind at least.'

'Perhaps,' said Frank, although he was not convinced. But the situation was so strange that he was not certain that he could think about it logically anymore.

'And he obviously wants his message, whatever it is, to be understood. That's why he is joining all the dots for you. If he simply wanted publicity, why not contact one of the daily papers?

No offence Frank, but the West End Weekly is a small paper,'
Ralston pointed out.

'Maybe he lives in the West End? I don't know.' Even now
that he now knew everything the police did, Frank could not see
where he fitted in to the killer's grisly picture. 'Maybe I've met him
in connection with a story somewhere locally? Or maybe he just
reads the paper and saw my name.'

'It could be any of these reasons, or none of them,'
McPherson said grimly.

'But we know that he is targeting gay men, so maybe his
motive is the obvious one,' suggested Frank. 'I've done some reports
on gay rights campaigns in the past, but I've never had anything to
do with gaybashers or homophobia. I assume you are looking into
offenders with that sort of history?'

'Of course,' replied Ralston. 'We're still working on that
angle. There are a couple of ex-cons that we are trying to track
down.'

'That may give you a suspect?' Frank suggested. 'He may
have committed lesser offences before graduating to murder?'

'We don't have long to figure it out,' said McPherson. 'The
time between his victims is getting shorter every time. Right now we
have no idea who the final victim could be.'

'Have you thought that it might be a prominent gay figure?
That would explain why he is going through this crazy build up?'

'That's a possibility, Frank,' replied McPherson.

'Here's another idea. What if the killer was a victim of a
sexual assault himself, perhaps by a gang of men? Maybe the
symbolism of the six victims is that he himself was attacked by six
men? And the final victim represents the leader?'

'Get onto that right away, Adam,' said McPherson,
realising the validity of the notion. 'Look into all sexual assaults
where a man was the victim. Although from what I've read, many of
this type of crime go unreported, even more so than rapes on

females.' Ralston immediately left the office to follow up on the new line of inquiry. 'Good idea, Frank.'

He nodded, accepting the praise. 'If the final victim is the big one for him, maybe he will give us a clue in advance or something? He will want to be sure that we get whatever his message is. And he will definitely want publicity for his final kill.'

'That makes perfect sense,' said McPherson. 'But while he can send us messages through you, the only way we have of communicating with him is through the media. We need to look carefully at what we say, so that we don't alarm all gay men in the city, but somehow encourage him to tell us more. Maybe we can use his desire for publicity to draw him out a bit?'

'Do you want me to write a press release for you?' asked Frank, keen to stay at the centre of the investigation.

McPherson seemed taken aback by the suggestion, but then appeared to reconsider his initial reaction.

'That would be very unusual, Frank. We have our own press team, of course, but you have the expertise and now the in depth knowledge. And it would mean one less person knows the details. Why not?' he concluded, the decision made.

Frank took a notepad and pen from his pocked. 'Give me some time and I'll draft something up for you.'

'Thanks Frank. I appreciate your assistance.' McPherson walked to his desk, leaving Frank with his thoughts.

He mentally ran through every aspect of the case, thinking how best to use the knowledge and structuring the press release in his mind.

Then he began to do what he did best: to write.

Chapter 10

Janice was feeling absolutely awful. She opened her laptop groggily and washed down two aspirin with a glass of water as she waited for it to boot up. Never again, she told herself as her head continued to pound. She didn't drink often and usually had the good sense to stop well before things got out of hand. So what had possessed her to try to match her friends with round after round of tequila shots in the Students' Union?

She answered her own question: she had been on a mission to get as drunk as possible in order to drive the twin thoughts of Glasgow's serial killer and Frank Gallen from her mind. And she had succeeded for a few hours. But she was certainly paying for it this morning.

When the computer was ready she opened her internet browser and went to the BBC news site. And there she saw the headline: 'Another Body Found in Glasgow'. Beginning to feel even sicker, if that was in any way possible, she clicked the link.

And saw a picture of the West End Weekly office.

Janice struggled as a growing feeling of nausea threatened to overwhelm her. The suspicion was that the murder was linked to the Glasgow serial killer.

Unable to read any more Janice ran out of her room and across the hall to the bathroom, just making it to the toilet before she vomited. She spent the next fifteen minutes with her head over the bowl, her hair held behind her head, until at last her stomach seemed to be emptied. She felt absolutely pitiful and wished that she was dead.

Janice stood slowly, finding that her head was still spinning, and walked over to the sink where she splashed cold water over her face. It didn't seem to do any good and she still felt wretched. Janice wasn't used to drinking to excess and felt worse than she could ever remember. This was the hangover from hell, she thought miserably.

Looking in the mirror she saw that she looked terrible too: pale and drawn with large black bags under her eyes. The phrase *death warmed up* had never been more appropriate. Thank goodness Frank couldn't see her.

Janice walked slowly back to her room and finished her glass of water in one long, greedy swallow. Unable to contemplate doing anything more active, she lay down on her bed and simply waited for the world to stop spinning.

When her mind was able to focus a little she looked over to her bedside clock to see that half an hour had passed. For a moment she felt relieved until she remembered the news report she had read.

Another killing, and so soon after Harrington. And why had he been killed at their office? Was this another message to Frank? Thinking of the link she had discovered between Harrington and Whitby, she wondered whether this victim was also connected to Longwell Homes in some way. She just had to find out, despite her fragile physical condition.

Frank would know, thought Janice. And then she wondered whether there had been another e-mail from the killer. She tried to remember where her phone was but found that she couldn't even remember coming home the previous night. She had said 'never again' several times in the past, who hadn't? But this time she totally meant it. Sitting up, even very slowly, caused another wave of nausea to hit her.

She thought she was going to be sick again, but a moment without moving calmed her stomach a little. Then she saw her jacket on the floor and rummaged through the pockets, finally finding her mobile. After a couple of deep breaths, she found Frank's number and hit the call button. It rang for a few seconds then went to voicemail. *God, he has a sexy voice*, Janice reflected, as she felt a shiver run down her back.

'Frank, it's Janice,' she started, then wondered what to say. 'I saw the news about the murder this morning. Call me back when you can?'

She ended the call and lay down once more, holding her mobile as she waited for the return call, longing to hear his voice once again. Still feeling particularly awful, she thought that perhaps some sleep was the best course of action. The room was spinning and so she closed her eyes, hoping for the relief of unconsciousness to come to her.

Janice held her mobile phone in her right hand, pressed to her heart, when sleep finally overtook her.

Saturday May 17 2008, 1:35pm

Frank walked out of police headquarters, his work completed. Now all he could do was wait until the media picked up on the press release that Superintendent McPherson had agreed with only minimal changes. And then hope that the killer would get in touch with him once more.

Not for the first time he felt torn between two conflicting emotions: the horror of the situation and the intense desire to get the story. His gut had told him when the first e-mail had arrived that he should follow the story and he was delighted that his instincts had not failed him. But how would it end?

As he walked along Pitt Street, Frank suddenly realised that he had not eaten at all and was extremely hungry, especially given the early start he had made that morning. He walked onto Sauchiehall Street, which was typically busy on a Saturday afternoon, and found a small café which was almost full with shoppers looking for respite, and hungover students looking for a late breakfast. He found a table for one in the corner and sat down.

Almost immediately a pretty young waitress dressed all in black approached, and Frank ordered a ham and cheese toastie and a diet coke. When she had left he fumbled in his pockets looking for his mobile phone to call John, and then realised that perhaps he shouldn't be discussing a serial killer in the middle of a busy café. He would have his lunch first and then call John before he made his way over to the East End to visit his mother, he decided.

Frank remembered that he had switched his phone off when he had entered the police station earlier, so he took it from his pocket and turned it back on. Inevitably his voicemail service called him within seconds and he took out his notepad. Three messages: firstly from John wondering what was happening, secondly from a contact on an unimportant story that he could ignore for now, and finally from Janice asking him to call her back.

He put his phone into his pocket and waited for his food to arrive, which it did shortly afterwards. As he ate he could only think about the killer who had seemingly chosen him as his conduit to the media. Surely it couldn't be someone he knew, could it? He racked his brains, but nothing at all came to mind. He could not think of ever dealing with anyone who was homophobic, well not beyond the bad jokes and snide comments that were common in the newsroom.

Frank wondered whether the killer would respond to their press statement. They had deliberately challenged him to contact the authorities. Of course, they had not made public the fact that he had already contacted Frank three times.

Now they could only wait and hope that his apparent desire for publicity would lead him to give them something that might help the police to track him down.

And before he got to his final, and most important, victim, whoever that might be.

Twenty five minutes later Frank had finished his meal. He walked quickly along Sauchiehall Street towards the main shopping area until he came to a bank. He stood in the doorway as it was closed on a Saturday, to return his calls in relative peace. First he called John, bringing him up to date with the police investigation and the press release, which, his editor told him, had already been distributed to media contacts by e-mail. Frank promised to call John again with anything he heard over the rest of the weekend and then rang off.

Then he returned Janice's call, and the number rang for a while before it was eventually answered.

'Hello?' He heard a rather sleepy voice from the other end of the line.

'Janice, it's Frank. Did I wake you?'

'Oh, just a minute.' She sounded flustered, Frank thought. Finally, she came back on the line.

'Sorry, I must have dozed off. It was a bit of a late one last night.' Frank could recognise the tell tale signs of a hangover at a hundred yards, but he was the last person to have a go.

'Good night, was it?' he asked her instead.

'Yeah, just a few drinks in the Union with some friends,' she replied, before abruptly changing the subject. 'I saw the news story about the body the found this morning. What's happening now, Frank?'

Once more he recounted the events of the day. Janice listened without saying a single word, only the odd gasp letting him know that she was still on the line,

'So the Longwell's link was just a coincidence after all?' she asked.

'It seems like it,' Frank replied, sensing that she was disappointed. 'But it was a good piece of work, though. In major stories like this, it's rare for the first idea to be the correct one. And the interview with Longwell will also be very useful for the other story.'

'That's true.' She sounded very rough, and Frank guessed that she must have had quite an amount more than just a few drinks.

'Now all we can do is to see if anything comes from the press release. John said that he had received a copy, so you will probably see it reported on the internet soon.'

'I'll look out for it.'

'Right, I'm going to have to go; I've got things to do. Enjoy the rest of your weekend and I'll see you on Monday.'

'OK, bye Frank,' she replied. 'Thanks for calling me back.'

Frank stepped out of the doorway and into a stiff wind that had suddenly come up from nowhere. It was beginning to spit with rain too, he thought, as he looked for a taxi to take him to his mother's in Parkhead. Within a few minutes he had managed to flag down a black cab and was on his way across the city to the East End.

Saturday May 17 2008, 4:35pm

'Come in,' shouted Superintendent McPherson.

DI Ralston walked in and took the seat opposite his boss's desk. He noticed that McPherson had now taken his tie off and was in his shirtsleeves, which he assumed would count as casual dress for him. Or perhaps a sign of the pressure they were under to solve the case, thought Ralston.

'The press release is out, sir. You and Frank did a good job,' he reported

'How did the PR boys take it?' asked McPherson, smiling. 'Did they try to make any changes?' He moved a large pile of papers from the middle of his desk to the floor.

'I decided not to tell them that we had outside help on this one. I said it was all our own work and that you had insisted it go out exactly as it was. They couldn't really argue with that, could they?' he finished, also smiling.

'Sounds like a good way to handle it, well done.'

'And we have extra phone operators coming in to field the calls from the usual lot that we will inevitably get.'

'Good stuff,' replied McPherson. Then his face turned more serious. 'So where are we with the investigation, Adam?'

Ralston took out his notebook and ordered his thoughts, preparing to brief his boss. 'There's a lot of activity and we have a great number of officers working very hard, but not too many positive results as yet.'

'Take me through it all,' McPherson instructed, sitting back in his chair to listen.

Ralston composed himself knowing that his report had to be a good one. 'Firstly, forensics have come back with some more details on the body,' he began. 'Cause of death is now confirmed as strangulation, but then we pretty much knew that anyway.' He looked up, saw McPherson nodding and continued.

'There were also traces of chloroform found around the victim's mouth, again as we thought, so he must have been subdued before he was killed. Time of death is estimated at between 11:30pm and 1:30am. The difficulty is that they don't know exactly how long his body was lying outside, so that makes an accurate time of death based on body temperature difficult to ascertain,' he explained.

'So do we still think that he was killed elsewhere and then taken to the West End Weekly?'

'That still looks most likely, they reckon, based on the lividity,' replied Ralston. 'And of course that implies that the killer must have access to a vehicle.'

The Super nodded. 'Go on.'

'The murder weapon was a very common type of rope, so there's nothing to help us there. And Stevenson had a high amount of alcohol in his body, which ties in with a night out. No sign of drugs of any kind, though.'

'So was he definitely drinking at the LGBT Centre?' asked McPherson.

'That's now verified, yes. We've talked to the two friends he met there and they confirmed that the three of them had quite a few drinks together. They met there around eight and were all in the bar for the rest of the evening. Stevenson was on the South Side and both of his friends lived in the West End, so he left on his own to get a taxi home somewhere around 11:30.'

Ralston moved to another page of his notebook. 'We've got him on CCTV leaving the bar at 11:39 and then walking west along Bell Street. That's the last sighting that we have of him. It looks like he turned south onto Albion Street and the camera lost him. We assume he was heading down to Argyle Street to look for a taxi on the main road.'

'That would make sense,' said McPherson, picturing the scene in his mind. 'Do any of the cameras around Argyle Street pick him up again? He could either have headed along Argyle Street into town or perhaps down onto the Saltmarket from there.'

'We're still looking at the footage, sir. I've also put his photograph out to the taxi companies just in case,' Ralston replied. He knew that any further sighting of the victim might also involve the killer himself.

'You know our killer could be a taxi driver,' suggested McPherson, pausing to let Ralston consider the idea.

'We know that all of the murders have occurred late in the evening or in the early hours of the morning. What looks less suspicious than a taxi at that time of night? And we know that at least two of the killings involved a vehicle: Ramage was knocked down and now we think that Stevenson was transported across the city,' he explained.

'It's a thought,' acknowledged Ralston, making a note. 'I'll have officers look into it. Now we are still examining all of the CCTV near where the body was dumped. The newspaper office isn't directly covered, unfortunately, but several of the approach roads are. I'll tell the officers on that to look out for taxis, too.' Ralston made another entry on his increasingly lengthy to do list.

'Have them note all of the taxis they see near to the office, then cross check that with taxis seen around the Merchant City,' ordered McPherson. 'See if any were in both locations around the correct times.'

'Will do,' confirmed Ralston.

'Good work. We've covered all of the bases and we just need a bit of luck. What about any leads on the killer himself?' he asked.

'We are due a break on this case,' agreed the DI. 'Now we've contacted all of the ex-cons we can find with attacks on gay men on their records. Most are ruled out; either not in the area any more or they have alibis for one or more of the killings. Four officers are still perusing the remainder of that list.'

'What about sexual assault victims?' asked McPherson, remembering the earlier suggestion from Frank Gallen.

'There are on average 30 incidents categorised as 'serious' where gay men are the victims in Strathclyde per year. That takes out the cases of verbal abuse and the like,' explained Ralston. 'I have an officer going through all of the reports for the last five years now, narrowing it down to victims in the city who suffered serious injures.'

'OK, keep looking. It may just get us somewhere.'

'We believe that only a minority of cases are ever reported but we might be lucky.' He considered his words for a moment. 'But look how many cases of child sexual abuse are coming out of the woodwork many years later. Our man could be a victim of something from way back.'

'I know,' admitted McPherson, 'and if he was it will be almost impossible to track down. Let's just keep working on what we have and hope that we get something turning up.'

'It's a massive operation. Checking the CCTV alone will take hours.'

'Tell me about it,' he replied ruefully. 'The Chief Constable was on an hour ago looking for something positive to tell the press. I only just managed to talk him out of another media conference at this stage. We've nothing to tell them at the moment, so there's really no point.'

'Is there anything else, sir?'

McPherson looked at his inspector for a few seconds before replying. 'Yes. Go home, Adam. That's an order. You're doing a great job but you're obviously exhausted. Go home and try to get a good night's sleep.'

'Thank you,' replied Ralston grateful for the praise.

'It's been a hell of a first week for you, hasn't it?'

Ralston smiled grimly. 'I didn't expect it to be easy.'

McPherson nodded. 'Well, get out of here and try to enjoy the rest of your weekend.'

'I'll just pass a few notes on to the team, check a couple of things and then I'll be off.' He closed his notebook and left the office.

McPherson stared into space for a long time, considering all that Ralston had reported. He was pleased that they had a number of leads to pursue, although none of the lines of inquiry looked immediately hopeful. But something would break soon, he hoped. Or was that just wishful thinking on his part?

Finally, the realist within him had to admit that they were a very long way from catching the killer.

Saturday May 17 2008, 4:50pm

Frank sat in the living room of his mother's small house in Parkhead while she made another cup of tea. He knew better than to offer any assistance in the kitchen: Helen Gallen was a proud woman who didn't considered herself to be old at the age of 67.

As always the house was immaculate, Frank thought. He had often wondered why his mother stayed there now that she was on her own, but she would not consider moving.

Frank looked around the living room, his eyes falling on the vast collection of family photographs that completely covered a large wall unit. Frank could see a couple of himself in younger days, in the background as always. Standing up front besides his parents' wedding photograph were a black edged shot of Kathleen and one of Tommy taken in the City Chambers. Some things never change.

His childhood had largely been a happy one, he remembered. He had enjoyed school and spent most of his free time playing football or just hanging out with his friends. But, back at home, he had always felt like an afterthought in the family: the late baby who had come along eleven years after the twins. He had spent many years trying to live up to what they had achieved. But never quite succeeding.

His mother returned with a tray containing two cups of tea, proper china cups with saucers as always, and a plate of biscuits. Frank took his and she offered him a biscuit. He took one just to keep her happy, not that he was really hungry.

'Are you eating well, Francis?' she asked him. How he hated that name. But she simply refused to call him Frank, always arguing that his father had called him Francis and that was how he had been baptised. The fact that his father had been Tommy, and not Thomas, to everyone all of his days didn't enter into things at all.

'Yes, mum. I'm feeling pretty healthy these days,' he replied.

'You're looking a bit thin,' she replied dubiously.

'Is that a bad thing?' asked Frank. 'I'm going to the gym when I can and trying to stay fit.'

'And you're still not drinking?' Somehow she always managed to make that simple question sound like an accusation.

'No, I've not touched a drop since I came out of rehab.'

'Well, that's something, the Lord be praised,' she replied, sipping her tea. 'What do you have planned for this evening?' He knew that was his mother's way of politely asking what time he would be leaving. The way his life was at the moment she was more likely to have plans on a Saturday night than he was, he realised sadly.

'Just a quiet night in tonight. It's been a very busy week.' Isn't that the truth, he reflected, looking back on a crazy few days.

'Well, I'm going round to mass at five thirty as usual and then we have a planning meeting for the summer fete with Father Dennis afterwards,' she replied.

''I'll walk you round when I go then,' offered Frank. 'It's on my way.'

'That's fine.'

'Mum, I know that you said earlier on the phone that Tommy and the family are coming round tomorrow,' he said, beginning the conversation that he wanted to have with his mother, but was dreading at the same time.

'That's right,' she confirmed, but with a look that asked several questions.

'Well, I was wondering. Would you have a word with him for me? It's been almost two years now since we last talked and this can't go on forever. I've changed a lot since them, surely you can see that?' He tried not to sound bitter or to plead with her, although he could hear the stress in his own voice.

His mother stared at him for a long time before answering. 'I don't like to see you boys not talking either, you know, Francis. But Thomas took what you said to him very hard. He was devastated when Kathleen passed, God rest her soul.'

'And so was I,' replied Frank with feeling. 'I still miss her. But when I was drinking I didn't know what I was saying half the time. I've tried to apologise but he just won't listen to me.'

'I don't know...' she began.

'Mum, isn't forgiving a Christian thing to do?' he tried.

'You don't need to tell me what Christianity means, Francis Xavier Gallen. When were you last in a chapel?' she retorted angrily. Frank always knew he was in trouble when his mother used his full name. But she surprised him with what she said next.

'I will try to talk to him, but don't be shocked if he isn't ready to forgive as yet. It can take time,' she counselled. 'I will talk to him, though.'

'OK,' Frank replied, knowing not to try to push her any further. 'Thank you for trying anyway, mum.'

Without another word his mother finished her tea and began to collect the crockery together onto the tray. She took them into the kitchen leaving Frank with his thoughts once more.

He wanted a reconciliation with his brother more than anything and wondered if his mother would somehow be able to persuade Tommy to talk to him, at least. That would be a good start.

When she had finished in the kitchen Helen Gallen walked back into the living room carrying her handbag, a clear signal that it was time to leave.

'I should be going,' she said. Frank nodded without saying anything and got up to walk out with her.

Saturday May 17 2008, 11:40pm

Were the police mocking him? What the fuck was this all about?

He read the article on the BBC news site from beginning to end for a second time, trying to quell the rage he felt rising deep inside. No need for the gay community to panic? Who did they think that little platitude would fool?

OK, they had finally got the link between his targets, but only after he had handed it to them on a silver fucking platter. Number five had been delivered to them via Frank fucking Gallen with a neon sign pointed straight to the body. And yet they still listed only four of the five names. What the hell did that mean? Were they really so incompetent they could still not have found number one? The police really were useless bastards.

He felt invincible. Superhuman. He had killed five times in the middle of the biggest city in the country and yet the police still had absolutely no idea who he was or how to stop him.

The appeal for him to contact them through "an intermediary, if he felt more comfortable" was nothing more than a thinly disguised cry for yet more help. Maybe he should send an e-mail to the BBC himself? Let them know that he had been in contact with one of them all along? Show up Frank Gallen for the useless bastard that he was.

He fought to control a growing need to do something. Anything. Just to take action in order to calm the beast that dwelt within him. But the sensible thing to do was to ignore this bullshit and continue with his plans. They would get the full story when he was good and ready to give it to them. And he wasn't quite ready yet.

Chapter 11

Sunday May 18 2008, 1:40pm

Frank Gallen sat in a small café on Byres Road with the Sunday papers spread out in front of him. He was stiff from a strenuous session at the gym, which had tired him out enough for him to get a good night's sleep for a change. And he was now feeling even better after a bacon sandwich with tomato sauce and two cups of black coffee.

The papers were, of course, full of the serial killer story. It looked to Frank that most had simply taken the press release and printed it almost word for word as their main story. Lazy journalism really, he thought cynically.

He studied the opinion pages, which had some analysis as well as some angry comments from leaders of the gay community in the city. It was easy to ask what the police were doing, but the insight he now had told him that actually catching the killer was a lot more difficult than most people might imagine it to be. The police were following every lead they had, he knew. What else could they reasonably be expected to do?

Frank wondered whether the inquiry had turned up any viable leads as yet. The thought that he might know the killer was still driving him crazy. But no matter how hard he tried, he still could not think of anyone he had ever known who he would consider to be even remotely capable of mass murder.

Unable to concentrate on the story any longer he turned to the back of the paper he was reading and the sports pages. The race for the league title was going into its final few games, with his team, Celtic, locked in a tight race with old rivals, Rangers.

His mobile phone brought him back from the football. He looked at the screen and answered.

'Hello, Janice.'

'Hi, Frank. Any news today?' She sounded much brighter this afternoon than she had yesterday, he thought, smiling.

'Nothing at all, I'm afraid. No more e-mail messages from him.'

'I saw the papers. They have pretty much the same story as was on the web last night. Do you think he will get in contact again?' She seemed excited by the possibility.

'I hope so.' He paused and looked around, then lowered his voice. 'If our theory about the cards is correct, then there will only be one more killing. And that will be the big one for him. They need to catch him before that happens.'

'But what happens if they don't find him in time, Frank? Surely he won't just stop after the next victim and go back to a normal life? I've been doing some research on serial killers and they all seemed to keep going until they were caught.'

'Bear in mind that the studies are only looking at those who did get caught in the end. Maybe some do just stop when they feel that they have accomplished whatever sick goals they had in the first place?'

'Do you think so?' she asked, not sounding at all convinced.

'I've no idea really,' Frank admitted. 'I've got so many thoughts going round my head that I don't know what to believe any more.'

'Maybe the police will have found a new lead by now? The story gave the time that Stevenson was in Bell Street on Friday night, so maybe someone saw something?' She sounded desperate to Frank, grasping at straws in exactly the same way as he was.

'Maybe,' he replied, not wanting to crush what little hope she seemed to have. 'But he has been pretty careful so far.'

'Let's just hope that they get something positive.'

'Sure. What time are you in the office tomorrow?' he asked, wanting to bring the conversation to a close.

'About two, probably. I've got lectures in the morning.'

'I'll maybe give the police a phone in the morning and see if anything has come up. See you tomorrow.'

'Bye, Frank.'

'Bye.'

Frank wondered how much more information he could possibly get from Superintendent McPherson or DI Ralston. The fact that he was the only one with whom the serial killer was contacting and that he had assisted with the press release gave him an in to the inquiry. But they would still be wary about giving information to a journalist. Especially as he was no nearer to recognising the killer from his messages. If he wasn't useful to them, he could lose his place at the centre of things.

Frank resisted an urge to call Ralston there and then. Hopefully he would soon have another e-mail to report on and could then ask for an update on the inquiry.

He had been thinking a lot about whether there was a book to be written about the Card Killer. *I need a better name than that for a start*, he told himself. But he knew that there were always true crime books on the bestseller list and this was the biggest criminal story that Glasgow had seen for years.

Frank pulled his notebook from his pocket and began to sketch out some notes on the story to date. Fifteen minutes later he paid his bill and left the café, making the short journey home as quickly as he could.

He had decided to write the book and was desperate to get to his laptop.

Sunday May 18 2008, 5:25pm

Thomas Gallen's mobile phone rang while he was eating. He saw that the call was from Alan Mathers.

'I have to take this,' he said, excusing himself from the table, despite his mother's disapproving glance. He walked into the living room and closed the door behind him.

'Alan? What do you have for me?' he asked, desperate for some good news.

'Just a hint of something, Thomas, but I thought that you would want to know right away.'

'Well, what is it?' demanded Gallen.

'I've just had a call from a contact in Stirling Council. There is apparently a rumour there that there is about to be an investigation into bribery of officials in the Planning Department. And Longwell's name has been mentioned as one of the developers who might be involved,' explained Mathers.

'How reliable is your source?' Gallen sat down, his mind calculating the implications. Maybe this was just the thing to put Mister Longwell in his place. If it turned out to be true, of course. Or could he simply use the rumours to regain control?

'Pretty good, I think.' Mathers seemed to be considering his words carefully. 'He is close to the Planning Convener over there, and he told me that there will be an official announcement made early next week.'

'If the primary focus is the officials then won't they keep the developers' names quiet at first? There could be legal issues if they made accusations.'

'That could well be true,' admitted Mathers. 'I'll talk to him again tomorrow and see what else I can get.'

'Keep on to it, Alan,' encouraged Gallen. 'You know how important this could turn out to be for us.'

'I will, Thomas,' Mathers assured him.

'OK. Bye.' Gallen ended the call and considered what he had been told in the quiet of the living room. Time was his problem: he simply didn't have any to spare. He needed to be able to put a spoke in Longwell's plans as soon as he could, and he knew that would be easier to accomplish before his planning application was submitted.

Then he thought more about what Mathers had told him. If Longwell was implicated in one area would questions be asked about the developer's dealings elsewhere? In Glasgow, for instance? He was now publicly allied to the man and even if he did manage to get him off his back there would surely still be questions asked about his judgement in getting involved with a crook in the first place.

But would that be the lesser of two evils? The situation wasn't getting any easier was all that he could say for sure. But perhaps Mathers could find out more in advance of the Stirling announcement. With that thought lingering in his mind he stood up and walked back to the dining room table.

'Sorry about that, mother. Business,' he explained. Now both his mother and Marie looked sternly at him. If looks could kill, he thought, smiling at the two women in his life.

After they had finished, Thomas was instructed to help his mother with the washing up. He immediately had a bad feeling about this, as she rarely let anyone at all into her kitchen. As soon as they were alone she closed the door, presumably so that Marie and the children wouldn't overhear whatever it was that she had to say to him. He braced himself, wondering just what was on her mind.

'Francis was here yesterday, Thomas,' she said, without any preamble. 'He asked me to have a word with you.'

'Mother, no,' he replied. 'I know what you're going to say and the answer is no. I'm not going to talk to him.' He crossed his arms obstinately.

'Look, Thomas, just listen to me,' she told him sharply.

Even at 43 years of age, Thomas Gallen found that he still obeyed his mother without question.

She leaned against the sink and continued. 'I hate to see you two arguing. You're all I have left now and this rift between you isn't doing anyone any good. Surely you can see that, Thomas? Do you know how much pain this situation is causing me?'

His mother was not beyond using emotional blackmail to get what she wanted; he knew that from past experience. But he resolved to stand firm for once.

'What Frank said to me that night was way beyond the pale. Way beyond,' he protested.

'And I was as hurt as you were when you told me about it, Thomas. But we have to stick together as a family. We've lost too much already,' his mother continued, still applying the pressure.

'I can't just forgive that easily, mother', said Gallen, mentally digging his heels in.

'I understand, but listen to me, "*For if you forgive men their trespasses, your heavenly Father will also forgive you. But if you do not forgive men their trespasses, neither will your Father forgive your trespasses.*"'

The Biblical quote stopped Thomas Gallen dead in his tracks. He knew that he had committed a heinous sin, and worse, he had not even had the courage to confess and to beg God for His forgiveness. Without fully knowing why, she had just delivered the most appropriate quotation of all to him. How typical of her that was.

He looked down to avoid his mother's eyes. Why did she have to bring this subject up today? Didn't he have enough on his mind at the moment? But he knew that he had to try to do the right thing; that was his only hope of eventual salvation. And perhaps if he righted one situation then another might fall his way too?

His mother still knew exactly how to play him, he realised. Thankfully his political opponents were not half as skilled, he thought ruefully.

Finally Thomas looked up again, a decision made. 'Alright, mother. I will talk to him and hear what he has to say at least. But please let me have a couple of days, I'm very busy at the moment.'

Helen Gallen merely nodded, obviously content that she had got her way, as she always seemed to do in the end. She turned to the sink.

'I'll wash and you can dry, Thomas,' she commanded. And of course, he obeyed.

Sunday May 18 2008, 9:10pm
Frank Gallen poured the last remnants of a pot of very strong coffee into his mug. He had hardly moved from his desk since returning

home except to change the CD. He liked music while he wrote; somehow it helped him to focus.

Hours hunched over his laptop had meant that he now had a substantial outline of the last week's events mapped out. Between his notebook and his memory he had managed to detail almost all of the major events that had occurred.

Frank sat back and listened to Bruce Springsteen sing about the tragedy of 9/11 for a few moments. He stretched out and felt his shoulders ache. Had it really been less than a week since the serial killer had first contacted him? It felt like so much longer. Five men had died so far and somehow the theory that there was only one more intended victim was not a comfort to him. After all, it was only a theory, and they could, of course, be wrong about the killer's intentions.

He heard his mobile phone ring from inside his jacket, which was hung on the back of the chair. He was tempted to let it ring out and continue to write, but curiosity got the better of him and he pulled the phone out while also fumbling for the remote control to turn the CD down.

'Hello mum, how are you?' he answered the call.

'Fine, Francis. Listen, I talked to Thomas this afternoon.' Typically, his mother was right to the heart of the conversation with no pleasantries or introduction.

'What did he say?' he asked, fearing that he already knew that the answer would be a negative one.

'Give him a few days and he will be in touch with you, Francis.'

Frank was totally thrown. After almost two years his brother was willing to talk to him, just like that? Somehow it was so surprising that it seemed to be unreal.

'How did you manage to persuade him?' he finally asked his mother.

'I simply reminded him what Jesus had to say about forgiveness. The answer was in the good book, as always,' she replied.

Frank smiled. 'I don't know how to thank you, mum.'

'You don't need to Francis. Do you think I enjoy seeing my two remaining children fighting? When he calls you, try not to start another argument, won't you? Just apologise and then you can get yourselves back on good terms with each other.'

'I will,' he said, and he sincerely meant it.

'OK, bye for now.'

'Bye.'

Frank laid the phone down and considered his mother's words carefully. He wondered just how he could manage to persuade Tommy that he was truly sorry for what had happened between them.

He knew that his brother did not understand his alcoholism, seeing it as nothing more than weakness. So he had to make him understand that the old Frank was now behind him. And of course that the new Frank was a much better man who could control himself.

With a sigh he turned back to his laptop, his spirit very much lightened, and tried to recount the conversation in McPherson's office the day before when he had learned the full details of their hunt for the killer.

But the words wouldn't come and he knew that his full concentration was not now on his writing. He saved his work onto the hard drive and also backed it up onto a portable USB drive before quickly checking his e-mails and then closing down his laptop.

Frank's mind was firmly in the past and he recalled the fateful Wednesday night almost two years before. He could remember almost every single detail so clearly.

It had all started when his brother had called him to tell him that Kathleen had been knocked down and rushed to the Royal

Infirmary. He had immediately left whatever pub he was in at the time, he couldn't even remember which one it had been, and caught a taxi to the hospital.

The whole family had been present when he had walked into the A&E department at the Royal: his mother, Tommy and Marie and their children. Kathleen's husband Colin had arrived a few moments after he did. No one seemed to know how it had happened or where Kathleen had been going that evening when a car had struck her just a few yards from their home in the Calton area of the East End.

The doctor had come to talk to them some time later and he recalled that they could all tell immediately from his stern visage that the news was not going to be good. He had told them that Kathleen had suffered massive internal injuries and that they should prepare themselves for the worst. A nurse had then showed them to a small room to wait.

Frank remembered standing as if in a trance as Tommy and his mother tried to find a priest to administer the last rites to Kathleen, which had seemed to be the most important thing to them at that moment.

He, on the other hand, just could not bring himself to concede that his big sister was about to die and had held on to that belief with nothing more than naïve optimism, clinging to the slim hope that she would somehow make it.

But late that night the same doctor had once more come to talk to them. And he had told them that Kathleen had died from her injuries without ever having regained consciousness.

Frank could still remember the devastation he had felt as if it had been yesterday. They had all huddled together; all crying and trying to take in the tragedy, before finally they had left the hospital, a family shattered and broken. Frank of course had headed for a late night drink.

Kathleen's funeral had taken place in the East End a few days later. Frank couldn't remember too much about the day itself: a combination of grief and a great deal of whisky left him with little memory of the service, which was probably no bad thing in the circumstances, he reflected.

Over the next weeks the family had spent a great deal of time together, trying to come to terms with the devastating loss. The police had become involved immediately and they had eventually tracked down the driver of the speeding car that had killed Kathleen.

The family came to know that the driver had been drunk at the time of the accident and had not stopped even though he told the police later that he had been certain that he had hit someone. He was only halted some miles further into his journey when he had run into the back of a stationary taxi.

Somehow knowing exactly how Kathleen had died had not helped to decrease the grief, probably because of the senselessness, the randomness of it all. And Frank recalled that the eventual imprisonment of the driver some months later hadn't helped to ease their suffering in the slightest. He was in jail, but Kathleen was dead and buried.

It had been three weeks or so after the tragedy that he and his brother had come to blows in the Chambers Bar in Glasgow city centre.

Frank could still remember every detail, indeed every word, of that Thursday evening, which was surprising given the amount that he had drunk.

He had been in the pub just across the road from the City Chambers for several hours, drinking with a fellow journalist. Tommy had come in with several other councillors. His brother was not a regular drinker and had probably come into the pub for political rather than social reasons.

When he saw his brother come in, Frank had called Tommy over to the bar where they were standing and bought him a drink. It had been a lager shandy, he recalled. His drinking partner had gone outside to make a telephone call and Frank had asked Tommy how he was coping.

'I'm getting by as best as any of us can' Tommy replied. 'Of course I'm trying to stay strong for mother. You could do more to help her, you know.' The last sentence had been delivered in an accusatory tone that immediately got Frank's back up.

'What can I do?' Frank replied, his tongue fatally loosened by several beers and more than one large whisky. 'It's her golden boy she wants with her, as always.'

'Don't be stupid. We all need to be there for her at a time like this.'

'If she's not in St Michael's, then she's praying at home. You know all that stuff means nothing to me,' he replied dismissively.

'Frank, you know how important our faith is to us, especially after a tragedy such as we have just suffered. You shouldn't mock,' Tommy chided.

'Don't. Just don't,' he replied tetchily. 'Kathleen's gone and none of your prayers or rosaries or whatever other mumbo jumbo you have will bring her back to us.' He lifted his whisky glass from the bar and swallowed the large measure in one, feeling the liquid warm his stomach with that familiar sensation.

'Everything happens according to God's plan, Frank. Even if you won't accept it, that's the simple truth of the matter.'

What a sanctimonious prick his once revered big brother had become. 'Well, you can tell him from me next time you're praying that his plan stinks.' He raised his glass to the barman who immediately went to pour him another large one.

'Don't you think you've had enough?' Thomas asked, looking down his nose at this younger brother.

'I've only just started, Tommy,' Frank replied, laughing with the black humour of the hardened drinker. 'I'll know I've had enough when it stops hurting. And I don't think that will be happening any time soon.'

'For goodness sake, Frank. It was a drunk who killed our sister and this is how you react? You're no better than him.'

The words stung Frank and he reacted angrily. 'That's just bullshit and you know it. You know, you could do with lightening up sometimes, Tommy. Come on, have a real drink with me.'

'No thanks. I've got a drink.'

'Come on, brother. You're not ashamed to have a drink with me, are you?' he persisted.

'I only came in here because I've got business to discuss with my colleagues,' he replied, gesturing to the group of councillors who were now sitting at a table in the far corner of the bar.

'Well, on you go, big brother. Is your political advancement all part of God's great plan too?' he sneered. 'Are you just doing his work for him?'

'I've had enough of your mouth, Frank. You drunks are all the same,' Tommy said, the disdain clear in his words.

'You know, by your twisted Christian logic that bastard driving the car was only doing God's work when he killed Kathleen, wasn't he? How do you explain that, Tommy?' Frank demanded angrily. 'Your god wanted our sister dead and that driver was just carrying out his part of the divine fucking plan.'

Frank stared at his brother, watching the furious expression that came over his face. And then he saw his brother's fist coming towards him an instant later, as if in slow motion, but he was unable to move to avoid the blow. He hardly felt the punch which landed on the side of his jaw and sent him sprawling to the floor. For some bizarre reason his brother's totally uncharacteristic loss of control took all the anger out of Frank and he was laughing as he pulled himself unsteadily to his feet.

His drinking partner walked back into the bar and looked at Frank with a look of shock on his face, 'Are you alright, Frank?'

Frank looked at his brother who was still standing perfectly still, as if unable to figure out what to do next. Frank lifted his whisky and downed it in one, then put the glass back down, throwing some money after it onto the bar.

'Let's go somewhere else and leave the revered city fathers to their important business,' said Frank with contempt, already walking towards the front door. A second later his friend walked after him. As he opened the door Frank looked back at his brother and laughed once more.

'You're no brother of mine,' shouted Tommy after him as Frank staggered down the steps onto the pavement below.

And that had been the last thing that his brother had said to him. *'You're no brother of mine.'*

Almost two years later they still had not talked. Frank remembered trying to build bridges when he came out of rehab but his brother would have none of it. Frank was not allowed to visit his mother if Tommy was going to be there. He had even tried making an appointment to see his brother in the Chambers, but Tommy's secretary had obviously been given specific instructions not to have anything to do with him.

Frank now knew how much his words must have hurt his brother. But he had been in the midst of his own grief at the time and was tackling it the only way he knew: by crawling deeper and deeper into a bottle. Looking back he could see that his drinking was already getting out of control by then, but of course at the time he hadn't been able to see that he had a problem.

Frank did not attend AA, the philosophy of appealing to a higher power for help being totally foreign to him. He knew that the problem was his and that ultimately only he had the power to beat it.

But he recognised that it worked for many people. And there was one part of their philosophy that he did agree with: making amends to those he had harmed during his drinking days. That had actually been pretty easy for Frank: he was so self destructive while drinking that the main person he hurt was almost always himself.

But now Frank knew that he had to try to make amends with his brother and to get Tommy to accept that he was no longer the person who had caused the fight between them. He longed for reconciliation with his big brother more than anything else in the world.

All he could do now was to wait for Tommy to get in touch, and then try to make an apology that was sufficient to begin to repair the broken relationship between them.

He had waited almost two years. He could wait a few more days.

Monday May 19 2008, 8:05am

Principal Officer Jim Mullins drove his Ford Focus steadily in the already heavy morning traffic and turned right into Hillfoot Street, to the east of Glasgow City Centre. It was a typically dull Glasgow spring morning and he found the drive along Duke Street with its collection of downmarket pubs and takeaway shops mixed in with vacant premises as depressing as ever.

Having just finished a night shift at Barlinnie Prison on the outskirts of the city, Mullins was feeling extremely tired and the only thing on his mind was whether enough of his car owning neighbours would have left for their work to allow him to find a parking space somewhere near his close. He turned onto Roslea Drive and drove slowly along the narrow one way street.

He knew from long experience that the first of his four nightshifts was the worst, as his body struggled to change its rhythms to match his nocturnal working pattern. And so he was looking forward to a long, hot bath before a few hours in bed. At least the prison had been quiet last night, he thought, as he slowed the car, approaching his flat.

This morning Mullins was lucky and he was able to park right outside the entrance to the second floor flat that had been his home since his divorce almost four years before. He parked expertly just a few inches from the kerb and shut the engine off. Then he got out of the car and took his bag from the back seat before locking the car behind him and walking into his close.

What he did not notice was the white van parked on the opposite side of the road. The red haired driver made an entry in his notebook, smiled, and then started the van before driving off slowly.

Chapter 12

Monday May 19 2008, 10:40am

Frank was at his desk going through the e-mails that had arrived in response to the Kelvingrove Park story in Saturday's edition. He was now glad that he had set up a separate e-mail address as over 100 messages had been received; the biggest response they had received to any story.

He hadn't yet made an accurate count, but his initial impression was that those against the proposed development were outnumbering those supporting it by a large margin, which didn't really surprise him. In his experience those opposing something were far more likely to do something about it than those who were supportive. The e-mails may not provide a true reflection of public opinion, although Frank would have expected a majority to be against Longwell's proposals.

His mind was already onto his follow up article which would include the interview with Longwell as well as, he hoped, one with a local councillor and a summary of the readers' e-mails. A nice centre page spread was already forming in his mind. He made a note to himself to ask John for a photographer to take some shots of the proposed site.

At that moment his computer let out a loud beep, startling him momentarily until he remembered that he had set it up earlier to alert him to an incoming e-mail. He quickly looked at the message.

It was from the killer.

To: Gallenf@wew.com
From: 8sg6wskl3@hotmail.co.uk
Date: 18/05/08 at 10:43

It's disappointing that a fellow Bosco boy hasn't figured it all out yet! I'll give you a few days before #6.

Frank's blood ran cold as he read: it contained the first real clue to the killer's identity!

Frank had attended John Bosco Secondary School in the Gorbals, as it appeared had the killer. The very possibility that he had been at school with someone who had committed five murders horrified Frank beyond belief.

'John!' he shouted, seeing that his door was lying open as usual. 'Come and see this!'

John Addison responded immediately and walked quickly to Frank's desk.

'John Bosco School? The killer was at school with you Frank! Or at least he attended the same school as you did.'

'I left school in 1992 and it was closed down in 1997,' said Frank, thinking back. 'So if the killer was there that would make him in his late twenties or thirties by now.'

'Sounds about right.'

'This is the first time he has given us any information about himself,' said Frank excitedly. 'And he says that number six will be in a few days. This message is a taunt, John. He's mocking us for not finding him and challenging us to stop him before he kills his next victim.'

'It definitely looks that way,' said John, nodding his assent, although his face was grim. 'You had better call the police and let them know about this, Frank.'

Frank took his wallet from his jacket pocket and extracted Superintendent McPherson's business card. He dialled the direct number and waited for a response.

'Murder Squad, DI Ralston speaking,' came the reply.

'Adam, it's Frank Gallen.'

'Morning, Frank. What can I do for you?' Ralston sounded down, he thought.

'Another e-mail has just arrived. I thought you should know right away,' he explained.

'Can you forward it to me?' replied Ralston, giving Frank his e-mail address. 'Send the e-mail and then stay on the line until I get the boss,' he ordered.

Frank typed in the address and sent the e-mail. A few moments passed and he heard Ralston's voice again.

'What does it mean, Frank?' he asked.

'I was at John Bosco Secondary School. It looks like our killer was too,' Frank explained. He could hear the two police officers talking animatedly and then McPherson came on the line.

'Frank, can you get down here right away?'

'Of course,' replied Frank. 'I'll be there as soon as I can.'

'Thanks, I'll see you soon,' replied McPherson and then he hung up.

'He wants me to go down to Pitt Street,' Frank told John. 'I wonder what they have. They might have some names of possible suspects that they want me to look at or something,' he guessed. 'Do they have a lead on someone already?'

'Just go,' said John, dourly. 'You'll find out what they want when you get there.'

'I'm on my way,' replied Frank, already standing and putting his jacket on. 'Can you get Janice to collate all these e-mails about Kelvingrove when she comes in? Maybe do a bit of analysis: for and against. And pull out a few good quotes?'

'Leave it with me Frank. Now you get going!'

Monday May 19 2008, 11:00am

Alan Mathers walked straight into Councillor Thomas Gallen's office. For once the sun had just come out in Glasgow and he had to shield his eyes against the strong sunlight coming through the massive window that looked onto George Square.

Councillor Gallen was behind his desk working his way steadily through a large stack of papers.

'Alan. Have you got something more on Longwell?' he asked instantly.

'Stirling Council are going to announce their investigation this afternoon,' reported Mathers. 'Apparently it relates to planning permissions which were granted for three large housing developments over the past couple of years and five planning officers have been suspended pending the outcome. My source tells me that one of the developers is definitely David Longwell.'

Gallen smiled. 'Good stuff. But will his name be publicly linked to the investigation?'

'Officially no,' replied Mathers, with a grin. 'But I believe that the names of the three developers concerned may well be leaked to the local Stirling paper later today and that the nationals will probably be alerted too.'

'That sounds positive. For us, not for Longwell of course.' Gallen was elated. This was exactly the break he had been hoping and praying for.

'But the down side is that you are linked to a crooked developer,' Mathers pointed out. 'What if questions are asked about Longwell's conduct in Glasgow?'

'We will just have to show that we are clean, that's all,' Gallen replied with a confidence that he didn't really feel. There was no way to get out without some damage, but this had to be the best way, he reasoned.

'So how do you want to play it from here, Thomas?' asked Mathers.

Gallen leaned back in his chair and thought for a moment before replying to his assistant. 'Let's just wait until Longwell's name is mentioned publicly. Then see if you can get a friendly journalist to ask a question to us about it.'

'Parklands is a controversial new proposal, and the developer is now being investigated by another local authority. Do you still support the Kelvingrove project, Councillor Gallen?' suggested Mathers.

'Well, it would be unfair to condemn David Longwell on the basis of rumour of course. But we will be watching the situation in Stirling and will be interested to hear the outcome of their investigation.'

'Sounds good,' replied Mathers.

'And I will tell Longwell that it might be best to delay submitting the planning application for a while, because all the bad publicity for him would be manna from heaven to our opponents.' Gallen smiled; contented that he could now buy some time, at least. 'Make sure that it all goes to plan, Alan.'

'Leave it with me' Mathers replied. 'Oh, and Rafique wants a meeting with you to discuss the planning application. He grabbed me in the corridor five minutes ago.'

'Put him off for now,' replied Gallen. 'I don't want to get into it with him until the news about Longwell has broken.'

'That makes sense,' agreed Mathers. 'Was there anything else, Thomas?'

'There are some budget issues we need to talk about, but those can wait. Let me know when Stirling make their announcement.' He turned his attention back to his pile of paperwork as his assistant went about his business.

Thomas Gallen knew that he wasn't out of trouble yet. But taking a publicity hit for associating with Longwell in the first place wouldn't be as bad as what might happen if the developer used what he might have on him.

He was absolutely certain of that.

Monday May 19 2008, 11:15am

Just under twenty minutes after leaving the office, Frank Gallen was once again sitting in Superintendent McPherson's office with the two detectives. He saw that McPherson was as elegant as ever in a dark pinstriped suit with a white shirt and a deep blue tie and wondered how he always managed to look so smart.

Frank also noticed that both detectives were looking tired and drawn. He could only imagine the pressure that leading the hunt for a serial killer brought and made a note to include something about the human side to the detectives and the impact that the case had on them in his book.

'It looks like our press release worked, Frank,' said McPherson. 'We wanted him to stay in contact and he has.'

'And he has given us a clue about his identity as well,' interjected Ralston.

'Does anyone at all come to mind from your school days, Frank?' asked the DI.

'You mean who was voted 'Most Likely to Become a Serial Killer'?' He smiled and then continued. 'There were a number of strange characters that I can remember and I'm sure that quite a few of them ended up in prison. But I can't think of anyone who seemed that vicious.'

'We've been on to the Education Department and they are sending us a list of former pupils from when you started there until the school closed. We'll do a cross check against absolutely everyone who has come up and see if anything pops out,' explained McPherson. 'We might just get something,' he concluded hopefully.

'None of the victims went to John Bosco, did they?' asked Frank.

'No and none of them came from the Gorbals either. This new piece of information doesn't give us a link between the killer and any of the victims, unfortunately. It looks like he has simply been selecting men pretty much at random from outside well known gay hangouts all over the city' explained Ralston.

'So what else do you have?' asked Frank. He knew that they must have called him into headquarters for something more substantial.

'We have a couple of leads from CCTV footage, Frank,' explained Ralston. 'We've had a team of officers looking at recordings from the Merchant City and from the area around your office on Friday night.'

'And what did they find?' he asked.

'Well, we wondered whether our man might be a taxi driver. We know he has a vehicle and a taxi would let him drive about at night without raising too much suspicion. We found three taxis that were in the Merchant City around the time that Stevenson was on the streets and later showed up near to your office.'

'Could just be a coincidence. There would likely be a lot of folk heading home to the West End at that time of night.' Frank was sceptical.

'I know,' replied McPherson. 'But we have the registration numbers of these three and I've got officers tracking down the drivers right now.' Frank nodded: every angle had to be covered, he understood. 'Anyway, they might just have spotted something suspicious even if they weren't involved.'

McPherson took three photographs from a folder and passed them to Frank. 'These are the registered drivers of the taxis. We got their details from their taxi licence applications. Do you recognise any of them?' He looked to Frank expectantly.

All of the photographs were of men who looked to be in their late forties or early fifties to Frank. He didn't recognise any of them.

'No, I don't know them,' he told the detectives, seeing their looks of disappointment. 'But I guess someone else could have been driving one of their cabs on Friday? These men all look too old to have been at school with me, but maybe one of them has a younger brother or even a son?'

'Anything's possible,' conceded the DI wearily. 'We will know more when the registered drivers have all been interviewed.'

'The other possible lead we have is a white van which was spotted driving towards your office at 12:25, not too long after Stevenson left the bar. It was also caught on a CCTV camera travelling the opposite way back down Maryhill Road at 12:43,' Ralston told Frank.

'And you're thinking that would be just enough time to dump the body outside our door and then drive off again?' Frank concluded.

'That's the theory,' confirmed Ralston. 'Now what makes it even more interesting is that when we ran the plates we found that the registration number shown on the van belongs to a Vauxhall Astra reported stolen last Tuesday night from an address in Carntyne.'

'So the plates were obviously switched?' said Frank and Ralston nodded.

'We've got officers looking for the van all over the city. But the problem is that he might well have changed the plates back to the originals after he was finished.'

'That would make sense,' Frank said. 'Otherwise why change them in the first place?'

'From the CCTV we can see that here is some sort of a circular logo on the side of the van,' said McPherson, taking up the story. 'Unfortunately, we don't have a good picture of it. It could be a rental company or a works van, so it might provide a lead to where the killer works. We're trying to track it down right now.'

'Well, at least there is something to go on,' said Frank, optimistically.

'Can you stick around for a while, Frank?' asked McPherson. 'If we get some names from any of these leads, I'd like to be able to run then past you immediately.'

'Sure,' replied Frank. He was happy to be at the centre of the investigation gathering material. And if he could play some part in identifying the killer, so much the better.

Wouldn't that be a nice conclusion to his book, he reflected?

Monday May 19 2008, 1:20pm

'Councillor Gallen, I've got David Longwell on the line for you.' Sandra's voice startled Gallen.

He wondered for a moment whether he should take the call. He could simply stall, given that he hadn't heard anything officially from Stirling as yet. But then he decided that he could play that to his advantage. 'Put him though, please, Sandra.'

'Thomas, good afternoon.' He heard Longwell's smooth tone and longed to shatter the developer's consistently calm demeanour.

'David, how are you?' he replied with all of the fake sincerity he could manage.

'I'm well, thank you. I just thought I would let you know the latest on the Kelvingrove preparation. We are all very excited about it.'

'So what's the news?' asked Gallen.

'Well, the planning application is almost completed. My staff are just finalising a few minor details and we should have it submitted by the end of the week.'

'I think that it might be better to wait a while, don't you, David?' asked Gallen, smiling to himself and wondering what sort of a response he would get.

'Why would I want to do that? Don't try any more tricks with me, Thomas. You know that I can make life difficult for you,' Longwell responded.

Gallen waited for just a few seconds. He was enjoying the telephone conversation very much, but how he would have loved to be able to see Longwell's reaction to his next statement.

'Given that you are about to be investigated by Stirling Council for alleged bribery of planning officials, I do think that a delay would be beneficial, for you as well as for me, David.'

There was a silence from the other end of the line. Gallen was almost disappointed at the lack of response, although shocking

David Longwell speechless was a pretty fair accomplishment, he thought childishly.

'What on earth are you talking about?' was all the developer could finally manage.

'Maybe I'm getting ahead of myself?' said Gallen, taking great pleasure in the moment. 'Perhaps the Council hasn't made an official announcement as yet?'

'Thomas, what do you know?' Now Longwell sounded worried, he was very pleased to hear. Was Longwell acting, or could it be that he knew nothing of the Council's actions? This was getting better and better.

'I believe that Stirling Council are to establish an investigation into the awarding of planning permission for a number of housing developments. I'm aware that several officials have already been suspended and there are three developments where they think illegal payments might have been made to the officers,' explained Gallen, in as even a tone as he could manage.

It wouldn't do to gloat, he told himself.

'And you think that involves me?' Longwell asked.

'I know that one of the three developments is yours,' Gallen replied immediately.

'How do you know?'

Gallen simply ignored the question. 'I'm surprised your man on the inside hasn't already warned you. You do have a man on the inside, don't you, David?'

'I'm not going to answer that.' Now Longwell was decidedly flustered, Gallen realised. And so it was time to go for the kill.

'Now once this all becomes public, where would that leave the Kelvingrove project? Do you really want to go out to a public consultation with this hanging over you, David? Think what the opponents of the scheme will be able to make of it all.'

'Thomas, I will have to get back to you,' said Longwell and hurriedly hung up.

That had gone better than he could have ever anticipated, thought Thomas Gallen.

Now he could sit back and wait for the enquiry to take its course. And even if Longwell were to be found innocent, the mud would still stick, he thought. This could very well be his way out of a very difficult situation.

He turned back to his work feeling pleased with himself, which had not happened in a very long time.

Monday May 19 2008, 1:20pm

'Daniel, get in here now,' shouted David Longwell as soon as he had slammed the phone back into its cradle. He stood up and walked to the window of his office, his mind in turmoil.

'What is it, Father?' asked his son as he entered the office.

'Have you heard anything from our contacts in Stirling Council recently?' he asked, trying to keep his anger in check. To be investigated was bad enough, but to be blindsided like that by Gallen was absolutely intolerable.

'What about?' asked Daniel, looking confused.

'About an investigation that they are apparently just starting regarding allegations of bribery in the Planning Department.'

'No. Not a thing,' replied his son, a look that could only be described as panic crossing his face.

'Why did no one tell us?' Longwell shouted. 'Get on to our contacts and see what you can find out. Call their mobiles using a pay as you go phone. We can't be too careful now.'

'Right away,' replied Daniel and immediately left to get on with his assigned task.

Longwell sat back down at his desk. Surely a few gifts for a job well done was simply part of the process? But was there anything that could be made to look more suspicious? And how could he limit the damage that this investigation could cause to his reputation?

'Get me the Director of Planning at Stirling Council,' he instructed his secretary. If something was about to be announced he wanted to get a retaliatory strike in first.

Monday May 19 2008, 2:10pm

Janice's mind was in turmoil as she walked along Maryhill Road, not even noticing the welcome spring sunshine as she strolled quickly along the busy street. Her weekend had been spoiled by the two topics that had dominated her waking thoughts all week: her knowledge of a serial killer and her love of a man. And not necessarily in that order, she thought grimly.

She had spent the previous evening sharing a couple of bottles of wine with two of her flatmates. They had noticed that she had seemed preoccupied and she had initially tried to blame the stress of the course and her work, but they were not put off. Eventually Janice had confided in them and unburdened herself, partially at least, explaining the depth of her feelings for Frank Gallen.

They had sympathised with her, but she hadn't really listened to them at first, simply being glad to talk about how she felt to someone at last. But then the conversation had turned serious and they had both advised her to tell Frank exactly how she felt. She had dismissed the idea, certain that he would reject her and unable to contemplate the humiliation that could cause. And then she had managed to change the subject.

But later in the evening, lying alone in her single bed, Janice had come around to their way of thinking. She had thought about the situation for a long time and had finally decided that she should be honest with Frank, and with herself, about her feelings and just hope that somehow he would feel the same.

So she had resolved that today would be the day to talk to him.

Janice turned off the main road and walked towards the office, remembering with a shudder how a dead body had been left just yards from where she was now walking. She entered a near deserted office, her stomach tied in knots, and dumped her coat and bag before wondering where everyone was. John came out of his office, alerted by the main door opening and walked over towards her.

'Hi, Janice. How's things?' he asked.

'I'm fine, John. Is Frank around?' she asked anxiously.

'No, he's been called in to the police station again. There was another e-mail this morning.'

'Has there been another murder?' Her heart missed at least one beat at the thought.

'No, no. But he told us that there will be in a few days, and he also revealed that he went to the same school as Frank,' John told her.

'Wow,' said Janice, shocked. 'Does Frank know who it is?' What a stupid question, she berated herself as soon as the words were out of her mouth. *Get a grip, girl.*

'I don't think so,' John replied, rather seriously. He was a pleasant enough man, but he didn't have much of a sense of humour, Janice had found. 'But they must have some sort of lead that they want to run by him. He should be back in later.'

'Do you think they will catch this guy soon?'

'I certainly hope so,' responded John with feeling. 'Anyway, Frank wants you to go through the e-mails that have come in from readers in response to the parks story last week. Can you collate the numbers and pick out a few good ones for this week's edition? Can I leave that with you?'

'Sure,' replied Janice switching on her PC. 'I'll get on with that.'

John walked back to his own office leaving Janice with her thoughts. She would try to concentrate on this piece of work, she decided, and then get herself ready to talk to Frank when he came in.

Monday May 19 2008, 2:40pm

Frank was sitting talking to two of the PCs who had been involved in looking at CCTV pictures for most of the day, a mind numbing task they had assured him, when he saw DI Ralston walk into the police canteen. Ralston spotted him quickly and walked straight over to the table where they were sitting.

'The boss wants you back upstairs, Frank.'

'Got to go,' he said to the PCs as he stood up.

'Thanks for the coffee,' said one as he stood and followed Ralston towards the door.

'Buying the PCs coffee? What's that all about, Frank?' asked Ralston suspiciously.

'Just gathering some background on the investigation. You know, how dull and boring tasks like looking through hours of CCTV can sometimes lead to breakthroughs,' he explained.

'Remember what you hear is off the record,' Ralston warned him as they waited for the lift.

Frank said nothing in reply. It was all good stuff for the book, he thought. And then he changed the subject. 'What has McPherson got then?' he asked as the approached the lift.

'I don't know exactly. I just came back in when he asked me to find you. One of the DCs upstairs said you had gone for a coffee.'

Finally the lift arrived and they rode up to the fourth floor in silence. Ralston led the way down the corridor to McPherson's office, the door of which was open and they walked straight in. The Commander of the Murder Squad was sitting at the meeting table with yet another stack of files in front of him.

'Hello Frank,' he said in greeting. Frank and Ralston joined him at the table and waited for him to bring them up to date.

'We've identified the company whose van was spotted on Friday night. It's an East End firm called Target Home Services. They do small joinery, plumbing and decorating jobs and the like around the home,' he explained

'I've never heard of them,' said Frank.

'So the circular logo was actually a target,' stated Ralston.

'It was,' confirmed McPherson. 'DC McIntyre was the eagled eyed one who had the idea and tracked the company down through their website. They're based in a yard in Carntyne and have ten tradesmen working for them as well as the manager and a secretary. The manager is the son of the owner, who's now retired,' he explained.

'What else do you know about this firm?' asked Frank.

'They have eight of these white vans: common or garden Ford Transits, all between three and eight years old. The manager said that they should all have been garaged in the yard on Friday night. He checked their files and they have no record of any late night call outs.'

'The stolen car that supplied the plates for the van on Friday came from Carntyne too, didn't it?' asked Frank.

'Very sharp, Frank,' praised McPherson. 'That's right. Now I've got a list of all their current employees and I've also asked them to supply details for anyone who has left recently in case any of them still have keys.' He passed a list of names and addresses to Frank.

He read through the names but once again no one stood out. 'None of them mean anything to me,' he replied, disconsolately. 'Some of the surnames are pretty common though. There's a McDonald and a Fraser here, so perhaps one of them was above or below me at school?' But what if the killer was using a false name, he thought?

'Well, I'll cross check it against our John Bosco list when we finally get it from the Council anyway,' said McPherson. 'Can you phone the Education people again, Adam? They are taking their time with that list.'

'Sure boss,' replied Ralston.

'Now most of their vans are out on jobs at the moment and are not expected back until the end of the day,' continued McPherson. 'I've got two forensics teams going down later on to go through them all.'

'Can't we call them all back in right away?' asked Frank, eager to get on with the hunt.

'I thought about that, but that might alert our man that we are onto him. At this stage he might just run if he knows we are getting close. Better to let them all come back in as they normally would without knowing anything is up.'

'Good thinking,' Frank had to admit.

'The secretary said that she has some photographs of their last staff night out. She's going home to get them later this afternoon and will drop them in later. Maybe you could have a look through them, Frank? See if you can recognise anyone?'

'Sure,' he replied. 'But I do need to get back to the office at some point.'

'Just give it a bit longer, will you?' asked the Superintendent. 'We might be about to make a breakthrough here.'

'Ok,' replied Frank. 'I'll stay for now.' He wondered whether they were indeed about to make the crucial discovery, or whether this was just another dead end along the way.

Only time would tell, he knew.

Chapter 13

Monday May 19 2008, 3:35pm

David Longwell was pacing his office, becoming more and more agitated as the afternoon wore on. No one had got back to him regarding Stirling Council and he wondered for a moment whether Gallen was trying to bluff him. Surely not, he concluded: the man wasn't that stupid. Although you never could tell with politicians, of course.

The phone on his desk rang and he returned to his chair quickly.

'Mister Longwell, I have the Director of Planning at Stirling Council returning your call,' he heard.

'Thanks, Fiona. Put him through.' He had been waiting for this call for almost two hours. There was nothing on the internet yet about the proposed investigation and he wanted to be able to take the high ground in this conversation.

'Mister Dunsmore. Thanks for returning my call. I know you must be busy.'

'No problem, Mister Longwell. What can I do for you?'

'I had a journalist on the phone to me earlier,' he lied. 'He wanted my comment on the fact that your Council is about to investigate my company for allegedly bribing your officials. Could you explain to me what that is about, please?' he asked with just the right note of indignation in his voice.

He heard a sharp intake of breath. 'Which journalist was this?'

'That's really not the point here, is it?' he answered. 'Could you tell me why you didn't have the common decency to inform me of this investigation before the press got word of it?'

'We haven't made any announcement yet, Mister Longwell.'

'That's not what I asked,' snapped Longwell. 'Why didn't I know about this?'

'When we do make a press statement, we will not be mentioning the names of anyone involved. Not the officers or the developers, believe me.'

'You had better not,' replied Longwell. 'My lawyer will be looking at this situation and advising me what to do next. If any allegations are made against me or my company, I will take action.'

'There's no need for that approach, Mister Longwell. If you have nothing to hide then the investigation will show that, won't it?'

'So there is to be an investigation? Can you give me details?' he pressed.

'I can't at this time. It relates primarily to our staff and is internal for now. But we may wish to talk to you at some stage.'

'I hope that you will be looking for the leak in your department first, Mister Dunsmore. Someone is talking to the press. Good day to you.' He hung up, leaving the man to question his own staff, he hoped.

So now he knew that there was an investigation, and that couldn't possibly be good news. He had to ensure that his company would not be on the wrong end of any bad publicity, not when his plans in Glasgow were so close to fruition.

And then he wondered whether Gallen was in some way behind the investigation. Did he have allies among the Stirling politicians, or was the timing purely coincidental? Or was he becoming paranoid, looking for conspiracies where none existed? He shook his head.

He would have to have words with his own political contacts back in Stirling to find out exactly what the truth of the situation was.

Monday May 19 2008, 4:15pm
Frank finally walked back into the office of the West End Weekly after a frustrating afternoon. On the positive side he had a lot of notes that would enable him to add some colour to his book from his

conversations with police officers. But on the negative side, they did not yet have a definite lead on the killer.

'Hi, Frank,' Janice called as he passed the reception desk.

'Hi, Janice,' he replied without stopping.

'I've got a summary of those e-mails you asked for, Frank,' she called after him.

'Just e-mail it to me, please, and I'll talk to you later. I need to talk to John now.' He continued through the office and saw John sitting in his office.

'Frank, any news?' asked the editor as he approached.

'Nothing definite as yet,' replied Frank as he took a seat before outlining the day's events at the police headquarters.

'So they think the killer might work for this Target company?' asked John when he had heard the full story.

'Well, it was one of their vans that they spotted twice near here about the time that the body was dumped. They're still looking to see if it was in the Merchant City too,' explained Frank. 'And it had false number plates on it late at night, so it's a fair bet that someone was up to no good. It's the best lead so far. Maybe they will come up with something tonight when they examine all the vans.'

'Or maybe it's just a coincidence that it happened to be in the area.'

'Anything's possible,' Frank was forced to admit.

'What about the John Bosco connection?'

'Nothing so far and I still can't think of anyone I knew at school who might fit the bill. They were still waiting on the bloody Council to come up with the former pupils list when I left. McPherson isn't happy about that at all, as you can imagine.'

'You sound sceptical,' John noted.

'I'm sure I would have remembered a mass murderer in my class by now if it were that obvious,' he replied. 'Although, since it's sixteen years since I left school, there are very few folk I can recall at all, to be perfectly honest.'

'There must have been a few bad apples,' prompted John.

'Oh, of course there were. I grew up in the Gorbals, don't forget. And I'm sure some of them ended up in trouble with the police. But a serial killer?' He considered the notion for the thousandth time, but still could not come up with a single likely candidate. 'Maybe it's all just a way of throwing us off the track?'

John thought for a few seconds before responding. 'It's the only thing he has given up about himself, so I would tend to think that it is true. And everything else he has told you in the e-mails has been on the money, hasn't it?'

'It has,' Frank confirmed. 'It's just so difficult to accept that I knew this bastard.'

'Well, maybe the police will have something tomorrow, Frank,' John suggested optimistically.

'Maybe,' he replied, although he was not feeling particularly positive at that moment.

'But remember that we still have to get a paper out this week. There are a few stories up on the board for you to cover and of course there's the parks follow up.'

'I know,' said Frank, wearily. 'I've got the Kelvingrove stuff pretty well covered already, and I'll sort out the other stories over the next couple of days, John.'

'Thanks, Frank. I know things are difficult but you seem to be bearing up well.'

'Is that a question or a statement?' he asked, smiling at his old friend.

'A bit of both, I guess. Look, I know how well you've done staying off the drink. I just don't want to see you slipping up because of the pressure you are under.'

'Don't worry, I can cope,' Frank replied, although in truth he was not nearly as confident as he tried to sound. 'I'll go and get on with things.'

He stood and left John's office, wondering if his boss had simply guessed at the state of his mind, or whether he had observed something. Either way, he knew that stress was a big trigger for him and he recognised that he would have to be very careful. Perhaps I should give the counsellor a call tonight, he thought, as he sat down and turned his PC on.

As usual he turned straight to his e-mail in box first, but there was nothing more from the killer. Most of the e-mails were routine and he dealt with them quickly, before looking at the white board for the new stories John had mentioned. As well as the parks follow up, there were a number of minor local events that he had to cover, none of which excited him at all. But he would force himself to cover them professionally as always, he resolved.

Frank saw two pink telephone message slips on his desk. He wondered whether one of them would be from Tommy, but that turned out to be a false hope. However he was surprised to see the name of Roger Bessent on the second message. He took a deep breath, wondering what Bessent could possibly want with him. The obvious answer was that his former News Editor wanted information.

Frank realised that Bessent would be looking for an in to the serial killer story. It was, of course, the biggest news item in the city and all the dailies would be fighting for the edge. Bessent couldn't possibly know about the e-mails, could he? Frank hoped that he didn't, although the man's sources were legendary.

Frank's strong reaction was to tear up the message and to throw it straight into the bin. But his natural inquisitiveness got the better of him. Could there possibly be another reason for the call? Although he quickly realised that it couldn't be a coincidence that Bessent had called him for the first time since he had sacked him and ordered him out of the Daily News offices.

There's only one way to find out, Frank concluded. Steeling himself, he dialled the number, which he recognised as a direct line that would bypass the main switchboard at the Daily News.

'Roger Bessent. Speak!' Despite his dislike of the man, Frank found himself smiling at his former boss's typically curt greeting.

'It's Frank Gallen returning your call, Roger,' he replied.

'Frank, how the hell are you? It's been a long time.' Bessent was obviously trying for friendly, but Frank reckoned that he had missed by a very long way.

'I'm well. What can I do for you?'

'Look, I won't try to bullshit you Frank, you're too smart to fall for some "long time no speak" crap. I'm sure you've guessed that I'm calling to find out what you know about the gay killer. Is there a reason that the latest body was dumped on your doorstep at the weekend?' Straight to business then, which was equally typical of the man, Frank remembered.

'Can't tell you anything Roger - police instructions.' At least Bessent was giving him some credit for intelligence, he reflected as he waited for the next question.

'Come on, Frank. You're in the middle of the biggest story in years, so you must have something for me. Anything?'

'Why the hell would I give you anything? You sacked me, remember?' The awful day was now in Frank's mind, as clear as if it had been yesterday. He had been drinking heavily and it had begun to affect the quality of his work, although he hadn't realised that at the time.

Eventually he was summoned into Bessent's office for the "shape up or ship out" speech. He recalled that he had denied having a problem and a shouting match had ensued, ending in a massive fight. Of course, there was only ever going to be one winner of that confrontation and ten minutes later two security guards were escorting Frank off the premises. Typically he had immediately drowned his sorrows in the nearest pub.

'It turned out well for you, Frank. I forced you to get your life together.'

The worst thing was that he knew Bessent actually believed his own spin. Frank said nothing,

'Can't we do some kind of deal, for old time's sake?' Bessent suggested.

'No can do. I've told you: the police would go crazy if any of the details that only I know ended up in the press.' Just a little tease, Frank couldn't help himself.

'Frank, come on. You've fallen pretty low, haven't you? You're better than some backstreets weekly, and maybe I can help you to get back up the ladder again.' And now an appeal to his self interest.

'Just forget it. You'll get nothing from me, Roger.' It felt funny being on the other end of the questions for a change, Frank noted with a wry smile.

'OK, but if you do want to talk, you know where to find me.'

Frank said nothing and eventually his former boss ended the call without another word. He replaced the receiver feeling somehow used. Bessent hadn't really given a damn about him, he was simply trying to use him to get a scoop, exactly as he had suspected.

Bloody journalists!

Monday May 19 2008, 4:45pm

He had woken up after only half an hour's sleep, the terrible nightmares again having thrown his mind back to that awful evening, forcing him to relive the horrific experience once more.

It will all be over shortly, he told himself, fighting for strength. Soon I will have my revenge and all the suffering will come to an end.

He only had a couple more days to survive until everything was ready. You can get through it, he told himself. The bastards will soon know what it has all been for.

He was pacing his room now, restless and still feeling terrible, when he heard a mobile telephone ring. It was the one he had been given from work, so he decided that he had better take the call.

'Hello?'

'Hey, it's Janey.'

'What's up?' he asked. Surely he hadn't been missed already? He had finished a job near to home earlier in the afternoon and decided to have a couple of hours off rather than head back to the yard and risk being given another call to make.

'The police were sniffing about the yard this afternoon for some reason, and they wouldn't tell me why. They're coming back tonight to have a look at all of the vans as they come in. I know you said that you have a homer on the go, so it might be best to have a wee clean out before you come in. I wouldn't want you to get caught with something that shouldn't be there, Stephen.'

If only she knew, he thought. 'I will. Thanks Janey, you're a star.'

'No bother,' she replied.

'I'll see you when I get back, honey.'

Christ, were they on to him now? His adrenalin levels shot up as he considered what he had been told. Had someone seen the van on Friday night? They must have, he concluded quickly. What other link could there be to Target?

Then he smiled. This was just an added dimension to the game. All he had to do was to drive in as if nothing had ever happened and answer a few questions from some stupid fucking plod. They couldn't possibly have anything on him.

After all, it hadn't been his van that he had driven on Friday night and he had made sure that the one he had used was well cleaned out afterwards. And he had put false plates on anyway, thinking of everything as usual. He was still well ahead of the police, he concluded, smugly. The bastards couldn't stop him now, not so close to the climax of his perfect plan.

This will be fun, he told himself as he lifted his keys and prepared to head back to the yard.

Monday May 19 2008, 5:50pm
Impressive, very impressive.

Finishing reading through the work that Janice had done for him earlier, Frank concluded that her writing had improved a great deal. Not only had she collated the e-mails and analysed the results, but she had also drafted a very good piece that pretty accurately summarised their readers' views.

As if she knew that he was thinking about her, Janice walked over to his desk at that very moment.

'I was just reading your piece on the readers' feedback. It's really great stuff, Janice,' he told her. 'Well done.'

She sat down, saying nothing and looking a little flustered, but clearly delighted with his praise.

'I think we will use it in the piece this week. Under your by line of course,' he said, smiling at her.

'Wow, thanks, brilliant' she gushed. 'That's great, Frank.'

'No, you deserve it. Your writing has really got a lot sharper over the last few months, Janice.'

'You're a good teacher, Frank,' she replied. 'I've learned so much from working here with you.' He noticed that she looked away from him as she spoke.

'You've got talent. If you apply yourself then you could have a bright career ahead of you.'

'Do you really think so? Wow, that's good to hear.'

'I was just about to leave for the night. What are you up to this evening?' he asked, logging off from his PC.

'Nothing,' she replied. 'I should be doing some Uni work I suppose, but do you fancy going for a coffee?' Frank noticed that she looked almost scared asking the question, which was very strange.

'Why not?' he replied. It had been another long day and he had nothing planned that night in any case. A coffee and then a walk home would be a good way to round off the day. 'Let's go round to Jaconelli's,' he suggested.

Ten minutes later Frank and Janice were seated in a red leather booth in the famous 1940s café near Queen's Cross, one of several of its type still operating in various parts of Glasgow. Frank preferred the genuine old time Glasgow feel of the small place to the many chain coffee houses that were now located all over the city.

'This place was used in Trainspotting, you know,' he remarked.

'Really, I had always assumed that was all filmed in Edinburgh.'

'I can't remember the full story behind it, but there was definitely a scene shot here. Two of the characters shared a milk shake,' he explained.

The waitress arrived with their coffees and placed the two cups on the table between them. Frank tasted his immediately: hot and very strong. Excellent as always. He had not been in the café for a while and was pleased to see that it was operating to the same high standards.

'I meant what I said, earlier at the office, Frank. I'm really enjoying working with you,' Janice said, only half looking at him as she added milk to her cup.

'I'm glad,' he replied. 'It's only a small paper, but the basic principles are the same whether it's a local weekly or a big daily.'

'What I meant was that as well as learning a lot, I really enjoy spending time with you.'

There was something about the way Janice was looking at him, a coy, sideways glance, which made him wonder where she was going with this, He said nothing, choosing instead to let her continue.

'Frank, I know that I'm a bit younger than you, but we do have a lot in common and we always get along really well together when we're working. And when we're away from the office, we get on too. I mean, we could be good for each other.'

Frank was sure he knew what she was trying to say, and he knew that he had to prevent her from going any further.

'Janice, stop for a moment,' he said, as gently as he could. 'I am much older than you, and you can do far better for yourself than a washed up old hack like me anyway. Please believe me when I say that I really like you, but as a colleague and as a friend too.'

He hoped that he had managed to let her down gently, as he genuinely did not want to hurt her. Janice was a lovely girl, Frank acknowledged and very attractive too. But he was totally the wrong man for her; there was no doubt in his mind about that.

'Frank, I'm not a girl, I'm a woman. I know I might seem young to you, but I'm very mature for my age.' She seemed close to tears, Frank saw guiltily and he tried once more to find the right words to sooth her without being patronising.

'I know you are. But it could never work. And I'm not looking for a relationship right now anyway,' he explained. 'I've got too much going on in my life to even think about it. I'm really flattered that you feel like this about me, Janice, honestly. And I'm sorry that I have to say this, but I'm afraid that I just can't. We have a really good working relationship, let's just keep things that way, can we?'

She nodded in agreement, but for a moment he thought that she was going to burst into tears. However, she managed to collect herself and held her head high. 'I had better go and get on with that course work,' she said, pulling her coat on.

'OK, I'll talk to you tomorrow. Will you be alright?' he said, still trying to speak as kindly as he could.

'I'm fine, really I am. Goodnight, Frank,' she said as she slid out of the booth and left the café as quickly as she could.

When she had gone Frank took a long drink of his coffee and sighed. That had been beyond awkward, and he wondered for a moment whether he had somehow led her on inadvertently.

Christ, that was all he needed the way things were at the moment. He couldn't shake the feeling that somehow he was responsible for the uncomfortable situation that they now faced, having to work together after that scene.

How had he managed not to notice that Janice felt like that about him, Frank wondered? He had always enjoyed teaching her and seeing her develop as a journalist, but that was all.

Still, I never did understand the way women's minds work, he told himself sardonically.

Frank suddenly felt extremely tired, so he finished his coffee and left some money on the table to cover the bill, plus a decent tip, before walking out the front door. A long walk, maybe picking up a pizza somewhere close to home and then perhaps an early night was in order, he decided.

Maybe things would look clearer after a good night's sleep.

Monday May 19 2008, 8:15pm

DI Adam Ralston followed Superintendent McPherson into his office following the conclusion of the day's final briefing session. It had been another long shift and he wasn't altogether sure they were any further forward than they had been when he had arrived at the office twelve hours earlier.

He sat down and waited for McPherson to speak. His boss looked tired too, he thought. This case was really taking it out of all of them: the frustration of working excessively long hours combined with minimal progress and the anxious waiting for a break.

'So where do we go from here, Adam?' he asked.

'Maybe the forensics boys will come up with something on the vans?' Ralston replied hopefully. 'We know that one of them was around the scene on Friday night, so if it was him then perhaps the killer has left us something to find.'

'We won't know until tomorrow. All of the van drivers have now been interviewed and no one sticks out as a possible suspect. They almost all have alibis for Friday night and those that don't seem to be covered for other killings.'

'There's a fair bit of work to be done to check out all of their alibis, though. One of them could always be lying,' pointed out Ralston. 'And then there are the former drivers to chase up too. The manager said that the locks haven't been changed in years, so there could still be a number of people out there who have keys to the yard.'

'That's true. So there may still be something in the Target angle. All of the taxi drivers have been eliminated though,' said McPherson.

'There are a few names from John Bosco that we still have to track down. One of them might give us a lead,' Ralston suggested hopefully.

'Let's talk to some of the teachers too, if we can track them down,' suggested McPherson. 'It's only eleven years since the school closed, so some of them will still be teaching, I would think. I would definitely like us to talk to the Head Teacher and guidance teachers anyway. See if they can remember who the worst troublemakers were.'

'OK, that makes sense.' Ralston noted down yet another area to be investigated. But it all felt very much like needle in a haystack stuff to him, rather than a definite lead that they could pursue with some reasonable chance of success.

'Do you fancy a drink, Adam? I've got a bottle of scotch in here somewhere,' said the Super, standing up and walking to his desk.

'Why not? Thanks,' replied Ralston. He was so tired that his mind was beginning to get foggy with so many details to try to keep straight. This was a large and complex investigation and he was now feeling the strain. But this was exactly why he had put in for a transfer to the Murder Squad, he reminded himself: to be involved in the big, high profile cases like this one. And he had to prove to McPherson that he was capable of doing the job.

McPherson returned to the table with a bottle of Bell's and two mugs, pouring a generous measure into each. He passed one over the table to Ralston.

'Cheers, Adam. I really appreciate all the work you're putting into this one. Hopefully it will lead us somewhere very soon.' He lifted his mug and drank.

'Thanks, sir,' replied Ralston, also taking a drink of his scotch. 'We're doing everything we can, but we just need that little bit of luck.'

'I can't help thinking that there's something we've missed,' said McPherson with a pained look on his face. 'Some angle that we should be looking into.'

'I can't think what it might be,' replied Ralston, feeling equally frustrated. 'This is already the biggest inquiry we've had in many years and we've got teams chasing every possible lead. We just need to keep going.'

'I know,' he replied. 'But the Chief Constable will be on the phone any time now wanting to know when we can tell the press that we are getting somewhere. He's desperate for something to announce. I think he is still being pressured by the gay organisations.'

Ralston flicked through his to do list which never seemed to get any smaller. He had a host of things to chase up, but none of them looked like the key to the case. He swallowed the remainder of his whisky and closed his notebook.

'I'll be going if there's nothing else, sir. See if my wife still remembers who I am.'

McPherson smiled at the feeble joke. 'You do that, Adam. Go home and have a good night.'

'Thank you, sir.' He stood and walked towards the door. Before he got there he heard the telephone on McPherson's desk ring and saw his boss move to answer it with a look of resignation on his face. The Chief Constable, he assumed.

Ralston walked to the lift feeling fit to drop. He couldn't even remember if he had eaten all day, and then he recalled half a leftover ham sandwich snatched some hours earlier in the car. Finally the lift arrived and he got in, pressing the G button and descending quickly.

He had walked half way along the corridor when he suddenly remembered that the secretary at Target was supposed to have brought in some photographs. He thought about going back upstairs to check whether she had delivered them or not, but then decided to leave it.

It could wait until the morning, he thought as he finally walked out of the office and towards his car.

Chapter 14

Monday May 19 2008, 11:45pm

How easy had it been to fool the fucking police? He was still streets ahead of them. They couldn't possibly stop him now.

Even when they had managed to get close, actually talking to him, he had still totally outwitted them. He felt invincible now, with only a few days left to go until his plan would come to a climax.

And what a climax it would be!

Of course, having the tip off from Janey that the police were in the yard had helped. But they were so stupid that he would have been able to talk his way though that feeble attempt at an interrogation anyway.

He remembered every detail of the conversation with relish. PC fucking Plod had waddled up to him, wanting to know where he was on Friday night. He told him he had stayed in on his own most of the night and then popped out late on for a couple of pints in his local. It was a busy pub, especially at the weekends, and it would be difficult for them to prove that he wasn't there.

Then Plod had asked him to open his van and let him into the back, which of course he did, oh so helpfully. Three bags full, officer, you stupid fuckwit.

The fat PC had climbed in with great difficulty while he tried not to laugh. He had examined the tools and spares inside as if he had a clue what they were and then told him that the forensics team would also be examining his van later on. Go for it, you'll find nothing at all of interest, he thought triumphantly. It's the wrong fucking van!

He would go down in history. The man who outwitted the entire police force. Even the clues he had given to Frank Gallen hadn't helped them. There was no way they could now catch up with him before the game was well and truly over.

He was unbeatable.

Janice lay awake in the dark of her room, the conversation with Frank replaying in her mind for the hundredth time. He had been very nice about it, but it wasn't the outcome she had hoped for, had longed for. But what could she do now? He had made his feelings clear and she would have to get on with her life knowing that she could never be with the one man she truly loved. And how could she even talk to him now, never mind work with him every day, after she had revealed her feelings? It was such a mess.

Perhaps she should just resign from the paper? She would miss the place and everything she was learning, but wouldn't it just be too awkward to see Frank every day after that conversation? But did it have to come to that? Surely she didn't have to give it all up now?

Janice thought long and hard before coming to a conclusion. She simply had to stay with the paper and prove that she was mature enough to deal with the situation. She would show that she was a professional; that she could work with Frank despite her feelings.

Maybe she shouldn't have said anything to Frank after all. Wouldn't it have been better to continue to suffer in silence, rather than facing the horror of rejection? But at least she knew where she stood now, she concluded. And she had been honest which had to count for something.

What had he called himself? 'A washed up old hack'. That was it. God, he was anything but washed up. But there was nothing she could do now. Maybe friendship would be enough, or was she just trying to kid herself? Definitely kidding, she concluded sourly. She still wanted him so much.

If only it didn't hurt like hell, Janice thought, trying not to give in to the tears she felt building in the corners of her eyes. If only Frank had felt the same as she did. She just knew that they could be great together given the chance. That was the most frustrating thing about it all.

Life just wasn't fair sometimes: that was the only conclusion she could reach.

Tuesday May 20 2008, 9:30am

Already at his desk with the inevitable mug of coffee beside him, Frank was catching up on the morning news. He found little new apart from yet more media speculation and growing public outrage that the police did not seem to have any definite leads.

The Chief Constable had issued a statement which said nothing other than that a number of lines of inquiry were being followed by the largest taskforce that Strathclyde Police had ever employed on a single case. Frank knew that the police must be feeling intense frustration as they continued to try to find a lead before he struck again.

And he knew exactly how they felt.

Another story caught his eye: Stirling Council had announced an investigation into alleged payments by developers to planning staff. And one of the developers named in the story as allegedly being involved was none other than David Longwell.

Frank carefully thought through the implications. He knew that the Council would take weeks to come to any conclusions; local government always worked slowly. But now that the suspicion was out there in the media regarding Longwell, would he press ahead with the Kelvingrove project or would he be forced to delay?

The antipathy to private developers that was at the core of the protesters' case would only be strengthened by any hint of corruption, he assumed. And that could increase public pressure on the Council to deny the planning application when it came before them. Of course, applications were supposed to be decided in the context of planning law only, he knew, but with elected members worried about their careers, public pressure could make a huge difference.

Frank wondered where this new revelation would leave his brother. He had publicly supported Longwell's company and was known to be close to the developer himself. For a second he wondered whether Tommy was a recipient of Longwell's favours, but he quickly dismissed the idea. His brother had many faults, but he was fundamentally honest, he was certain of that.

But it wouldn't take long for the accusations to start, he realised. Politically Tommy could get into a lot of hot water over this one. He wondered when his brother would contact him, and for a moment was tempted to make the call himself. But his mother had been clear that he had to wait for Tommy to get in touch with him, so he resisted, but only with the greatest of difficulty.

Instead he lifted the phone and called David Longwell's number. As always his secretary answered the call.

'Could I speak to David, please?' he asked, trying to sound as if he was close to her boss.

'Can I ask who is calling?'

'It's Frank Gallen from the West End Weekly. I just have a few things to follow up with David from our meeting on Friday,' he explained.

'I'm afraid Mister Longwell isn't taking calls from journalists today. We will be issuing a press release tomorrow,' came the reply.

'I just need a few moments of his time,' he pressed.

'He isn't in the office anyway. And as I said, he is not talking to journalists today,' she replied with the obstinacy of a good secretary. And Frank knew that he simply wasn't going to be allowed to talk to Longwell.

'Could you tell him I called anyway? Thanks.'

Frank wasn't surprised that Longwell was not speaking to the press. With his name already in the papers he would have to be very careful what he said. Frank wondered how much of this he should use in his own story. Well, he had a couple of days before his deadline to see what else came out before he had to decide, he concluded. And, looking at his watch he realised that it was time for him to leave to cover one of the other stories for this week's edition.

He locked his computer and put on his jacket, preparing to go out and do his job.

Tuesday May 20 2008, 11:20am

'The forensics report from the Target yard has just arrived, boss,' said DI Adam Ralston as he entered the office. He noticed that McPherson's tie was loose around his neck, rather than tightly knotted as it usually was. 'They worked all night on the vans at the yard and have just submitted their initial findings.'

'What does it say?' asked McPherson, looking up briefly from the stack of paperwork he was working his way through. He continued to write but Ralston knew that he was also paying attention to him.

Ralston sat down, opened the folder and began to skim through the summary, hoping for something positive that would take the investigation forward. He began to pick out the key points for his boss.

'Minute traces of blood were found in two of the vans. They've taken samples to the lab to compare it with Stevenson's.'

'But he was strangled, wasn't he?' asked the Super, proving that he was as alert as ever. 'I don't recall anything about wounds being found on the body.'

'You're right,' replied Ralston. 'It could be something as simple as a workman having cut himself, I suppose. Still, it can't do any harm for them to check, can it?'

'What else is there?' he asked, with his eyes on the papers in front of him.

'Lengths of rope were found in five of the vans. Again they are doing further tests to see if they can get any link to Stevenson. But that will take a few days.'

McPherson looked up, frustrated at a further delay no doubt, but said nothing, so Ralston continued.

'Nothing else of interest in the seven vans in regular use, but there is a note here on the spare van that was in the building the whole day. Apparently it has been thoroughly cleaned out using industrial strength bleach, and very recently too.'

'That seems unusual, doesn't it?' asked McPherson, his full attention on Ralston.

'None of the other vans showed any traces of bleach. In fact the report states that they all looked like they hadn't had a decent clean out in ages.'

'Get down there right away, Adam,' said McPherson. 'Find out from the manager if he knows when that one was last cleaned out and why. Also, who last used the van, who had access to the keys and so on.'

'Right away,' replied Ralston, eager to follow up the potential lead.

'That could well be the one that was used on Friday night, Adam. Have a look at the number plates too: see if they look like they've been changed recently. And did we get those photographs of the drivers that we were promised?'

Damn, thought DI Ralston remembering that he was supposed to have followed up on that this morning. 'I'm not sure, but I'll check again on my way out,' he replied, trying to cover his omission.

'Was the Target van spotted on the Merchant City CCTV cameras, do we know?'

'I haven't heard. They were still looking through all of the footage when I last spoke to that team. There are a lot of cameras to cover, sir,' he explained.

'OK, get to the yard. And report straight back to me on this, Adam,' ordered McPherson.

'Yes, sir,' he replied as he strode out of the office.

Tuesday May 20 2008, 11:40am

Frank returned to his desk, another short article almost written in the taxi on the way back. The office was quiet again this morning, he thought as he sat down and took his jacket off. First, he checked his e-mail and found nothing and then checked his voicemail, having noticed that the reception desk was unstaffed. One message: from his brother's secretary asking him to return her call. He immediately did so, dialling the number with great anticipation.

'Glasgow City Council. Leader's Office.'

'Hi, it's Frank Gallen here. I got a message to call this number,' he said, expectantly. His heart was pounding, he realised.

'Oh yes. Councillor Gallen asked me to see if you could make an appointment with him this afternoon here in the City Chambers,' came the immediate reply.

'Of course! What time would suit?' asked Frank.

'How does 3pm sound to you?' she asked.

'Great, I'll be there,' he confirmed. 'Thanks a lot.'

Frank was both expectant and more than a little apprehensive about facing his brother after all of the time that had passed. He knew that he would have to be very controlled and contrite. But at least Tommy was now willing to see him after almost two years. That had to be a major step forward, he thought positively.

Frank got to work, excited at having the chance to put things right with his brother at long last. He quickly typed up what he had written in the taxi and then completed the story on his earlier visit to the opening of a new sheltered housing complex and sent it off to John.

Then he turned to the news sites to see if anything had broken while he had been out.

Tuesday May 20 2008, 11:50am

DI Adam Ralston pulled into Target's Carntyne premises and parked his car beside two others in a corner of the yard. It wasn't much to look at: a couple of rusting and rundown old industrial units and a yard completely enclosed by a barbed wire fence, located on an East End back street. The state of the place certainly wouldn't encourage anyone to give business to the company, he concluded. Still, he supposed they probably didn't expect to pick up much in the way of passing trade.

Ralston walked across the dusty yard towards the two units and saw a small painted sign saying 'Office' with an arrow pointing to the left hand one of the pair. He entered and looked around, finding it deserted. He could see one of the white vans towards the rear of the unit and then he noticed a door on the right. He knocked and then entered the tiny office.

'I'm looking for the boss,' he said.

'He's out right now. Can I help?' The bottle blonde behind one of the two desks crammed into the small space looked to be in her early thirties, although with the heavy make up she was wearing, her true age could have been anywhere between mid twenties and early forties. And her bright pink top seemed totally out of place in the dingy office.

'I'm Detective Inspector Adam Ralston,' he said, showing her his warrant card. 'I have a few follow up questions to our enquiries from yesterday. What time will the manager be back?'

'Not until late on this afternoon. I'll help if I can,' the blonde replied eagerly, as if the police investigation was the most exciting thing that had happened to the company in a long time.

Which was probably not far from the truth, Ralston realised.

'What's all this interest in our company about, anyway?' she asked, smiling.

'And you are?' Ralston asked her, deliberately not answering her question.

'I'm Jane McDougall. Call me Janey, everyone else does. I try to keep the paperwork and the drivers in line,' she said, smiling again in what Ralston assumed was supposed to be an alluring manner.

'Ah yes,' replied Ralston. 'You were going to bring in some photographs to the station yesterday, weren't you?'

'Yesterday afternoon was hectic,' she said, looking guilty. 'I couldn't leave here until the boss came back, because your forensics guys were all over the place, so I didn't have time to get them in to you last night. I had to pick up the kids from my sister's,' she explained.

Janey reached down into her bag, rummaged for a moment and then pulled out a wallet of photographs.

'Thanks,' said Ralston, opening the wallet and removing the ten or so snapshots, which looked like they had been taken in a bar somewhere.

'I took them about two months ago. We all got our annual bonus in our March pay packets so we had a night out on it. Great night it was too,' she said, smiling once again.

Ralston looked through the photographs. They appeared to be the usual badly focused group shots followed by several individual and smaller group pictures. And as the night went on, the camera had got less and less steady. He picked out a half decent snap which showed ten men crowded around a small table covered with many pints of beer and a single bottle of white wine.

'Could you write me out a key to this one for me please?' Seeing her blank look he explained. 'Match the faces to the names of the men.' Not the sharpest tool in the box obviously.

'Got you,' she replied, reaching for the photo.

'I've got a few more questions, too,' he said. 'Can you tell me about the van that you call the spare one, with the registration ending MNS?'

Janey seemed confused, as if the task of answering a question while thinking about the photograph was too much for her. She tore a piece of paper from a notebook and pulled a pen from the drawer in her desk before answering.

'It's in the other unit, right at the back. It's an old one that we only really use when one of the others is in for repair,' she finally replied.

'When was it last used?' asked Ralston. 'And who would usually clean it out?'

'Just a minute!' Janey exclaimed, looking flustered. He was clearly overtaxing her now. She grabbed a hard backed book from the corner of her desk and flicked slowly through it. 'That one was last used on the 16th of April. I would doubt that anyone has cleaned it in months. The drivers are supposed to keep their own vans clean and tidy, but no one bothers too much.'

Very interesting, the detective thought. 'And who has keys for that van?' he asked.

'All of the keys are kept up there when the vans are in the yard,' she answered, pointing to a cork board on the opposite wall that was covered in hooks.

Ralston could see that there were only two sets of keys hung on it at present, which he presumed would corresponding to the van he had seen on his way in and the spare.

'And I keep a complete set locked in my drawer in case anyone loses theirs,' Janey added.

'What about the keys to get into the yard and to the units? Who has them?'

'Everyone who works here has a full set of keys,' she explained. 'The drivers often get back late or have to go out in the evenings if an emergency call comes in, so they need access.'

Any one of the company's employees could have taken the van out on Friday, cleaned it out afterwards and returned it without anyone ever being the wiser, he concluded. That gave them at least a dozen suspects, or maybe more if any of the former employees still had keys. Or had made copies before they left, he considered.

'Can you finish that list of names while I go and have a quick look at the spare van?' he asked. Janey nodded and got to work.

Ralston walked out of the office and then entered the second unit. A white van was parked exactly where Janey had told him it would be. He bent down and carefully examined the front number plate. It was caked with dirt, like the outside of the van, which certainly hadn't been cleaned lately. But the heads of the

Phillips screws holding the plates on were clean and shiny. He checked the back and found exactly the same story.

Now they were getting somewhere, Ralston realised excitedly. This was the van that had been used to carry Stevenson's body from the Merchant City to the West End, he was sure of it.

All they had to do now was to find the driver.

He walked back into the office and found that Janey had finished listing the names of the men in the photograph. She handed both the photo and the piece of paper to Ralston.

'Thanks for this,' he said. 'I think that's everything I need for now.'

'Just get back to me if you need anything else,' she said. Janey clearly enjoyed being in the spotlight, he realised. Hers couldn't be the most exciting of jobs, he supposed. But it looked like the possibility that she worked with a killer had not occurred to her. And she had not asked again why there was suddenly so much police attention on the company. Was that because she already knew something, or was he just being overly suspicious, Ralston wondered.

As soon as he was back in his car he took out his phone and called Frank Gallen. He wanted to show him the photograph as soon as possible. Gallen was in his office and he told the journalist to stay put as he would be there in fifteen minutes.

Ralston pulled out of the yard and headed towards the motorway with rather satisfying feeling. He was getting somewhere at last.

Tuesday May 20 2008, 12:05pm

'So what do you think, Alan?' asked Councillor Thomas Gallen, passing a printed draft of his press statement to his assistant. 'After I talked to the Head of PR I had a chat with Rafique and this is the line we agreed to take. I want to keep him on side if at all possible.'

'Looks good, but just a few little changes, I think,' replied Mathers as he read the draft. He made some suggestions, not all of which Gallen agreed with, as the Leader finalised the statement on his PC.

'Here's the final version then,' said Gallen. '*In light of the internal investigation announced yesterday by Stirling Council into alleged illegal payments by developers, Glasgow City Council is now reviewing its own internal procedures. While we are certain that nothing illegal has taken place in the Planning Department, we wish to ensure that the citizens of Glasgow can continue to have absolute confidence in our officers. We have no comment to make at this time on Longwell Homes or any other company that may be involved in Stirling Council's investigation.*'

'Sounds good,' said Mathers, smiling. 'If I was a journalist this would raise more questions. It doesn't scream cover up, but it does give a hint that there might to something to look at. And it also firmly links Longwell to the Stirling investigation.'

'That's precisely the point,' replied Gallen, smiling slyly. 'But of course I won't answer a direct question on Longwell while the investigation is going on. It wouldn't be proper, would it?'

'Well, it certainly keeps the pressure on him. There's no way he can submit a new planning application in this climate,' Mathers concluded, pleased that the inevitable seemed to have been stalled.

'Exactly right,' said Gallen. 'It buys us time and the Stirling people might just come up with something. Keep in touch with your contact over there, Alan. I want to know what they are doing and when they come to any conclusions about Longwell. And preferably before he does.'

'Will do,' answered Mathers. 'Let's just hope that they nail Longwell for us.'

'Amen to that.' replied the Leader of the Council with real feeling.

Frank stared at his computer screen, not really taking in the story. He was hoping that Ralston would arrive soon, anxious as he was to see the photograph. Could he finally be close to discovering the identity of the killer?

Finally he heard the door open and saw the detective enter the office.

'Adam, over here,' he called from his desk. As Ralston walked over he saw that he had an envelope in his hand.

'Here it is!'

Frank Gallen grabbed the photograph from DI Ralston and looked closely in turn at each of the ten men grinning drunkenly at the camera. Frank was desperate to find someone he recognised in the snapshot.

But on a first look no one stood out at all.

He took a closer look, studying each face individually, taking his time. One man, standing at the back of the group, looked vaguely familiar, but it had been sixteen years since he had left school. It wasn't a great photograph, but there was definitely something about that man that he recognised.

'This guy here with the red hair,' said Frank, pointing to the man at the back. 'I don't know his name, but there is something about him that seems sort of familiar to me.' He gave the photograph back to Ralston, wishing he had found something a bit less vague to offer him.

Ralston consulted the piece of paper where Janey had written the names. 'That's Stephen Fraser,' he replied. 'Does that mean anything to you, Frank?'

But the name didn't sound right to Frank somehow.

Ralston saw the look on his face and his excitement was tempered a little. 'You don't recognise the name, do you, Frank? Or do you think it is someone else?' It was not unreasonable to think that the killer was using a false name, he realised.

'Just give me a minute,' Frank responded, picking up the photograph once more and looking very closely at the face.

The name didn't seem to match with the half thought that his memory was now teasing him with. He could feel it hanging tantalisingly just beyond his consciousness. He closed his eyes and tried to think back to when he was a boy. And suddenly, just like the light bulb appearing over the character's head in cartoons, a name was clear in his mind.

'Kevin Fraser! I'm sure that's right. He was in the same year as me at school, but not in any of my classes, I don't think.' He picked up the photograph one more time. It could be him. He had worn his hair longer at school but there was a definite likeness. And then he suddenly remembered something else.

'Freaky Fraser! That's what we called him at school, Adam. He was a strange boy back then. You know the type: a loner, not at all interested in sports or girls. He didn't fit into any of the typical secondary school crowds.' Now Frank was certain who the man in the picture was.

'I've definitely got Stephen here for his first name. Maybe your man has a brother who looked similar?' asked the detective.

Frank tried to cast his mind back to his school days. Living in the flats, walking to John Bosco School every morning come sun or rain, playing football on the waste ground at night.

'Let me call my mother,' he suddenly thought. 'She knew everyone in the Gorbals and her memory is still as sharp as ever.' He pulled his phone from his pocket and dialled her number as Ralston walked away from his desk.

'Francis, what a surprise,' his mother answered. As if he never phoned her at all, he thought angrily, then got his mind quickly back to the business at hand.

'Mum, just a quick question. I need to test your memory from the old days. Do you remember a family called Fraser? There was a boy, Kevin, in my year at school.' He waited with baited breath.

'Of course,' she said, just a few moments later. 'Eileen Fraser. She lived in the next block to us. Her husband was a fireman and died in a fire when you were in primary school, God rest his soul. Kevin was always a strange boy, very close to his mother. He never left her side when he was young. And there was an older brother, Stephen, I think. Yes, that's right, Stephen. He was called after the father and became a plumber or something like that when he left school.'

'You don't know how helpful that has been, I need to go now.'

'What do you suddenly want to know about the Frasers for, Francis?' she asked curiously.

'I can't tell you now. I'll call in a few days. Bye.' He knew that she would pull him up later for his rudeness, but he had what they needed. Frank noticed that Ralston was also on his mobile phone and waited impatiently until the detective was finished.

'I was right,' he explained urgently. 'Kevin Fraser was in my year at school and his brother Stephen Fraser was a few years older. And when he left school he became a plumber, my mother thinks.'

'I got one of the DCs back at the office to check the John Bosco list,' Ralston told him. 'Kevin Fraser left school in 1991, the year before you did.'

'That makes sense,' replied Frank, nodding. 'I stayed on for fifth year and left in '92, so he must have left straight after fourth year.'

'But there is no Stephen Fraser on the list at all. Could he have gone to another secondary school?' asked Ralston.

'Some kids from the Gorbals went down to Holyrood in Govanhill,' Frank recalled. 'But it would be unusual for a family to send their two children to different schools, wouldn't it? I can't remember anything about the older brother at all, to be honest.'

'Well, Stephen is the name we have so that's what we have to go on for now. And if he became a plumber that would fit with his working for Target, wouldn't it? Maybe he just looks a bit like his wee brother, Frank?'

Frank wasn't altogether convinced, but the evidence seemed to support Ralston. Perhaps he was just confusing the two brothers in a poor photograph so many years later. And he didn't really know Stephen at all, so it was probably natural that Kevin was the name that had come to his mind.

'Could be,' he told the detective.

Ralston opened his phone and called the Target office.

'Janey, its DI Adam Ralston again.'

'Oh, hi,' she replied brightly. 'What can I do for you now?'

'Are any of the drivers back in as yet?' he asked her.

'Oh no,' she told him. 'It can be anywhere between three and six before they're finished, just depending on how long the jobs they have on take them.'

'Alright, thanks Janey.'

'Were you looking for anyone in particular?' she asked.

'Yeah, I need to speak to Stephen Fraser about something that was in his van yesterday. Could you get him to give me a call when he gets in?'

'Sure, no problem,' replied Janey.

Ralston hung up and then called his boss. He quickly explained the breakthrough that they had made and the conclusion that Stephen Fraser was the man they were after,

'Need to go, Frank. The boss wants me back at HQ immediately. Thanks for your help.'

'But what's happening now?' Frank asked, desperate to know.

'I'll call you later, Frank,' said Ralston already rushing towards the door.

Damn, thought Frank. Maybe this was what they had all been waiting for. If they now had the correct name for the killer then they would bring him in for questioning.

Had he just missed the chance to be there when they arrested the serial killer?

Tuesday May 20 2008, 12:45pm
His mobile phone rang as he was lying on the floor at his final job of the day, painting a skirting board in the kitchen of a Springburn flat.

'Hello?'

'It's Janey. Look, a Detective Inspector was on the phone asking about you.'

'What exactly did he say?' he asked. Now this sounded serious, he thought, a slight tendril of fear creeping up his back.

'He just wanted to know what time you would be back in to the yard tonight. He said it was to do with something that you had in your van yesterday. What's going on, Stephen?'

Thinking quickly he told her, 'I've got a big homer on the go, Janey. A friend of a friend got me the paint for it. You know, off the back of a lorry? I must have left a tin in the van yesterday.' He managed to put just a bit of exasperation into his voice. Lying came effortlessly to him by now. Nothing at all could faze him.

'But I warned you,' she whined.

'It's nothing, just a tin of bloody paint. Not exactly the Great Train Robbery, is it?'

'So what are you going to do now?' That's an intelligent question for such a stupid girl. But she had her uses.

'I'll have to get the job done tonight and tomorrow, and stay away from the yard until I'm finished. Here's what to do. Don't tell them anything today at all. You've not heard from me. Then in the morning tell everyone I've called in sick with a dodgy tummy. That will give me the time I need to get it done.'

'Are you sure? I don't like lying, especially to the police.'

Oh, stop the bloody whining, woman!

But could he trust her, he wondered? There was no choice really, he concluded. Surely she could manage to keep her big mouth shut for a few hours? 'Just do it for me, babe. I'm going to make a fortune on this job and then maybe we could go away for a few days? Just you and me, somewhere expensive.' That should secure her help.

'Alright, but call me when you're finished tomorrow, OK?'

'Of course I will. Bye for now.'

He hung up the phone and wondered what the police had. There couldn't possibly have been anything incriminating in his van, so that had to be a ruse they had used. But how could they have made the leap from Target to him? Had Frank Gallen finally managed to put things together?

He quickly made a plan. He would finish this job off, which would only take half an hour or so. If they were waiting for him at the depot that would work out fine. They wouldn't be looking anywhere else.

Then he would get out of the city. When he didn't turn up at the depot at the end of the day they would eventually come looking for him, so he had to get right out of Glasgow. He had to stay free until Thursday. Then his plan would be completed.

This was so exciting; he could hardly stand it as his adrenalin levels went through the roof. The bastards now thought they knew who he was and where to find him. But he was too good to be caught now.

He would outsmart them one last time.

Chapter 15

Tuesday May 20 2008, 2:30pm

Frank was incredibly frustrated.

He knew that the serial killer case was coming to its climax at any minute and he was sidelined at the crucial moment. He had tried to find out anything he could on the Frasers, but for once the internet offered him next to nothing.

He could only wait until he got a call from Ralston, he realised. He was continuously checking the news feeds, just waiting for the capture of the killer to be announced. What a tame ending to his book this would make, he realised gloomily.

And then it was almost time to go and meet with Tommy. In all of the excitement he had barely thought about the meeting with his brother, which was probably a very good thing, given how nervous he suddenly felt.

Frank saw Janice walk into the office and wondered how she was today. He still felt extremely bad about their conversation, but knew that he had done the right thing and could only hope that Janice would one day see that too. He realised that it would be awkward between them, and decided that the best thing to do was to try to get their relationship back to normal as soon as possible.

He walked over to the reception desk where Janice was settling in.

'How are you?' he asked.

'I'm fine thanks,' she replied, not even looking at him. 'What can I do for you?'

I don't have time for this right now. 'Could you call me a taxi to go to the City Chambers?' he asked her, as politely as he could.

'Oh, so am I off the Kelvingrove story now? Going to meet the local councillors, are you?' She obviously wasn't reacting well to the situation but what else could he say?

'Look, Janice, this meeting is personal. It's nothing to do with the story at all, honestly. I wouldn't do that to you. Could you just call me a cab and I'll explain everything to you later on, I promise?' He hoped that he wasn't being too harsh with her.

'OK, Frank,' she replied and picked up the phone. But he knew that he had only delayed dealing with the problem, not solved it. He would have to talk to Janice again when he got back. But for now he had to think about his brother and how to gain his forgiveness.

Fifteen minutes later the taxi dropped Frank outside the front door of the City Chambers on George Square. He had always loved the imposing building that dominated Glasgow's most famous public space, although he had to admit that he had never grown used to the red tarmac that had covered the Square for several years. The newspapers had come up with the obvious name: Red Square, but thankfully it hadn't made its way into common usage.

Frank strolled through the main door, entering the building for the first time in months and remembered the many times he had been there before, covering Glasgow's big political stories. He walked up the magnificent marble central staircase to the second floor and turned through a massive set of engraved glass doors onto what was known as Councillors' Corridor. This was where the Committee Rooms were situated, as well as the Members' Dining Room, the Library and various offices, including those of the Lord Provost and the Leader of the Council.

Frank asked one of the Council Officers, the elaborately dressed officials who looked after the elected members, to show him to his brother's office, which he did. He walked into the anteroom where Tommy's secretary sat and gave her his name. She told him that the Leader would be with him shortly.

Frank sat down looking around the grand office, with its wooden panels and ornately decorated ceiling. He could have been in the nineteenth century were it not for the computers and telephone switchboard on the desk in front of him.

A few minutes later he was told that he could go in. Taking a deep breath Frank walked into his brother's office, a grandly decorated space with windows looking out onto the Square itself.

'Tommy, it's so good of you to talk to me,' he began as he walked in. His brother was sitting at the meeting table by the window. He smiled and indicated that Frank should sit opposite him.

'It's Thomas,' he reminded him. That's a good start thought Frank. He always forgot that his brother had used the full version of his name ever since he started his political rise to prominence. Did Tommy sound too working class for New Labour, he wondered, and then he dismissed the thought as irrelevant.

'Sorry, sorry,' he said. 'So how are things going? This is some office,' he remarked, looking round at the heavy wooden furniture and the elaborate decoration.

'I have a few difficulties right now, Frank,' replied Thomas. 'But I didn't ask you here to interview me about being Leader of the Council.'

He said this with a smile, Frank was glad to see. Perhaps he was attempting to break the ice? Frank decided that he should get straight to the point.

'Look, I know I owe you a massive apology, Thomas. What I said to you after Kathleen's death was inexcusable and I deeply regret every single moment of it. I know that I hurt you, but I can only give you my sincere apology. I was in a bad way at the time, but I should never have taken it out on you.' He looked anxiously at his brother, wondering how he would respond.

'Mother told me that I should forgive you,' replied Thomas. 'Or rather she quoted a piece of scripture to me that made the point very eloquently. Frank, I know that you were very upset at the time too, and I can understand that it was your grief allied with your drinking that made you act as badly as you did.'

'As you know, I've changed my life totally since then, Thomas. I've not had a drink in over a year and I'm feeling very much better for it.' It appeared that Thomas was at least willing to consider forgiving him, Frank realised. This was going better than he had even dared to hope.

'That's good. It can't have been easy for you,' he said.

Now Frank could see the compassion of a big brother rather than the public face of a politician. Tears came to his eyes, but he held them back.

'No, and it's still murder at times to be honest, but I've got through it so far. If we could rebuild our relationship then I would feel that my life was getting properly back on track at last. I really am so sorry for the pain I caused you, Thomas.'

His brother seemed to consider his words for a long time, staring down at the table between then. Frank said nothing at all, simply waiting in silence, trying to anticipate what his brother might say next. Would he offer his forgiveness as Frank hoped so fervently that he would?

Finally Thomas raised his head, looking to Frank like a man who had just made a very big decision.

'This is the quote that mother used on Sunday: "*For if you forgive men their trespasses your heavenly Father will also forgive you. But if you do not forgive men their trespasses, neither will your Father forgive your trespasses.*" Again he paused.

'It's so true. I have to forgive you, Frank, so that we can all move forward with our lives. But I also have a more selfish reason. There are sins I have committed, grievous sins, that I must one day find the courage to beg God's forgiveness for, and so I must find forgiveness in my own heart first.' He bowed his head, as if in prayer.

'I'm not sure I understand, Thomas. I'm sure you can't have done anything nearly as bad as I did.'

'You don't know the half of it, Frank. I've committed a vile sin which has put everything I've ever worked for at risk. My political career and much more importantly my marriage and my family.'

Frank frowned, wondering what exactly his brother had done. He had an idea that Thomas needed to get something off his chest, and he had a very strong sense that he was the one to hear about his brother's sin.

'Thomas, I'm not trying to invade your privacy, but if there is something you need to talk about I'm here for you. And it goes without saying that I won't tell a soul.' He hoped that he had judged the situation correctly. The atmosphere was tense and he could not face another rift with his big brother.

Thomas turned his head away for a few seconds and then looked directly at Frank. Now he could see tears and he wondered again exactly what his brother could possibly have done that was so awful.

'Frank, I appreciate that more than you can know.' A tear rolled down his cheek. 'Back in the dark days after Kathleen's passing, God rest her soul, I was in the depths of despair. I committed a heinous sin. And now it has come to haunt me in more ways than one.'

Frank said nothing. He realised that his brother had to be given the time to tell his story in his own way.

'Frank, I had an affair. It only lasted a week and I knew it was so wrong, but I needed some comfort to get me through what was the most difficult time of my life. Losing a sister is so very difficult, you know that of course.' Now he was weeping openly.

'But losing a twin is like suddenly finding that a part of yourself has died, that something is missing from your very soul. I still miss Kathleen every single day that passes.'

The tears were flowing down his brother's face. Frank felt powerless, unable to comfort his brother in any way. He tried not to let his shock show on his face. Thomas was the last person he would ever have expected to cheat on his wife.

'I'm not trying to excuse what I did,' he said, looking up and taking hold of himself. 'I'm just trying to make you understand why I was so weak. I was tested and I failed the test, that's the simple truth of the matter.'

'I can understand that, Thomas. Kathleen's death was a terrible time for all of us. But you finished it quickly and got on with your life.' He could see from his face that it wasn't working. 'You are a good husband and a wonderful father to two terrific kids. I'm sure your God would forgive a momentary lapse in judgement, given the circumstances.'

Again he hoped that he had found the right words in an awful situation. There was nothing worse than Catholic guilt, as he remembered very well from his own school and Sunday school days.

'What you don't understand is that my affair was with a young man, Frank.'

His breath was momentarily taken away. The thought of his brother with another woman had been difficult enough for him to accept, but with a man? That would have been the last thing, the very last thing that he would ever have expected from his big brother.

'Not only did I break my wedding vows made before God; I sinned by lying with another man. And what made it even worse was that he blackmailed me. He knew just what it would do to me if it all came out, and he told me that he had ... videos of us ... well, I think you can guess.' His voice tailed off into nothing and Thomas looked at Frank with eyes that seemed to beg for forgiveness.

'Thomas, that's terrible. How could someone use your weakness against you like that? Did you give him money?'

'It wasn't money he wanted, Frank. Let me explain it fully to you. His name was Phil Whitby and...'

'Whitby?' interrupted Frank, amazed. 'Is this the same Phil Whitby who was murdered by the serial killer?'

'That's him,' confirmed Thomas. And then he told the full story from when he had first met Whitby to their brief affair, through

Whitby's blackmail and then the way that David Longwell had used the situation to his own advantage.

Frank was stunned by Thomas's revelations. But then he saw how his brother's fate and his had now become tangled together.

'Thomas, I may just be able to help you,' he said, smiling.

'What do you mean?'

'Let me tell you a story. For the last week or so the serial killer has been e-mailing me.' And now it was his brother's turn to look absolutely astounded.

Frank he took his brother through everything that had happened from the first e-mail to the identification of Stephen Fraser.

Thomas Gallen simply shook his head in disbelief.

'Thomas, I have Phil Whitby's laptop. It was taken from his flat when his cousin cleared it out and given to his mother. Then she kept it in a cupboard in her house until I took it last week,' he explained. 'There's no way that Longwell could possibly have those videos. He was bluffing you about that as he tried to do about Whitby's death.'

'That changes everything,' said Thomas animatedly. 'Where is the laptop now?'

'In my desk in the office,' replied Frank. 'As soon as I get back I'll make sure that those videos are destroyed once and for all.'

'I was right to trust you again, Frank. God has shown me the way to make this right. Once I know that the videos are gone, I will confess my sins to Him and then to Marie.'

He was now smiling, relieved that there was a way out, Frank concluded. But was telling his wife the best thing to do in the circumstances?

'Does Marie really need to know everything, Thomas?' he asked gently. 'I can understand that you want to be totally honest with her, but you would be risking your marriage if you told her about Whitby.'

'I've already done that, Frank' he replied. 'No, my mind is made up and this is what I have to do. If she can't forgive me then so be it, I have to take whatever punishment God decides in His infinite wisdom is fit for my sins.'

At that moment there was a knock on the door and Sandra came in. 'Sorry to interrupt, but your next appointment is here, Councillor Gallen.'

'Two minutes, Sandra, thanks,' he replied.

'Frank, this has worked out probably better than either of us expected. Thank you for not giving up on me.' He stood and put his hand out.

'No, Thomas, thank you for your forgiveness.' The brothers hugged warmly and Frank felt at peace with himself for the first time in a very long time. 'I'll call you later on tonight.'

Thomas nodded as he walked towards the door, already preparing himself for whatever was next on his agenda. Frank walked out through the anteroom and back to the main staircase. He looked at his watch and was amazed to find that it was almost six o'clock. He had been in his brother's office for almost three hours, he realised.

Frank felt more emotionally drained than he had at any point since leaving rehab. His mind was all over the place, filled with thoughts of what Thomas had told him and the strain that his brother had clearly been under. At that moment he had a fleeting desire for a very strong drink. But he put that behind him and walked back down the marble staircase as swiftly as he could, desperate to get back to his office and to Phil Whitby's laptop.

The videos had to be on the laptop; that was where Whitby had kept anything of importance. And that meant that he could provide the assistance that his brother needed.

Frank Gallen walked out onto George Square, urgently looking for a taxi.

DI Adam Ralston was worried. And he was getting more worried as the hands on his watch told him that time was slowly moving forward. Three hours he had been sitting in his car waiting. Where the hell was Stephen Fraser? Why hadn't he come back to the yard yet?

His mobile buzzed and he reached to answer it. Damn, it was the boss.

'Hello, sir.'

'What's happening, Adam? Do you have him yet?'

'Not yet, sir.' He could hear a sharp intake of breath and quickly summarised the situation for McPherson. 'I'm in the yard waiting with three squad cars just around the corner. Six of the eight drivers have returned to the yard so far. We just need to wait until Fraser gets here, that's all.'

'Get into the office right now and find out exactly when he is expected,' ordered McPherson. 'And call me right back.'

'Yes, sir,' he replied before realising that McPherson had already put the phone down. He got out of his car and strode quickly across the yard towards the office. It had all seemed so simple: just wait until the suspect drove into the yard and pick him up. How the hell had it gone wrong?

He calmed himself as he entered the office. Janey was putting her coat on, obviously finished for the day.

'Oh, hello again,' she said. Ralston immediately noticed that she did not seem as pleased to see him this time.

'Where's Stephen Fraser?' he asked.

'He's not back as yet,' replied Janey, unable to meet his eyes. 'There are two drivers still to come back in, but I need to go home now. It's past my finishing time as it is.'

She seemed desperate to get out of the door. What was she hiding?

Ralston realised that Janey could have tipped Fraser off. And that was his fault, he realised with a sickening feeling in his stomach. He had asked her about Fraser on the phone.

'Where should Fraser have been this afternoon?' he demanded, desperate to retrieve the situation.

Janey frowned at him for a moment, looking as if she was going to refuse to answer. He gave her his very best stare and she sat back down at her desk. 'I need to put the PC back on to check the job lines. Maybe he is just running late? It happens sometimes.'

'Just get on with it.' Should he have her call Fraser, he wondered? If she had already told him of his interest, it wouldn't achieve anything, he decided. And if she hadn't it would alert him that something was wrong. No, just find out where the hell the man is now and deal with it from there, he concluded.

'It's an old PC and it takes a while,' explained Janey, still with her coat on. Finally she appeared to be into the system. 'He had two jobs to do: a washing machine repair in Maryhill and then a decorating job in Springburn.'

'Give me the names and telephone numbers of the customers.' He had to make this right.

'I'm not sure if I should without authorisation from the manager. Data protection ...' she started.

But Ralston was in no mood to be stopped.

'Listen, if you want me to arrest you for Obstruction right now then I will,' he threatened.

That did the trick: she pulled a pad and a pen from her drawer and wrote the details down for him.

'Stay there,' he ordered her as he took the pad from her trembling hands.

He picked up the phone on her desk and dialled the first number. It was answered immediately.

'Mrs Williams?'

'Yes, who is this?'

'It's Adam from Target, Mrs Williams. I believe that you had one of our men out to see to your washing machine today?'

'That's right, he fixed it for me this morning and it's going fine now,' she answered.

'That's great. Please call us again of you have any further problems. Goodnight.'

One down, he thought, as he dialled the second number. It rang for a fair time before an elderly lady answered.

'Hello?'

'Good evening. Is that Mrs McIntosh?' he asked with exaggerated politeness.

'Yes, it is.'

'It's Adam from Target here, Mrs McIntosh. You had some decorating done by one of our men this afternoon, I believe?'

'He did my kitchen for me, son, and a lovely job he made of it too. I'm so pleased with it,' she said.

'What time did he leave you, Mrs McIntosh?'

'Let me think.' *I don't have time for this.* 'The nurse came in to see me at two o'clock and he had gone by then. It must have been between half past one and two o'clock then, son.'

'Thanks very much,' he replied.

Fraser had finished his work over four hours ago! Where the hell had he gone and why wasn't he back at the yard? Maybe he was simply skiving somewhere, he considered desperately?

Or maybe he was on the run. Fuck! What had he done?

'Janey, think very carefully before you answer this question. It will decide whether you go home or spend the night in the cells.' A look of terror crossed her face. Good. He knew that she would be truthful now.

'Stephen Fraser finished work on his second job hours ago. Where the hell is he now?' He started at her, demanding an immediate answer.

Janey's eyes widened as she seemed to consider her words very carefully. 'Maybe he just went home? If he finished his jobs early he might have taken a few hours off. I know some of the men do it in case they get given another job if they come back here early.'

'Janey, tell me the truth. This is very important and I'm fast losing my patience. I will arrest you.' Ralston was certain she knew something.

'Where is he?' he suddenly shouted.

'He's doing a homer,' she finally replied, speaking softly and looking close to tears. 'I don't know where. Honestly, he didn't tell me. He's decorating a house somewhere, cash in hand. And he was using knocked off paint, that's probably why he is avoiding you. That's all I know.'

What to do now? Of course the address of this homer wouldn't be in the office.

'If I find out that you're lying to me ...' He left the threat unsaid.

'Honestly, I have no idea exactly where he is,' she replied, tears now rolling down her cheeks. He was sure that he now had everything that she knew. He called his boss back, readying himself to give him the bad news.

'Adam?'

'Fraser has finished for the day, sir, but apparently he's doing a decorating job as a homer. I don't know where.'

'OK, I'll get every officer looking for his van. You call Technical with his mobile number. Tell them to put an immediate trace on it and to call me directly as soon as they get a location. And you get to his house and see if the van is there. Leave the other cars at the yard in case he does come back.'

'Yes, sir.' Again, he had hung up and immediately called the Technical Support team. When he had passed on McPherson's instructions he turned back to Janey.

'Has Fraser called in today, Janey?' he asked in a soft voice, He knew that she was now scared enough to cooperate fully.

'No, he hasn't called me,' she replied. 'He told me about the homer this morning before he went out. Said he was going to earn a packet from it, too.'

'Give me his home address and mobile number,' he ordered.

Again she turned to the PC and this time wrote down an address on Roystonhill, just to the north east of the city centre and a telephone number. He put it into his jacket pocket.

'Ok, you can go now.'

'Thanks,' she replied, looking very relieved indeed. 'I need to lock up.'

He walked out of the office, leaving her to close down the PC. Ralston got into his car in a foul mood, and screamed out loud in pure frustration at his own stupidity.

Had the killer managed to elude them because of his actions? But if Janey was telling the truth, and she was probably too scared to do anything else, then he was probably OK. But that didn't excuse his error.

He called the control room and had them relay Superintendent McPherson's message to the squad cars. He also insisted that he be called immediately if Fraser's van was spotted.

With a squeal of tyres he sped out of the yard. It was only a ten minute drive from Carntyne to Fraser's address and as he drove quickly along the road he wondered again whether he had blown the arrest. Or was it just a coincidence that Fraser had not come back to the yard tonight?

Soon he was on Roystonhill, a long winding street just off the main road. He drove slowly uphill, looking for the correct number. The area had changed dramatically, Ralston was astonished to see. The last time he had been along here it had been a succession of old, poorly maintained tenement flats. But now there were new family houses in their place.

At the crest of the hill he slowed as he approached a church spire that had somehow been saved when the church it had been a part of was demolished. He saw families walking and children playing in a new park. This was all very different.

But where was Fraser's house? He sped up as he headed downhill, overlooking the M8 motorway, which was gridlocked in both directions. Finally he came to an older set of flats near the end of the road and found Fraser's number

There was no sign of Fraser's van on the street. And there was nowhere to hide it either, so it looked like the suspect wasn't at home. He called the station and asked for an unmarked car to take over at Fraser's flat.

Ten minutes later he recognised a blue Ford Focus as a CID car and drove off, heading back to the station.

Tuesday May 20 2008, 6:55pm

The videos weren't on Whitby's laptop, Frank concluded, sitting alone in the office. He had now been through every folder on the computer and the only videos he had found were music ones. He was irritated by the failure and desperate to find them for his brother's sake.

He had been so sure that the videos would be there. After all, Convery had told them last week that he kept everything on his laptop. So where else could they possibly be?

He called Mrs Whitby and asked if he could come by once more to have another look through Phil's things. She readily agreed, desperate for any news of the hunt for her son's killer. He simply explained that he would tell her what little he knew when he got there and ended the call. Then he phoned a taxi to take him to Pollok and prepared to leave.

Frank put on the alarm and locked the front door to the office, then stood outside waiting with extreme impatience for his taxi to arrive.

'Does he know we are onto him, Adam?' Superintendent McPherson seemed to be eyeing him suspiciously, or was he just imagining that, Ralston wondered?

He considered his answer very carefully. 'The only person who could have conceivably tipped him off is Jane McDougall, sir. And she told me that Fraser had not called in today.'

He decided not to tell his boss the full story, knowing that he was in the wrong. And telling him everything wouldn't help them to find Fraser anyway, he rationalised.

'Maybe it's just a coincidence that he has a homer on the go at the moment. Although I suppose it isn't exactly a rarity for a tradesman, is it?' McPherson commented.

Ralston thought that he was off the hook for now.

'We've still got cars at the yard and at his house. And every officer in the city is on the lookout for his van. His mobile is switched off according to the technical boys. They'll call immediately with the location if he switches it back on again.' Ralston couldn't think of anything else that they could possibly do.

'It's back to a waiting game, then.'

'Seems like it, sir. But we don't know how long we have until he goes after his next victim. He said 'a few days' in the last e-mail. Could he be getting ready to strike tonight?' asked Ralston.

'What do we know about this Stephen Fraser? Maybe we can figure out what this is all about now that we have a name. If this sixth target is the one he is really after as the profiler suggests, then there must be a reason.'

Ralston opened his notebook and found the page that detailed the little they had discovered.

'Stephen Fraser. Born in the Gorbals in December 1970, and now 37 years of age. Went to Holyrood Secondary School in Govanhill. He has no criminal record, not even a parking ticket. Worked as a plumber in various places throughout the city since leaving school. Lived in Springburn for ten years then moved to

Royston in March of this year. Unmarried and no children. Joined Target in March of this year,' he reported succinctly.

'So he moved jobs and home earlier this year? Might that mean something?' asked McPherson.

'I can't think what,' replied Ralston.

'The other thing that stands out for me is that he didn't go to John Bosco. Was that just an attempt to throw us off the scent?' asked McPherson.

'It looks like it,' Ralston responded. 'Although Frank Gallen was at school with Fraser's younger brother Kevin. It still seems odd that two brothers would go to different schools though'

'So maybe he used that to lay a false trail?'

'That looks like it,' replied Ralston. 'Why should we expect a serial killer to tell us the truth?'

'Good point,' mused the Super. 'We've got the bases covered, Adam. Now we just need to wait for him to come to us.'

But Ralston had a very bad feeling that Fraser wasn't going to make it anywhere near that easy.

Tuesday May 20 2008, 7:45pm

For a third time in just over a week Frank Gallen found himself in Margaret Whitby's neat and tidy living room, sitting on her leather couch and drinking tea.

He explained a little of the hunt for the man who had murdered her son, without giving too much away, and tried as best he could to reassure her that the police were closing in on him. That much was true, he thought, but would they catch him before he killed again?

Frank thought that Mrs Whitby looked brighter than she had the last time they had been here. And she wasn't wearing black, he noticed, which had to be a good sign. Perhaps knowing that her son hadn't killed himself had given her some crumb of comfort.

'Could I take another look through Phil's things, Mrs Whitby?' he asked, trying to sound as casual as possible. 'Now that I have more idea what has been going on there might just be something that gives a clue to who killed Phil?'

He hated lying to the woman, but simply didn't have the heart to tell her that her son had been a blackmailer. Anyway, the less people who knew about the compromising videos of Whitby and his brother together the better.

'Of course,' she replied. 'Anything you can do that might help is fine by me.' At that moment her telephone rang. 'Look, you know where the box is, help yourself,' she said before answering the call.

Frank nodded to her and walked into the hall. He opened the cupboard and pulled out the box, which was exactly where it had been the last time he had taken it out. He realised that he didn't know exactly what he was looking for. Computer disks or perhaps a USB drive? There was nothing like that in the box.

But there were CDs.

The covers showed a variety of bands that he had never heard of, but he opened each one to see what was inside anyway. And there, contained in the cover of a bootleg of a band called The Black Arrows, whoever they were, was a Verbatim CD.

Written on the CD in red felt tip was 'TG!!'

Frank slipped the CD into his notebook; he was sure that he had found what he had come for. He looked through the remaining CDs, but every other one seemed to match its cover.

He put the contents back into the box and returned it to the hall cupboard before rejoining Mrs Whitby in the living room. She looked expectantly at him but he simply shook his head. Again, he hated lying to her, but it had to be done.

Fifteen minutes later Frank was in a taxi heading home. He was sure that he had the videos of his brother and would be able to destroy them once and for all. At least one mystery was solved, he thought, wondering what the latest on the killer was.

Had the police arrested Stephen Fraser yet, he wondered anxiously?

Chapter 16

As soon as he walked into his flat Frank turned on his laptop.

As it booted up he walked through to the kitchen and took a bottle of water from the fridge. He drank and then sat in front of his computer to input his password. He turned the CD player on, unable to remember what he had last played. The sound of Snow Patrol filled the room and he decided that was as good an album to listen to as any.

When the laptop was ready he went straight to the BBC news headlines, but there was nothing new. Surely it would have been a major story had they captured Fraser by now? So it looked like the police hadn't got hold of him yet. Buy why?

Next he loaded Whitby's CD into his laptop. The file list told him that it contained four videos. He loaded one and saw a bedroom. Then he saw Phil Whitby walk up to the camera and adjust it until it pointed exactly at the bed. A burst of static filled the screen and then the picture suddenly became clear. He saw Thomas standing by the bed, undressing.

That was enough.

He immediately ejected the disk and broke it in half, tiny shards of plastic showering everywhere, catching the light as they fell around him. He found a pair of scissors in his desk and cut the remains of the CD into pieces before putting the shredded remnants into the bin. It was over; the evidence was now destroyed.

He took his mobile from his pocket and dialled Thomas's number.

'It's Frank,' he said

'Have you got them?' his brother asked.

'Yes, Thomas. They weren't on the laptop, but I found four videos on a CD in Whitby's stuff at his mother's house. I've destroyed it. It's over, Thomas.'

He heard nothing for a long period and then a sigh.

'Thank you, Frank. That means a lot to me, I won't forget it. Now I need to make this right if I can.'

'Thomas, can I ask one thing of you?'

'What is it?'

'Sleep on it? I know that you think that you are certain about what you should do now, but one more night can't hurt, can it? Just take the time to make sure that you are doing the right thing here.' Frank could only hope that his brother would listen to him.

'Alright,' he replied, sounding dubious. 'I'll do that, Frank.'

'Thanks, Thomas. We'll talk soon,' he said, finishing the call.

Frank and his brother were back on speaking terms and the blackmail videos were gone for good. But if Thomas did decide to tell Marie everything, then another problem would definitely present itself.

That's one for tomorrow, thought Frank wearily. He turned back to his laptop and opened the draft of his book.

It had been another long day and he had a great deal to write about.

Tuesday May 20 2008, 11:10pm

Ralston walked along the corridor towards Superintendent McPherson's office once more. He was absolutely shattered and his nerves were frayed from the hours of waiting. Despite the hour he wasn't at all surprised to see that the light was still on in McPherson's office.

'What have you got for me, Adam?' he was asked before he even had a chance to sit.

The boss looked as tired as he felt, thought Ralston. And he was in even earlier than me, he recalled.

'Nothing at all, I'm afraid,' he reported, sighing wearily. 'The only activity after I left was the other Target driver returning, but there's still no sign of Fraser. And he hasn't come home either. There's no sign of his van and no lights on at his flat, back or front.'

Ralston felt drained, disappointed and, most of all, guilty they had not yet apprehended the suspect.

'Fuck it!' exclaimed McPherson. Ralston was taken aback: he hadn't heard his boss swear before. Mind you, under the circumstances, who could blame him? Any thoughts he had of admitting to his error vanished entirely from his mind.

'There's more bad news, I'm afraid: Fraser's mobile hasn't been switched back on and we haven't had a single sighting of that van anywhere in the city.'

'Maybe tonight is his night, as we suspected, Adam?' suggested McPherson. 'The problem is that we still have absolutely no idea who his final target might be.'

'I know,' Ralston said, feeling as dispirited as he ever had.

'Get them to run the details of the van to every station every hour throughout the night. We need to know the moment it is sighted. Especially if he is about to kill again.'

'Will do, sir.'

'And get some PCs to start going through all of the CCTV from around Springburn. See if we can pick him up after he left that last job this afternoon. We know the time and the van shouldn't be too difficult to spot.'

'That's already in hand, boss.'

'Well done. And Adam? Go home after you've done that. You've been here far too long today.'

'With respect, sir,' he replied. 'I'm not going anywhere. I'll try to get some sleep later, but I want to be here for the moment we finally catch up with Fraser. I don't suppose you were planning on going home, were you?'

McPherson smiled for the first time during their conversation. 'No, you're right, Adam. Let me know the moment anything happens.'

'Of course I will, sir.'

McPherson pointed to an empty in tray on the corner of his desk. 'At least I'm up to date with my paperwork for the first time in months,' he said, trying vainly to bring a little humour to the situation.

Wednesday May 21 2008, 2:25am
All he had to do was stay away from the city for one day.

The police would never find him out here in the countryside. In fact, he wasn't exactly certain where he was himself. The drive north had been an easy one with little traffic around and the last place name he remembered seeing was Aberfoyle. He reckoned that he was at least thirty miles out of the city.

He sat drinking coke and eating crisps in a deserted picnic area on the edge of a forest. The van wouldn't even be visible to anyone driving past on the main road. He didn't taste what he was putting into his mouth, chewing mechanically and trying to keep a lid on the nervous energy that threatened to overwhelm him.

Thursday was the day.

There wasn't a cat in hell's chance of him being found by the fucking police, he concluded. He had been way too clever for them yet again. They thought that they could trap him, but here he was, out of the way and safely hidden.

His only regret was that he couldn't send another e-mail to Frank Gallen taunting them one last time.

It wasn't too cold in the van, he thought, wrapping a sleeping bag around himself. Not that he would sleep tonight in any case. He was too hyped up to consider rest. Besides he wanted to savour the feeling of complete and utter control that he now had of the situation.

He smiled, knowing that he was totally in charge and there was nothing that the fucking police could do about it.

One day out here and then the drive back towards the city early in the morning. He would have to park the van somewhere outside Glasgow and finish his journey in on public transport. Surely they would be looking everywhere for the van? They wouldn't expect him to travel any other way.

And for the final time he would outwit the entire fucking Strathclyde Police force.

He felt the gun in his inside pocket and smiled. In the North East of Glasgow a man was at his work right now, and he didn't know that he only had thirty six hours to live. And what a death the bastard would have!

Yes, his plan was all coming to its conclusion very nicely.

Chapter 17

Wednesday May 21 2008, 7:45am

DI Adam Ralston looked into the mirror in the locker room. He could see that he looked like hell.

He washed his face with cold water in a vain attempt to revive himself after three hours of fitful sleep. He ran an electric razor over his face, brushed his teeth and put on a fresh shirt. This case was getting to him in a way that no other ever had: finding Fraser now felt like a personal challenge.

And it was a challenge he was determined to win.

Ralston walked into Superintendent McPherson's office, seeing that the door was open. His boss was still sitting at his desk and Ralston wondered whether he had actually moved from his seat during the night. But somehow he still looked neat and tidy, with his tie tightly knotted around his neck and what looked like a clean white shirt on.

'Adam, is there any news yet?' he asked in a measured tone.

'Still nothing, sir,' he replied, frustrated. 'Fraser didn't come home last night and there are no reported sightings of the van anywhere.'

'And no incidents last night?'

'I've had a look through, sir, but there's nothing that would appear to be linked to our man. A few serious assaults as always, but I can't see a link anywhere in any of them. And any incident involving a gay man anywhere in the city is being flagged up to us right away.'

'Wake up Frank Gallen and see if there has been another e-mail,' McPherson commanded. 'Right now. We don't have a clue where Stephen Fraser is or what he might have done. No one has seen him since half past one yesterday afternoon. He can't have just vanished.'

'I'm on it,' replied Ralston, pulling out his phone and dialling. Gallen answered quickly.

'Frank, sorry to phone so early. Did I wake you?' he asked as soon as the call was answered.

'No, I just got up,' the journalist replied. 'What's happened? Have you got Fraser yet?'

'Afraid not, Frank. We need you to check if there has been another e-mail from him.'

'OK, give me five minutes. I can log on remotely to the office system from here. I'll phone you straight back.'

Ralston explained the result of the call to McPherson and they waited quietly for Frank Gallen to get back to them, neither man saying anything. After a few minutes of a silence that was fast becoming oppressive Ralston's phone finally rang.

'Frank. Anything?' he asked.

'No, nothing,' came the reply. He shielded the phone and told the Super the news.

'What's going on, Adam?' asked Gallen.

'Honestly, we really don't know, Frank.' Ralston was as downhearted as he had been at any time. 'We have no idea where Fraser is. He hasn't been at work since yesterday afternoon and he didn't come home at all last night. All we know is that he is likely to strike again soon.'

'Have you tried tracking down his brother, Kevin?'

'That's our next step; to get onto his family and see if they have any idea where the hell he might be.' He saw the expression on McPherson's face. 'Look, I have to go, Frank. Bye.'

'Nothing?' asked McPherson and Ralston nodded glumly. 'Get on to the family angle then. Mother, brother and anyone else you can find. See if Fraser has another place somewhere or even a spot he likes to go to. Just find him, Adam.'

'Yes, sir.' Ralston left the office and walked back towards the squad room. He would get as many detectives as he could rustle up to begin the search for Fraser's family.

They had to find him before he killed again. Ralston could not face having a death on his conscience. But had Janey tipped Fraser off following his call? He still thought it unlikely, given how much he had frightened her. Surely she had told him the truth.

Or was he just trying to convince himself?

Wednesday May 21 2008, 7:55am

Principal Officer Jim Mullins was not having a good day.

He sat at his desk writing up an incident report, detailing how two of his officers had come to blows in the middle of the shift. Some nonsense about insults to each other's family had started an argument and then it had all kicked off. It was bad enough having to keep the inmates in order without worrying about his staff fighting too, he grumbled. Mullins completed the detailed report, shaking his head at the stupidity of it all.

He stood up, glad that the shift was finished and looking forward to going home, but then winced as a sharp pain shot down the back of his left leg. That was all he needed: his bloody back to start playing up again.

Maybe this time he should see a doctor, Mullins thought, as he waited for the wave of pain to subside. But he had always prided himself on his fitness: nine years in the Army followed by over fifteen as a prison officer and never more than a cold.

Well there had been one incident at Shotts where some bastard had bit his arm, but that had only put him out of action for a few days. And he had taken his revenge on the inmate later, of course. You had to let them know who was in charge, didn't you? He smiled at the memory.

Mullins walked towards the door feeling tired and not at all looking forward to the drive home. He signed out and headed for the locker room to pick up his jacket. As he crossed the corridor, he felt another wave of pain, this time so strong that he almost lost his balance. But he managed to grab onto a chair to steady himself and waited for it to pass once more, hanging on grimly. When the pain finally ended he was relieved.

I don't need this, he thought. He had a headache too, perhaps from the strain of everything he was dealing with. A couple of painkillers and straight to bed this morning, he decided, as he walked towards his locker. At least there was only one more nightshift to go and then he had a couple of days off. And his son was coming over on Thursday at lunch time too, he suddenly remembered. It was an in-service day at school and so they could spend the afternoon together.

There was something to look forward to for a change, Mullins decided, smiling.

Wednesday May 21 2008, 8:40am

'Morning, Frank. Any news?' John asked as soon as he walked into the office.

He was surprised to see Frank in so early. John knew he hadn't been sleeping well recently, which was of course a bad sign. Truth be told he was worried about Frank. He was taking the serial killer case very personally and the longer it went on the more stress he was putting himself under, which surely couldn't be good for him.

'Nothing at all. No more e-mails and the police now seem to have lost all track of Fraser,' Frank answered.

How did he know that, John wondered?

'Ralston phoned me at home just before eight wanting to know if he had been in touch again. That's why I'm in early. There didn't seem much point in going back to bed.'

'He must be worried,' replied John. 'The dailies are slaughtering the police. Five dead and no real leads. Of course the press don't know that they are onto Fraser, I suppose.'

Frank sat down and turned his PC on. 'There's still something about this that doesn't seem quite right to me.'

John sat down opposite him. He had learned over the many years that he had known him to trust Frank Gallen's hunches. 'Tell me what you're thinking,' he encouraged. Maybe he could help Frank to work it through.

'The only personal thing that Fraser has told us is that he went to the Bosco.' He looked over at John, a questioning expression on his face. 'Why would he lie? Why tell us he went to his brother's school instead of giving us accurate information?'

'To throw us off the track?' suggested John, playing devil's advocate. Not the best phrase given the circumstances, he thought, wincing.

'But I think he enjoys the chase. That's why he is giving clues. Or else, why e-mail me at all? We would never have known about Whitby and the link between the other murders might not have come out either. No, he wants what he is doing to be in the public eye, I'm sure of it, John.'

'That would fit with the profiler's view that the last kill is the most important. He would need it to be publicised, wouldn't he?' John asked.

'So he needs the police close to him, but not close enough to stop him,' said Frank.

'Maybe the police are getting too close and that spooked him?' Was the killer worried that he wouldn't get to his final and most significant victim, John wondered?

'But that e-mail when he mentioned the school came on Monday morning and the police were not onto Target,' Frank pointed out.

'I don't know,' replied John, shrugging his shoulders. 'Maybe he isn't rational at all? He has killed five people. Why should anything he does make sense?'

'He is very much in control, though, John,' Frank pointed out. 'He has killed five men and left precious little in the way of clues. The whole of the police force is after him and they are nowhere near to catching him. That takes some doing.'

'That's true,' he replied. 'But why do you feel that something's wrong? Try to work out what's giving you that feeling, Frank.'

'I don't know.' He responded, obviously frustrated. 'I can't put my finger on it, John, but I know there is something.'

'Try thinking about something else,' John suggested. 'Then it might come to you.'

'Maybe you're right. I'd better just work on another story.'

'Alright, you've got plenty to be getting on with,' John said, standing up. 'But keep me up to date with anything you hear.'

'Sure, boss,' replied Frank.

John smiled back at Frank, worried that he was under so much pressure at the moment. Truth be told, he felt little like smiling.

Just after ten, Frank saw Janice come into the office. He suddenly remembered that he had promised to talk to her the night before. Damn. It had simply gone out of his mind, as Thomas and Whitby's videos had been the only thing he could think of. He knew that he should have called her to explain though. That was stupid, he berated himself.

He walked over to the reception desk.

'Morning, Janice.'

'Hello,' she said, not even looking at him.

This was going to be difficult, Frank concluded. 'Janice, I'm sorry about last night. Can I explain what happened?'

She nodded without saying a word.

'I told you that my meeting yesterday afternoon was personal, not to do with the parks story. Well, that was true. I went into the Chambers yesterday to meet my brother. We hadn't talked in almost two years following the death of our sister, but I think we might have just about finally sorted things out.'

He saw that she was now looking intently, hanging on his words. He hadn't told her any of this previously, and still found it very had to divulge anything of his personal life to anyone.

'I can't explain just how much that meant to me, Janice. My family was torn in two after Kathleen's death and it was all my fault.'

'Why? What happened?' she asked intently.

'It's a very long story. Let's just say that I was drinking a great deal in those days and I behaved abominably. I hurt my brother at a time that he really needed me and I can understand why it took him a long time to forgive me.'

'So things are OK with you two now?'

'I think so. Look I really didn't mean to ignore you yesterday, honestly. I simply had to sort things out with Thomas. I know I could have called, but I just had so much on my mind,' he explained

'I thought you were just avoiding me,' said Janice in a very small voice.

'I wouldn't do that, Janice,' he assured her. 'I do want us to continue to work together and to be friends if we can. It would be a real shame if we couldn't manage to get through this.'

'OK, I guess I understand,' said Janice, looking down at her desk. Then she changed the subject. 'So what's happening with the killer?'

He explained what he knew from his conversations with Ralston, but didn't go into his gut feeling that something was wrong with the Stephen Fraser lead.

'So everyone is just waiting for him to kill again?'

'Well, the police are doing what they can to track him down. But if everything that the profiler has said about the playing cards is true, then he has one more victim lined up. And from his e-mails I think he will go after him very soon.'

'And no one knows who it will be?' she asked, wide eyed.

'That's the problem. They are looking into Fraser's family background to see if they can find out where he is, or get a lead on why he is doing this,' he explained.

Before Janice could ask another question the phone rang and she turned away to answer the call.

'It's for you, Frank. Roger Bessent.'

Frank noticed that she hadn't muted the call before speaking to him and he had to curb the urge to swear. He really didn't want to talk to Bessent again but the man would know that he was there so he had to.

'Put it through to my desk, please?' He walked slowly back, letting his former editor wait for a few moments before he finally picked up the phone.

'Roger, I hope this isn't going to be the same conversation as we had on Monday.'

'Look, Frank, I'm just doing my job. You know what the pressure is like when there's a big story on the go. I know you have an in on the gay killer story and I want to know what you can give me.'

It was more of the same then. 'Nothing. That's what I can give you, Roger.'

'Frank, we were friends once, there's no need to be like this.'

The man had some nerve, talking like that after everything that had happened between them thought Frank, struggling to keep himself in check. 'It's not personal, Roger. I told you: police instructions.' This was getting very tiresome.

'Look Frank. Just one question: have the police caught up with Stephen Fraser yet?'

How the hell had he got the name? It looked like Bessent's sources were as good as ever.

'Forget it Roger, I can't ...' he began.

'Your pause told me that I have the correct name, Frank.' The man was relentless. 'It will become public knowledge very soon anyway. Why not just tell me what you know?'

'Roger, I'm giving you nothing. That's my very last word on the matter,' he said, trying to control himself but to be as assertive as he could.

'OK, your loss,' his former boss said and hung up.

What a day, thought Frank. Everyone seemed to be on his back and he was getting nowhere with anything. Time for a coffee, he thought, although the idea of something much stronger was never far from his mind.

Wednesday May 21 2008, 10:25am
David Longwell was also having a bad day.

He slammed his hand down in frustration. The morning newspapers were spread out on his desk and as he read through their stories on the Stirling Council situation he wondered how he would ever be able to repair his reputation. He considered whether he could sue, but quickly realised that the papers had been very clever. None of them were directly accusing him of anything, merely reporting that accusations were being investigated.

His thoughts were interrupted by his son.

'Is there any news?' asked David Longwell.

Daniel took a seat opposite his father's desk. 'I've managed to talk to all of our main contacts in Stirling Planning now, Father. Two of them have been suspended and they were both extremely reluctant to talk to me at all.'

'So where do we stand, Daniel? Do we know what the Council has?'

Daniel smiled, looking as if he was the cat that had the cream.

'Spit it out, boy. What do you know?' He had no time for games. Did his son not realise how much was at stake?

'I went over to Stirling yesterday, as you know, and I had a drink with the Planning Director's secretary. Turns out she is a big fan of cold hard cash,' replied Daniel. 'And in return she told me that we are not the main target of this investigation.'

'So who is?'

'Alan Freeland,' Daniel said.

'So where do we come in?'

'They just named three developers to hide their main target a bit. The word is that two of us will be cleared by the investigation but Freeland will be hammered. And then it all looks good from their point of view: an impartial investigation.'

Perhaps Freeland simply hadn't been as good as he was at covering the little gifts. But if it was true, one of his biggest rivals would take a very heavy blow indeed.

'So what do they have on him?'

'I don't know exactly, but she told me that her boss met with the Council solicitors yesterday and they are now preparing to go public. They think they are fireproof.'

'Great work, Daniel,' said Longwell. 'But how long will all of this take?'

'I don't know exactly. A week or two at least.'

That wasn't the answer Longwell had been looking for. He knew that the longer his company was under suspicion then the worse it looked. No one would remember that there was no fire at the end: they would simply recall the smoke.

Perhaps it was time for another discussion with the Director of Planning, he concluded.

Wednesday May 21 2008, 10:25am

'Any good news this time, Adam?' asked McPherson. He sounded annoyed.

These briefings must be as frustrating to receive as they were to give, Ralston concluded.

'Not exactly,' he replied. 'We've now got Fraser's van on CCTV from yesterday afternoon. We have him heading up Maryhill Road and then driving through Milngavie. But the CCTV loses him heading north on the A81.'

'Damn, he could be anywhere by now. Somewhere to the north of Glasgow isn't exactly a very specific location, is it?'

'We've alerted Central Police that the van could now be in their area. But there are no sightings to date.'

'Anything else?' asked McPherson with what Ralston thought was just a hint of desperation.

'His mobile still hasn't been turned on. He hasn't come home and hasn't showed for work today. Total blanks everywhere, I'm afraid. And it doesn't look like he killed last night either. He must simply be hiding and getting ready for his final victim.'

'So not only don't we know where he is, we also have no clue where he is going next. This just gets better.' McPherson looked down at his desk for a moment, apparently deep in thought.

Ralston said nothing. But inside he was in turmoil.

'We think that he has one more target, yes?' The Super continued without waiting for a reply. 'But do we know if his target is necessarily in Glasgow? Maybe his final victim is somewhere else?'

'The profiler did say that the victims to date might be symbolic,' Ralston reminded his boss. 'But that the final one was very personal. So anything or anywhere is possible right now, I suppose. But Fraser has always lived in Glasgow, so you would have to think that anything significant in his life would have happened in the city.'

McPherson paused to mull this over. 'Are there any other leads at all?'

'The full forensics report on the vans at Target has come back but there's nothing useful. The blood in the two vans doesn't match any of the victims and the ropes have no traces at all on them,' explained Ralston. 'And we have talked to the former Head Teacher at John Bosco. He gave us a few names from his memory of the troublemakers and they all have criminal records, but we've found no connections to Fraser as yet.'

'Dead ends everywhere. What have you got on Fraser's family?' 'asked McPherson.

'His father, also called Stephen, died in 1982. He was a fireman and was killed while attending a house fire. His mother, Eileen, died of cancer in 2005. Now his brother, Kevin, is interesting.' Ralston turned a page of his notebook to find the details he was looking for.

'Kevin Fraser has a criminal record. Some juvenile stuff and then a string of housebreakings. He did two short spells inside. Then three years clean, followed by three years for aggravated assault after a fight in a pub. He got out of Barlinnie in January this year.'

'Have you contacted his parole officer?' asked McPherson.

'He doesn't have one. Got himself into trouble a few times in Barlinnie and ended up doing his full sentence. How unusual is that?'

'So where did he go when he came out?'

'We have him in a couple of hostels in the city back in January and February but then no trace. I've got uniforms checking all of the hostels right now to see if anyone knows him. He was signing on initially, but the Department of Work and Pensions don't have any record of him claiming benefits after March. There is no record of him having worked either. He has no credit cards in his name and there is no record of any activity in his bank account since March. He seems to have just disappeared,' concluded Ralston.

'This just gets stranger,' remarked McPherson. 'So where is he now?'

'There are a number of possibilities,' said Ralston. 'Ex cons sometimes move on, try to start again somewhere else, or drop out of circulation if they are going back to their old ways. He could be working cash in hand, of course. Or maybe he is helping his brother after all.'

'So Stephen Fraser could be at his brother's but we have no idea where that is? Doesn't help us much, does it?'

'It might if we can track Kevin down.'

'Do we even know for sure that Kevin Fraser is alive, Adam? Could he be another of his brother's victims?'

The idea had crossed Ralston's mind and he wasn't surprised that his boss had also considered the possibility. But there was no evidence to support the theory. Kevin Fraser simply seemed to have vanished two months previously.

'Right now it's just another mystery. We've talked to Stephen Fraser's neighbours but they didn't give us much. One said that he was rarely at home and another couldn't remember seeing him with anyone else at all.'

'So to sum up,' said McPherson dourly 'All we can do is keep waiting for Stephen Fraser to show up somewhere.'

'That's about the truth of it, sir,' agreed Ralston.

'Get a warrant and search Fraser's house. Maybe we should have done that last night. He's obviously not coming home, so we may as well do it now. Perhaps we will get some clue as to where the hell he is. Or maybe even his brother's address.'

'Right away,' replied Ralston, desperate to do anything that might give them a lead.

He simply could not bear to think of Fraser killing again before he captured the bastard.

Chapter 18

Wednesday May 21 2008, 12:40pm

'Mister Dunsmore, I thought we should have another chat,' said David Longwell. Again the man had made him wait for a return call; not a good idea when Longwell wasn't in the best of moods to begin with.

'What about?' the Director had the gall to reply.

'What do you think? Your little investigation of course. Now I have been talking to my solicitors and they have advised me to react aggressively. But in light of the good relations my company had always enjoyed with your authority, I thought we should talk first.'

'Is that some sort of threat?'

Longwell simply ignored the question. 'I am happy to talk to you and your investigators on the record. I have a number of developments at various stages of completion as you know and I wish to clear up this misunderstanding as quickly as possible. The continuing bad publicity is making my solicitors rather anxious.'

'The inquiry is taking its course, Mister Longwell. As I mentioned the last time we talked, it is primarily internal and relates to the alleged conduct of some of my staff.'

'That's a disappointing response, Mister Dunsmore. My solicitors advised me that I should have them write formally to you. It looks as if that is what I will have to do now.'

'That's your prerogative,' replied Dunsmore. He was trying to say as little as possible, Longwell realised.

'As you know I am receiving some very unwelcome press attention following the leak from your office. Now I will have my solicitors write asking that you either make public any charges against me and my company or release a statement exonerating us. The letter will be with you very shortly.'

'It sounds as if we have nothing left to discuss, doesn't it?'

'You are correct. Good day,' said Longwell snappily, ending the call.

The next stage of his plan was to get the politicians involved. His sources had told him that the investigation had come from the Director's office, not from the elected members. But they were always vulnerable to pressure.

And David Longwell would be applying as much pressure as he could.

Wednesday May 21 2008, 2:45pm

Councillor Thomas Gallen sat alone in his living room staring out of the window. He was unaccustomed to the quiet, probably because it was so rare for him to be at home in the middle of the day. He had been sitting for over an hour, and the only activity he had seen was a single delivery van.

Gallen looked at the piece of paper in front of him. He had only managed to scribble a few notes for a press statement before finding that it was not at all easy to explain the situation. He decided to seek help with the wording, so he dialled his brother. Who better to write a press release?

'Frank, it's Thomas.'

'Hello, how are you?'

'I've been better,' he replied. 'I've told Marie.' He heard his brother's gasp and realised that this was just a small taste of what he would have to face as a consequence of his decision.

'What happened?' Frank eventually asked.

'I waited until the children were gone, then told her everything. The whole sordid story.'

Thomas Gallen paused, the image of his wife's face at the moment that her world had fallen apart etched on his mind as if burned permanently into his brain.

'It broke her heart, Frank,' he confessed, feeling the tears coming once again. 'I broke her heart. She shouted at me, called me all of the names under the sun. I felt like I wanted to die. The pain I caused her was almost too much to take. But I deserved everything that she threw at me, and more besides.'

'Has she left you, Thomas?'

'She told me to leave her alone to think, so I went to chapel. My second confession was to God. Better late than never, I suppose.' His voice trailed off as he recalled his priest's shock.

'I stayed there for hours, praying and seeking His forgiveness. It was awful, Frank, thinking of her alone and in so much pain. And knowing that it was all my fault. I truly hate myself for what I've done to Marie.' Thomas Gallen wept, the tears rolling down his face as he struggled to tell the story to his brother.

'Finally I came back here and Marie was sitting waiting for me. She gave me a choice. She is willing to give me another chance, Frank! We can work on our marriage and try to resolve the situation together. However, her one condition was that I resign from public life without mentioning Whitby to anyone, and make my marriage and my family the only priorities in my life. And of course I agreed. I would have given her anything she wanted just for the opportunity to try to make things right again.'

'Wow,' replied Frank.

'She is a remarkable woman, my Marie. I would have understood if she had never wanted to see me again after what I've done to her.'

'But Thomas, your career?'

He smiled for the first time in hours. 'It means nothing to me compared with my family. It was an easy decision to make. If I lost my family then I don't think I could carry on.'

'This is incredible, Thomas. I don't know what to say.'

'I need your help now, Frank,' he said looking again at the piece of paper on his lap. 'Marie is staying with her sister for a few days until I sort everything out. I've called my secretary and told her that I am ill, so she will cancel all my meetings. Now I need to sort out my resignation letter and a press release. But I'm finding it very difficult to find the correct words.'

'I'm on my way,' his brother replied immediately.

Thomas Gallen put the phone down and sighed. He took a tissue and dried his eyes, thinking how lucky he was to have married such a wonderful woman.

Wednesday May 21 2008, 3:05pm

DI Adam Ralston sat at his desk looking through his notebook as he waited for the search warrant for Fraser's house.

Had he missed something? Was there an action not taken that could lead them somewhere? He was becoming more and more desperate to atone for his error, the desire to make amends driving him on. He simply had to find Stephen Fraser before …

But what else could he possibly do?

Ralston read through his action list once more, ticking off everything that he had done. He had called his contact in Central Police for an update, but there had been no sign of the Target van in their area. He had called Technical again but Fraser's mobile still hadn't been switched on. He had talked to the team looking for Fraser's brother but they had nothing new to offer him. There must be something else to try, he thought grimly as he waited.

Adam Ralston simply hated doing nothing. Where the hell was that search warrant? Surely they were not having trouble with it? The case against Fraser was strong.

Finally a DC approached his desk waving a piece of paper in his hand. 'Got it, sir!'

'Is the team ready to go?' demanded Ralston.

'In the yard, waiting.'

'Right, let's go. Call me if anything at all happens,' he instructed before grabbing the all important document and walking briskly to the lift.

Ralston stood in the middle of a small, untidy living room that had a smell he could not identify. It seemed to be a mixture of rotting food, stale sweat and several other unpleasant odours. He wondered what the profiler would make of Fraser's flat. His killings may have been neat and tidy, but his home certainly wasn't. He had been in cleaner drug dens. There were clothes strewn everywhere and the remnants of several weeks worth of takeaway food littered the small kitchen.

They had found nothing useful so far, frustrating Ralston yet again.

Ralston suddenly realised that there was not a computer in the flat. Perhaps Fraser carried a laptop with him? Several of the e-mails to Frank Gallen had been sent in the early hours of the morning, so an internet café seemed unlikely.

A PC passed him a pile of papers and he leafed through them eagerly. Payslips from Target. Bank statements showing only one income and a lot of cash withdrawals. Council Tax and electricity bills. Nothing that added to the little that he knew of Stephen Fraser's life. The search had so far yielded nothing useful.

'Sir, in the bedroom!

Ralston quickly pushed past other officers in the hallway to get to the bedroom, desperate for a lead. When he got there he saw that a PC was holding a pack of playing cards in his hand. Ralston took them and opened the box. He quickly rifled through the pack laying all of the spades face up on the bed.

All activity stopped as every officer in the room realised exactly what the DI was doing. When he was finished eight cards lay on the dirty duvet covering Fraser's bed. The two, three, four, five and six of spades were not there.

But the ace of spades was!

What the hell does that mean, wondered Ralston?

The five missing cards had ended up on Fraser's victims, of course, but why was the ace still here? Had Fraser intended to come back to prepare for his final kill, but ran when he had found out that the police were onto him? Had they managed to disrupt his plan? And did that mean that he would not now make the final kill?

But then he could always buy another deck of cards, Ralston realised.

'OK, keep searching,' he ordered and the activity immediately recommenced. There simply had to be a clue in this dive of a flat, he told himself desperately.

'Here's something!'

From the small bedside cabinet a PC pulled a large collection of what looked like pretty hard core pornography and a photograph album.

'Give me that album,' Ralston instructed and it was passed over to him.

It was an oversized red book with the name "Stephen Fraser" written in thick black writing on the front cover. Ralston opened the book, which appeared to be almost full.

The album started with baby photos and seemed to catalogue Fraser's life. Ralston read the carefully printed notes under each photograph which told when it had been taken and where. Now they were getting somewhere, he realised triumphantly.

School pictures came next: Fraser at St Francis of Assisi Primary and Holyrood Secondary. Not John Bosco as he had stated in his e-mail then, he noted.

Family photos came next and then Fraser as an adult, with various women and assorted cars. Finally Ralston saw a number of very recent shots of Fraser with a younger man who looked very much like him. The same build, the same red hair, presumably his brother. There was no text below these pictures; perhaps they had only recently been added to the album?

Ralston suddenly felt a thunderbolt strike him.

It was the younger of the two brothers pictured who was the Stephen Fraser who worked for Target. He was almost certain of it. He realised he had to get back to the office immediately with the album to make absolutely sure.

'Get the forensics team up here now,' he shouted. Seconds later the small flat was overflowing with bodies as the technicians mingled with the police officers. Ralston found the head of the team and called him over.

'I need recent prints of the man who lives here. Check the fast food boxes, plates, cups, anything,' he instructed. 'Get them back to the lab as soon as possible and run them through the system. Let me know immediately if there is a match. This is top priority. Is that absolutely clear?'

The technician didn't seem to appreciate Ralston's tone, but he nodded anyway. Ralston immediately left clutching the photograph album with a sinking feeling in his stomach.

Wednesday May 21 2008, 4:35pm

'Are you absolutely certain this is the way you want to do it, Thomas?' Frank Gallen asked as he finalised the wording of the statement.

'Totally sure, Frank,' replied Thomas.

He seemed to have a serenity about him that was very odd in the circumstances, Frank thought. Perhaps he was just relieved that the whole thing was soon to be over.

'I'll tell the Labour Group first at the meeting tomorrow morning and then we will issue our statement to the press.'

Frank nodded. 'Let me read it to you one last time: "*Councillor Thomas Gallen, Leader of Glasgow City Council, announces that he will be standing down from the Council with immediate effect. Mr Gallen is suffering from a serious health problem and asks for privacy so that he and his family can deal with this issue on their own.*

"*I wish to place on record my thanks to all of my colleagues and my officials, whom I have enjoyed working with over the past eight years. I wish them all well for the future.*"

"*Mr Gallen will not be answering questions.*"

'Perfect' replied Thomas. 'Thanks for helping me, Frank.'

'Hopefully it will keep the press at bay for a while. And then you can vanish back into private life with Marie and the children.'

'Sounds good to me,' replied Thomas, grinning.

'Are you alright?' asked Frank, concerned that the calm with which his brother was dealing with the issue was unnatural.

'I'm relieved if anything,' he replied. 'The strain has been enormous recently, and it's now over. I've confessed and been forgiven by God. I know you don't believe, Frank, but that means so much to me. I should have done that at the time, but I was too afraid.'

'And what about Marie? Will she be alright?'

'I think so. I've done exactly what she asked me to do, and I will now have the time and space to be with Marie and the children as we try to rebuild things.'

'That won't be easy, you know,' advised Frank. 'It might take a very long time for her to trust you again.'

'I know, but I'll do whatever it takes.'

Frank smiled, recognising that the resolve his brother always took into any challenge would be of great use to him in the difficult times he would have ahead.

'Well, if that's what you want.' Frank's mobile rang. DI Ralston. 'I have to take this.'

'Frank, how soon can you get to Pitt Street?' Ralston demanded.

'What's happening?' he asked, taken aback by the urgency in the detective's tone.

'I think you were right about the Frasers after all. Just get here and I will explain it.'

'OK, give me twenty minutes' he answered, puzzled. Ralston immediately ended the call without saying another word.

'What's up?' asked Thomas, seeing the look on Frank's face.

'I have to get into Pitt Street immediately,' he answered. 'Something to do with the serial killer case. I don't know exactly what it is, Thomas, but the police seem to need my help.'

'I'll give you a lift,' replied his brother.

Wednesday May 21 2008, 5:35pm

The trip to Pitt Street through the rush hour traffic had taken longer than Frank had estimated, but he had finally reached the police HQ. DI Ralston was waiting at the lift, his impatience obvious.

'Frank, come on in,' he said. 'I've got a photograph to show you.'

They walked silently into a large open plan office, full of officers working hard. Ralston opened the photograph album and waited for Frank to look at it.

'To me, that looks like Kevin Fraser on the left and that might possibly be his older brother on the right. I didn't really know him but there is a definite resemblance.'

'Exactly what I thought you would say,' replied the detective, his face lit up by a smile. 'But compare this photograph.'

From a folder he took a blow up of the picture of Stephen Fraser cropped from the Target staff night out. 'What do you think?'

'That's Kevin Fraser, not Stephen,' Frank realised immediately. And from Ralston's reaction, Frank realised that he must have come to exactly the same conclusion.

'A team is taking fingerprints from what we thought was Stephen Fraser's house in Royston right now. Kevin Fraser's prints are in the system of course, so we will know very shortly.'

'So what does this mean?' asked Frank, confused by this sudden turn of events. 'Has it been Kevin all along? Is he the killer? That certainly explains the e-mail reference to John Bosco.'

'Kevin Fraser came out of Barlinnie in January this year, Frank. We can trace him for a couple of months but then he seems to have vanished off the face of the earth. And the records show that Stephen Fraser moved house in March and started work with Target a week later,' Ralston explained.

'So Kevin has assumed his brother's identity?'

'That's what I think,' agreed Ralston, nodding vigorously.

'Where is Stephen Fraser now then? Did Kevin kill him too?'

'We don't know, but given he has killed five others …'
Ralston left Frank to reach the obvious conclusion.

'So what happens now?' asked Frank.

'We still don't know where Fraser is. The last sighting of him was heading North on the A81 yesterday in the Target van, so he could be anywhere by now.'

'But where is he heading?'

'That's the question I wish I could answer, Frank. For all we know his final victim could be miles from here. I've got officers chasing down his prison records and talking to anyone who he came across inside, trying to get some clue.'

'OK, but that will take time.'

'Frank, I need to try to work out why *Kevin* Fraser would have done all of this. You knew him, didn't you?'

He sensed the desperation in the detective's question.

'Adam, I was at school with him but that was years ago, and we weren't even friends. All I can remember about him is that he was a strange kid, a loner and very close to his mother. I think he was quite intelligent, but he didn't really try at all at school.'

'Anything at all could be helpful.'

Ralston was almost pleading now. He searched his memory but came up with little.

'His father was killed when he was young, that must have had an effect on him, I suppose?' he suggested.

'He was killed in a fire though. If Fraser had become an arsonist I guess we would have a motive. Is there anything else at all?' Ralston continued to press him.

'He had no real friends at school from what I recall. He was always the last picked for any sports teams. He did a piece for the school magazine once, I remember!' Frank suddenly recalled what had probably been his only direct interaction with the boy who had gone on to become a killer. 'A story about a lion or something. It was awful and we didn't use it in the end. Sorry, there is nothing else.'

'There wasn't anywhere he liked to go outside the city?' prompted the detective.

'We grew up in the Gorbals, Adam. None of us made it out of Glasgow terribly often,' he replied. 'We didn't have holiday homes, either. Or rarely even holidays come to think of it.'

'We can only identify his final victim if we can work out why the hell he is doing this. Do you have any ideas at all, Frank?'

'I know Kevin Fraser was picked on a bit at school, but nothing serious. Just the usual teasing of anyone a bit different. But there isn't a major incident or anything like that which stands out. I'm sorry, Adam.'

Ralston slumped in his seat with a resigned expression on his face while Frank tried vainly to recall anything that might help. But his mind was blank.

The chatter and noise throughout the office filled the space between them.

Wednesday May 21 2008, 9:05pm

Ralston prepared to leave the building. McPherson had ordered him to go home, although Ralston had left word that he was to be contacted if anything broke.

He still had officers watching Fraser's house and the yard, although he really didn't expect him to turn up at either location. And Ralston had ordered officers to interview all the Target employees again to see if any of them knew anything of Fraser's real identity. It was a long shot, but that's exactly what he was reduced to.

Fraser had simply disappeared somewhere to the north of Glasgow and he had no idea where he would turn up next. Ralston imagined Kevin Fraser getting ready to make his final kill and knew that it was his fault that another man was at risk.

A uniformed PC walked into the office and handed Ralston an envelope. He saw that it was from the lab and tore it open immediately.

The fingerprints in the Royston flat were confirmed as belonging to Kevin Fraser, rather than his older brother, he read. At least he had got that right in the end, Ralston tried to console himself. Although it didn't bring him any closer to catching the killer.

Adam Ralston couldn't stop berating himself for making that dammed phone call to Janey McDougall. If only he hadn't been so desperate for a result and had shown a bit of patience, Fraser may well have returned to the yard at the end of the day and would now be in custody. It had to be his fault that he remained on the loose, he had concluded, despite what Janey had said. She must have warned Fraser somehow.

Finally he switched off his desk light and put his jacket on. A few hours at home with his wife and maybe even a proper meal would be a welcome break from the hunt, he thought.

But perhaps he should go and visit Janey first.

Wednesday May 21 2008, 9:25pm

Janey McDougall lived in a flat in Tollcross just a couple of miles from the Target yard. Ralston arrived at her close, climbed to the first floor and knocked on her door. She did not look in the least bit happy to see him.

'I talked to another copper earlier tonight. Do I have to let you in too?' she asked.

'I could call a squad car and have you hauled away in handcuffs in front of all your neighbours,' he threatened, in no mood for any more nonsense. She reluctantly opened the front door and let him in.

Ralston walked into the living room and sat down. The room was incredibly warm, with a gas fire burning brightly. Toys and magazines covered the floor, which was almost as untidy as Fraser's flat. He waited while Janey came in and shut the door behind him.

'My kids are in bed,' she said. 'Can we do this quietly?'

'All I need to know is whether you were totally honest with me yesterday, Janey.' She didn't seem able to meet his eyes and he knew that she must have lied. Damn, he had been so sure that he had got everything out of her.

She said nothing, suddenly seeming to find a picture on the wall fascinating.

'You told me that Fraser was doing a homer and that you had no idea where it was. Is that right?'

She nodded, still not meeting his gaze.

'And was that the truth?'

'Yes,' she said defiantly, now staring straight at him. 'He didn't tell me where the job was. Honest.'

'Did you talk to him at all yesterday after he left the yard in the morning?'

Bingo! Now she didn't look as confident. Janey looked away and then met his eyes for a second.

'Yes,' she finally admitted in a small voice.

'Well?' he asked quietly, giving her his best glare.

'After you called me, I called Stephen on his mobile to let him know that the police were asking about him,' she told him quietly, beginning to cry softly.

Shit, thought Ralston. She had warned him off after all! This was a disaster. Why hadn't he asked for Fraser's mobile records? He had got stuck on the fact that the phone was switched off and missed the obvious.

Another terrible mistake. You bloody idiot!

'And what did Fraser say?' he asked Janey, seeing the tears in her eyes. But he had to have the full story, whatever it cost her.

'That's when he told me about the homer, not in the morning,' she confessed.

'Go on!'

'He told me that he wouldn't be back in the yard until he had finished the job because of the dodgy paint in his van. I told you about that. He said he would call me today when he was finished but he didn't. You can check.'

The defiance had returned and he knew that he now had the full story. Anyway, Fraser's mobile hadn't been switched on all day.

'Is there anything else that could help us find him, Janey? He is in a lot of trouble and if you are covering for him …' He let the threat dangle.

'Honestly, I don't know anything else.' She was beginning to cry again. 'I don't. Are you going to arrest me?' she asked,

'Here's my card,' he said, deliberately not answering her question. 'Call me on my mobile immediately if Fraser gets in touch with you. Do you understand?'

She nodded.

'You had better, Janey. This is serious.'

He left the flat without saying another word and went back to the car.

Ralston sat in the dark. He realised that he had blown it after all. Firstly by letting Janey know that he was looking for Fraser and secondly by not finding out from her that she had warned him. And then by not checking Fraser's phone records, which would have showed the call from the office.

If he had not been so stupid then perhaps they would have Kevin Fraser in custody by now. And the killing would be over.

He drove off heading for home, tyres screaming, feeling shattered, but he knew that he would not be able to sleep. For a moment he considered going straight back to the station, but decided against that. He did not want to face Superintendent McPherson until he had decided whether on not to tell him about this mess.

Ralston was close to tears, the consequences of his stupidity pressing down on him. McPherson would have his warrant card for this. And, more importantly, if they didn't catch Fraser before he killed again he would have a death on his conscience.

How the hell was he going to get out of this?

Frank Gallen was very pleased with the way his book was shaping up. He turned the volume up as Jim Morrison and the Doors played Moonlight Drive and sang along.

The latest revelation that Kevin and not Stephen Fraser was behind the spree of killings had added the kind of twist that he knew every good thriller needed. He finished his coffee and backed up his work before switching off the laptop for the night. A good story needs a strong ending, he thought, and not for the first time he wondered how this one would conclude.

Where had Fraser been heading as he drove North? Was he on his way to carry out his final murder, the one that really meant something to him? Frank instinctively thought that he would have to return to the city: his first four victims, or five if his brother was included in the count, were all killed in Glasgow.

It was just a gut feeling, but somehow he knew that the key to Fraser's killing spree must lie in the city. That was where he had spent all of his life, after all.

His own brother's predicament came back into his mind and he wondered whether Thomas and Marie would manage to rebuild their relationship. They had been married for eighteen years and he had always thought that their marriage was as strong as any he had ever known. But then he had never expected something like this to come along and test their commitment to each other.

Frank was momentarily amused by the sudden realisation that he had probably the biggest political story in recent times in the city, the shock resignation of the Leader of the Council, but he could not use it.

If it hadn't have been such a personal issue he would have been tempted to leak it to one of Bessent's competitors just to spite the man. Childish he realised, but it would be fun nevertheless.

Feeling more serious, Frank wondered how the press would treat his brother. Hopefully the illness ruse would put a stop to the inevitable questions, although he realised that rumours would probably run rife for a few weeks.

Frank walked over to the couch and sat down. He knew that he should probably go to bed and try to sleep, but his mind was far too active to consider that. In the old days a few drinks would have done the trick of course, but he didn't have that possibility now. Perhaps some dull late night TV would have the required soporific qualities he thought as he reached for the remote control.

Thursday May 22 2008, 7:40am

Kevin Fraser sat in the corner of a near empty train, an anonymous man in a grey jacket with a baseball cap pulled low over his head and a rucksack at his feet. Just another man heading to his work.

This was the third leg of his planned four part journey. And so far everything was going exactly as he had expected.

Firstly, he had driven the van back down the empty A81 to the northern outskirts of Milngavie, just outside Glasgow. He had left the van in car park of a golf club. Someone would find it in a few hours, but he planned to be long gone by then, so it wouldn't matter.

The second leg had been the walk into the centre of Milngavie, only a mile or so, to catch a train. He knew that there would be CCTV at the station, so he made sure that his hat covered as much of his face a possible, looking down as if he was not looking forward to the day ahead, which in fact couldn't have been any further from the truth.

This was the day that Kevin Fraser had been longing for.

And now he was sitting on the 7:27 train that would soon be arriving at Glasgow Central. It was only a short walk from the station to Argyle Street, where he would get a bus to Dennistoun.

He would be at his destination in under an hour.

Adrenalin was coursing through his veins and it was struggle to sit still. He grasped the handle of his rucksack tightly to quell the shaking in his arm. He looked out of the window trying to find something to focus his overactive mind on. The feelings of relief mixed with triumph and anticipation were now almost unbearable. Months of planning were finally coming to fruition and it wouldn't be long until his ultimate target was at his mercy.

He couldn't wait.

Simply fucking couldn't wait until that bastard was his at last!

Chapter 19

Thursday May 22 2008, 8:15am

DI Adam Ralston was back in the office. He had come in early as he always seemed to, much to the annoyance of his wife, who was left with their two young children. He had tried to tell Helen that the case would soon be over, but she had refused to believe his assurances.

But his wife's criticism was the last thing on Ralston's mind.

He scanned through the large pile of reports that had gathered on his desk, hoping that he would have something positive to tell the boss, but none of them seemed to lead anywhere. Several former cellmates of Fraser's had been interviewed, but all had refused to co-operate. None of the Target staff had known of their workmate's secret identity. And there were still no sightings of that damned van anywhere.

Ralston finished looking through the night's serious crimes, but there was nothing that appeared to be linked to Fraser. He sat back in his chair and sighed deeply. There was still time to catch him before he killed again.

Adam Ralston came to a decision that he knew could have serious consequences for his career. He had spent most of the night trying to find a way to avoid telling McPherson of his error, but had finally admitted to himself that he had to bite the bullet.

The Superintendent was a fair man and he knew instinctively that admitting his error to him would be nowhere near as bad as what would happen if he later found out about it from someone else. In all likelihood McPherson would want him off his team, but perhaps he could salvage something of his career.

Ralston realised that being a police officer was all that he knew. He simply couldn't face the thought of having to start again in some other profession. He was a detective, and until now he had always been very good at it.

Steeling himself for what was to come, Ralston walked quickly along the corridor, not relishing his conversation with the Super in the slightest.

'Adam, come in,' said McPherson. 'I was just about to call you.' He was sitting at the meeting table with another man whom Ralston did not recognise.

'DI Ralston, this is Tom McLaren from the PR section. The Chief Constable called me late last night and he has decided that it is almost time to enlist the public in the hunt for Kevin Fraser. If we don't have anything definite we will go public in time for the evening news programmes.'

McLaren nodded to Ralston. He was a small, pale looking guy in a shiny suit. For some irrational reason Ralston took an instant dislike to the PR man.

'Now is there anything new overnight?' he asked.

'I'm afraid not, sir,' replied Ralston. He quickly brought his boss up to date with the numerous dead ends.

'What about Fraser's prison records?' asked McPherson.

'Are they not here yet?' Ralston had expected them to be delivered the previous evening. 'I'll get right onto them, sir.'

'Now Tom here will be putting the script together for a media conference. Please give him your full cooperation, Adam.' Ralston nodded, resigned to the idea. As if he didn't have enough to do.

'I'll go get on with the draft of the press release,' said McLaren, standing. 'It will be with you before lunch.'

The Superintendent nodded as McLaren left the office. Ralston closed the door after him and returned to the table. McPherson looked at him quizzically, obviously realising that he had something to say.

'Sir, I have to tell you that I've made an error that may well have cost us the chance to capture Fraser.'

McPherson's face remained impassive. 'Tell me about it.'

'On Tuesday afternoon when Frank Gallen first identified Fraser, I telephoned the Target office to see if he was there. When the receptionist told me that he wasn't, I left a message asking for him to call me as soon as he got back to the yard.'

Ralston looked at McPherson and saw that his expression somehow seemed to be darkening. He took a deep breath and finished his sorry tale.

'I found out late last night that she then called Fraser to warn him that the police were after him. And I didn't check his phone records because his mobile was turned off. If I had it would have shown the call from the office.'

'So that's why he didn't come back to the yard on Tuesday night?' McPherson appeared to by straining to keep his temper in check.

'I assume so, sir,' replied Ralston miserably, waiting for the inevitable explosion.

McPherson shook his head with what appeared to be a mixture of anger and disappointment. Ralston felt like a raw recruit.

'That was such a bloody stupid thing to do, Adam. Never, ever alert a suspect that we are on to him. You're experienced enough to know that, surely? He was bound to run, wasn't he?'

'Yes, sir.' Ralston studied a spot on the carpet intently, finding himself unable to look at his boss.

'There's nothing we can do about it now,' McPherson said, but Ralston could tell that he was still very angry. 'You've done such a good job on this case up to now, Adam. But now I'm really disappointed in you. I had thought that you were such a good addition to my team, but now I'm not so sure.'

Ralston found that there was nothing he could say. He wished that the ground would open up and swallow him. The sense of failure was so profound that he wondered how he could carry on.

McPherson appeared to come to a decision. He stared at Ralston for several seconds, as if he could see right into his soul.

Finally, he spoke in a harsh tone. 'Get back onto the case and see if you can make up for your stupidity, Inspector. Prove to me that you deserve to remain on my team. There is still a murderer to be caught.'

'Yes sir,' said Ralston, desperate to get out of the room. Somehow Superintendent McPherson's calmly expressed disappointment in him had made him feel much worse than the rollicking he had been expecting. He knew that he had let him down, and that hurt more than anything.

Ralston walked quickly back along the corridor, resolving to do everything he could to catch Fraser.

He returned to the main office and sought out one of his DCs.

'Why don't we have Fraser's prison file yet?' he asked. 'I need it right now.'

'Bureaucracy, sir. They couldn't get authorisation to release the file last night so it should be with us this morning.' What a typical answer, thought Ralston. Even a multiple murder inquiry stopped for red tape.

'Don't they realise what we are dealing with here? Get on the phone to whoever needs a rocket up their arse. I want that file here right away,' he ordered gruffly.

'Yes, sir.'

Ralston quickly realised that he was taking out the frustration of his own failure on the DC and returned to his desk, not trusting himself to say anything else. Was there anything more he could do, he asked himself for the millionth time that morning?

But nothing came to mind. He was hoping with all of his heart that they caught Fraser before he killed again.

Ralston simply could not even bring himself to think about that.

Thursday May 22 2008, 8:40am

Kevin Fraser walked slowly along Roslea Drive, head down. He saw Mullins' car parked directly outside his close and walked up to the controlled entry system at the side of the main door. He pressed the service button and was immediately admitted to the close. With a smile, he walked right through and out the back door into the small back court. He looked up at what he knew to be Mullins' bedroom and noted that the curtains were closed.

Everything was going perfectly, he thought calmly. But then he had planned it all down the finest detail, so what could possibly go wrong? He was in control.

Fraser crept back into the close and opened his rucksack. He pulled out the pistol and screwed the silencer on, just as a former friend from Barlinnie had instructed him. He realised that he didn't even know what type of gun he had, but what did it matter? He knew that it was lethal at close range and that was how he intended to use it.

He put the weapon into the inside pocket of his jacket. Returning to the rucksack he took out a roll of duct tape and put it into his side pocket and also removed his lock picking kit. It had been a while since his housebreaking days, but he was confident that his old skills would come back to him.

Fraser then walked as quietly as he could up the two flights of steps to Mullins' flat. He knew that he was vulnerable here and hoped that none of the neighbours would come out at exactly the wrong moment. But he reached Mullins' front door without being seen and had it open in thirty seconds. He was just as good as he had always been!

Then he crept inside, put the snib on quietly and located the bedroom door. It was slightly ajar and he could tell from the sounds of snoring coming from it that Mullins was asleep. Again, exactly as he had planned. This was all going so well, he thought smugly. Everything was all falling into place nicely for his grand finale.

Walking slowly into Mullins' bedroom he looked down at the sleeping figure of the man he hated more than any other and had to resist the temptation to blow the bastard's fucking head off there and then.

No, a quick death was not what he had planned for Principal Officer James fucking Mullins.

What authority he had at that moment, he realised. He was godlike; he quite literally had the power of life and death over the man lying on his back asleep just a few feet away. Fraser suddenly noticed that he had an erection, the painful swelling irritating him. Christ where did that come from, he wondered? He took a few deep breaths to try to calm himself, then continued with his plan.

Slowly, he tore a long strip of duct tape from the roll and than reached down and quickly attached it over Mullins mouth. The man was suddenly awake; eyes wide open with shock as he sat up. Fraser took a step back, quickly removed the pistol from his inside pocket and mercilessly put a bullet into Mullins leg.

Mullins' eyes bulged as he tried to scream and then his hands went to his leg, instinctively trying to stop both the pain and the blood, which was already soaking through the bedclothes.

The recoil from the gun had forced Fraser to take a second step back, but he quickly focused the gun on the whimpering Mullins once more. But he was no threat. No threat at all. He had Mullins exactly where he wanted him: helpless and in agony.

Mullins looked up, dazed by pain and shock. And then he recognised Fraser.

What a moment that was! The bastard was hurting and confused, awoken to a terrible ordeal and frightened for his life.

And he knew exactly who his assailant was.

Fraser moved quickly forward and hit Mullins firmly on the side of the head with the butt of the gun. He fell back onto the bed, unconscious. Fraser then worked quickly, pulling four lengths of rope from his rucksack and tying Mullins' arms and legs firmly to the frame of the bed. The prison officer was a big man and he filled the bed with ease. Fraser made sure that the gag was secure, wrapping more tape around Mullins' head.

Thankfully Mullins was wearing a t-shirt and shorts, although being naked could have added another dimension to his torment he supposed.

Fraser then picked up a t-shirt from the floor and tied it securely around Mullins' leg. The bullet had hit him just above the knee, he noticed, and he was bleeding steadily. Fraser didn't want him to bleed out. His death had to be a long and slow one.

Exactly as the bastard deserved.

He stepped back from the bed and leaned against the door. He was in no hurry at all: he would simply wait for Mullins to regain consciousness. He had waited a year for this. What harm would another few minutes, or even hours, do? And as he stood, silent and motionless, he stared intently at the tattoo on Mullins' right forearm.

The ace of spades.

Thursday May 22 2008, 10:10am

'Here's Fraser's prison file, sir.'

Finally, he thought. He took the file and immediately read through it. Ten minutes later he made an urgent telephone call and then ran along the corridor towards McPherson's office.

He entered without even knocking on the door. McPherson looked up and appeared to be about to berate him when he noticed the look on his face.

'What do you have, Adam?' he asked instead.

'We finally got Fraser's prison records. I think I know what all of this has been about!' he exclaimed.

'Explain,' McPherson commanded, gesturing for Ralston to sit.

'While Fraser was in prison he got into a number of fights. We knew that: it's why he served his full sentence,' he began. 'But about a year ago he alleged that he was sexually assaulted by five other prisoners in the showers at Barlinnie with the assistance of a senior prison officer. There was a hearing but they all stuck together and denied anything had ever happened, and the officer backed them up. The whole thing was dropped in the end.'

'So going on what the profiler told us, the five gay men Fraser has killed would represent the prisoners who attacked him. Then the sixth target, the one he is really after, would logically be the prison officer?' McPherson quickly concluded.

'That's exactly it, sir. I'm thinking that he blamed the officer most of all for the whole thing, especially for covering it up,' confirmed Ralston. 'I telephoned the Governor at Barlinnie and the officer involved is still working at the prison. His name is Jim Mullins, but he had just finished a night shift and gone home. They're trying to reach him now and will get back to me as soon as they hear from him.'

'Where does this Mullins live?'

'Dennistoun. If Fraser is after him then he will have to come back into the city. I always thought that the answer would lie in Glasgow.'

'Have there been any sightings of Fraser or his van as yet this morning?'

'No, nothing at all.'

'So maybe we will be in time. Good work, Adam.'

Ralston's mobile phone rang. He listened for a few seconds, asked a question and then pulled out his notebook to write down some details.

'Sir, that was Barlinnie. There's no answer on either Mullins' home number or his mobile. The Governor talked to another warden who is doing a double shift and he told him that he had talked to Mullins before he left. He said that he was going home for a sleep as his son was coming round later today. I've got his car registration and telephone numbers here.'

'Get a trace on Mullins mobile. And then get over to his flat as soon as you can. I'll put an alert out on Mullins' car.'

'Yes, sir,' replied Ralston, tearing the page from his notebook and leaving it on the desk as he walked quickly out of the office.

Now they knew where Fraser was heading. Could he finally get a step ahead of him and stop the final part of his awful plan?

He prayed that they would be in time to save Jim Mullins' life.

Thursday May 22 2008, 10:40am

Frank Gallen was sitting in his brother's office waiting anxiously.

Councillor Thomas Gallen had left him to go to the Council Chambers for the Labour Group meeting where he would announce his resignation to his colleagues. He would then return to the office and summon the Council's Head of PR. And the statement that they had written the day before would be released to the press. Finally, they would go home to try to avoid the commotion that the announcement would inevitably cause.

He should be back any minute, thought Frank. Thomas's plan had been simple: open the meeting, drop the bombshell on his colleagues and then leave. No questions and no fuss. Knowing politicians as Frank did, he was certain that their minds would be on the fight for the vacant leadership the moment Thomas left. Who would stand, who to back, the usual political infighting.

The door opened and Thomas walked in. Surprisingly he had a broad smile on his face.

'How did it go?' asked Frank.

'Exactly as planned,' his brother beamed. 'The response was a totally shocked silence and then a lot of good wishes before I left. You know, it feels great to be free of the responsibility now.'

'That's good,' Frank replied, glad that this brother was still so positive.

'Anyway some of them will be planning their leadership bids by now, and the others will be wondering who to back,' he said, echoing exactly what Frank had been thinking.

'Now for the press.' He pressed a button on the intercom. 'Sandra, have the Head of PR come to my office immediately.'

'Will do, Councillor,' came the reply.

'Soon all of this will be behind me. I'll be plain Tommy Gallen again, husband and father. And I'll make Marie and the children proud of me again, whatever it takes,' he vowed.

'I know you will,' his brother told him.

Thursday May 22 2008, 10:50am

Mullins had been out cold for not far short of two hours now, Fraser reflected. Perhaps it would be better to revive him? After all he didn't want someone to miss the man before he had time to reach the beautiful climax of his plan.

The telephone had rung twice in the living room, Fraser remembered, but he had ignored it. Now he decided that he had better check in case there had been a message left. When he walked into the living room, very neat and tidy for a single man he noticed, he saw an answering machine with a blinking light, so he hit the Play button.

'Jim, it's Helen at the prison. Can you call the Governor's office as soon as you get this message? It's very important.'

Fraser wondered whether the message was in some way related to him. It was fairly vague but she had emphasised the importance of a return call. Had they finally managed to figure it all out? They would have had to get both his real identity and the reason for his revenge before they could have got to Mullins. Could the stupid bastards have finally managed to put his clues together?

Maybe it was time to speed things up a bit, he decided with a smile. He wanted them to find him, but not before he had some fun. And of course the best part of the entire plan was still to come.

The part where Jim fucking Mullins finally paid the ultimate price for what he had done to him.

Smiling manically, he walked into the kitchen and filled a glass with cold water. Christ, the man even kept his kitchen as clean as a bloody showroom. What sort of freak was he? Shaking his head, Fraser left the kitchen and entered the bedroom. Unceremoniously, he emptied the full pint of water over his head.

Mullins woke and tried to scream, but the gag stopped any sound from coming out. Fraser watched as he realised that he was now tied up. Mullins tried to free himself, but he had no chance of getting out of the thick bonds. He finally stopped struggling and looked up at Fraser, pleading silently.

Fraser responded by putting a bullet into his arm.

Mullins' jerked violently and the agony was immediately evident on his face. His entire body shook and a second pool of blood began to form on the sheet below him.

This was beautiful. There was nothing Mullins could do to stop his torment. Fraser knew that he has in complete control and could continue to torture Mullins for as long as he wanted. He debated whether he should take the gag off. It would be great to hear the bastard plead for his life, but what if he screamed? Maybe later, he decided.

Then he heard a knock at the front door.

He stood as silently as he could; waiting to see if the caller would simply go away when there was no answer. It could be the postman or a delivery, he realised. But then he heard a voice shouting through the letterbox.

'Anyone in? Mister Mullins? It's Strathclyde Police here. Are you alright in there?'

Showtime, he thought. The game was well and truly on now.

They had managed to track him down after all. Not bad, considering how fucking useless they normally were. Although without his clues they would have had no chance. No fucking chance at all. He had given them the answers and just waited for them to come to him. It was all still going exactly to his plan.

With a quick look back to make sure that Mullins was still secured he walked out into the hall.

'Identify yourself!' he shouted.

'I'm Detective Inspector Adam Ralston of Strathclyde Police. Who am I talking to? Is that James Mullins?' came the reply.

Fraser had to resist the impulse to laugh.

'I've got a gun. Don't make a move or Mullins will be killed. Is that clear?' He heard a gasp.

'OK, look, just tell me your name and we can talk about this calmly and sensibly,' the response came through the letterbox. 'No one needs to get hurt.'

The usual nonsense, as he could have predicted. And of course someone was already hurt. But not as badly hurt as he was going to be. Now he laughed loudly, the perfection of the situation was almost more than he could take.

'My name is Kevin Fraser, but then you probably know that by now, don't you? The only person I will talk to is Frank Gallen. Get him here immediately. If he's not here in thirty minutes, Mullins dies. If you try anything stupid, Mullins dies. Now go do what I say. Is that fucking clear?'

'Alright, leave it with me.'

Fraser smiled. Of course the copper would do exactly as he had been told. He had no choice.

Kevin Fraser was running the show and he would soon have the only audience that he wanted.

Thursday May 22 2008, 11:05am

Ralston ran back down the stairs to his car. They had been too late after all. If only they had received the bloody prison file earlier. They would have worked out the target and got to him before Fraser did. But that did not excuse him from blame, Ralston knew. He felt physically sick, well aware that Mullins was in extreme danger.

He took out his phone and called McPherson.

'Adam, have you got Mullins?'

'No, Kevin Fraser has,' he replied, hearing a groan.

'He confirmed his identity and told me that he has a gun. He wants Frank Gallen and says that he is the only person he will talk to. And we have thirty minutes to get him here'

'For fuck's sake,' replied Superintendent McPherson, swearing for only the second time in Ralston's recollection. 'You stay there, Adam, but get well back from the house. I'll get a tactical team down and some of the local boys to close the street off. And I'll call Frank Gallen too.'

'Yes, sir,' replied Ralston, already turning his engine on to reverse back down the narrow street.

Thursday May 22 2008, 11:10am

Frank and Thomas Gallen were finalising the arrangements for the press release with a shocked Head of PR when Frank's mobile rang. Seeing that the caller was Superintendent McPherson he immediately moved to the far corner of the office to answer the call.

'Frank Gallen.'

'Frank, John McPherson. I really need your help.'

'What's happening?' He could tell from his terse tone that the situation must be grave.

'Kevin Fraser has a prison officer held hostage and he insists that you are the only person he will talk to. Can you meet me in Dennistoun? I'll explain fully when you get there.'

'OK, I'm in the City Chambers right now, so it shouldn't take long to get there. What's the address?' he asked.

'It's on Roslea Drive. I'm on my way there now. We will have the street closed off, but I'll let them know that you can come through,' he replied.

'On my way,' said Frank. He turned to his brother. 'Thomas, I'm going to have to go. It looks like the serial killer saga is about to come to an end, one way or another.'

'What's happening?' asked Thomas.

'He has a hostage and he wants to talk to me. I need to be there.'

'Of course, Frank. Go to the front door on George Square. There will be a car waiting for you.'

The Council's Head of PR had looked shocked when told of the resignation of the Council Leader, but he had almost fallen off his chair when the conversation had casually turned to the hunt for the serial killer.

'Thanks Thomas. I'll call you later.'

Frank Gallen was already heading for the door.

It looked like he would soon have an ending for his book after all, he realised. Frank found that he was excited and scared in equal measures when he thought of the prospect of coming face to face with the killer. He wanted the story of course, but what was Fraser going to do now?

And why did Kevin Fraser want to talk to him?

Thursday May 22 2008, 11:15am

Fraser was extremely pleased with the situation. He had it exactly as he wanted. They knew where he was and presumably why. Mullins was at his mercy. And Frank Gallen was on his way to listen to his tale.

Absolutely perfect!

And the tape could come off from Mullins' mouth; it would make no difference if the bastard screamed now. In fact, it would probably add to the fun, Fraser realised, smiling.

The room was dark and the smells of fear, sweat and blood mingled to give the atmosphere a hint of menace. Mullins was struggling, still trying to break the ropes, but Fraser knew that he would have no chance. All he would achieve was to use up what little strength he had left.

He pulled out his pocket knife and moved slowly towards Mullins. He could see the terror in the man's eyes as he focussed on the blade. Slowly Fraser moved it towards Mullins' face, enjoying the way his eyes widened. His hand shot forward suddenly, stabbing into the pillow just inches from Mullins' right eye.

Fraser laughed.

He pulled the knife out and brought it close to Mullins' face once more, revelling in his panic.

'Don't worry. I'm only going to cut the tape off your mouth. Calm down, you stupid bastard,' he finally said. Mullins lay still as he cut the tape. 'The police are already outside so there's no point in screaming. I've told them that you'll die if they try anything stupid.'

And you'll die even if they don't, he said to himself. Control. It was all his.

'Kevin Fraser,' said Mullins in a weak voice.

'You remember me. That's good,' replied Fraser softly. 'I've thought about you a lot since I got out. About how I would get even with you one day. And, guess what, Mullins? This is the fucking day that it happens.'

'Please...' he started to say.

'Don't even think about it,' Fraser cut in before the pitiful bastard could beg for his life. 'Did you show me any mercy when those five animals attacked me? Did you stop them when they pulled my clothes off and did those filthy, vile things to me? Did you say anything when they hosed me down afterwards? Did you speak up for me at the hearing?'

Mullins made no reply.

'Of course you fucking didn't. You told everyone that nothing had happened, you lying piece of shit. And now you will pay for it.'

He was close to losing control, he realised. The urge to kill Mullins was so strong that he had to lean against the wall, breathing deeply.

'I'm sorry.' Mullins said. 'But I ...' his voice trailed off.

'Don't even have an excuse do you, Mullins? You really are just a bully, aren't you? But I have the upper hand now, don't I? You're the final step in my revenge. Five men have died so far and you know why.'

'Was it really you? All those killings?' asked Mullins incredulously, struggling against the obvious pain of two bullet wounds.

'Oh yes. I'm the killer that the whole of Glasgow has been trying to catch,' he said proudly. 'All because of what you and those bastards in Barlinnie did to me. How does it feel to know that all of this is your fault? Those deaths are on your conscience, Principal Officer James Mullins!'

Oh, now he was crying. This just gets better and fucking better, Fraser thought as he watched the man he hated lying in front of him, bloody, scared and now weeping. He had reduced Mullins to this.

He had used his power to humiliate the bastard totally.

Thursday May 22 2008, 11:25am

The black Daimler dropped Frank Gallen at the junction of Hillfoot Street and Roslea Drive. A marked police car was stationed there, blocking the narrow street. Frank thanked the driver and approached the police officers.

'I'm Frank Gallen,' he said, starting to explain himself. The PC didn't wait for him to finish: he simply grabbed his arm and showed him along the quiet street. They walked quickly until they reached DI Ralston's car.

'Frank, thanks for coming,' said Ralston. 'I take it Superintendent McPherson told you what was happening?'

'Not really,' said Frank. 'Just that Fraser has a hostage and that he wants to talk to me.' He could see the strain that Ralston was under from the grim expression on his almost colourless face.

'Ok, here's the short version of the story.'

It all became clear to Frank, the reason why Fraser had carried out the murders. And had now taken the man he presumably held as primarily responsible as a hostage. He was the sixth man, the one who was so important to Fraser.

His ace of spades.

What had happened to Fraser was obviously terrible. Frank could only imagine the ordeal that he had been put through and the psychological damage that the experience must have caused. But he found that it was hard to feel any sympathy at all for a serial killer.

McPherson joined them at the back of Ralston's car. And behind him, a large black van was trying to negotiate its way along the street, which had cars parked on both sides.

'Frank, has Adam explained the situation to you?'

'Briefly, yes,' he replied.

'OK, we need to make contact with Fraser. I'll call the flat and see if he will pick up.' McPherson was calm and completely in control, Frank noticed. He looked like he came across situations like this every day. Frank watched as he dialled Mullins' number.

'Answering machine ... Kevin Fraser. Fraser, are you there? This is Detective Superintendent John McPherson, Fraser. Talk to me,' he demanded. 'I have Frank Gallen here as you asked. Call me back on this number.' He closed his phone. 'Let's give him a few minutes.'

McPherson turned to the armed officers, who were emerging from the black van. 'Who's in charge?' he shouted.

'I'm Sergeant Kennedy, sir.' A tall, well built officer all dressed in black and carrying a machine gun moved forward. 'What's the situation? I believe that there is a civilian hostage?'

'Superintendent McPherson, Murder Squad. I'm in command of the scene. We have one armed man and one hostage in a flat. Which one is it, Adam?'

Ralston pointed up to Mullins' top floor flat.

'Any idea of their positions within the flat, sir?' asked Kennedy.

'There's no sign of anyone in the front room there that I can see. Did you check out the back, Adam?'

'Yes sir,' replied Ralston. 'What I assume to be Mullins' bedroom window has the curtains closed. He's a prison officer and just come off a nightshift at Barlinnie,' he explained. 'I reckon that he was probably in bed when Fraser entered the house this morning.'

'We need to confirm that if possible,' replied Kennedy, frowning. 'It's not a great location for us: that church opposite is the only clear position for our snipers. I'll go see if anyone is in and also send someone to recce the back court.'

'Have the other flats in the close been cleared?' asked McPherson, just as his mobile phone rung. 'It's him.' He looked up to the front window of the flat before answering but couldn't see anyone.

'McPherson.'

'Put Frank Gallen on the line. Now'

'He wants to talk to you, Frank,' McPherson explained, his hand over the phone. 'Try to get him talking and see if you can find out if Mullins is OK. He might well be: if Fraser simply wanted to kill him he could have done it by now and been on his way. And find out what the hell he wants.'

He handed Frank his phone.

'This is Frank Gallen,' he said, hoping that his voice was steadier than his hands. McPherson and Ralston were standing close; trying to hear what was said on the other end.

'Frank Gallen! It's so nice to speak to you again after all this time. You managed to follow my clues in the end, then?' He sounded strange, Frank thought. His voice was high and loud and he was speaking very quickly. Had he been drinking, Frank wondered, or perhaps taking drugs?

'What's happening, Kevin?' he asked. 'Is Jim Mullins with you?' He looked up towards the window but there was still no sign of movement inside.

'Oh, Frank that's funny,' laughed Fraser. 'Of course Mullins is here, but he can't talk right now. He's a bit *tied up* at the moment.' Fraser laughed loudly, a strange sound, almost a bark. He sounded like he was losing control, Frank surmised, and he realised instantly that couldn't be at all good in the circumstances.

'What's this all about, Kevin? Why did you ask to speak to me?' he asked, trying to keep his voice as calm as he could.

'Always the hot shot journalist, Frank. Questions, questions, it's always fucking questions with you, isn't it? I'm in control here, not you,' Fraser shouted. 'This goes my way from here on in. To the end, right to the very end.'

'Alright Kevin,' replied Frank, speaking softly. 'What do you want from me?'

'Now that's the right question! I want to give you my story, Frank Gallen. That's why I was e-mailing you all along. You will be the one to tell my story to the whole fucking world. I've chosen you. You have ten minutes to get up here.' And then he cut the connection.

'Did you hear any of that?' Frank asked the two detectives, a strained look on his face.

'He wants me to go in there.'

Chapter 20

'John, I think you should come out here,' shouted Janice, horrified at what she was seeing.

Her eyes were fixed on a television set the corner that was tuned to a 24 hour news station. John walked quickly through the office and joined Janice in front of the screen.

'What's going on?' he asked trying to take in the information on the television. *"Glasgow Serial Killer: Armed Siege"* was the dramatic headline below a shot of a reporter looking along a street lined with tenements. John could see a lot of police activity, including what looked to be armed officers. They seemed totally incongruous: police officers with machine guns on a quiet city street.

'They think that the serial killer has a hostage and is holed up in his flat in Dennistoun. And he has asked to speak to a journalist. There are no names but surely it has to be Frank given that he has been e-mailing him, doesn't it, John?'

All he could do was to nod his agreement.

'It has to be Frank,' Janice repeated.

She felt intensely frightened that Frank was anywhere near the killer, but also strangely proud of him. He was where he should be as a top journalist, of course: at the very heart of the story. Janice once again felt the intense sorrow of her unrequited love for Frank Gallen.

John had pulled out his mobile phone and she watched him dial a number: clearly he was trying to reach Frank. But he was frustrated in his attempt.

'Switched off,' he said grimly. 'I just hope Frank doesn't do anything stupid.'

He had a shocked expression on his face and Janice could only imagine what he was thinking. Frank wouldn't do anything silly, would he? But in her heart she knew that the man she loved would put himself in danger without thinking about it if there was a big story to be had.

And this was the story of the decade.

Suddenly Janice found that all of the feelings she had been experiencing were replaced by a single overwhelming emotion: fear.

Thursday May 22 2008, 11:40am

'Frank, you do realise that he is crazy? Fraser has killed five, maybe six men that we know of. You don't know what he might do,' said Ralston. He was slumped against the car, looking down as if unable to face the situation.

'He wants his story to be told, Adam,' Frank replied. 'He needs the world to know what this has all been about. That's why he was giving me the clues all along. He didn't want to be caught until he had got to Mullins, but he did want the publicity. Mullins is obviously his last target and now he will tell us everything.'

'You seem very sure of this, Frank,' said Superintendent McPherson, clearly not convinced. 'It would be a hell of a risk for you to go in there.'

'He won't kill me,' Frank stated simply and clearly. 'He needs me alive to tell his story.'

At that moment Kennedy returned to the makeshift command post. McPherson quickly filled him in on the events of the past few minutes.

'OK, sir. I've got two snipers on the roof of the church across the road, but there is no sign of the target. The back curtains are still drawn so we have no idea exactly what's happening in the bedroom. The infrared scope shows two people in the room, though.'

'Anything else, Sergeant?'

'We could get onto the roof of his building and come in through the bedroom window, although that's clearly very risky with a hostage in the room.'

'No, let's leave that for now,' decided McPherson. And his phone rang again.

'McPherson.'

'Where the fuck is Frank Gallen? Your ten minutes are up.'

Before McPherson could say a word Frank gestured that he wanted the phone given to him. The detective frowned but then handed it over.

'Kevin, it's Frank,' he said calmly, once again trying to placate him. 'I will be up in a minute. I just need to know that Mullins is OK first.'

'Well, he is still alive. Just,' replied Fraser, giggling manically. What did that mean: was Mullins hurt?

'Can I talk to him?' he asked. There was a long silence on the other end. Frank waited, picturing Fraser in the flat and hoping that he was taking the phone to Mullins. And then he heard a weak voice.

'It's Jim Mullins here and ...'

'Satisfied?' demanded Kevin Fraser. Frank put his hand over the phone and turned to McPherson.

'Mullins is alive, but he doesn't sound too good.'

'We have proof of life. That's something,' Ralston remarked. He appeared relieved that the prison officer was at least still breathing.

'I don't know if he is injured or just terrified. There's no choice: I have to do what Fraser wants. I'm going in.'

'I'm still not convinced that's a good idea, Frank,' Ralston told him.

'Kevin, I'm about to come into the close,' Frank said. He wasn't going to let anything stop him from getting the biggest story of his career. 'I'll be alone, just like you wanted. Will you open the front door for me?'

Fraser immediately ended the call. Frank handed the phone back to McPherson and smiled. 'I've got to get the story. It's the only thing to do. Fraser will have to let me back out, or else what's the point in his talking to me?'

'I don't like it, Frank.' McPherson's face was grim.

'What else can we do?' He tried to reason with the detective, deciding on a different approach. 'If I don't go in, he will kill Mullins, and you have no way to stop him. I'm his only hope of getting out of there alive.'

McPherson looked at Ralston who shook his head. The senior detective thought for a moment while Frank stood impatiently beside him. He could almost see McPherson's mind ticking over.

'OK, do it, Frank,' McPherson finally said.

Frank felt his heart lift. Everything that had happened had been leading up to this moment. He was about to get the full story behind Fraser's murderous spree directly from the killer himself!

'Be careful, Frank. I mean it,' the detective emphasised, waiting until Frank had nodded his assent before continuing. 'Try to get him into the front room if you can. Let the boys on the roof have the chance of a clear shot at him.'

Frank nodded again and then walked away from the two detectives.

He headed towards Mullins' close, feeling like a gunslinger in town to face the bad guy. The street was very quiet, eerily so. It was the middle of the day but there was not a single person in sight, no signs of life at all. A black cat crossed his path, running across the road, and he wondered whether that would bring him luck.

Frank walked up the path, feeling very alone, and found the name Mullins. Everything looked so normal, thought Frank as he pressed the button. He turned around and saw two police snipers on the roof of the church opposite. Maybe it's not so normal, he realised.

He heard the buzz that he knew meant the front door was open and he could enter.

Despite what he had said to persuade McPherson, Frank recognised that he was putting himself in a very dangerous situation. Fraser was clearly not entirely rational and therefore could not be depended on to behave in a predictable manner, or even to remember that he had to let Frank leave once he had told him his story.

This was either the story of a lifetime or the craziest thing he had ever done. Well, the craziest while sober anyway, Frank decided.

Taking a deep breath he pushed the heavy door open and walked into the close.

Thursday May 22 2008, 11:50am

Gallen was coming, just as he had known that he would in the end. He is still dancing to my tune, Fraser thought, delighted.

Now he could tell the world what it had all been about, and whose fault all the deaths really were. And then they would all know why Jim fucking Mullins had to suffer, just as he himself had suffered back in Barlinnie.

Fraser dropped the cordless handset onto the floor and looked Mullins in the eye. Christ, he was pissing himself now, quite literally. Mullins' humiliation was almost complete.

'Not the big man now, are you Mullins?' he sneered. 'You're just a snivelling coward lying in a pool of his own piss. I've broken you Mullins. You were a bully and a coward all along, only acting the tough guy when you had five thugs to back you up. Very different now, isn't it? I've got you where I want you!'

An uncontrollable rage shot through Kevin Fraser's mind. It was like an explosion inside his brain, burning bright and painful behind his eyes. Electricity sparked through his body, bringing all of his anger and hurt to a head.

Mullins had driven him to this. Mullins had made him do everything. Mullins had turned him into a killer.

Mullins had to pay the ultimate fucking price.

He lifted his gun and pointed it at Mullins' head. The bastard cringed and looked away from him, a coward to the very end. One quick movement of his finger and the bastard's head almost disappeared in a shower of blood and brains. The recoil forced Fraser back against the door. He found that he was shaking and sweating, his breathing loud and ragged.

Shit! He hadn't meant to kill him so soon. That wasn't the way that the plan was supposed to finish. Gallen was supposed to witness his final act of revenge.

But now he had blown it, quite literally fucking blown it.

Still breathing heavily, Fraser surveyed the scene. What a mess! Mullins' body lay still and lifeless in the bed, which was covered in blood. Bits of something grey were attached to the headboard amongst more blood, bright red and dripping down onto the sheets.

Fraser did not feel a shred of pity for Mullins, simply regret that he had killed him earlier than he had planned and thereby ended his suffering far too soon.

Think, Kevin, what now? He tried to regain his composure. This was the first break from the plan and realised that he had to recover quickly. Now he didn't have a hostage and Gallen was on his way up. How could he get his story out now? Taking a deep breath he attempted to calm himself.

But then he realised that as long as they thought that Mullins was still alive he would be alright. Nothing had really changed after all, he told himself. He could still get what he wanted. He laughed; he was still in charge.

Then he heard a buzzer sound: the controlled entry.

Fraser closed the bedroom door behind him and walked into the hall. Frank fucking Gallen was here at last! He pressed the button on the wall to let him into the close and then waited, imagining Gallen walking up the stairs, fearful of what he was going to find.

There was a knock at the door. Fraser could see the figure of a man through the opaque glass that covered the top half of the front door, but had no idea if there was anyone else behind him. Would they try something?

Think, Kevin, think. This is your game. You're the one who is in control. What happens now, he asked himself?

'Stand back from the door and I will unlock it,' he shouted. 'And remember that I've got a gun, Gallen.'

'Alright, Kevin.'

He saw the figure move away and he walked slowly forward, the gun held in front of him, pointing it sideways like he had seen in the films. He was half expecting the police to try to rush him, but at least he was prepared. He was still in charge, he told himself once more.

Fraser unlocked the door and pulled it inwards towards him. He saw Frank Gallen standing well back, alone at the top of the stairs with his hands up. He smiled and pointed the gun directly at him. Now Gallen looked really scared. Perfect!

'Sit down, Frank. Sit on the top step and I will talk to you from here.' And then he shouted, 'If anyone is listening I've got Gallen in my sights. Make a move on me and he dies. Do you hear me?'

There was no response.

Gallen sat just where he had instructed him, he was pleased to see. Now he could tell his story and then Gallen would make sure that the world knew exactly what Jim fucking Mullins had done to him.

Thursday May 22 2008, 11:55am

Frank sat down on the top step as he had been told to do. He looked up at Fraser, taking in the staring eyes, the crazed expression on his face and the gun pointing at his head. And he immediately wondered whether he had done the wrong thing by coming anywhere near the man.

He could not count on Fraser being rational enough to remember that he needed him. That was the problem, Frank concluded. He knew that he had to remind Fraser of the role that he had to play. Then he noticed the bright red blood sprayed across the killer's face and shirt. There was an awful lot of it, but no obvious wound. He must have shot Mullins, he figured, and got caught in the spray.

And with a sickening feeling he then realised that he could now be Fraser's only hostage. Fraser needed him to tell his story, but could he now let him leave? There would be nothing to stop the police from storming the building if Mullins was already dead.

Fraser was looking behind him, staring down the stairs, as if waiting for something to happen. It seemed like he finally decided that everything was OK and he turned his attention to Frank.

'Frank Gallen. You were always the great writer at school, weren't you? And then the star fucking journalist? But then it all went wrong, didn't it Frank? Too much of that, wasn't it?' He mimed drinking, a strange, crazed smile on his face.

Frank said nothing, trying to figure out how he could keep Fraser calm.

'Not the star of John Bosco now, are you, Frank? It's easy to lose everything isn't it? I know that. And that's how we ended up here, really,' Fraser said, almost wistfully.

'What do you want from me, Kevin?' asked Frank simply. He had decided that letting Fraser talk as much as possible was probably the safest course of action. And doing nothing that might annoy him, obviously.

'I want to know how much you managed to work out. I gave you all the fucking clues, but did you manage to solve the puzzle? You tell me what you know and then I will fill in the blanks for you. Deal?'

Fraser seemed a lot calmer, but Frank knew that he would still have to keep his wits about him.

'OK, it's a deal,' replied Frank. 'But I need my notebook, I'm going to take it out of my inside pocket very slowly. Is that alright, Kevin?' Fraser nodded and Frank did exactly as he had said, sliding his notebook slowly out and onto the stone step.

'Why don't we go inside and sit down, Kevin? It would be more comfortable for both of us?' It was worth a try, Frank decided. Fraser seemed a little calmer, so why not ask the question?

'No, we're fine here. I can see you and I can see if anyone comes up the stairs.' But then his eyes narrowed. 'Or do you want me to stay here? Are they going to come in the window? Are you bluffing? Or double bluffing?'

Frank realised that paranoia had set in and that Fraser could be close to a complete breakdown.

'I'm not doing anything or trying anything. I just thought that you might want a seat, Kevin, that's all.' Keep calm, he told himself, feeling his heart beating wildly in his chest.

'But then what happens?' Definitely paranoid, Frank concluded.

'Nothing's going to happen, Kevin. I'll tell you what we know, just like we agreed, OK?' He couldn't risk pushing Fraser any further he realised. He had to follow his instructions in order to stay alive.

'Right, get talking,' commanded Fraser. He was still holding the gun out in front of him, sideways in gangster style, but his arm was trembling, Frank noticed. He took a deep breath. And then he started to take Fraser all the way through the investigation.

'It all started when I got your e-mail about Phil Whitby,' he began.

Thursday May 22 2008, 12:05pm

David Longwell put down the phone, feeling a little better about the situation than he had in a few days. He had talked to several members of Stirling Council and they had reiterated their support for him. Of course it had helped that he had reminded them of the donations that he had secured to their election funds. None of which had been in his own name, naturally.

Now all he had to do was wait for the politicians to put pressure on the Director of Planning and a press release would be made clearing his company. Then he could get on with his business here in Glasgow.

Daniel burst into his office, shouting, 'Father, have you heard the news?'

'What news, Daniel?' he asked.

'Thomas Gallen has resigned from the Council. It was on the radio just now. Something about a serious health problem,' he explained.

'Are you sure?' asked Longwell. Now this was something that he hadn't foreseen.

'Of course. It's definite. He resigned from the Council this morning with immediate effect.'

Another twist to the situation, thought Longwell. He sighed wondering whether Gallen was really ill or if he had simply had enough. Not that it really mattered: he was no longer any use to him at all, that was the key fact. But how would this affect things? Every time he got close to finalising his dream project, something else seemed to get in the way.

'Father, are you OK?' his son enquired.

'Yes, yes. I just need to work out what this means for us. Tell me, what do you think, Daniel?' he asked, interested to hear what his son could come up with.

'There will be a leadership contest of course. Which will take a couple of weeks, and during that time nothing will get done in the Council. We will need to wait for now, see who the new leader is and then try to persuade him that our partnership with the Council is a good one and should be continued.' He looked at his father, expectantly waiting on his verdict.

'Pretty good, Daniel, pretty good,' he said, nodding slightly. 'But I've never been much in favour of waiting to see what happens as a strategy. Find out who the leading candidates are likely to be and who is likely to win. And then we will decide what to do.'

Thursday May 22 2008, 1:10pm

Frank had been talking for a very long time and he was getting hoarse. And his backside was numb from sitting on the cold stone step. He finished telling Fraser everything that had happened, closed his notebook and sat back.

'Could I have a glass of water, please Kevin?' he asked, as casually as he could.

Fraser looked at him, instantly suspicious. He merely shook his head, and then started laughing.

'That's pretty impressive. You did fairly well, Frank, but not nearly as well as a star reporter like you should have.'

'What didn't we manage to get, Kevin?'

Fraser smiled at him, a strange lopsided grin. For several seconds he did not move at all and his eyes did not even blink. Frank thought that he was in some sort of a trance. But then he laughed once again.

'You haven't found my brother's body for a start. Yes, I killed him and buried his body in the woods near his flat. After everything I went through he wouldn't help me to get my revenge. Bloody refused to get involved. He never helped me,' he whined. 'Never. But after I killed him I decided that I could just become him. It was so easy. He gave me a whole new identity. That was the first useful thing that he ever did for me, I suppose.'

'What else?' asked Frank.

'And you didn't find my first victim. The six of spades. You didn't find him. Some rent boy I left down by the river. He deserved to die, the pervert. Tried to rob me, but I was too strong for him. I strangled him with my bare hands,' he explained, his eyes now bright as he relived the moment.

'OK, we will look into that,' Frank replied.

'I had to e-mail you after Whitby as no one had made the connection. I forced Whitby to call his mother, I wanted to raise suspicions. But they thought that he had jumped and no one got the connection to the first two. That's when I had the idea of e-mailing you,' Fraser explained, speaking very quickly.

'Was there anything else?' asked Frank.

'I knew the police were onto Target. But of course I had used the spare van, not mine. A PC even interviewed me and searched my van, but he was too stupid to realise what was going on. Then when the police started getting interested in me I got away again. Janey in the office told me they were looking for me. I knew that daft tart would come in useful eventually.'

'Right,' replied Frank, wondering how he should play it. He had finished his story: how long would Fraser keep talking? And, more importantly, what would happen when he stopped?

'And that's almost everything, I think,' said Fraser, reflectively. An almost peaceful look came across his face and he lowered the gun to his side.

Frank hadn't heard a sound from the bedroom in the whole time he had been there. Combined with the blood spatter on Fraser, he was now pretty certain that Mullins was dead. And that meant that he had to get away in case Fraser turned on him.

'There is still your most important failure to discuss, Gallen,' Fraser said suddenly, animated once more.

'Tell me, Kevin,' he urged.

'Even when I gave you the calling cards, you didn't manage to take it all the way to its conclusion, did you?' Fraser taunted Frank. 'You couldn't work out exactly what they meant.'

'Mullins was the ace of spades, the ultimate target. He was the one you really wanted all along, wasn't he?' Frank asked.

'Oh yes, but why that card, Frank? Why?' asked Fraser smiling and staring at Frank intently, as if the answer was of extreme significant to him.

'The death card,' Frank stated. But Fraser simply laughed once again. A long and deep laugh that seemed to rumble on and on. What had they missed, wondered Frank?

'In a minute you can have a look at Mullins' body and then you will know the real answer,' said Fraser, looking serious once more.

Frank now knew he was right about Mullins being dead, but still wondered what Fraser had meant. And he was now very scared indeed.

Fraser lifted the gun up again and looked directly at Frank.

'You didn't get the most important detail. You fucking failure. But now you know it all and you can make sure you tell my story to the world. That's my gift to you, Frank Gallen. You have my story to tell.'

Frank didn't know what to say. He found that he was completely unable to move.

'And now it's all over.'

Kevin Fraser very calmly put the pistol to his right temple and pulled the trigger.

Frank recoiled at the muffled sound of the shot and watched in horrified fascination as blood and brains sprayed from Fraser's head. He heard a wet sound and saw blood drip slowly down the white wall to the side of him. Fraser seemed to stand comically still for a moment and then he toppled to the floor.

Kevin Fraser was very obviously dead.

It took several seconds before Frank could even move. He was shaking. His heart was pounding. But it was over and he was now out of danger. He had his story, but at the cost of Mullins' life and now Fraser's life too.

Composing himself, Frank stood painfully then walked slowly and unsteadily past Fraser's prostrate body and into the bedroom. He saw Mullins' body tied to the bed with most of his head missing. Resisting the impulse to throw up, he saw the tattoo of the ace of spades on his right forearm.

Now Kevin Fraser's final taunt made sense.

Frank staggered back into the hall. He tried not to look at Fraser's body as he passed, not to think about the fact that two men had died here. He ran down the stairs, desperate to get away from the sights and smells of death.

He made it to the front garden before his breakfast was splattered over the grass.

When he looked up there were two armed officers pointing guns at him, so he quickly put his hands up. He also saw Ralston and McPherson running towards him.

'It's OK, that's our man,' shouted Ralston.

Thankfully the guns were immediately lowered.

McPherson looked at him and asked 'What happened?'

'Fraser killed Mullins, gave me his story and then he killed himself,' was all Frank could say before he had to sit down. He saw Ralston's face turn a deathly shade of white and his eyes close as he took in the news.

Superintendent McPherson however took charge of the scene.

'Sergeant Kennedy, you can stand your men down. Thank you for your assistance,' he said to the tactical commander. 'Adam, make sure that the scene upstairs is secured and then get back to the office.'

'Yes, sir,' replied Ralston, still clearly shaken by what he had heard from Frank, as he walked towards the close door.

McPherson turned to a uniformed sergeant. 'Did Mullins son turn up?'

'I don't know, sir,' he replied. 'I'll check with the officers at either end of the street.'

The thought of the prison officer's son coming to visit only to find that his father was being held hostage was horrific enough to Frank. But now he would be told that his father was dead. Frank felt tears forming and he sighed deeply, desperate to get away from the horrific scene.

'Frank, I'll need you to fill us in on exactly what happened up there,' said McPherson. 'But it can wait until later.'

Frank was profoundly grateful to the detective. He was shaking uncontrollably once more and all he could think about was the sickening sight of Kevin Fraser blowing his brains out in front of him.

He knew that the image would never leave him.

Thursday May 22 2008, 4:25pm

Superintendent McPherson put the telephone down and relaxed into his chair. The past week had been the most difficult of his long career, but thankfully the case was now over. The Chief Constable was pleased that it had been concluded and that the killer was unable to harm anyone else, but McPherson knew that they should have caught up with Fraser sooner.

And if they had, Jim Mullins would still be alive.

He reflected on what could have been done differently, and as usual found himself searching for a perfection that simply couldn't exist in the complexity of a multiple murder case. He knew that mistakes would always be made, that what looked like trivial details would often turn out to be important leads. But he always reviewed cases when they were over and tried to learn something from them.

There was a knock at the door and DI Adam Ralston walked in.

'Sit down, Adam,' he said. Ralston did so without saying a word. 'Is everything sorted out at the scene?'

'Yes, sir,' replied Ralston. 'Both bodies have been removed.'

'Well, the Chief was pleased with the result. His press conference got plenty of attention too, so he will be off our backs for a while.'

'Yes sir,' replied Ralston edgily. McPherson could see that the man was anxious and he knew exactly why.

'We should talk about what happened with Fraser at the yard, Adam,' he began. 'You made a mistake and that's perhaps understandable given the pressure I was putting you under. This was the biggest case for the Squad in many years and something of a baptism of fire for you.'

McPherson paused, choosing his words carefully.

'I know exactly how hard you were working, Adam; what you put in to try to solve the case. But you should have told me about that phone call immediately.'

'Yes, sir, I know that now.' Ralston was a picture of misery, his face grey and drawn.

'But apart from that error, you did a tremendous job keeping such a complex investigation together and juggling so many different lines of inquiry. We can all learn from our mistakes, Adam, and you're a good copper. Go home and get some rest, you deserve it. I don't want to see you before Monday,' concluded McPherson with a smile.

'So I'm still on the team?' asked Ralston, sounding surprised.

'You are,' he replied, nodding. 'Now get out of here. That's an order.'

'Yes, sir, thank you,' said Ralston, relieved and excited as he walked swiftly out of the door.

McPherson sat back in his chair once more, feeling a weariness that threatened to overwhelm him. He knew that Ralston would do whatever he could to atone for his error. But he wondered whether he would be able to move beyond the fact that a man had died because of it?

McPherson concluded that it would be very difficult for him, but that Ralston had exactly the strength of character that could allow him to move forward.

He had faith in DI Adam Ralston.

Chapter 21

Sunday May 25 2008, 7:40pm

'You picked absolutely the perfect day to resign as it turned out, Thomas,' joked Frank Gallen.

'It certainly ended up that way, didn't it?' laughed his brother, as they drank coffee together in the living room of his house. 'But then I didn't know that the papers would be filled with the story of your confrontation with a serial killer, did I?'

The sudden and totally unexpected resignation of the Leader of Glasgow City Council, Scotland's largest local authority, should have been a major news event. But it had been relegated to the inside pages by the biggest story of the year.

'I'm glad that they have largely kept away from me,' remarked Thomas. 'Marie and I really need the time together.' He smiled and Frank knew that the work to repair their marriage was well under way.

'Does anyone else know the true story of why you resigned?'

'I haven't told a soul, Frank. I kept to the 'mystery illness' line and no one has had the audacity to ask for more details. Not even Alan Mathers, and he lost more than most when I quit,' explained Thomas. 'And now things have moved on and I'm not a story any more.'

'Don't you miss it?' asked Frank.

'Not really,' laughed the former Councillor. 'All the endless meetings, the pressure, the telephone calls night and day. I can live without any of it, thank you very much.'

Frank thought that he looked more relaxed than he had ever seen his brother. Stepping out of the public eye can't have been easy, he assumed, but Thomas was certainly looking very good on it.

'You achieved a lot during your time in public life, you know. You should be proud of yourself, Thomas.'

'There are a few things I'm proud of: some of the improvements we managed to make for people in the East End most of all.' Then he shook his head. 'But it is true that power corrupts, Frank. I nearly threw everything that is important to me away. I'm lucky that I now have a second chance with my family.'

'Marie really loves you, Thomas. She wouldn't be trying to make things right if she didn't.'

'I know, and I thank God every day for her understanding and forgiveness. She amazes me Frank. I don't know if I could ever forgive a betrayal like that,' he confessed.

'You forgave me, Thomas,' Frank reminded him.

'It wasn't the same at all,' he replied, smiling.

Frank felt his mobile phone vibrate and pulled it from his pocket, glancing at the screen. Seeing the call was from Janice he hesitated before pushing the red button. He still felt bad about turning Janice down, although he knew it was the correct thing to do. She was young and would find someone more suitable in time. He hoped that he could continue to encourage her career though: Frank was sure that Janice would turn into a very good journalist one day, and also intended that their friendship would continue.

Seeing Thomas staring at him, Frank turned his thoughts back to their conversation.

'So Asif Rafique is to be the new Leader? How do you think he will do in the job?' asked Frank.

'He will be elected unopposed by the Labour Group. In the circumstances, I don't think anyone wants a protracted contest, and he was the obvious candidate. Asif is a very able man and I'm sure he will do a great job. And it is also tremendous for the city to have its first Asian leader.'

'Maybe I'll get an interview with him,' mused Frank.

'Asif telephoned me this evening, Frank. Just before you arrived actually. He asked me if I had any advice for him.'

'And what did you tell him?' Frank asked, finishing his coffee and leaning forward to hear what his brother had said.

'I told him to be his own man and to stick to his principles.' A smile came across his face. 'And I told him to have absolutely nothing at all to do with David Longwell and his bloody Parklands projects!'

Frank laughed at the reply.

'I didn't tell him why, obviously, but I did make it clear that I thought Longwell couldn't be trusted and I am sure he got the message. He was never totally convinced by Longwell's ideas anyway.'

'So what do you think will happen there?'

'Longwell will try to get him on side, but it won't work,' he predicted. 'And if he does eventually put in a planning application I think Asif will persuade the Group to reject it. I'm pretty sure that his damned project will never see the light of day now.'

'That's good,' replied Frank. 'Longwell deserves to have someone stop him in his tracks.'

'Anyway what are you going to do with yourself now that the excitement is all over?' asked Thomas.

'Well, I need to tidy up my book. It's close to being finished, but I have a few things still to do. And I've had three different publishers on the phone looking to buy it from me. They're promising big advances, too.' Frank knew that the inside story of the hunt for, and the demise of, a serial killer was a certainty to sell.

'You will be the one in the public eye soon then. Frank Gallen, best selling author. It sounds good to me!' laughed Thomas.

'I prefer to write the news rather than being in it,' he replied wryly.

'Are you going to stay on at the paper?'

'For now, yes I will,' Frank said. 'Would you believe that Bessent called me and offered me a job back at the Daily News?'

'You're not going to accept, are you?' asked his brother in astonishment.

'No way,' replied Frank, laughing at the notion. 'But I might end up at one of his competitors eventually. I really would like to get back to front line journalism one day.'

'Great. There might be big changes on the horizon for you, too,' said Thomas.

'It's been a crazy couple of weeks for both of us,' replied Frank.

Both men were silent for a few moments, reflecting on the events that had changed their lives forever. And had also brought them back to each other.

Sunday May 25 2008, 11:20pm

Adam Ralston sat in a near dark kitchen, a cup of tea that had long gone cold in front of him on the small table. He smiled as he reflected on a long weekend spent with his family, relaxing and gathering strength from them as always. What a contrast it had been to the investigation that had consumed his time, indeed his life, over the previous two weeks. Smiles and laughter rather than murder. Games rather than cryptic clues. Joy rather than pain.

But even in the midst of such pleasure Ralston had found that he could not stop thinking about the man who had been murdered because of his error of judgement.

He longed to be able to go back and change things. He knew that if he hadn't alerted Fraser that they were on to him, then they would have caught up with the killer much sooner and Jim Mullins would still be alive. Everyone makes mistakes, thought Ralston morosely. But not everyone had to live with such horrific consequences.

Staring out of the window to the lights of the city, Ralston picked up his cup and took a sip, immediately recoiling at the feel of the cold liquid. He thought of putting the kettle back on but then decided to go to bed instead. Perhaps tonight he would manage to sleep without those awful images from Mullins' flat invading his mind.

Adam Ralston knew that there would be many other cases. He could not now do anything for Jim Mullins or his family, so he resolved to do a better job for other victims and their families in the future. And he could only hope that if he could learn from his mistake, and become a better detective because of it, perhaps one day he would be able to make peace with himself.

Ralston sighed deeply, thinking, not for the first time, that he was lucky still to be a part of the Murder Squad. He remembered how difficult it had been to hear McPherson's words of praise that had contrasted so sharply with the disappointment that was clear to see in his face. He felt a pain that was almost physical at the memory, knowing that he had let McPherson down.

Adam Ralston knew that he now had a great deal to prove to his boss.

But he also knew that he had even more to prove to himself.

THE END

ABOUT THE AUTHOR:

Gordon Johnston

Gordon Johnston lived in Glasgow for over 25 years before moving to the countryside of Clackmannanshire. He graduated from the University of Strathclyde in 1982 with a degree in Applied Physics, but chose not to work in the scientific field. Instead he has had a successful career in the public and voluntary sectors in jobs that have included urban regeneration, managing European and National Lottery funding and IT project management.

Gordon has spent the past five years conceiving a series of psychological thrillers set in Glasgow, of which *"Calling Cards"* is the first completed novel. He has almost completed the second, *"Cold Roses"*, featuring DI Adam Ralston, which should be published by Ringwood in 2015, and is currently working on a third, *"The Lion's Den"*. He also has many further ideas to continue the series.

He is currently Editor Scotland for the UK music website and e-zine Glasswerk and a Director of a number of Scottish charities in the mental health field.

He is an active member (and former Organiser) of Glasgow Writers' Meetup Group.

Good Deed by **Steve Christie** is a fast paced crime novel that captures the reader from beginning to end.

The gripping story of Good Deed rattles along relentlessly, leaving the reader breathless but enthralled. Good Deed introduces a new Scottish detective hero, DI Ronnie Buchanan, who is certain to quickly attract a legion of fans.

The events crammed into Good Deed take Buchanan from his base in Aberdeen on a frantic journey around all the major Scottish cities as his increasingly deadly pursuit of a mysterious criminal master mind known only as Vince comes to a breath-taking climax back in Aberdeen.

"The pace of Good Deed is exceptional and unremitting. It is the kind of book that demands to be read in one sitting, but most readers will be so breathless as the saga unfolds without pause that they will need occasional rests before eagerly returning for more."

Good Deed is Steve Christie's first novel. Based in Edinburgh, the good news is that he is already hard at work on the follow up to Good Deed, which will also feature Ronnie Buchanan. Ringwood is confident that both Steve Christie and Ronnie Buchanan are names that will become very familiar to all lovers of quality crime fiction.

 Good Deed can be purchased on www.ringwoodpublishing.com for £9.99 excluding p&p, or ordered by post or e-mail for the same price. It is also available online from Amazon.co.uk and from all good booksellers.

The e-book version is   available for £4.99 from the Kindle Book Store or Amazon.co.uk

Torn Edges by Brian McHugh is a riveting mystery story linking modern day Glasgow with 1920's Ireland.

When a gold coin very similar to a family heirloom is found at the scene of a Glasgow murder, a search is begun that takes the McKenna family, assisted by their Librarian friend Liam, through their own family history right back to the tumultuous days of the Irish Civil War. The search is greatly helped by the discovery of an old family photograph of their Great-Uncle Pat in a soldier's uniform.

The McKennas quickly realise that despite their pride in their Irish origins they know remarkably little about this particular period of recent Irish history. With Liam's expert help, they soon learn that many more Irishman were killed, murdered, assassinated or hung during the very short Civil War than in the much longer and better known War of Independence. And they learn that gruesome atrocities were committed by both sides, atrocities in which the evidence begins to suggest their own relatives might have been involved.

Parallel to this unravelling of the family involvement of this period, Torn Edges author Brian McHugh has interwoven the remarkable story of the actual participation of two of the McKenna family, Charlie and Pat, across both sides of the conflict in the desperate days of 1922 Ireland.

"Torn Edges is both entertaining and well-written, and will be of considerable interest to all in both Scottish and Irish communities, many of whom will realise that their knowledge and understanding of events in Ireland in 1922 has been woefully incomplete. Torn Edges will also appeal more widely to all who appreciate a good story well told."

TORN EDGES can be purchased on www.ringwoodpublishing.com for £9.99 excluding p&p or ordered by post or e-mail. It is also available online from Amazon.co.uk and from all good booksellers. The e-book version is available for £4.99 from the Kindle Book Store or Amazon.co.uk.

Paradise Road by **Stephen O'Donnell** is the story
of Kevin McGarry a young man from the West of Scotland, who as a
youngster was one of the most talented footballers of his generation
in Scotland. Through a combination of injury and disillusionment,
Kevin is forced to abandon any thoughts of playing the game he
loves, professionally. Instead he settles for following his favourite
team, Glasgow Celtic, as a spectator, while at the same time
resignedly and with a characteristically wry Scottish sense of
humour, trying to eke out a living as a joiner.

It is a story of hopes and dreams, idealism and disillusionment, of
growth in the face of adversity and disappointment. Paradise Road
examines some of the major themes affecting football today, such as
the power and role of the media, standards in the Scottish game and
the sectarianism which pervades not only football in Glasgow but
also the wider community. More than simply a novel about football
or football fandom, the book offers a portrait of the character and
experiences of a section of the Irish Catholic community of the West
of Scotland, and considers the role of young working-class men in
our modern, post-industrial society.

The road Kevin travels towards self discovery, fulfilment and
maturity leads him to Prague, enabling a more detached view of the
Scotland that formed him and the Europe that beckons him.

*"Written in a thoughtful, provocative yet engaging style, Paradise
Road is a book that will enthral, challenge and reward in equal
measure. It will be a powerful addition to the growing debate on
some of the key issues facing contemporary Scotland"*

Paradise Road can be purchased on www.ringwoodpublishing.com
for £9.99 excluding p&p, or ordered by post or e-mail for the same
price. It is also available online from Amazon.co.uk and from all
good booksellers.

The e-book version is available for £4.99 from the Kindle Book
Store or Amazon.co.uk